"What if a city and the people you meet there get so under your skin that you see once more that life is full of beauty and possibility? *I Make Envy on Your Disco* will remind you that growing older is not just about what you leave behind but also about new beginnings, new relationships, and new ways of living in the world."
—**Anton Hur,** National Book Award finalist and author of *Toward Eternity*

"The characters in this hilarious, wistful, and moving novel will live with you long after you've read the last, aching page. *I Make Envy on Your Disco* is pure pleasure—a celebration of the intense, even transcendent connections we can make when traveling far from home."
—**Carolyn Turgeon,** author of *Godmother* and *Mermaid*

"In Eric Schnall's fast-paced and funny debut novel, a successful New York art advisor finds himself perpetually discombobulated on a short business trip to Berlin. Moment by moment, we tag along as he continually loses—and eventually recovers—himself in a city that comes as vividly to life as the eclectic cast of characters he meets along the way. I loved this sharply observed and deeply touching book."
—**Bill Hayes,** author of *Insomniac City*

"This is a pendulum of a book, swinging between rolling in smoky Kreuzberg techno clubs and strolling the preppy lushness of New York's Upper West Side, and never being quite sure when or where we're going to slip off and land. A love letter to Berlin, to travel, and to saying yes to life."
—**Alan Cumming**

"An amazing feat. Wonderful books are like foreign travel itself. You're dropped someplace unfamiliar, lost in a new language. You begin to feel your way around, and in the hands of a skilled writer like Eric Schnall you slowly but surely fall in love with place, with character, with words, ultimately gaining a new sense of self. I finished *I Make Envy on Your Disco* completely enchanted, and I can't wait to book a return trip to Schnall's work."
—**Steven Rowley,** *New York Times* best-selling author of *The Celebrants*

"One of the most delightful, smart, surprising, and unexpectedly affirming books I've ever read. Not unlike protagonist Sam Singer—who has fled his life in New York for an exquisitely rendered Berlin—I fell in love with every character who crosses his path."
—**Steve Adams,** Pushcart Prize–winning author of *Remember This*

"Eric Schnall's gorgeous debut is everything you want in a novel—perceptive and witty, melancholy and honest, kind and full of heart. Better yet, his story is populated with the most hilarious and singular characters you could hope to meet on the page."
—**Jenny Jackson,** *New York Times* best-selling author of *Pineapple Street*

I MAKE ENVY ON YOUR DISCO

I make envy

Zero Street Fiction   SERIES EDITORS
Timothy Schaffert
SJ Sindu

on your disco

A Novel   **Eric Schnall**

University of Nebraska Press   LINCOLN

The University of Nebraska Press is part
of a land-grant institution with campuses
and programs on the past, present, and
future homelands of the Pawnee, Ponca,
Otoe-Missouria, Omaha, Dakota, Lakota,
Kaw, Cheyenne, and Arapaho Peoples, as
well as those of the relocated Ho-Chunk,
Sac and Fox, and Iowa Peoples.

Library of Congress
Cataloging-in-Publication Data
Names: Schnall, Eric, author.
Title: I make envy on your disco:
a novel / Eric Schnall.
Description: Lincoln: University of Nebraska
Press, 2024. | Series: Zero Street fiction
Identifiers: LCCN 2023048996
ISBN 9781496239013 (paperback)
ISBN 9781496240040 (epub)
ISBN 9781496240057 (pdf)
Subjects: BISAC: FICTION / Literary |
FICTION / LGBTQ+ / General |
LCGFT: Queer fiction. | Novels.
Classification: LCC PS3619.C446544 I43
2024 | DDC 813/.6—dc23/eng/20231023
LC record available at
https://lccn.loc.gov/2023048996

Set and designed in Miller Text by N. Putens.

For Shax

For my parents

For Berlin

Berlin tasted of the future,
and that is why we gladly
took the crap and the cold.
— CARL ZUCKMAYER

I MAKE ENVY ON YOUR DISCO

Nothing Translates

Everything is a puzzle. The windows open differently here, from the top, the corners slanting inward. There's no radio, no clock in the room, yet the floors in the bathroom are heated by a switch next to the door. To flush the toilet, I must step on a metal lever. There is no UP or DOWN button on the panel beside the elevator. Instead, I punch in the number of the floor I'm going to. I'm on the third floor, but I press 0 to get to the street. When I ride the train, I buy my ticket from one machine and get it stamped by another, but no one checks my ticket. I just get on the train and sit. When the train reaches my stop, I push a button so the door slides open and I can exit. I've forgotten to do this a few times already and have twice missed my stop. Though I have no use for warm marble floors, I'll leave them on for the length of my stay, because they're there, I'm paying for them, and they're controlled by the one button in Berlin I seem to understand.

Some hotels overlook mountains or the sea. My hotel sits at the end of a tramline, tucked away on a side street, hidden from the bustle of Mitte. My room has its own peculiar view: one window faces the street, its slim glass doors opening to a balcony just big enough to step outside for a cigarette, if I still smoked. A cluster of yellow trams sleep below and a maze of wire dangles a few yards from my window, feeding power to the machines. Across the street, an apartment building is covered entirely in graffiti, and in big red letters: FUCK BUSH.

And in the distance stands the Fernsehturm, the TV Tower that hovers over Alexanderplatz like a giant steel dandelion.

The other side of my room overlooks a courtyard. Strands of flowering vines crawl up walls, defying the October chill. A small koi pond is lit from below. A few tables and chairs are scattered in the yard, but it's hard to imagine they've gotten much use. It's been cold and rainy since I arrived in Berlin rather suddenly, less than two days ago.

I go down to the breakfast room. A wall of windows faces the courtyard. German tourists and businessmen sit at square tables eating cake, salami, and muesli. Outside it's gray and drizzly and the wind is gusty, but they all seem used to it. Most of them, like me, have blue eyes.

The hotel is staffed almost entirely by young women dressed in black. They are all very beautiful. "*Guten Morgen,*" one says as she leads me to a table. Her name tag reads Astrid. "*Kaffee?*" she asks, tilting her head to the side. I nod. As Astrid pours the coffee, her blond hair drifts down her shoulder and she sighs, "*Soooo . . .*" Everyone says this to me. I eventually discover that it means *here you go,* but not quite. Nothing is what it seems here. Nothing translates. The word *bitte* means *please* and *you're welcome* and *may I help you?* When I walk around the city, streets don't have names like 14th Street or Avenue A. My hotel is between Grosse Präsidentenstrasse and Oranienburger Strasse. That's two streets and sixteen syllables.

I've come to Berlin to see an exhibit at Klaus Beckmann's Zukunftsgalerie, curated by the owner himself. The latest show at the "gallery of the future" is all about the past. Its theme is *Ostalgie,* the nostalgia for the products, objects, and way of life that disappeared from the East almost overnight, after the Wall fell, less than fifteen years ago.

I'm an art advisor in New York. I specialize in contemporary art and tell people what to buy. Sometimes I consult for corporations, but mostly I deal with private collectors, which means that these days, I spend a lot of time with the newly wealthy—hedgefunders, trophy wives, Europeans, that sort of thing. I often find myself trapped in their cavernous apartments or strolling arm in arm with them through galleries in Chelsea, dining out with their families, making small talk, just hoping to close a sale.

Walking around Mitte, the neighborhood that bridges east and west, I see graffiti everywhere. But it's not fuck-you graffiti. It's beautiful, the wild bursts of color and ridiculous taglines. Art is everywhere—painted on buildings, stenciled on doorways, plastered on pipes. It is raw and, like much of Berlin, reminds me of New York in the seventies and early eighties, the city of my youth.

I picture Times Square: the crowds, the lights, television screens and scrolling headlines, the stock quotes, kidnappings, and natural disasters. Endless information pouring across pixilated walls. It's the core of my city now, an advertisement for everything and nothing, the void filled with a million things.

There's nothing about Berlin that's on similar display. It's a cagey peacock with its dazzling tail spread, walking away from you while looking backward. It seems an insular and introspective culture, happy to be on its own, connected by the dark threads of its knotty history.

Daniel would say that I've got it all wrong. A city unfolds, takes its time. "Sleep," he'd tell me. Because first impressions are never right.

German is a language of scissors and knives. *Z*'s, *p*'s, *k*'s, *s*'s, and *w*'s are chopped into an orgy of consonants: *Platz, Strasse, Kuchen, Wasser,* and *Schnitzel.* I'd been told that everyone would speak English. But now it seems that many Berliners don't speak English, or if they do, they try hard not to use it. When I ask the front desk for directions, I am repeatedly handed a map.

I walk down an endless number of streets in East Berlin. The entire city is under construction. New office buildings are being erected, town houses restored, austere Soviet-era structures torn down. Much of the city is draped in tarp and plastic, which hangs from it like peeling skin.

And then there is the Wall. A few slabs are on display, scribbles of love and desperation, pleas for help, a reminder of a once divided city. Though the Wall is almost entirely gone, its scar remains. A brick line snakes through the pavement, showing where the city was separated. With no wall, Berlin is now a city with two hearts and no center. You feel like you're in the middle of everything and totally lost no matter where you are. Or maybe that's just how I feel after thirty-six hours of jet lag, overcome with the sort of traveler's depression that makes you feel like your brain has fallen into your throat.

Everything would be easier if Daniel were here. Someone to speak the language, just a little bit. Someone to tell me where to eat. Someone to know what to do.

Everyone smokes. The clouds rise lazily above me in restaurants and cafés, instead of being sucked down in greedy gasps of nicotine outside office buildings. My clothes absorb the stench and carry it with me. Pretzels, beer gardens, blue-eyed pretty boys walking dachshunds down the street—they are all here. Young women huddle in the *Bäckerei* scarfing down pastries and espresso, yet they are thin and porcelain skinned. I don't see a gym or a pink packet of Sweet'N Low. No one seems to drink water. I don't ask for decaf. I don't eat dinner before 9:00 p.m. It is not allowed.

One of the first things I like to do in a foreign city is absolutely nothing. I just stay in my hotel room for an entire day. I read magazines, take a bath, listen to my iPod, watch foreign TV, lie on the bed and jerk off, then order eggs from room service. I don't worry about crumbs or spooge on the sheets. It feels almost deviant to do this in Berlin, sort of kinky, when I should be out Seeing Everything. It makes me feel disgusted with myself, but that's okay. It's become my ritual. I always need one of these days when I travel alone, and by nighttime, I stumble onto the street looking for food.

I go downstairs. A bar sits to the side of the reception area, its windows to the street. The lounge has remained closed since my arrival, but the hotel still plays that ubiquitous trip-hop soundtrack that follows me wherever I go. I don't see many guests wandering around, and though the lounge is closed, a chandelier still glows at its center and dozens of candles are lit each evening along the mahogany bar. Berlin seems to be big on atmosphere. People are almost beside the point, or additional decoration.

Magda sits behind the reception desk, my least favorite of the women in black. We've gotten to know each other quickly. When I first arrived at the hotel—yesterday at seven in the morning—she told me my room wouldn't be available until midafternoon. "Fifteen and thirty hours," she said, needlessly referring to 3:30 p.m. in the European way, watching me do the math. And so I wandered around, fueled by endless espressos. It was during this zombie walk that I dropped my BlackBerry while trying to check my email. The trackball fell off and bounced down Rosenthaler Strasse. I watched in amazement as the tiny ball rolled past a man walking his dog, then disappeared behind a tram.

When I finally checked in that afternoon, I asked Magda where to have my phone repaired. She kept repeating "*Zatoone* by Alexanderplatz! *Zatoone* by Alexanderplatz!" So I walked to Alexanderplatz but couldn't find the store. When I returned and asked for the street address, she shook her head and repeated "*Zatoone* by Alexanderplatz! It is so big, you cannot miss it!"

After my third attempt, she wrote down the information with such exaggerated detail that I found even her rendering of a street address totally aggressive. But as I looked down at the paper I realized *Zatoone* is how Germans pronounce "Saturn," an electronics superstore the size of the moon. I found the store, located an English-speaking salesman, and showed him my injured BlackBerry. He shrugged his shoulders and scoffed, "We carry no balls."

Since then, I've tried unsuccessfully to connect my laptop to the internet in the hotel room. Magda has supplied me with cables and endless codes on slips of paper, but nothing seems to work. ("This is your problem," she told me yesterday. "The World Wide Web is working in the hotel. Your computer *ist kaputt!*") The other ladies seem almost interchangeable, but Magda, the manager of the Hotel Hackescher Hof, she's different. She sits behind the front desk like a bored young queen on her throne, her long brown hair tied into a tight bun, black designer glasses resting at the tip of her nose. Whenever I approach her, she clasps her hands and sighs, as if to say, What now? Cautiously, I walk up to her. "Hi, Magda."

"Good evening, Herr Singer." A sprawling saltwater aquarium sits behind her. I watch the striped yellow clown fish dart back and forth, no doubt pleading for escape. "Did you enjoy your nap?"

I ignore her question, annoyed by the judgment I sense in her voice. "Magda, can you recommend a restaurant to me?"

"For dinner?"

"Yes."

"Herr Singer," she sighs, "really, I do not know."

"You don't know?"

"Yes, I do not know." She flashes her blue eyes at me. "They are all good."

Please, I think, just tell me where to eat. This is how our conversations go.

I leave the hotel. It's cool and damp and my breath hangs in the air. It's Saturday night and the streets are crowded. I survey the restaurants by the Hackesche Höfe, but I can't choose. There's Japanese, Italian, Russian, German. I look into the windows of Cibo Matto. Berliners line the banquettes, drinking wine, laughing. A table of Dietrich lesbians in suits puff cigars and stare at me, bloodhounds at their feet.

When I'm traveling by myself, dinner is the loneliest time of day. It's too dark to read a book, and I feel self-conscious staring into space with a glass of wine and a blank smile on my face, trying to indicate to people I don't know that I'm happy to be on my own. This feeling is even more pronounced in Berlin, where every café is lit by the soft glow of candlelight, every table filled with lovers and friends, and each empty seat seems filled with the absence of Daniel and the mess I've left back home. After circling the street, I buy a beer and a Döner kebab from an Imbiss stand. I take it back to my room and wolf it down over the bathroom trash can.

At night, by the hotel, there are these prostitutes, about eight of them. I stare at them from my window. They stand in a line next to the tram stop, perfectly spaced, like dominoes. These women have had plastic surgery and their faces and bodies look exactly alike; their cheekbones, lips, and breasts cobbled from a blend of Eastern European porn star and Britney Spears, their noses lifted from a Modigliani. They wear tight white jeans and puffy satin jackets of different colors: shiny pinks, greens, and silvers. I could grasp their tiny waists between my hands.

I haven't seen any takers, but the ladies are kind when tourists ask for directions or to have their pictures taken with them.

I think of my old apartment in the Meatpacking District, back when you still tripped on a calf's heart on your way to the A train. I would lean out the window for hours, smoking cigarettes, watching transsexual prostitutes approach cars in the middle of cobblestone streets. I'd put in earplugs before I went to sleep to shield out their come-ons and the mad hum of meat trucks idling outside my window as slabs of beef were hauled into the warehouse below. In the morning, when the white sun blasted through my windows and I removed my earplugs, the first thing I heard was the surprisingly loud sound of high heels against cobblestone, like a hammer missing a nail. The meat trucks would be gone, but the ladies stayed until at least seven. I'd run across Washington Street to the bodega for cigarettes and coffee and they'd say hello, wink at me, make me feel safe.

We Are Nice Here

Since it's Saturday night and I'm in Germany, I decide to go to a club and hear some techno. Never mind that I haven't been out dancing in years, or that I now find myself listening to Lite FM and enjoying the music in Starbucks.

The clubs in Berlin have weird English names. Tonight, I must choose among Butter Club, Polar TV, and Delicious Doughnuts. Polar TV has the edge because it's been recommended by an artist back in New York who is ten years younger than me and has a DJ, Woody, whom I've actually heard of.

When I arrive, Polar TV looks like an enormous hut between a row of broken train tracks and an empty lot. It's drizzly and the wind is vicious, but there's a line at the door. The bass pounds from inside, the stairs shake as I climb them. I watch people show their IDs and panic that I don't have my passport. Then I remember that I'm thirty-seven with flecks of silver in my hair—sparkles, Daniel calls them—which I always seem to forget.

I don't get carded. I follow a group through a dimly lit corridor until we spill into the main room. My heart breaks just listening to the music and seeing everyone in their incredible fashions and silly haircuts, all of these young people with big smiles on their faces. DJ Woody is hunched over the turntable while a screen behind him flashes blue and white. The beat just repeats and a hundred people throw their hands in the air. The room quivers, the bass thumping from the center like a heartbeat. The disco ball gleams above the dance floor like an alien relic, the shining jewel of some galactic tomb.

I buy a Coke and perch on a bench by the side of the dance floor. A beautiful girl with short brown hair and a white tank top sits next to me. I study her, the way her head rocks forward then sways to the beat. She reaches over and grabs the bottle from my hand, takes a sip, and returns it. I love this girl, that she wanted a sip of my Coke and just took it. I hand her the bottle twice more, because I want her to stay with me. I lean into her. "What's your name?"

She shrugs her shoulders and smiles.

"I'm Sam," I say.

"I'm Sam," she repeats, shrugging again. "Sam?"

I point to myself. "Sam."

"Aye, Sam!" She laughs, then taps her chest. "Uli."

I extend my hand but she grabs my shoulders and hugs me. I feel her cheeks, soft and warm, against my face.

A boy—small, lithe, pale skinned—sits down on the other side of me. He is long but miniature in his slinky jeans and tight black T-shirt, his eyes gazing sideways. There seem to be many serpentine boys slithering around Berlin, and that's fine by me; they all leave me breathless. The boy smokes, and I'm surprised at how happily I ingest the haze. Uli says something to him in German. He reaches over my lap, grabs her hand. For a few minutes we just sit, their clasped hands resting on my thigh. The boyfriend takes a puff from his cigarette and puts his fingers on my back, tapping to the beat. Then he offers me a pill.

"You speak English?" I ask.

"A lee-tle," he says.

We introduce ourselves. His name is Markus.

"Is it ecstasy?"

"*Ja*," he nods. "It is good, the tablet. You will take it, no?"

I begin to pull out my wallet, but he grabs my wrist. "No," Markus says, "it is not necessary." He deposits the pill into my hand. "This is Berlin. We are nice here."

"Thanks." I lean into him. The music is blaring. "How old are you guys?"

"*Was?*" he shouts.

I rephrase my question. "What is your age?"

"Ah." Markus rests his chin on Uli's shoulder and translates. Uli looks at me, closes her hands, and opens all of her fingers. Ten. She does this again. Ten more. I wait, but that's it. They are twenty years old. Was I this cute when I was twenty? You can get away with anything at that age. But I only realize this now, after three more hands and two fingers have slipped away from me.

"Enjoy the tablet," Markus says. He takes Uli by the hand and leads her to the dance floor. She blows me a kiss. I watch them dance, her hands on his waist, staring into each other's eyes. They move closer and start kissing. It's so beautiful and intimate that I look away.

I find the bathroom, go into a stall, and examine the pill under the dim blue light. It's yellow with a Motorola logo imprinted on its top. I haven't taken ecstasy or done any drug in a long time. I used to be an expert on all the "brands": BMWs, 007s, Smurfs, CK1s. I had my own ecstasy testing kit. I slept with some boy once just to get the name of his dealer and kept my pills in a velvet-lined box. But now I'm boring. I have no vices anymore. No cigarettes, no pot, no pills. Half a beer makes me sleepy. I'm usually in bed by eleven o'clock with my dog and my boyfriend (my partner, my lover . . . whatever I'm supposed to call him).

I decide to take only half of the pill. This seems to be my new thing lately: half an Ambien, half-caffeinated coffee, half-naked sex with my boyfriend—or more often, half-naked sex with myself.

I go into the lounge and buy another Coke. I shield my mouth with my hand and bite the tablet straight down the middle. The taste is instantly familiar—synthetic, chemical, nostalgic. It has the bitter, artificial taste of laundry detergent. Daniel used to say that ecstasy tastes like the future, like space. I swallow it, take a sip of Coke, and put the other half in my pocket.

I sit down and watch the kids. That's what they are to me now—young, dancing, smoking, running around. No one here uses Rogaine.

No one worries as much as I do. No one has a perfectly fine one-bedroom apartment that costs $3,000 a month and is told that it's a Great Deal. Now I'm in this club with these beautiful people, and I can't even sleep with anyone. Or can I? I don't know the rules anymore.

The rush arrives sooner than expected—first an electric buzz in my cheeks, then I feel warm and cozy, slipping under the covers, relaxed. I take a few deep breaths. The air tastes good, cool, filled with particles of music. I touch my cheeks and they are hard like stone.

DJ Woody is switching from techno to house to trance; no rules, no darkness. I hear a snatch of horn, I see drums in the air, and a thick booming synth line vibrates in front of me. A disembodied woman's voice purrs "all you need is me" over and over again, and she is right. I'm starting to fly. The disco ball shimmers, swollen, throwing sparks in the air. The music twists and snaps like rubber bands. People smile as they walk past me like they know everything about me. A nerdy boy in a polo shirt dances in front of me with a deranged grin that might get him arrested in the middle of the day. I wonder if it's his first time on ecstasy because he looks ridiculously happy. The boy may never feel this free again. It's diminishing returns after the first pill, always searching for that original high.

When Daniel and I went out in New York, we'd be happy just to sit, watching everything, tingly from the pills. Our defenses down, we'd get wrapped up in conversations with strangers: a dominatrix and her slave, boys with glitter on their cheeks, rough girls in fishnets, lonely musclemen on the prowl. We'd have to remind ourselves to dance.

I stand up and experience a head rush: waves of water sloshing in my brain. The teeth grinding begins, and soon my jaw starts to hurt. I see Uli, or a swirl of her, churning toward me. Markus runs up to us. "We go to Sternradio. It is big party, it is huge." He spreads his hands in the air. "You come, no?"

I look at them, so pure and beautiful, like angels. "No, thanks," I say into Markus's ear. My nose brushes against his wet black hair. It smells good, the sweat, salt, and smoke. "I'm going to stay right here." And I walk onto the middle of the dance floor, under the disco ball, and begin to dance.

A girl with butterfly wings glides over to me. Her pupils are the size of quarters. She lifts my shirt and puts her ear to my stomach, smiles up at me. Her ear is cold. The girl says something in German. I think she must be telling me that I'm warm, because she seems so happy with her freezing ear pressed against me. We dance like this for a while. Then I bring my shirt down. "I. Need. To. Sit." I say this loudly, slowly. I feel like a robot now, my jaw controlled by metallic joints. I go to the bench and sit down. I'm dizzy. Did I dance for one song? Ten? I have no idea.

Some people describe the effect of ecstasy as "rolling." You ride a wave of high and then a little less high, then roll back up again. You circle euphoria but never quite land. And it occurs to me that I feel awful, like the back of my mouth has been stapled shut and I'm about to throw up, that I'm practically forty and know better than to be in some German club, the Tin Man fucked up on ecstasy. I feel like crying, but it's concentrated above my eyes, tears traveling upward, inside my skull. I didn't come to Berlin to do drugs and be wrecked for three days. Waiting for a moment that never comes.

Nights, like people, can turn a corner. Suddenly I feel totally alone. Strangers flicker in and out of view, whirls of color trailing behind. The music has grown darker, the crowd thinned out, everyone on their way to someplace else. A wave of dry ice rolls across the dance floor. Beams of yellow light glide over the room, illuminating faces that look like ghosts. I'm trapped inside myself and it feels slightly tragic; all of these designer chemicals lodged in my brain, synthesizing a new mood for me every ten minutes. I want my neurotransmitters back. I want to get the hell out of Polar TV and go home.

History in Berlin seems to be a living thing, swirling through the air, seeping into dreams. When I leave the club, I smell something in the dawn, acrid and burning. My mind goes to a dark place. It's hard to smell something bad in Germany and not have your mind wander.

When I get back to the hotel, I'm confronted by another smell in my room, something sharp, nasty. I can't trace where it's coming from. I put my nose everywhere—by the window, inside the closet. I smell the walls, get down on my knees and sniff the carpet. It has a blue diamond pattern. I rub my finger across one of the diamonds. At its tip, a splash of red, like blood. I examine the rest of the diamonds and they all contain this smudge of red. It's a disturbing pattern, and with the smell, and the fact that I'm tripping and flying so low, I find myself unable to sleep. I want to reverse the night and reclaim my chemistry. Instead, I take half a sleeping pill. And just as the light of another gray day trickles into my room, I close my eyes and I am gone.

I wake up a few hours later and the smell has disappeared. I look at the carpet and it doesn't look so bad. I walk into the bathroom and sit down to pee, take my time so I can feel the warmth of the floor. I could get used to these heated floors. Maybe they're better than a radio.

I don't feel as cracked out as I'd expected. I have a headache, but I have Advil and a bed to sleep in. There is coffee, cake, and cold cuts downstairs. It's good that I only took half a pill. I used to take three pills in one night, back in the day. I always hated that expression, but now I use it a lot.

It's raining, and thunder echoes in the distance. I stare out the window and wonder what Markus and Uli are doing. I imagine them dancing. He's holding her tight now, fused at the hips, smiling at the morning, at what's to come. I try to remember that feeling, but my thoughts are interrupted as the phone rings in its warped European drawl. Why does everything sound not quite right here? The whoosh of the S-Bahn, the burr of the police sirens, the clomping of boots on pavement.

"It is time to get up," a woman says.

As I begin to thank her, she hangs up.

Schmuddelwetter

I go into the bathroom and look in the mirror. My pupils are dilated—little black marbles, Olive Oyl eyes. My skin is perfectly clear. Whenever Daniel and I took ecstasy, he would turn to me at some point in the night and tell me I was glowing. "You're luminescent," he'd say. "Your skin looks beautiful." He'd stroke my cheeks with the back of his fingers and tell me how warm I was. We'd kiss for a few minutes and then he'd look at my face, hold it in his hands. "You're so delicate, like fine bone china." It was a weird thing to say while dancing in a sea of boys at four in the morning, but that's Daniel.

Things change. I have a headache. I splash water on my face. I look in my toiletry bag for Advil and see the bottles of Rogaine, Ambien, Metamucil. When did I become such a balding, sleepless, bowel-challenged man?

I go downstairs to find I've nearly missed breakfast, but Astrid pours me a cup of coffee, which is all I really need; the pill has left me with no appetite. The breakfast room seems to have three CDs on continuous shuffle—the greatest hits of Elvis Presley, Frank Sinatra, and Ace of Base. They all sound unexpectedly melancholy in the context of this gloomy room. Even Ace of Base takes on shades of disconnect I've never noticed before, their songs reverberating with an awkward in-betweenness that feels entirely fitting: Jamaica by way of Sweden, upbeat yet depressing, lyrics that make no sense at all.

Two British ladies linger at a nearby table, staining their teacups with identical shades of purple lipstick. I listen as they talk about their husbands back in England.

"Harvey has no idea?"

"None. He's a daft man now, isn't he?"

"The wanker."

They giggle and smear jam on their croissants. One of them gives me the eye, probably trying to determine if I speak English. I sip my coffee and stare ahead. She decides I'm German and they resume their gossip and plan their day: Checkpoint Charlie, tea at the Adlon, and, if it ever stops raining, a boat tour on the Spree. Just contemplating their itinerary makes me want to go upstairs and take a nap. Unfortunately, I have plans of my own: a ticket to the Berlin Philharmonic later this afternoon. Daniel arranged it; a gift, he called it, one prime seat above the orchestra. It seemed like a nice idea at the time, but now I find myself wishing it away. Ecstasy lingers in your system, and its aftershocks—exhaustion, depression, a heightening and distortion of senses—can last for a few days. Taking the drug, even half a tablet, is a commitment.

Everyone has a plan for me in Berlin. One of my clients wants me to take her nephew—a wannabe DJ newly relocated to the city—to coffee. And when I told my mother I was traveling here, she suggested I find the nearest concentration camp. "I don't know which one is closest to the city," she said. "But you'll be in Germany. One can't be very far."

That's not the kind of trip I'm taking, I told her. I was coming for work. And I couldn't tell her about Daniel. My parents had visited Theresienstadt when they went to Prague and found the experience to be soul-depleting and profound. But I wasn't in Germany to explore my identity. Besides, we were hardly super Jews when I was growing up, and I find her newfound religiosity random and disorienting. Still, my mother called on my way to the airport. "I googled it, Samuel. The nearest camp is Sachsenhausen," she said. "You take the train forty minutes. I'll send the info over email. There are no excuses."

I promised her I would go. But not today. Still, I look up Sachsenhausen in my guidebook and see that it's sixteen stops away on the

S1. Perhaps I'll go tomorrow after my meeting with Klaus Beckmann from the Zukunftsgalerie.

Astrid brings me a piece of black cake. Elvis Presley's "Can't Help Falling in Love" plays in the background, languid and lonely, the perfect soundtrack to my soporific mood. I force myself to eat the cake, which sits in my stomach like a fistful of copper.

I head upstairs and find Magda behind the reception desk. Always Magda, even on a Sunday. "*Guten Tag*, Samuel," she says with a sigh. I've asked Magda not to call me Herr Singer. It just sounds creepy. So now she calls me Samuel, but still it doesn't sound right with her clipped, metallic accent.

"Hello, Magda," I say. "Are there messages for me?"

"No," she says. "Of course not."

I cock my head. "Of course not?"

She bats her enormous blue eyes. "Samuel, if you have message, of course we give it to you. And how is your email? Is it still no-go?"

I shake my head. "Yup, no-go." I look out the window, everything gray and damp, the glass fogged over. I have time before the concert; perhaps I'll visit a few galleries down the street. "Well, do you have an umbrella I could borrow?"

"I am sorry, Samuel. It is borrowed already by another guest."

"The hotel has only one umbrella?"

"Yes," she says. "That is correct."

I watch the fish darting across the tank behind Magda's head. If I squint, it looks like the fish are eating her face. "Do you know of a store where I can buy one?"

"Let me think," Magda says, pausing for a few seconds. "No. I am sorry." She stares into me. I wonder if she's looking at my black eyes. If they give me away.

"Is it supposed to keep raining?" I ask.

"Through the week, yes. More of the *Schmuddelwetter*. It is too bad that you are not here the last week. Ah, it was so beautiful."

"So, Magda, there's really no place to buy an umbrella?"

"Really, Samuel, there is no place that I know."

"Okay." I clear my throat. "One more question."

She adjusts the pearls wrapped around her neck. "Yes, Samuel. One more."

"Is it possible to have some laundry done?" My clothes from Polar TV reek of smoke and sweat. A few pairs of socks and pants are wet from the rain. "Just a few things."

"Shirts? Socks? Underwear?"

"Yes," I say. "Exactly."

"I am sorry, Samuel." Magda tilts her head to the side. "We are not doing this at the hotel."

"Really? Can't I just have a few things washed? I'll pay of course."

"I do not think so. Maybe for you I investigate, okay?"

I hear a woman outside in the distance screaming German through a megaphone. People clapping. Another demonstration, at least the third since I arrived. "What's that one about?"

Magda shrugs. "Who knows." She looks out the window to the street. "Something is always wrong, *ja*? The people of Berlin are *gegen alles*."

"What does that mean?"

"*Gegen alles*?"

"Yes."

"Against everything."

I am beginning to hate Magda. Since it seems she works the day shift, I decide to avoid her like I avoid the subways of New York at three o'clock, when the kids get out of school.

It's afternoon when I leave the hotel. The *Ampelmann* traffic lights glow brilliantly, greens and reds shimmering like jewels, a lingering effect as the pill works its way through me. I hear each sound as separate from every other: every foot on the street, each car churning, a tram twisting down the avenue.

I head down to Auguststrasse, but it's Sunday and the galleries are closed. It's just as well. I'm in no mood to hunt for art or make chitchat with German galleristas. I walk back to the hotel and pass the Hackescher Höfe. Inside, a maze of interlinking courtyards is hidden from the street. As I wander through the labyrinth, I find myself in a square filled with boutiques, bars, a cabaret, and a cinema. A garden is located in the center, strands of white lights strung along its brick walls. I watch a pair of stick-figure women stare at dresses through store windows. Two boys hold hands on a bench. One of them hoists a red umbrella above them.

The walls are painted with graffiti. I walk over to a drawing of a face sitting on two feet with black squiggly lines around them. The face says: *Kind Bleiben.* I look up the words in my dictionary: *Child Remaining.* I take a picture. I translate more phrases that I see on the walls. *Harm Is Harm. Remember the Pickles? Fashion Is the Cat.*

I go through another alley so narrow that I turn sideways to pass through it. It leads to a small square with an enormous metal sculpture of an owl perched on a platform. The owl's eyes are closed and adorned with black wire lashes. I notice a coin slot and deposit a euro. The owl's mouth drops open, its silver wings unfurl, its eyes move from side to side. At first, the only noise comes from the metal moving and rubbing against itself. It sounds very German, all rust and industry. And then, from a rusty speaker at its base, the owl speaks: "U-hu u-hu." I wait for more, but the owl is done. Its eyeballs settle into a cautionary position, its wings stop midspread.

I don't know what I was thinking, taking the pill. I'm lucky I have time to reassemble my brain before my meeting tomorrow. As I stare at the owl, I realize that a cluster of men have been standing behind me. One of them taps me on the shoulder. "*Gefällt Ihnen die Eule?*"

I look at him, confused.

"Ah," the man says. "*Er ist Amerikaner!*" He winks at me. How does he know? "Have a great day," he says in perfect imitation of an American accent.

After a failed attempt at a nap, I take a shower and get dressed—white shirt, black jeans, gray blazer—my New York armor. I head west to the Philharmonic. Daniel thought I should see the building: a "paradigm of organic modernism," designed from the inside out. Whatever that means. The massive structure sits at the edge of the Tiergarten like a metal-clad space station from a 1950s B movie. Standing in front of it,

I can't decide if it looks truly amazing or more like the world's greatest Lego project. I buy a glass of sparkling water in the lobby, stand on the steps, and watch Germans sip champagne and smoke cigarettes. Then the bells chime softly, and I head to my seat.

The auditorium is astounding, a zigzag of seating areas that entirely surround the stage. Sitting in the concert hall, hovering above the orchestra in my hundred-euro seat, I wonder if anyone else is about to listen to Simon Rattle conduct Bach's Brandenburg Concertos under the waning influence of a mind-altering substance. This is not, I am sure, what Daniel envisioned. The music starts—first the tap of a piano, then the chords of a violin—and I close my eyes. I don't sleep, exactly, but when it's over I remember floating above the music, horns and cellos drifting through the air. After a long ovation, the man next to me ushers his wife into her fur coat. She swats me across the face with her belt strap. The woman bends down to apologize, but I'm grateful for the wake-up call.

After the concert, I walk toward the train station, the wind whipping down the street, an ambulance whooshing by. The streetlights glow warm and bright, but I feel like I'm sleepwalking. Like a refrigerator, I am humming low, electric, tucked away in a corner, seeing everything. I find myself standing under balconies, taking shelter while umbrella-less Berliners soldier past me, immune to the spitting rain and wind. *Schmuddelwetter*, as Magda called it.

It's dark when I exit the train. I see my breath in the air. The space-age prostitutes seem over it already, hands tucked in pockets, teeth chattering. It's windy and they sway slightly, a row of sunflowers nodding in the breeze. One of them, the blond, winks at me. "*Hallo*, muffin," she calls.

"*Hallo*," I whisper back.

I find a cybercafe so I can send a note to Daniel. A note, I've decided, is preferable to a call. I wind up at Surf & Sushi, where young people eat dumplings and check their email. I reserve a computer for five euros, only to discover that the keys are in a slightly different order on the German keyboard, just enough to fuck you up. There are extra letters in the alphabet too, letters like *ß*, which is pronounced "ess" even though there is already an *S*, which seems to do the job perfectly well. Dozens of fingers clack around me, but it takes me half an hour just to access my email. After one macchiato, my heart is pounding, and I've only managed to send Daniel a two-sentence note in response to his four emails. "Hallo, muffin," I write. "Miss you and the pooch. More later, trouble with the keyß!"

It's all I can manage, but it's all I want to say.

I read an email from my mother, wondering why I haven't called, nudging me to go to Sachsenhausen. There are a few dozen work emails that can wait because of my out-of-office message, but I reconfirm my meetings with Klaus Beckmann tomorrow and the collector Leopold Koch later this week. There's a message from Greta Hoss, an art consultant here in Berlin, already providing the time and place for our appointment on Thursday. And then *three* notes from my client Debra, wondering if I've contacted her nephew. "Please do, Sam," she writes, although there is no way I'll be taking some twentysomething American kid out to coffee. "I'll try to work it in, of courße!" I write back.

When I eat dinner at Cibo Matto, the restaurant is empty except for the occasional tourist and the newspaper man wandering in selling copies of *Zitty* and *Tip*. By the time I finish my pasta, the restaurant is full. Forks clank, drinks are ordered, people lean back in chairs, exhaling smoke. Outside, the streets buzz with couples holding hands, bands of people with arms around one another. I don't know if it's because I'm alone and buzzing, this feeling that everyone else is connected.

I make one final stop: the magazine store under the arches of the Hackescher Markt train station. I buy some bottled water and a copy of *Tip*, a what-to-do guide for the city. The boy behind the counter has a snub nose, icy-blue eyes, and white-blond hair. He looks like a spoiled white cat, the kind that hisses, even when you're nice to it. Every time I come here to buy water, he looks at me as if I've shit on the floor. He types into the cash register with one hand and holds the other on his hip. The boy hands me the bottle. "Do you have a bag?" I ask.

He stares at me, says nothing. "Hot in Herre" by Nelly hums from a tattered boom box, a fluorescent light clicks overhead.

"I'd like a bag," I repeat. "For the water."

"*Nein,*" he says. "You must pay for it."

"Forget it." I leave the store.

I return to my room. From my window I observe a woman on her terrace. She's wearing her nightgown and stringing laundry along a clothesline. I think of the view from my window at home, the apartment I share with Daniel and Harry. We have a nice place, but our bedroom faces an air shaft, opposite a small tenement across the way, looking into people's kitchens (the Woody Allen view, my mother calls it). Standing by our window, looking one floor down, we see this couple making incredible meals for themselves, gutting chickens, pounding meat, kneading dough. It's something out of a Brueghel painting. The woman is always in a nightgown. The man cooks in his tighty-whities and nothing else. When I wake up in the middle of the night to go to the bathroom, they are often still up. They sit around the kitchen, watching each other cook, drinking wine, eating, and laughing.

Daniel and I used to be like this. He'd make eggs and coffee, wearing only his pajama bottoms, his blond hair tousled, always barefoot.

I stare at my open suitcase, barely unpacked. I see the clothes Daniel assembled for me, and his green winter hat, the one with the snowflakes on it, lying flat on top of a sweater. I pour a glass of water and remember when we lived in separate apartments downtown.

There was a blizzard one January. It happened during the night, two feet of snow as a Sunday slipped into Monday, and Daniel and I slept at his place. That morning, he woke up first. "Come on," he said, crawling on top of me. "Get your boots, we're going for a walk." Work was canceled, schools were closed. He made us coffee and poured it into a thermos, which he placed in a backpack. He put on his boots, his gloves, and his green wool hat with the snowflakes. He wore this hat everywhere in winter. When I told him I loved it, he said well, you can't have it. Two men dating shared many things, but some were off limits.

The streets were deserted, and only a few had been plowed. Mountains of snow rose from corners, parked cars were covered entirely in white. We walked right in the middle of the street. Looking down West Tenth Street, it could be any day of the week, another year, a different century. Our boots disappeared in the snow, and there was Daniel in his hat, drinking his coffee, staring at the second floor of a town house. "My God, those windows." We stared up at the building, its floor-to-ceiling casement windows lit from inside with a warm glow. Two balconies adorned the parlor floor, and at street level, a garden was planted with gnarled ivy and twisted conifers.

By this time, Daniel and I had stopped going to clubs. Instead, we walked endlessly around the city, mostly at his prompting, and he always led the way. He loved this block, one of the only intact mid-nineteenth-century tree-lined streets. He'd find something new on every walk. This time, it was this town house, these windows. And the snow. "Look at the city," he said. "Isn't it the most beautiful thing you've ever seen?"

"You're so corny."

"Sam. Just because you were born here doesn't mean you have permission to take New York for granted. Not for one second."

"Well, I don't. And I'm still here. And I want to live in a town house someday."

"You and everyone else," he said. "I'm in, if we can have those casement windows. I'll install them, I don't care. By the time we can afford that town house, we can afford those windows."

"We?"

"I like having goals," Daniel said. "And you know I'll need to renovate. But trust me, you'll love it."

"So I'm one of your goals?"

"Sam, don't go fishing." He walked ahead of me. A traffic light switched from red to green. But there were no cars, just me and Daniel making our way down a row of endless white. "You know I love you," he called to me. I stared at him. Even in his boots and puffy winter jacket, his legs were long and lean. I walked over to a parked car, rolled some snow between my hands, and threw the ball at him. It hit him in the back. He lost his balance. "Hey!" he yelled as he fell to the ground.

I trudged over to him. "I used to throw snowballs at the sides of buses with my friends. After school."

"I'm not a bus."

"No, you're not. And I still can't believe you love me."

Daniel grabbed my hand. I lifted him up. "Let's move in together," he said.

"What?" I held his hand tightly. "Where? Your place? My place? Another apartment?" I felt blood rush to my head, nearly panicked with excitement.

"We'll figure that out. I don't care. But listen, Sam, I want to live with you."

"You've thought about this?"

"Maybe." Daniel stopped and looked at me. He began to list things he wanted us to do together: reading the paper, hosting dinner parties, falling asleep watching reruns of TV shows, arranging a window full of bonsai and succulents. "And I don't even want to think about the mess you'll make in our bathroom," he said, his arms now around my waist.

In a moment, I saw everything he described, a blur of domesticity that was too good to be true. We were thirty years old, but I saw us at every age, felt every emotion we might someday feel. The collage overwhelmed me. I stepped away. "Daniel. It's too much."

"It's not too much. It's just enough."

"You haven't had a boyfriend, Daniel."

"I've had lots of boyfriends, Sam. Lots."

"That's kind of my point. It's not the same thing."

"Well, none of them have stuck."

"Also my point. You've never lived with someone. What if it doesn't work?"

"Sam, tomorrow the snow will be dirty and melting and dogs will be staining it yellow. There will be puddles of water at every corner and we won't know how to cross the street. But right now it's perfect. It's mountains of white. So can you just be in a moment, for once, and we'll deal with the rest later?"

A man appeared with a poodle in his arms, trying to find a flat space for the dog to do its business. He climbed over a mound of snow and placed the dog in the middle of the street.

"Fine," I said. "But I want a dog."

"You do?"

"Yes. If we move in together, I want a dog. Like, immediately."

"What kind of dog?"

"A Boston terrier. A dachshund. A small dog that I can take to work and to galleries."

"So you've been thinking, too."

"I have. And maybe even, someday, a family."

"Of people?"

"Yes, of people!"

"Let's start with the dog." Daniel grabbed my hand, opened the gates to a town house, and led me down the steps.

"What are you doing?"

"You must be cold."

"Someone lives here, Daniel."

"Someday, maybe, it will be us." He removed my furry hood, took off his gloves, and rubbed a thumb across my cheek. He took off his hat and put it on me. "You look cute in it, but you still can't have it." He pushed me against a wall and pinned my arms against it.

"Seriously, what are you doing?"

Daniel moved closer and put his hands on my face. "I'm happy," he said, his breath filled with coffee. "And I'm going to kiss you."

I feel something in my pocket, a little pebble. I cup it in my palm and stare at it: the other half of the pill from last night. That's probably why I still feel like this, like my head is falling through the floor. I think of my meeting tomorrow with Klaus Beckmann. What am I going to say? My neurotransmitters are rebelling. My synapses are tired and angry and on strike tonight.

I find my eye mask and mouth guard. I squeeze toothpaste on my toothbrush. I don't have to do this at home; Daniel puts paste on the brush for me and lays it by the sink. He started to do this in his old apartment, after we'd had sex and were getting ready for bed. Back then I thought it was the sweetest, sexiest thing in the world. Now I think it's just codependent. Still, I find myself missing this ritual here in Berlin, this order imposed upon me, a small act of kindness, a connection to another person.

Montag

Monday morning. I stare at the blinking light on the telephone alerting me to a message. Daniel and I were supposed to check in last night, but I was in no shape to talk to anyone, let alone him, so I turned off the ringer and went to bed.

I grab my watch. I can't believe it. I've slept for eleven hours. I do the math in my head—it's nine thirty in the morning in Berlin, smack-dab in the middle of the night back in New York. Daniel must be asleep—but who knows? Two nights ago, I was stumbling home from Polar TV, my synapses sputtering serotonin like a busted lawn sprinkler.

I listen to the message but it's not Daniel. It's Kerstin from the Zukunftsgalerie, informing me that Klaus had an emergency and left for Bonn last night. He's unable to meet this afternoon and will return Wednesday. We'll reschedule for then, she says, details to follow, and reminds me of the time and location of the opening. I take a breath. Everything gets instantly lighter. Perhaps it's the relief of a newly free day replacing the dread of meetings, of having to be on when I feel so off. It's like I've been handed a Get-Out-of-Jail-Free card.

I open the curtains. Gray clouds blanket the sky, but for the first time I see sunshine piercing through. It's startling to see light bouncing off windows and illuminating concrete, a glimmer of another dimension. A new Berlin.

I catch myself in the mirror. I look ridiculous in my pajama bottoms, eye mask and mouth guard. I should be at a rave in the desert. If I was fifteen years younger, if it was fifteen years ago. I take a shower and get dressed. Not long ago, I couldn't go a day without hearing Daniel's voice. Now I'm relieved the message was not from him, that it's too early to call home.

On my way to breakfast, I notice a copy of the *Herald Tribune* in the reception area alongside stacks of *Berliner Zeitung* and *Der Tagesspiegel*. Magda sits at the front desk, checking in a tall man in a fur coat, a set of snakeskin suitcases at his feet. I wonder if I can swoop in and steal the paper without her noticing me. I take my chance and fly through the lobby, grab the *Tribune*, and escape down the stairs to the breakfast room.

Astrid pours me coffee, and with her help I discover the nougat croissant in the pastry basket, so warm and sweet it makes my eyes roll back. After a full day of the pill wreaking havoc on my appetite, I'm suddenly so hungry that, after the croissant, I eat three boiled eggs in a row. I haven't looked at a newspaper in days, but nothing has changed: bad president, scary stock market, dangerous pills, people are fat, fires burn in some other country. I set the paper down.

Today feels different. The sun throws light into the courtyard, rippling the koi pond into a mirage of diamonds. And the breakfast room is more crowded. A German family dressed entirely in white feasts on plates stacked with cold cuts and cheese. The British ladies spread honey on their muffins and continue discussing Harvey the Wanker. And an Asian couple sit in the center of the room: An elegant girl wrapped in a tan shawl, her dark hair almost scraping the floor. Her boyfriend is unshaven in black jeans and a baggy sweater three sizes too big for his slender frame. They don't talk. He just smokes, stares into the girl's eyes, and dips his croissant into her coffee.

Though my meeting is canceled, I pull out my folder with information about Klaus Beckmann and the Zukunftsgalerie. *Immediate/ Present* is the first show he's curated since his gallery moved into a former bread-making factory in Kreuzberg, abandoned since the war. The invitation came in the mail, with a handwritten note from Klaus himself. A mutual friend suggested he contact me. *Dear Comrade*, he wrote, *I am told you like adventure, dogs, wine, and art. I promise you will find at least three at my opening so why not come to Berlin?* I had no intention of coming or even responding to the invite. I get twenty a week. *Ostalgie* felt obscure, Germany too far to travel. But then things took a turn at home, and an invitation from a stranger begot this hastily planned trip. Before I left New York, I found a few articles on Klaus and printed them. As it turns out, he's a real character, a well-known director of theater and performance art in East Germany before he opened his first gallery, in the West, after the wall fell. He's an iconoclast, a provocateur.

I'd heard people rave about Berlin, the ever-changing city with the complicated history. The Nazis. The Wall. The decadence. I'd read about the "new" Berlin—streets dotted with galleries, covered in graffiti, bursting with art; clubs and restaurants that pop up out of nowhere, then disappear like a one-night stand; an entire city exploding with creativity. Clients began to nag me. *How can you care about art and not go to Berlin?* But caring about art has grown complicated. For someone who makes a living from the cutting edge, my knife has grown pretty dull.

I decide to use these remaining days well. No clubs, no pills, no hiding in my room. I'll prepare for my meetings, cross some galleries off my list, eat great food, find inspiration on the streets. In the afternoon I'll take the train to Sachsenhausen. At least, that's my plan as I down my fourth cup of coffee, lucidity returning, caffeine rattling my veins.

Berlin is nine times the size of Paris. Walking around in the middle of the day, it's like the entire city is taking a disco nap. I pass a playground, so recently built that the red slide and much of the swing set are still wrapped in plastic. Damp leaves cover the sandbox. Three perfect trees lie on their sides, their tangled roots waiting to be planted. I take a picture.

I wander the streets of Mitte. I pass gray buildings whose incredible flatness and girth make it impossible to gain perspective on them; they tower over narrow streets like gravestones over a row of dominoes.

Scaffolding twists down blocks like vertebrae. Bullet-scarred walls await restoration. The smell of tar is everywhere.

I notice an umbrella lying in the middle of the street, twisted inside out, its metal skeleton exposed like a dead bird's wing, the fabric torn and flapping in the wind. I once knew a photographer who took to the streets after a storm, capturing pictures of discarded umbrellas. She had a gallery show many years ago on Broome Street, three rooms of umbrella remains. It was the saddest exhibition, desperate and disturbing, each picture more lonely than the next. It was the first time I understood that objects could be as emotional and complicated as the humans who owned them, and oftentimes more mysterious. I wonder what happened to her. Like so many people I knew in my twenties, she disappeared.

I walk over the Friedrichsbrücke and cross the Spree. Most of Museum Island is submerged in reconstruction. Cranes neck above museums as roofs are replaced and facades are cleansed. Entire buildings look like they are visiting the dentist. Two massive winches hover over the Pergamon. Apparently they've been restoring the roof for thirteen years, and there are still thirty more to go. Sometimes I think, What's the point, we'll all be old or dead.

The Altes Museum sits across the street. With its endless lawn and hulking facade—colossal columns stretching across its face like a row of teeth—the building looks like it could eat the Met for breakfast. I walk down Unter den Linden, past the libraries, memorials, museums, and opera houses. There's something freakish about this parade of monumental architecture, each building asserting its history, scope, and style. I pass tourists eating strudel at Café Einstein, old women selling newspapers and scarves, a man in army pants selling maps and gas masks.

And then, out of nowhere, it starts to pour. Men don't magically appear selling three-dollar umbrellas like they do in New York. I run back toward the Pergamon and buy a ticket for admission. My socks are wet. My soggy jeans feel like anchors. Red-and-blue euros slide out of my pocket like wet leaves. People cut in front of me as I stand in line. In New York, I'm so full of hate for the person who cuts me off, who stands in front of me in line for the bathroom, who kicks the back of my seat at the movie theater, who shoves their ass in my face as I sit on the subway. I can hate somebody, want to kill them, decide they are among the stupidest people living, for just a few seconds. Then it's on to the next thing. But here I feel inferior. There's a vibe, and the Germans are positively right to step all over me. In just a few days, the city has made me submissive, strangely passive. In a way, it's a relief.

Like jerking off in my hotel room, the Pergamon is another check off my list: Must Do Something Cultural. It's strange that for a person who works in the art world, a trip to the museum still feels like a chore. Daniel can look at a porcelain bunny for twelve hours and then read an entire book about it. But put me in a museum, surrounded by art, the first thing I want to do is find a bench and go to sleep.

When I stop to buy an audio tour, the woman looks at me and hands me a headset.

"English, please," I say, returning the contraption to her.

"Eng-leeesch is what I give to you," she says, handing it to me again.

"How did you know?"

She looks me over. "I know."

The first exhibit is gargantuan: the Pergamon Altar, a marble shrine the height of a three-story building. A skylight casts distorted shadows on the green-gray walls as gods battle giants on a never-ending frieze. Tourists sit on the temple stairs and cling to its gigantic columns. As I climb the vertiginous steps to join them, my wet sneakers squeak like a pair of rodents. People flick their heads and stare at me. I reach the top, grab on to a column, and sit for a while. The sound of Germans chattering is so different from English—like glass breaking, motors starting, wood being chopped.

When I finally reach the Ishtar Gate on the other side of the museum, I'm shrined out. I sit on a bench in front of some Islamic water jugs and notice the bulge in my pants. I get hard-ons in the weirdest places. When I moved in with Daniel, I'd get erections in Pottery Barn and Bed Bath & Beyond. I felt so suffused with possibility, looking at all the side tables, sheets, and espresso machines. One day, while shopping at Crate & Barrel, I went into the men's room and jerked off. It took only two minutes, I was so turned on by all the plates and furniture.

I leave the Pergamon and walk along the Spree. It's sunny again, but the air is damp and smells of rain. I'm lucky my meeting with Klaus Beckmann has been postponed. I'm so used to not speaking in Berlin that I feel nervous when physical words are called for. I find myself having conversations in my head. I've noticed that I've started to grunt and laugh out loud.

I look at my watch. Somehow, it's three o'clock. I should check my email, call Daniel, hop on the train to Sachsenhausen. But I don't. I just sit on a bench by the river and dig my fingers into my scalp. A woman sits down on the opposite end of the bench. She reeks of perfume and smoke, her fingers and lips yellowed from nicotine, her hair a poof of cotton candy. An unlit cigarette dangles from her mouth. "*Haben Sie Feuer?*" she asks.

"*Nein,*" I say. I get up and walk away.

An unusual development: When I return to the hotel, Magda is nowhere to be seen. Instead, a young blond man sits at the reception desk, chatting on the phone. He looks up. I nod and head toward the elevator. "*Hallo!*" he calls. "*Haben Sie ein Zimmer hier?*"

"Hello," I say, walking back to the desk. "Do you *sprachen* English?"

"Oh," he groans at my terrible attempt at German. He cups the receiver with his hand. "Sir, if you are *wisi-tor*, we must call up to your friend."

"There is no friend. I have a room here. My name is Sam Singer."

He repeats my name, pronouncing it *Zahm Zinger*. He removes his hand from the receiver and signs off to the person on the other end—"Ciao, kisses"—and hangs up the phone. "So . . . Zinger," he says. "Like *zee zoh-ing* machine."

"Yes. No relation."

"Singer, this is German name."

"I know."

"I *zoh,*" he says. "Just a lee-tle bit, sweaters and things like this . . ." He shows me evidence, unspooling the black scarf around his neck. "It is nice, as you can see."

He presents it to me as if it's a delicate animal I may only gently pet. I brush my fingers against it. "It's really soft," I tell him.

"*Kasch-mir*," he explains. "Only zee best for Frankie." I look at his name tag: M. Frank Rinkert. He looks me over. "Burberry?"

"What?"

"Your scarf."

I forgot I was even wearing a scarf. "Oh—well, I don't know."

"You do not know?" Frankie holds out his hand and I place the end of my black-and-tan scarf in his palm. He rubs the fabric between his fingers, then turns it over, finding the label. "*Nein*," he sneers. "Banana Republic." He shoos the scarf away, my fashion sense instantly demoted. "So . . . where were we?" He clacks away and stares into the computer screen. "Zinger, Zinger, Zinger."

"This is my third day at the hotel," I tell him.

"On zee weekend I am not working," he says. "Of course! I must not miss my night at Casino. I am needing all of my Sunday just to recover. And tomorrow there is Cookies." He raises an eyebrow conspiratorially. "Have you been yet to Cookies?"

"I don't even know what that is. So no, I have not. Is it a bakery?"

"Oh my God. *Nein*. It is a club. A disco."

"Great. Well, anyway, I didn't think I'd have to check in every time I come and go. I have a key." I dig into my pocket and present it to him.

"Ah! Super!" he exclaims, looking into the computer screen. "Here you are, Zinger. Room *drei-hundert-zwei*, very nice." He continues reading something on the monitor. "Oh!" he says dramatically.

"What?"

"No, there is nothing. It is just, there is note here, it is interesting, *ja*?"

"What is it?" I peer over the counter and into the computer screen, which is pointless, as everything is in German.

"Herr Singer, sometimes zee hotel staff makes lee-tle notes next to name of guests, what he like and he don't like. Just lee-tle things."

"Really? What does it say about me?"

"Ah, many things." He looks up and whispers, "*Zay are zee-cret*."

"What is this, the Stasi hotel?"

"Funny," he says. "You have that New York funny thing."

"How do you know I'm from New York?"

"Remember, Herr Singer, here at Stasi Hotel, we know everything!"

He giggles. "I must tell your funny to Magda. She will love it." Of course they're friends. I can imagine Frankie and Magda together, cackling about the hapless guests like a pair of hyenas. He stares at the computer, suddenly serious. "So, it say here you move rooms."

"I wanted a bathtub."

"Of course. And then you move again."

"I wanted a view of the TV Tower."

"Ah, yes, our guests from New York, they know always there is the better room."

"Well, it's usually true."

"*Natürlich.* And it say also you prefer coffee to tea with breakfast. *Milch mit ein bisschen Zucker.*" He translates for me: "Milk but not much sugar."

"It says that?"

"*Ja,*" he says. "This note is from Astrid. At zee hotel, we very much like to please our guests."

Oh really?

"I prefer tea," he continues, "and of course it must be green. Coffee, it is not so good for zee skin." He bats his long white eyelashes. I don't know what to say, so I stare at the aquarium behind him, the day-glo sea creatures darting back and forth, trapped. I once read that fish have no memory. By the time they reach one end of the tank, they've forgotten all about the other side. In a way, this sounds incredibly liberating.

"Listen, Frankie—or is it Frank?"

"For you, Herr Singer, it is Frankie."

"And please, Frankie, call me Sam."

"Okay. Sam."

I look at him. Were it not for the snippy voice and the overflowing attitude, Frankie might actually be quite handsome in a baby-faced sort of way. "Now that I've made it past Checkpoint Charlie, can you tell me where I can do my laundry?"

"Herr Singer, we do it for you here, of course. Bring it downstairs in zee morning. We wash it."

"Really? Yesterday Magda told me it was a whole big to-do."

"What is it, a big to-do?"

"A to-do, is, you know, a thing."

"A thing?"

"Forget it. So I can just bring you some laundry in the morning and I'll get it back in the evening?"

"*Ja.*" He waves his hand. "Abracadabra, as you say."

"That's fantastic, Frankie. Have a good night."

By the time I reach the elevator, he's back on the phone. Before I even press the button, the door slides open, revealing a young couple pressed into the corner, making out. The boy wears a business suit, the girl a red silk blouse and a tight-fitting black skirt. They seem unaware that they've reached the lobby. I don't know what to do, so I step into the elevator. But they don't leave. The doors close. I try not to watch them, but it's difficult to ignore in this tight space. We begin to go up.

They kiss like they do in the movies, like they're starving and eating each other. The boy stares at me from the corner of his eye. Suddenly, the girl pushes him away. "*Nein!*" she shouts. She wipes her lips with the back of her hand.

"*Nein?*" He looks at me and laughs, then asks something in German, his voice unexpectedly gravelly for someone barely in his twenties.

"I don't know what you're asking," I say.

The boy walks up to my face. "*Wie findest du meine Freundin?*" he asks, pointing to the girl. The language sounds sharp, like bits of glass being thrown into my brain.

"I really have no idea what you're talking about," I answer. What a lame thing to say. I sound like a stuffy English butler. The boy shakes his head, loosens his tie. He grabs her hand. They start kissing again. She wraps one of her legs around him and pulls him in. And I wonder: Where am I? Who the fuck are these people? This doesn't happen to me, not even in New York.

The elevator reaches my floor and I take my leave. The girl looks at me. "Ciao," she says, waving at me with her free hand, lipstick smeared across her cheek.

A Stranger in Berlin

I lie sideways on the bed. In the hush of the hotel room, this empty feeling spreads through me, a pocket of sadness behind my eyes. I must be experiencing the forty-eight-hour dip, the black hole that follows a few days after an ecstasy trip like emotional whiplash. The serotonin rush is over and the cylinders are empty. You just have to wait it out.

I switch on the TV. The weather lady talks cheerlessly in front of a map—a brown blob of land the shape of a berry. She looks into the camera, shivers, and rubs her hands together. From what I can tell, it looks like three days of rain and then a burst of cold air. Great. More *Schmuddelwetter*.

I press the mute button and call Daniel, finally. The phone rings several times. For a moment I think I'm saved, that I'll get the machine. But he picks up. "*Guten Tag*, Herr Singer." He says this so cheerfully that it makes me a little angry.

"Hey. I thought you'd be at work."

"You called when you thought I wouldn't be here? I was at the office all night working on the Boston project, so I slept in. I'm getting ready to leave."

"We don't have to talk now."

"Sam, I've sent you four emails."

"I know. I haven't been able to get online."

"I thought you had internet in your room."

"There were all these issues. And my BlackBerry is broken. I should have told you that."

"Yes, you should have."

"I went to a cybercafe and sent you an email. Didn't you get it?"

"All three sentences? Yeah, I got it."

"So . . . what's up?"

"Well, you're in Berlin and I'm in New York."

I feel nervous and sad, a knot in my chest. "I mean, how's it going?"

Daniel tells me about the library he's designing: geothermal heating, paneling lifted from a castle in France, wooden planks salvaged from the floor of a schoolhouse. I half listen. I say "uh-huh" and "yeah" a lot. But I've barely talked for days, and the last traces of the pill are exiting my system, which of course Daniel doesn't know. "Anyway," he says. "It's a lot of work."

"Well, it could be worse," I offer.

"Thanks a lot," he says. "So tell me about Berlin."

"It's crazy here." I tell him about the Pergamon, the hidden courtyards, the painted streets. "And everywhere you turn, there are boutiques and galleries, all these young people selling clothes and making art."

"Sam, you sound like you're a hundred-and-two."

"Whatever. It still breaks my heart. You never see that in New York. It doesn't exist anymore."

"Have you been to Nolita lately? Or Williamsburg? Or Smith Street?"

"Oh, Daniel." I sigh. "I guess you're right."

I miss him. I want to tell him this. Instead, I ask about our dog. "How's Harry?"

Harry's become everything to us. In New York, I take him on the subway in a little carrier. No one knows he's with me; I just tuck him under my seat. Harry is a dachshund from a farm in Georgia where he ran with horses and lived with a pack of fifteen dogs. Then we found him on the internet and brought him to the city to live with us. I'm convinced Harry dislikes New York, but Daniel thinks I'm projecting. Harry doesn't like strangers, and he doesn't like other dogs. It doesn't matter if they're friendly. In fact, that makes it worse. But we thrive indoors. Harry spends the day at my desk curled in my lap. Every so often he looks into my eyes and lets out a multisyllabic sigh that encapsulates everything I'm feeling. I love Harry and our undiluted need for each other. And without him, I don't know what it would be like for Daniel and me. When I consider the future, my future, I think: But what about Harry?

"Harry is keeping me warm," Daniel says. "He's lying next to me. He's doing that thing with his paw."

"Are you letting him sleep with you?"

"No," Daniel says. "Just naps."

Harry sleeps in his crate with his blanket and toys. If he slept in our bed, Daniel and I would never touch. When we nap, Harry squirms in between us, needs to be in the middle.

Daniel and I have what I call Dog Bone Sex. If Harry's sleeping in the living room and Daniel and I start kissing in the bedroom, Harry wakes up. He can sense any sort of bonding, fun or sex, even a hug, and runs into the room barking. So we bribe him with strips of rawhide. It usually takes Harry about ten minutes to tear through the bone before we hear his feet scraping at the bedroom door. These days, that's all we really need: ten minutes.

Daniel and I used to take a lot longer. We did things that make me blush now. Sometimes, when I'm alone, I jerk off and think about having crazy sex with Daniel, like we used to, and when I come it's amazing and intense. And then I think, How sad, I'm imagining sex with my own boyfriend, the person who left the apartment five minutes ago.

I wonder if Daniel really was up all night working on the Boston project. The names of his buildings always sound like code for a secret affair, or a bomb being built. I lie back and sigh.

"Are you smoking?" Daniel asks.

"No, I just inhaled deeply."

"I think you're smoking. Have you gone out?"

"No," I lie. "I've just stayed in and read."

"You went out and you smoked. I can smell it from here."

"Daniel, we stopped going out a long time ago."

"A stranger in Berlin," he says. "Brokenhearted. Lonely. Must be tempting."

"Daniel, please don't."

"I know you looked at my phone, Sam."

I hear layers of sound: the hum of the elevator through the wall, someone unlocking their door.

"I didn't do anything. I promise. It was lunch." That's what you said last time, I think. "You didn't need to run away," he adds.

"I didn't run away."

"Sam, you could come home, you know."

"I have the opening, Daniel." I change the subject. "You know, they have these marble floors in the bathroom."

"*That's* what you're going to say?"

"They're heated somehow, like magic."

"Sounds like something the Germans would like," Daniel says, giving up. "Function, function, function. Everything must have a function."

"Well, they make me happy."

"At least something does. Maybe I'll get you some hot floors for Christmas."

"I'm Jewish."

"So you're in Germany and suddenly you're Jewish?"

"I *am* Jewish, Daniel."

"Oh, please, Sam. We have a Christmas tree. You're bagels-and-lox Jewish."

"Daniel, can we talk about something else?"

"I've been trying," he says with a sigh. "Fine. How's the pooping?"

"Pretty good," I say. "I'm glad I have the Metamucil."

"I packed that for you."

"I know. Thank you."

I can't believe we're talking about this. That it's the first time I feel close to him during this conversation.

"Did you see what else I packed?"

"The hat?"

"Yes. I thought it might get cold. And I thought you might like it."

I stare at Daniel's green hat, which I've placed on the nightstand.

"So, did you call the guy?" he asks.

"What guy?"

"Debra's nephew. What's his name again?"

"Jeremy," I groan. He moved to Berlin nine months ago. With his aunt's nudging, we swapped emails before I left New York. In his last note, he asked me, a total stranger, to go to his storage space in Brooklyn and bring over a few of his sweaters. It was getting cold, he explained, and he was not prepared for his first Berlin winter. Only four hours of daylight, he wrote, that's what it would be like in January. He sent his phone number in Berlin and the combination of his locker at Red Hook Mini-Storage. I did not respond to that email. "You know what," I say to Daniel, "I don't really want to meet a stranger."

"Sam, he's your friend's nephew."

"Debra is not my friend. She's a client."

"Well, she helped pay for our new kitchen. And isn't he like twenty-four? You know what it's like to be alone in a big city."

"He's young and in Berlin," I say. "He should be getting into all sorts of trouble."

"Just call him, Sam. Take him for a beer."

"I don't take people for beer."

"Oh, God, then take him to coffee."

"Fine," I say, even though the prospect of meeting Jeremy Green—a.k.a. TheGreenDJ@aol.com—is not exactly appealing, especially since the only reason we'd meet is that we happen to be in the same city, connected by a pretty flimsy thread. "You know if that boy and I were in New York, we'd probably never meet at all."

"Well, guess what, you're both in Berlin," Daniel says. "Be nice. You owe it to Debra. She's been good to you."

"She's been good to my wallet."

"And she invites us to all of her parties."

"Exactly. I hate parties. I don't want to go to any more of her gang bangs."

"You are such a pain in the ass, Sam. When did you turn into such a curmudgeon?"

Good question. And with that, Daniel and I say goodbye. We don't say I love you.

I lie down on the bed, pick up my book, and read the same three sentences over and over again—a child, a village, an earthquake, a flood. But I can't stop thinking about Daniel.

Distance is no longer distance. Daniel sounded like he was around the corner, in the next room, beside me. I liked it better when long-distance calls echoed, reverberated, made you feel the eight-hour plane ride, the time zones, the far away. I still remember when calls crackled like an old movie. There was something reassuring in the delay of talking to someone half a world away, the static letting you know that you might as well be on the moon. But talking to Daniel just now, the dead air on the line was just so there, an awkward pause enhanced by technology, not caused by it.

I slide under the covers and pick up the *Vanity Fair* left over from my plane ride. I turn to the back page and find my horoscope:

Prepare for the new moon, for a perfect storm is brewing. Key relationships will be affected. But fear not, because romance is in the air. Get ready to come out of your shell, little crab. Expect fireworks.

When you're single, you read your horoscope looking for signs of love, and everything resonates. Then you meet someone and find yourself reading two horoscopes. Maybe you even read them to each other, in bed, at brunch, or on the plane to your first vacation together. You're in love, and for one perfect moment, everything is in its place. You stop reading horoscopes. You stop reading magazines. Really, what is there to know? You live in the present, not thinking about the future. You're sure it will always be like this.

Days, months, years pass. You drift away, first in bits. Then suddenly, on the street, your eyes begin to wander. Longing returns. You don't act on it. Your partner, however—now that's another story. And one day you find yourself reading your horoscope again. You look for signs of change in your future, seismic shifts, cosmic overhauls. Now, in a hotel bed in Berlin, a gusty breeze whistling through the trees outside your window, your horoscope says that romance is in the air. You wonder from where and with whom it will come, even though, undeniably, you're taken. You glance at your partner's horoscope, think about reading it, but don't.

I once read that the deepest spot in the ocean is in the Pacific, near Guam. It's over thirty-five thousand feet deep. I wonder what lives down there, if the fish are black and flat with long feelers coming out of their smushed heads, two eyes looking up at nothing. I wonder what it feels like to see nothing but darkness, and what it's like if that's all you've ever known.

I take a breath and rub my eyes. Forty-eight-hour dip, indeed.

I turn off the light and think of us, Daniel and me, back when we were "just friends." I'd met him at a party eight years ago, but it took us nine months to fall in love—or rather, for him to fall in love with me. We'd talk on the phone every night and go out on the weekends, supposedly to have fun and meet other people when really I was starved to be near him. We'd come back to my apartment and sleep side by side. I'd make a smoothie, pour us water, and give us Advil. We'd sleep off the pills we'd taken at the club.

Then one night, we kissed under a disco ball. We still don't know who kissed whom, but the moment our lips touched is frozen in my brain.

Before I go to sleep, I call Jeremy Green on his cell phone, praying for voice mail and expecting it because it's late. But he picks up. "I didn't think I'd hear from you," he tells me. "I gave up." I propose coffee tomorrow and, in an effort to contain things, tell him I'm on a tight schedule and have approximately ninety minutes between two meetings that don't actually exist. "Where's your first meeting?" he asks.

I glance at the map on my nightstand and choose a neighborhood close to Mitte. "Prenzlauer Berg," I tell him, tapping it with my finger. "But the next meeting is across town, in Charlottenburg." The lies just fly out of me. "So I should leave time to get there."

"Cool. Let's meet in P-Berg and take a walk through Mauerpark. Maybe you can buy me a sandwich."

It's best to just get these sorts of obligations over with. "Sounds like a plan."

The St. Bernard, or a Proper Sandwich

We're off to a bad start. He told me to meet him under the train tracks, but the station stretches an entire block, and he's fifteen minutes late. The U2 runs above me on an elevated track, slicing Schönhauser Allee right down the middle. I pace back and forth, searching for someone who might be Jeremy ("maybe the only redhead in all of Berlin," he told me last night), watching the punk mommies in their plastic table-cloth dresses, the construction workers eating sausages on their lunch break, the faux-hawked men zipping by on their bicycles. Then this guy rushes toward me wearing a brown trench coat, combat boots, and a black wool cap. "Hey, you're Sam, right?" He's out of breath, his voice low, booming, and American.

"That's me," I say, shaking his hand.

The boy is enormous. Not overweight or particularly tall, just stocky with broad shoulders. Solidly built, like a Volvo. "Sorry," he says, huffing and puffing. "I missed the damn tram. In New York I'm late all the time, it's like big fuckin' whoop. But in this city it's a criminal offense."

Jeremy takes off his hat, and a mop of orange hair falls over his eyes. He is not what I expected. He's scruffy, with the beginnings of a beard, and though he's twenty-four, I notice a few flecks of gray in it. His lips are chapped and red, as if they're popsicle stained. He looks nothing like his aunt, a pocket-size, highly strung woman who yaps in some mysterious transatlantic accent. Behind her back, I call her the

Chihuahua. But if this guy were a dog, he'd be a St. Bernard—imposing but harmless, with two big brown eyes set a little too close together. He says, "FYI, that's the best currywurst in town," pointing to Konnopke's Imbiss, a food stand underneath the train tracks.

"What's currywurst?"

"The fuck if I know. But it's meat, it's cheap, and it's fuckin' good."

I stare at him. Who says "fuck" three times within a minute of meeting someone? Who cares. It's reassuring to hear an American accent and carry on a conversation that is about absolutely nothing. I take a breath and decide to go with the flow (It's a choice, Daniel always tells me. A strategy). "Well then, let's procure some currywurst, shall we?" I reach into my pocket, scoop out some coins, and hand them to Jeremy.

"Thanks, Pops." We both laugh. A little awkwardly.

As we wait in line, I dig into my pockets again and take out another handful of coins. "What is it with the Europeans and all this change? I feel like I'm walking around with anchors in my pockets."

"I guess."

"I mean, what does everyone do with all of these coins? A dollar should be a dollar, something you fold up and put in your wallet. Maybe I'll just give them to you at the end of my trip."

He gives me a look. "Thanks, man, but I don't know you well enough to take cash donations. I'm not, like, the maid at your hotel."

"Right," I say, afraid I've already offended him. "Sorry."

"Buying me food, however, is perfectly acceptable."

We step up to the white-haired lady in the window at Konnopke's Imbiss. She looks stern and clean, more like a nurse than a purveyor of sausage. Jeremy orders for us. The currywurst stand is a model of efficiency: one man places our sausages in a contraption that slices them into perfect bits; another takes a spatula and flips the meat onto a paper plate; a woman pours a red sauce on top and sprinkles it with a brown powder; then the sausage nurse presents the plates to Jeremy, and to my surprise, she hands me two bottles of beer. Beer for lunch on a Tuesday? I guess it's going to be one of those days.

We stand at a table in a nook under the train tracks, strands of ivy and white lights crawling up a rickety trellis beside us. I stare at my sausage. It doesn't look promising. I take a bite with a tiny plastic fork. The meat is spicy and sweet, the sauce perfectly tangy. "Oh, wow," I say. "This is delicious."

"Right? The Germans are way into their street food. Which is convenient, as I'm totally broke." Jeremy asks what I've been doing in Berlin. I tell him about the owl, my trips to the Philharmonic and the Pergamon, my dinner at Cibo Matto. "You've done more in a few days than I do in a month," he says. "I thought you were here for work."

"Well, work for me can mean a lot of wandering around, popping into galleries, that sort of thing. But the weather's been terrible, and it's a bit overwhelming. This city is huge."

I tell him about the space-age prostitutes outside the hotel. "Ah, yes," he says. "I know where you are. The lovely ladies of Oranienburger Strasse."

"Exactly. I look out my window and watch them give directions to tourists. It's bizarre." I take out my camera and show him a picture: one of the ladies leaning against a yellow tram, smoking a cigarette. "The view from my window," I explain.

"Yep. Hookers and a tram stop. That's Berlin glamour for you." He leans back and cocks his head to the side. "So, you here for something specific?"

"I am, actually. There's this gallery owner, Klaus Beckmann. He runs the Zukunftsgalerie." Jeremy shrugs his shoulders, suggesting this means nothing to him. "He has a new show that's about *Ostalgie*."

"Oh, I know all about *Ostalgie*," he says. "It's like, a thing."

"Yes, well, he invited me to the opening."

"Impressive. Let's see the next picture," he says, eyeing my camera. "Unless it's dirty." A glint in his eye.

"Sadly, no." I take a sip of beer and push the camera toward him.

Jeremy presses the button for the next photo: the TV Tower gleaming at night. "Ah, the giant disco ball in the sky." He scrolls through the next dozen or so—digital snatches of graffiti from the street; the gloomy, spectacular view from my window; and the TV Tower shot from different angles, capturing light like a supermodel. I stare at him. Who is this strange guy going through my camera?

Jeremy pops a final slice of meat into his mouth. "Thanks for the wurst, by the way. So, you wanna head to Mauerpark? We can wind our way through P-Berg."

"I'll just follow you."

We throw our trash away and walk down Schönhauser Allee. As we pass the Wall Street Institute of English, he tells me about Friedrichshain, the neighborhood where he lives. "It's punk, and sorta trashy, which isn't something I should mind. I lived in Williamsburg for three years, before it became, you know, *Williamsburg* . . . but that was like *Sesame Street* compared to this place. Last week, my neighbors burnt down their apartment."

"What? Why?"

"Don't know. Just 'cause."

"Okay, that's pretty punk."

"It is what it is. But it's pretty disheartening to be around so many people who have zero will to do anything. And it's not just the punks. Unemployment is like twenty percent. I haven't figured out if it's for lack of jobs or lack of motivation, not that I should talk, but it's ironic that these self-professed anarchists are, like, dependent on the government. And then you've got the unemployed yuppies and the so-called artistes who just sit around in cafés or hang out in the park with their babies. But here the state takes care of you. Even the hookers have health care." The wind whips down the street, throwing newspapers out of a garbage can and cycloning along the gutter. "Jesus, it's cold," he says, sticking his hands in his coat pockets.

"You're not used to it yet?"

"Dude, I never get used to it. It's like walking around in borscht."

We cross a square near Helmholtzplatz; the remains of yet another construction site have been turned into an impromptu playground. A girl runs through a row of tires toward her father, arms open, laughing. "This city is weird," I say. "The construction is insane."

"I know. All this fancy shit, the foo-foo architects, the 'urban renewal.'" He makes quotation marks with his fingers. "Every day you see new buildings going up, but they'll just sit empty. And still, you got the junkies pissing on their stoops. Mayor Wowi says 'Berlin is poor, but sexy.' That's like his thing."

We walk by a man passed out on a bench, lying sideways in his overcoat, a beer bottle by his side. The girl runs past him, chasing an enormous cluster of crows down the street. The flock of birds takes off, flying over us like army planes. A row of large gumdrop-shaped containers lines the corner—a relic from the GDR, Jeremy tells me. With mouths open, waiting for the recycling of glass, paper, metals, and plastic, they remind me of the ghosts from *Pac-Man*. It occurs to me that Jeremy is my unlikely conduit to a different Berlin, a make-shift tour guide. And not so bad, as these things go. I turn to him. "So why did you come here?"

"Oh, man. The Question. First off, there's just the legend of Berlin. You know: Iggy, Bowie, Isherwood. All that punk stuff I told you about. But really, I wanted to try the whole DJ thing, and Berlin is the place for techno . . . the innovative, cutting-edge minimal stuff. And that's what I do." Jeremy nods as if he needs to affirm that this is, in fact, what he does.

He tells me about the parties he threw in Brooklyn, that they brought in a few hundred people to an abandoned loft every other Sunday, just enough to make his rent. "They were super fun, great vibe, everyone dancing. But we got shut down, and then we had nowhere to go. In New York you need a license for this, a permit for that, it's such post-Giuliani fascist bullshit. So I got a job doing marketing for an indie label, but they practically paid me in jelly beans, and besides, the music industry is fucking imploding, so that was loads of fun. Plus, I had a girlfriend, and let's just say things did not work out."

"Yikes," I say. "That sounds like a lot."

"Hence the one-way plane ticket." He lights a cigarette. "I quit two years ago. But it's like, you can't really live here and not smoke."

I stare at the cigarette, the burning orange crackle at its tip. "So how's it been?" I ask. "Living here."

"It's been okay." A stream of smoke pours from his nose. "You hear about these expats moving to Berlin and forming these communities, all these artist types hopping into bed with each other, all that bohe-mian romantic stuff. Somehow, that has eluded me. It's a big fucking city. You can get lost."

"Well, seems like it was the right thing to do anyway. For the whole DJ thing."

"Yeah, turns out a whole mess of people had the same idea at the same time. So, Sam . . . *sprichst du Deutsch?*"

"Um, that's a big '*nein*.' I suppose you knew the language before you got here."

"Not a word. But I picked it up eventually. Bought the CDs, crashed a bunch of walking tours. Mostly I learned from watching *The Simpsons*."

"You're kidding."

"Nope. I know every episode by heart, so it was only a matter of time. At first I barely spoke to a soul. Sometimes I'd meet people on the tours, but they're just visiting, in and out. Usually, it's just me, Bart Simpson, cold cuts, and beer."

"Speaking of which, I know we had sausage, but I did promise you a proper sandwich."

Jeremy laughs and walks ahead of me. I notice his chunky black boots; they must have fifty lace holes, but he's not wearing any shoe-laces. "What's so funny?"

"You are, dude."

"I am?"

"Hilarious. A *proper* sandwich," he says. "Who says that? I love it."

"Well, shall we grab lunch? Maybe I can further amuse you."

"Absolutely. I was thinking, there's this new place by Kollwitzplatz that's perfect for you. They have a florist next door, so you can buy flowers while you wait for your crepe. But hey, don't you have to be somewhere?"

"Oh, my meeting? It got canceled."

And as we turn onto Husemannstrasse, I wonder why I seem like the sort of person who'd want to buy flowers while he waits for his crepe.

We sit outside Café Anna Blume, warmed by heaters built into its awning. I forgo the crepe and order the special lunch for two—a ridiculous three-tier tray overflowing with cheese, salmon, meats, olives, salads, fruits, breads, and jam. It's so over the top that I find it mildly embarrassing but also fantastic in a rococo sort of way. I order a glass of pinot blanc and Jeremy gets a beer.

While we eat, Jeremy tells me that he fell into a depression after his girlfriend left and the parties were shut down. For months he barely left his apartment. To pay his rent, he uploaded every piece of vinyl he owned onto a hard drive and sold all his records to stores on St. Marks Place and his CDs on eBay. A few days later his friend came over and spilled a Corona onto his computer. When he turned it on, he heard a clicking sound. The computer was dead. All of his music disappeared: 7,237 tracks.

"Had you backed it up?"

"Nope. I know. I'm an asshole. It's like my entire history was erased. And let me tell you, digital sucks. If it's fucking invisible, it does not exist, and besides, it's totally degraded. So be warned. The future, in general, sucks ass."

"Noted," I say.

"So all I had was the crap marketing job and everything was falling apart. My girl was gone, my tunes erased, and the towers had fallen pretty recently. Which, as you know, cast a mood."

"To say the least."

"And I realized there was nothing left for me in that city." Jeremy pauses for a sip of beer. "Because here's the thing: if you're over New York, and it's over you . . . well . . . there's gonna be a big fucking problem. That city will chew you up, spit you out, and send you the bill." He narrows those St. Bernard eyes, waiting for me to say something. "Sorry, dude, I'm rambling. It's just, I haven't been able to converse like this in a long time."

"It's okay," I tell him. "I know what you mean. I get it."

"You do?"

"Yes, I do."

"Then one day I'm in a Starbucks, and I felt, like, if I'm in a Starbucks one more time and see people chewing their cupcakes and chatting on their fucking Sidekicks, I'm just gonna lose it. Because that's what New

York had become to me: tacky people and bottle service and twelve million cupcakes." He looks up at the sky. "All my life I had this vision of what New York would be. I'd watch the graffiti-bombed subway cars zip by, dance in some giant loft with a thousand strangers. You know, *Taxi Driver*, skateboarders, Danceteria, Keith Haring . . ."

"I think you missed that by a few decades."

"Tell me about it. And you know what? I don't have a thousand dollars for a bottle of mango Stoli at some tacky-ass club. Seriously, who are those people sitting at those fucking tables?"

"I don't know. But I'm sure some of them are my clients."

"Oh man. Well, I hope you take them for a ride."

"Are you sure you're Debra's nephew?"

"Very sure. And trust me, we'll get to Aunt Debbie later."

"Aunt *Debbie*?"

"Yeah, that's what I call her sometimes."

"She's just so not a Debbie."

"She is if she's your aunt," he says. I laugh. "Anyway, I was always winding up in the damn Starbucks with my headphones on, hating the world. So . . . I left."

"Just like that?"

"Just like that."

"I saw this funny cartoon of two women sitting in a Starbucks and one of them says, 'Are we in this Starbucks or the one across the street?'"

"Yeah, that is funny." Jeremy surveys our tray—we've barely made a dent—and creates a sandwich with a pink meat of some kind. "So I went back into the office and quit. And I thought: Berlin."

"Had you ever been?"

"Are you kidding? I'd never left the country. But you know what it's like when you just need a change. Like if you don't do something, it'll be the same forever and it's your own fucking fault?"

"Yes," I say, a rush of recognition flying through me. "I guess I do."

"At first, no one would help me. Not my lame-ass folks in Albany, not my evil sister. They were like, 'you loser asswipe, you wanted to go to New York, we helped you, and now you want to go to Berlin? No!' But Aunt Deb, she's cool. I only see her once or twice a year, and I know she can be a pill, but we just have always been able to connect. And besides, she hates my fucking mother so much that she'll do anything to get at her. So I called her up and said, Debra, I'm freaking out, I have to get out of New York. Next day, she took me to breakfast. I told her everything. I said, Aunt Debra, I want to go to Berlin. It's imperative. She didn't ask why. She just said, Jeremy, if you need to go, do it now and do it fast or you'll stay in New York forever."

"I can hear her saying that. Did she say it in that funny accent of hers?"

"Of course. Let's just say she acquired that in New York, and it stuck. But it's cool, you go to New York to become a different person. That's the whole point."

I wonder where that leaves me, someone actually born there.

"And then," he continues, "she takes out her purse and gives me four hundred smackeroos, which like totally saved my life."

"Debra did that?"

"Totally. Aunt Deb is the only person who doesn't grill me or ask me what the fuck I'm doing every other minute or look at me like I'm some colossal disappointment. I don't care that she's all schmancy now, or that she got her fortune from that sketchy ex of hers. She gets me. That's a pretty great thing."

I have to say, listening to his story makes me think about Debra differently. Like so many insanely rich New Yorkers, his aunt has always displayed a weakness for bohemians, the down on their luck, the pursuit of art. Normally, I find this pretentious, but perhaps I'm being cynical. Jeremy goes on: "Next day after our breakfast, her driver knocks on my door and hands me an envelope. Debra bought me the plane ticket. It was Thursday and the ticket was for that Monday. Seat 17A. And here I am."

"That's an incredible story."

"I think so, too. Me and Debra, we don't talk much, and I definitely don't want to ask her for anything more. But then she sent me an email about you. Man, she loves you."

"Really?"

"Fuck yeah. She thinks you're all smart and hip and totally know your shit about art and pretty much everything."

"Well, that's nice to hear."

"It's true. She worships you. Anyway, hopefully I'll have a job by New Year's and can pay her back before I get fucking deported." He takes a sip of beer.

I finish my wine and look up at the bright-orange beams built into the restaurant canopy, emitting waves of warmth. I tilt my face toward it. "Wow, that feels good."

"Right? It's freezing outside, but right now I'm at the beach with a beer and my buddy, getting a tan. It's fucking great. I feel relaxed."

"Me too." I lean back and close my eyes. "And I haven't felt relaxed in about four years."

"You live in Man-fucking-hattan, what do you expect?" Jeremy extracts a creamy pastry from the top tier. "Oh Jesus, look at that," he says, his eyes landing on a young couple sitting side by side at a table not too far from us, a plate of cake in front of them. They're both gorgeous, the man with his shaved head, exquisite cheekbones, and black turtleneck sweater. With her clipped blond hair, pale skin, and dark-red lipstick, his companion resembles a young Annie Lennox. The couple stares into each other's eyes, caressing each other's faces.

"Have you noticed this yet?" Jeremy asks. "The way couples love each other in this city . . . there's this sense of ownership." The woman feeds the man cake with her fork. They begin to nuzzle. Jeremy practically swoons and almost winces, overcome by what looks to be envy.

For a few moments, Jeremy and I stare at them, spellbound, but our trance is interrupted when an American couple sits down next to us. The man throws his keys on the table and sighs. The woman falls into the chair and says, "I need coffee."

"I'm tired," the man says.

"And I can't feel my foot," his girlfriend says.

I raise my eyebrows. "Perfect timing," I whisper to Jeremy. I take out my wallet and we walk inside to pay the bill.

Jeremy thanks me. "I'm totally paying you back." I tell him not to worry about it. "Well, I'll make it up to you. I promise."

We leave the restaurant. "I didn't buy flowers," I tell him. "While I waited for my crepe."

"Yeah, but the point is you could have if you wanted to."

"So is it me or are Americans always complaining?"

"Totally. But just to clarify, Sam, Germans complain too. And they complain about everything."

"They are *gegen alles*," I say.

"Exactly! Hey, where'd you learn that?"

"Oh, just from someone." I picture Magda sitting behind the desk. She's probably there right now, doing something irritating. "It doesn't matter."

We pass more establishments with weird English names: Fat Ass Pizza; Negativeland; You're Welcome Bistro; No Socks, No Panties. We walk by a health club with windows swung open, techno music blaring, an aerobics instructor shouting commands in clipped German. Outside the club, two women smoke on a bench in striped running pants, their legs crossed toward each other. Jeremy stops at the corner and folds his arms, lost in thought.

"What is it?" I ask.

"Nothing," he says. "Well, there was this girl. She lived around the corner. I took her to a movie, and afterwards we passed this boutique." He points to a store across the street. "That one. There was this can of orange juice in the window. It was all by itself, like on display, with a light over it. And the girl, she just stared at it. We must have stood outside that store for five minutes, looking at that can of OJ. It was raining and we were getting wet. The window fogged up and she took her palm and rubbed the fog away so she could stare at the can some more."

"When was this?"

"Maybe a month after I moved here. We barely spoke, but I thought there was a connection. But it was not meant to be. I found out later that the can of juice was from the GDR. It was basically the only juice you could get in East Germany before the Wall fell. And then it disappeared."

"Sounds like *Ostalgie*."

"That's exactly what it is. Everything means something different here. You're walking some delectable *Fräulein* home from the movies, just hoping for a kiss, and then she breaks down on you while staring at a can of orange juice. I mean, who has to deal with this sort of history? And so much of it is recent. We're talking decades, not centuries. Okay, so you have the Nazis. Obviously it doesn't get worse. But then there's the Wall. Come on, that is some intense shit. That can of OJ is about the Wall."

"What happened with her?"

"The OJ girl? Next subject, please."

We pass an old bathhouse on Oderberger Strasse, its giant doors propped open. They are setting up for a party, tables and chairs and flowers are being carried inside. Jeremy wants to take a peek, so I follow him. He tells me that he often does this, just walks into a space with an open door. You never know what you'll find, he says, especially in the East. That's how he met the OJ girl, he tells me, just walked into a building on Marlene-Dietrich-Platz and there she was, sitting on the steps of a stairwell, reading a book about trees. His curiosity is another thing he's acquired from his aunt. Debra told him there are two types of people in the world: Yes People and No People. At an early age, she made him promise to try, whenever possible, to be a Yes Person, to always be curious, to march to the beat of his own drummer. Hearing these stories about Debra makes me further reconsider my notions of her, as well as her appreciation of the most conceptual art, which I often view with suspicion in my clients and see as a contrivance, a rich person's personality quirk.

Inside the building, an indoor swimming pool sits empty. The space is ecclesiastic—vaulted ceilings, light streaming through stained glass windows. A plaque says it was built in 1902; that much I can read. Tables are being assembled on the floor of the sunken pool, temporary stairs leading to the bottom, elegant centerpieces of red and black flowers on every table. Soft German voices echo across the hall, but no one pays attention to us; they're too busy setting up for the party with a seriousness that fascinates me. It's the same energy I noticed at the currywurst stand. A hushed orderliness. A togetherness. A sense of peace.

As Jeremy and I return to the street, I realize that something has shifted. I find myself experiencing a serenity, too. The city takes on new shadings as I experience it with someone else. The trees are more beautiful, dropping their giant yellow leaves like parachutes; the Soviet-meets-Parisian architecture of Prenzlauer Berg even more incredible. Even the leashless dogs dutifully following their owners make me smile. I find myself happy to be with Jeremy now, relieved to talk to someone who shares both my language and my heavy mood. Unexpectedly, I find myself opening up. "I went to Polar TV a few nights ago."

"Yeah?" Jeremy looks surprised, as if this does not compute. "How'd you like it?"

"I thought it was cool. What do you think?"

"It's cheesy," he says. "That trancey shit."

"I like the trance."

"To each his own. This is Berlin. There are other places to go."

"Well, there are always other places to go."

"True, that."

Jeremy offers me a cigarette. I wave it away at first. "Actually, wait." I take the cigarette; he cups his hand by my mouth and tries unsuccessfully to light the Marlboro. A newspaper flies past us. Jeremy is enormous, but no amount of protection can block the squall that's appeared out of nowhere, whipping the streets as if from below. "Wow, where'd that come from?"

"Fucking windy, this city," Jeremy says. "I grew up in Albany. I'm no stranger to cold, dark, and hopeless. But this *Herbstwind* is brutal."

We find shelter in a phone kiosk and he lights me up. I take a puff and get a head rush. "Oh man," I say, coughing, "talk about a cliché."

"What do you mean?"

"Guy is sad, comes to Berlin, smokes a cigarette for the first time in six years."

"Yep, that is pretty bad. So what ya sad about?"

"Let me enjoy my cigarette first." I take another drag. "This will be the only one."

"Who're you kidding? One puff and the wall comes tumbling down."

"Thanks a lot. You're corrupting me."

"Sorry, man, 'tis my duty."

I feel so lightheaded from the cigarette that I almost lose my balance. I steady myself as we head into the park, hoping he doesn't notice. "You're more fancy than I expected," Jeremy says.

"Fancy?" The timing of this observation is odd, as I'm about to collapse onto the pavement. "What's that supposed to mean?"

"You're so nicely dressed. You've got the shirt, the pants, the haircut."

"I do?" I try to regain my equilibrium. "Is that a bad thing?"

"No, man. Who wouldn't want classy footwear like that?" he says, looking down at the John Lobb shoes Daniel bought for me last year. "It's just, Debra was telling me that you work with all of these artists and, you know, downtown types."

I think about this. I want to tell him that I was one of those people, one of those downtown types. I danced in a loft with a thousand strangers, smoked a thousand cigarettes. I did all the things he wanted to do in New York, before they disappeared. But I don't feel like explaining this right now. And besides, is there anything more depressing than telling someone that you used to be wild? "Well, I guess there are the artists and the downtown types. And then there's the guy in the suit standing next to them."

"Making shit happen," he says.

"Right. There's always the guy in the suit making shit happen. I guess that's me."

"Interesting. And you have this lilt in your voice, this well-bred thing."

I tilt my head. "Me? But what do you mean?"

"See, there it is!" He laughs. "A prop-ah sandwich!"

"Oh stop. I'm just a Jewish guy from New York."

"Where'd you grow up?"

"Upper East Side," I say.

"Well, there you go. Fancy art guy from the East Side."

"It's not like that." I turn to him. "You know, I have a tattoo."

"No way." He looks me over. "What's it of? Where's it at?"

"You'll never know." I take another drag from the cigarette. I haven't smoked in years, and my body is unused to it. My heart beats faster, my tongue tastes like soot, and I'm nauseous, like there's a tennis ball lodged in my throat. It feels great.

"So tell me where your tat is. Is it all kinky? Maybe it's on your ass. You gay guys are obsessed with ass."

"It's on my shoulder," I say.

We walk through the park. Even though it's cold and windy, clusters of Berliners lie on the hill. Beyond the hill, the walls of a sports stadium fly into the sky, its silver night-lights stretching upward like a bug's antennae. On top of the slope, graffiti artists—kneeling on the ground, standing on ladders—paint on slabs of concrete wall that once separated Prenzlauer Berg from the West. I follow Jeremy as he climbs the hill. He sits on a patch of grass, leans back on his elbows, and looks at me. "So, do you like your boyfriend?"

"What a question." I stare at the cigarette between my fingers. Jeremy blows a perfect stream of Os into the air. "On a good day, yes, I like him a lot." I walk over to the steps. "Things have been hard." I drop my cigarette and crush it with my foot. I take out my wallet and find the picture of Daniel holding Harry on the beach. Daniel's eyes are incredibly green, the color of sea glass, and Harry's mouth is hung open, his pink tongue hanging to the side. They're both smiling. I almost lose my breath, my heart drops, looking at the picture. I sit down and pass the photograph to Jeremy.

"Aw, you got the dog and everything. What? Did the boyfriend diddle on the side or something?" He hands the picture back to me.

"Why would you say that?"

"Something about the way you pulverized your cigarette. Whatever. Stuff happens. The girlfriend back home got pregnant last year."

"Oh, man. It was yours, right?"

"*Nein.*" He wraps his hands around his knees. "But she pretended it was for like four months."

"No!"

"Yes." He flashes his eyes at me. "Can you fucking believe it?"

"Yuck. I'm sorry. That's terrible."

"And then *she* dumped *me*. It's like, *what*? It was so Jerry Springer. Hence the breakdown."

"So you have a breakdown in New York and then come to Berlin, is that the deal?"

"And the meltdown continues. But here, it's easier to hide. Berlin is fucked up. Sometimes the sun is shining and I think this is the most incredible place I've ever been, the flowers coming up through the train tracks, the crazy-ass architecture, and you walk by these terraces with satellite dishes and red flowers spilling off the railings. And if you want to party, come on, there's no place like Berlin. You can go to an after-hours in an abandoned kindergarten or pop shrooms in some old Nazi bunker or go to an outdoor graffiti party with all these artists doing their thang."

"And you do all these things?"

"When I got here, yeah, I was crazy. My first day in Friedrichshain, the Turks and the punks were literally having a food fight on the bridge at Warschauer Strasse. There were hundreds of them—yelling, dogs barking, food flying everywhere. I was so happy to be here, I just picked up some eggs and joined in."

"Really? Wow." I would have run in the other direction.

"And the next night I went to this party in a bombed-out warehouse by Treptower Park. It went on for three days. These rusty trucks and car parts were still there, but everyone just danced around them. I went home, slept for four hours, went back and it was all still happening. I couldn't believe it. No stupid cabaret laws. No lame bottle service. You want to do something in Berlin, you do it." Jeremy nods defiantly, then looks off into the distance, at a group of friends sitting cross-legged on the grass. "But I've been seriously stuck in my head for the past few months. It's like I'm watching everything, but it's all happening to other people. Nothing's happening to me."

"I've been here for a few days and I already feel that way."

"You're just jet-lagged. But I don't know what's wrong with me. It's like, if I go through an entire week and don't talk to anyone, did that week really happen? Most days it's gray and damp and I feel like I'm in a dream, and I never wake up. I evaporate on the street every day. And I'm a friendly guy. I didn't know you, but I sought you out, right? I was like, dude, I'm starved for affection, come buy me a sandwich."

"Well I'm glad you did."

"But I haven't been able to click with anyone here. A few weeks ago I went to this sex club, which is not something I ordinarily do."

"Jeez. That's pretty bold."

"Well, for some Berliners a trip to the sex club is like going to yoga class. But let's face it, I did it out of sheer desperation. I sat there for three hours until finally some girl went down on me. I asked her to coffee right after I came, but she just got up and left. It was terrible." Jeremy looks into my eyes, waiting for something, but I don't know what to say. "I'm so fucking lonely. I sit in cafés all day, wearing my headphones. See, you can't just leave your stuff back home. It'll find you eventually."

Jeremy stands up. He offers his hand, but I lift myself off the grass. It's grown later, and the air, carried by the *Herbstwind*, has turned bitter. Jeremy looks like he might cry, or try to hug me, and for some reason I step back. Whatever the instinct, it passes, and we begin to follow the two-brick-wide line that snakes through the park. Where the Wall once stood. Jeremy changes the subject. "So, what did you take at Polar TV?"

"Well, I went sober," I say. "That was my intention."

"Yeah. That's like going to a whorehouse to read a book."

"Whatever. This guy at the club gave me ecstasy."

"You rolled? That's so 1998."

"I had my personal renaissance around that time. So it was nice to try and relive it."

"No wonder you haven't done much work. What'd you do yesterday?"

"Well, my plan was to hop on the train and go to Sachsenhausen."

"Jesus, man. Do you have some psychological death wish for yourself? Nothing like a good trip to the camps after a comedown from pills."

"Nothing like it," I say. "Anyway, it didn't pan out."

"That's for the best. You should go, though. You're Jewish, right?"

"What makes you say that?"

"You told me a few minutes ago."

"I did?" I look at him skeptically, but Jeremy nods. "Not super religious, but yes, I'm Jewish. You?"

"Me? Nah."

"Oh, right." I'd nearly forgotten he shares blood with Debra Belle, who sends an elaborate arrangement of green tulips on St. Patrick's Day. Daniel calls her Miss Lucky Charms.

Jeremy turns to me. "So maybe it's not a cool question, but do you feel anything, being here? As a Jewish guy?"

"What I feel most is that I should be feeling something more, if that makes sense."

"I kinda sorta get it."

"Yeah, me too. When I first got here, I'd hear a sound, or smell something, and my mind would wander. But now I'm not really thinking about it. Is that wrong? I think that must be wrong." I stop and look down. There are metal markers imbedded in the brick line where the Wall used to be. I stare at a silver plate in the ground, which says something in German.

"They're reminding us that the Wall once stood here," Jeremy says. "Berlin is always reminding its people of everything. It's pretty exhausting."

We leave the park. The streets are practically deserted. There are just a few people in the restaurants. Every so often a bike or two flies past us, Berliners zipping by with babies, dogs, or groceries in their baskets. No one wears a helmet.

We wind our way through a beautiful part of Prenzlauer Berg, right down Rykestrasse, past rows of immaculate apartment houses on cobblestone streets dotted with antique stores and tiny bookshops. At the end of the street is a cylindrical stone tower sitting at the edge of a park. Jeremy tells me that the park covers a reservoir built in the 1800s, and that the building at its tip is the Wasserturm, the old water tower. A structure alongside the Wasserturm was used as an underground terror camp by the Nazis. Now, the tower has been converted into apartments, the terror camp demolished and turned into a playground. "So, people live there?" I ask him.

"I told you this place is fucked up. Everything used to be something else." Jeremy tucks his hands into his pockets. "There are things you can't comprehend. Sometimes you have to just keep walking."

And so we do. We pass a row of cafés. One of them, Anita Wronski, looks especially pleasant, a two-story café filled with interesting-looking Berliners reading books by candlelight or staring into the glow of laptops. It's a romantic vision, right out of a movie, an ideal spot to spend a few hours reading and people-watching. Perhaps I'll come here tomorrow to prepare for my appointment with Klaus Beckmann. The meeting. I almost forgot about it.

As we stand on the street, I realize that I'm cold, it's about to rain, and my feet hurt. We must have walked for miles. Fancy footwear or not, I should have worn sneakers. Jeremy looks at me as if to say, *What's next?* I could suggest another coffee or a quick beer or . . . I could just head back to the hotel. I've been so stuck in my head for the past few days that spending four hours with another person has left me totally wiped. I feel the urgent need to be alone, before I get cranky. I look at my watch. "You know, I should get going. I have all this work."

"Yeah, of course, no prob." Jeremy shrugs his shoulders. "I'll walk you to the tram."

And with that, we head to the tram stop at Prenzlauer Allee. We pass a row of taxis, lined up and waiting for passengers. I contemplate taking one back to the hotel, but I'll let Jeremy walk me to the tram instead. He already has the impression that I'm some aristocratic luddite and I don't want to validate that right now. As we cross the street, I notice the TV Tower hanging over Alexanderplatz, a mile or so away. "It's amazing," I say, "how you see that tower from everywhere."

"I know. And depending on the time of day, and the weather, and where you are in the city, it never looks the same."

Right now, the giant orb—so silver and shimmering in the blue sky yesterday—looks dull and yellow. "There's a revolving restaurant in the sphere of that tower," Jeremy tells me.

"That's depressing." I remove my camera from my pocket. "Let me take a picture of you. With the giant disco ball in the background."

"Of me?" Jeremy looks confused, like he can't believe I'd want a photo of him.

I nod. The picture will be a souvenir of our day together, and proof for Daniel and Debra that I more than did my duty. Jeremy stands with his hands in his pockets and a smirk on his face, the lights of Berlin and the tower behind him. I take the picture. After the flash goes off, he deflates instantly, as if he has a history of being asked to smile on cue. "When the sun is out," he tells me, "the light reflects off the globe and creates a glittery cross, right on the tower. Back in the GDR, the West thought it was hilarious, a giant F-U to the commies who built it. They called it 'the Pope's revenge.'"

"Another tidbit from your walking tours?"

"*Genau*," he says. "Which means, exactly."

We sit on a bench. A digital sign tells us the tram will arrive in three minutes. How civilized. How much angst I'd be spared if we had this back home. But New York is not a city that gives a crap. You can be verbally assaulted and sideswiped by a skateboarder before even leaving your apartment building.

Jeremy stares at a beautiful girl crossing the tracks in chunky black boots, a sundress, and a leather jacket. "Oh, man," he whispers. He puts his hand to his mouth in amazement. "Sam, I really need some TLC."

"It can't be that hard," I say. "You're a nice-looking guy."

"Thanks, dude." He stares longingly as the girl crosses the street. "I don't know what it is, but German chicks just won't look at me."

"So what's your plan for tonight?"

"Drink beer. Smoke joint. Watch TV." He says this like a robot, as if this routine replays every night. Jeremy looks at me as the tram emerges. "It's okay, by the way, about the sweaters."

"Jeremy, listen, this trip came out of nowhere. And I was so busy before I left."

"I know. I just don't want there be any weirdness between us, because you seem like a cool guy. But it's pretty obvious you didn't bring my sweaters, right?"

"Right."

"And maybe it was an unusual thing to ask a stranger. But now that you're here, and we're shooting the shit, I just want you not to worry about the sweater thing."

"Well, I wish I had brought them for you."

The tram pulls in. For a moment, I think Jeremy might follow me on board so he won't have to go home. I turn to him. "So I guess this is goodbye. *Auf Wiedersehen*, as they say."

"Actually, no one really says that here. They say '*Tschüss*.'"

"How do you spell that?"

"T-S-C-H-U with an umlaut . . ."

"Ah, well," I say, interrupting him. "Goodbye, then." I extend my hand, afraid he's about to give me one of those straight-boy handshakes with the complicated choreography. They always seem like a trick, these awkward hand-dances.

Instead, Jeremy grabs my back and gives me a quick hug. He looks into my eyes. "You're a cool guy, Sam. I'm very glad to have met you. Have an awesome time in Berlin."

I watch him from the tram. Jeremy stands on the corner, hands tucked in his pockets. He looks lost, like he doesn't know what to do. Then he cracks his neck and lights a cigarette. He crosses the street, the tram pulls away, and he disappears.

Discombobulated

Magda continues to confound me. This morning I took the stairs down to the lobby, impatient with the rickety elevator. Clearly she was used to the ding of the elevator alerting her to a new arrival, because I caught her by surprise. I think she was meditating. She was chanting softly, her eyes shut, her head held high and erect. I thought about creeping back up the stairs unnoticed, but then her eyes blinked open. "Oh. Samuel. I am sorry."

I walked over to the desk. "Don't worry about it."

She took a breath and collected herself. "How can I help you?"

"I was coming to ask for—well it seems so stupid, but dental floss."

She mouthed the words—*butdentalfloss*—her face punctuated like a question mark. I thought about explaining it—string for your teeth—but decided to forget it. "Magda, are you okay?"

"Of course." She cleared her throat. I saw books piled by her side, her hands folded on top of them, and two tissues bunched up, one with lipstick, one wet with snot or tears.

"What does that say?" I indicated the German words on her half-empty mug of tea.

"Ah, it says: Be kind, for everyone you are meeting is fighting a difficult battle."

"I've heard that before."

"Yes, some say it was Plato. But now, it is just words on a coffee cup."

"Did someone give that to you?"

"I get it for myself." Magda stared at me, trying to divert to another subject or simply get rid of me. "Samuel, down the street there is the bakery. And I recommend the *Laugenstange*. You must get it warm, *mit Butter*." She wrote it down on a yellow sticky, so certain I'd never remember it. She waved her finger toward the door.

I went to the bakery and of course I got two. I thought perhaps it was a hint, or a test, or simply a command. I thought we might share it together, a momentary détente, but I took one bite at the *Bäckerei* and before I knew it had devoured the entire thing. And it was delicious— warm and salty and sweet—neither pretzel nor breadstick but an otherworldly concoction, dough creased and drizzled with butter that seemed to be infused with sugar. It seemed impossible that you could just walk to the corner and eat this every day.

When I returned to the hotel, Magda was gone. Two men in uniforms were servicing the fish tank, cleaning the algae, feeding prawns to the rainbow creatures behind the reception desk. I wanted to ask what happens to the koi in the pond in the winter. But there was no way to ask, and they wouldn't understand.

I studied the fold-up map on the counter. I decided I'd take the long walk back to Prenzlauer Berg and find that café from yesterday. I traced the route with my finger and realized that I could simply take Rosenthaler Strasse to Neue Schönahauser Strasse to Alte Schönahauser and then Schönahauser Allee in more or less a straight line. If you could call that simple, or straight.

I placed the bag from the bakery on the counter. No doubt she'd know where it came from. I felt like I was leaving food for a difficult pet, hoping it might coax her out of hiding. As I began to head toward the elevator, Magda appeared. "What is this?" she asked.

"It's the *low-gen* . . ." I walked back to her. "It's the baked thing."

"For me?"

"For you."

"I cannot accept this." She pushed the bag toward me.

"Magda, it's a piece of bread."

She blinked. "*Nein*. Maybe it is nice, but no."

The two men handed Magda a clipboard, which she signed, and they left.

"What happens to the koi in the pond? In winter?"

"Samuel, I do not know, okay?" On another sticky, she wrote down another word: *Zahnseide*. "This is for the apothecary."

I left the bread on the counter and walked away, hoping that she would eat it, and in some way be grateful for it.

When I returned to my room, I looked up *Zahnseide*. Dental floss, it said, or literally: teeth silk. As I made my way to Prenzlauer Berg, I went to the *Apotheke* and managed to pronounce the word correctly. I walked out with a strange-looking tube of floss. And an umbrella.

Just when I'm convinced I'm lost, there it is again: the park surrounding the Wasserturm, the water tower I passed yesterday with Jeremy. Hopefully I'll find Café Anita Wronski on the other side. There's another, smaller tower uphill from the Wasserturm, its bricks stained with graffiti and surrounded by scaffolding as it, too, is being restored. It looms over this corner of park like a scene from an apocalyptic fairy tale. A field of loose bricks is marked off by construction tape, and in its center, a square of rubber, a do-it-yourself trampoline. A few boys with faux-hawks jump up and down, their laughs echoing. Two women play table tennis at a court right on the street, cigarettes dangling from their mouths.

I dreamt about Jeremy last night, imagined him alone in some dark room with his headphones draped around his neck. When I was his age, I was ridiculous. Ambitious and successful, I had it all figured out. I was never home. I was always doing something. And I was a slut. Sometimes, in the haze of nostalgia, I pine for those years: the way men would wind up in bed with me, the way I flourished in New York. I didn't think about anything. Because if I'd stopped moving, if I had started to think, I would have realized I was choked by loneliness.

I suppose that's your twenties: you're having more fun than anyone else, and yet you're totally miserable. No amount of drugs or money or sex could buy what I needed, and I learned that quickly. I'd be out until sunrise, each night a new chapter in a collection of stories, but after a few years of urban hedonism, I just wanted to be at home with someone, reading the paper, making eggs. It wasn't until I met my first boyfriend, Zachary, that I hit a semblance of a groove. But that relationship only lasted two years. When you're in your twenties, it's fun to play grown-up, but it can only go on for so long. Because your most distinguishing characteristic—besides your briefly flat stomach and your full head of hair—is that you're an idiot.

And then, some years later, I found Daniel. I thought, perhaps, that was it.

Oprah says that life begins at forty. Sometimes that's what keeps me going, this coffee mug platitude by a billionaire talk-show host.

But then there's Jeremy. Lonely, broke, brokenhearted, lost. He's in his twenties and not having any fun. So why do I find myself in awe of him? When it was time to leave and find something new, he did it. *Just like that.* A one-way ticket. A Yes person. Someone who walks into buildings to see what's inside.

I think I'd take the empty days and lonely nights just to start over again. To stare at someone longingly as they cross the street and wonder, what if? To feel a sense of possibility one more time.

I turn onto Knaackstrasse, and there it is, the Wasserturm, and the row of cafés—Bar Gagarin, Pasternak, and finally, Café Anita Wronksi. I kick my way through a sea of leaves and walk up to the entrance. A sticker on the door shows beams coming out of a computer. Perfect—a wireless hotspot.

Two floors are crammed with wooden chairs and tables. It's barely three o'clock and each table is lit by candlelight. I walk up the staircase to the second floor. Couples kiss, hold hands along maroon banquettes. Everyone has a coffee in one hand and a cigarette in the other. Trails of smoke rise from fingers like strings on a puppet. I find a chair by the window with a view of the water tower. It's strange that people live there now. It looks like a giant brick thermos.

I unzip my bag and remove my laptop. I flip through *Tip*, study the German words attached to the pictures, advertisements for futons and pianos, for movies I've never heard of, shows I'll never see. I try to decipher the specials on the blackboard but play it safe and order a macchiato and a glass of sparkling water.

Café Anita Wronski is submerged in a gray haze. Ceiling fans slice cigarette smoke and already, my eyes sting. Everywhere I go, the smoke overwhelms me. And now the craving has returned. It was a mistake to smoke with Jeremy, my system instantly poisoned and newly addicted. Just one lousy cigarette after all these years—is that all it takes?

Paintings of birds hang on the wall: parrots and crows, all in profile, black eyes staring out suspiciously. Music plays in the background; Louis Armstrong fades into "Bette Davis Eyes."

I try to get online, but all the prompts are in German. I restart my computer, try to log in, but nothing works. I've spent most of my short time in Berlin struggling to do the simplest things: finding a place to eat, buying an umbrella, opening a window, getting online. When I look up from my computer, I notice that my coffee has arrived. So I begin to read the press materials for the *Ostalgie* show:

IMMEDIATE/PRESENT at Zukunftsgalerie

Notes by Holger Höckel / English translation by Flora Mehrling

What is past? What is present? Where do artifacts/images live? Jars of pickles, traffic signs, a box of cookies, your favorite lipstick. In *immediate/present*, we explore Ostalgie, the wave of nostalgia currently gripping Berlin. You will travel through time. You will crash through walls. You will remember, and then you will forget. You will, we hope, arrive at a new destination: home. Your Immediate/Present.

Ostalgie—a fusion of Ost (meaning *east*) and Nostalgie (*nostalgia*)—is the desire to remember and understand the irretrievable past; to search for things that disappeared when the Wall fell. Products that were once the only choice in the GDR are now sought after, bartered, traded and collected. But mostly, they are remembered. A tin of coffee, a bottle of sparkling wine, a box of cookies: they have become fetishes. Everyday objects are now artifacts. The items of yesterday have become fossils buried in our collective minds.

Nearly fifteen years after the collapse of the Wall, East Germans are still struggling with a sense of loss. Not the loss of the tyrannical police state, but of the intimate rituals that disappeared in the new Germany. It is one thing to mourn one's youth, to obsess, to remember. But what happens when your past literally vanishes? Nothing can sate the loss created by memory, the deep tug of nostalgia. For Ostalgie is a disease. It is contagious. As with any sickness, it reveals symptoms that lay dormant within us, and thus we feel things like never before. East and West, newly unified, still crave a shared experience and reconciliation with their different but singular pasts. The East mourns the loss of an entire way of life; and the West Germans are curious about a life they knew little about.

Ostalgie is a phenomenon of memory, a desire to collect and obsess on things that have vanished. And so in *immediate/present* we dig into our past. Looking for fossils, searching for clues.

I stare out the window, my heart strumming from caffeine. The show is so crammed with ideas; it's going to be brilliant or terrible. I can't believe I came to Berlin for this, a show with concepts so tied to Germany. And is there even anything for sale? But then I think of my conversation with Jeremy. Be a Yes person. Walk into buildings.

I'm on my second macchiato when I notice a man searching for a seat. He's pale and thin, probably in his late twenties. He walks over to my table with his cup of coffee and a glass of water. His eyebrow is pierced, a small black hoop slipped through it. He's so handsome—beautiful and raven-haired—that I glance away.

I survey the other tables. There's nowhere to sit except the chair across from me, and he's just standing there, tight yellow T-shirt barely tucked into his black jeans, dried paint on his fingers. He looks at me and I see his green eyes, and when he smiles, my eyes fall to the floor, where they land on his blue Puma sneakers. I look up again, and he stares at me, perhaps waiting for an invitation to use the seat. So I do the thing that I always do when I get nervous. I ignore him and pretend to read.

I'm saved when the woman at the table next to me leaves and the Puma man sits there instead. He's arranged himself so that he, like me, faces the window. He exhales deeply, whispers to himself. I stare into my folder but I feel like I'm being watched. I'm grateful for the patch of distance between us now. I'm not attracted to many men, but when someone catches my eye, I might as well be run over by a bulldozer.

I glance at the folder and read absolutely nothing, then turn to see a sketchbook balanced on his lap. "*Hallo,*" Puma man says, relaxed. Another smile, and this time I notice a gap between his front teeth, which I find pleasing. As I try to smile back, his sketchbook drops to the floor between us. We both swoop down to retrieve it. His hand knocks into his glass and spills his water. It falls onto the table, my pants, my shoes, the floor. "*Scheisse!*" he yelps, leaping from his chair. "*Ich bin ein Idiot!*" He puts his hand to his forehead. "*Ah, Entschuldigung.*"

"I don't speak English," I say.

"*Was?*"

"No. I mean, I speak English. I don't speak German."

"Ah, okay. I speak not so great Engleesch. I speak only a lee-tle." He has a deep voice that hangs low in the air. "Your computer is okay?"

Under normal circumstances I'd be panicked about my laptop. But I calmly run my fingers across the keyboard. "It's fine. You missed it."

"Ah, *gut.*" I stare at his mouth, the way his lips part in a slightly crooked, highly attractive way. He brushes my shoulder with his hand, which startles me, and I flinch. "There is water," he explains. He shows me the wet tips of his fingers and walks away. I watch as he twists his long body through the maze of tables and disappears—another one of those serpentine boys.

He returns with a roll of paper towel, knees to the floor. I bend down to help, but he shakes his head. "You, please, sit," he says. I do as I am told. "I am sorry."

"That's okay," I say. "It happens."

"*Ja.* It happens." He says this quietly, shyly, then smiles again. Looking at him now, I feel like something else is happening. "It is wet still," he says, then flies away to the bathroom. I close my laptop and put it in my bag. I look out the window and watch the mommies push their babies across the cobblestone street and head into the park.

He returns, presenting two fistfuls of napkins as if they are bouquets of flowers. He bends down, squeezes between my legs, and wipes the floor. "Soooo," he says, twisting his neck back toward me. I try not to stare at his perfect little butt, his endless legs. But they're right there. It feels intimate, bordering on inappropriate. I don't know what to do, looking down at him wiping the floor. It's like the moment in a porn movie right before someone whips out his dick.

I start laughing.

"*Was*?" He looks concerned. "What is funny?" His T-shirt has come loose from his jeans. I see the edge of his back, the skin clinging to the chain of his spine.

"I don't know," I say. "I'm just a little discombobulated."

"Hmmm. The big words I do not know." He stands up and takes a sip of coffee. "My name is Kaspar." He holds out his hand. We share a leisurely handshake, longer than it normally takes. Enough time for me to notice the beginnings of a blue tattoo disappearing up his sleeve, the chipped black paint on his fingernails, the worn leather band around his wrist. "And you?" Kaspar asks. I watch his Adam's Apple move up and down, how it makes the stubble on his neck quiver.

"What?"

"What is your name?"

"Oh. Sorry."

"Sorry is your name?"

"No, sorry. Sam."

"*Hullo*, Sorry Sam."

"No, no. It's just Sam. My name is Sam."

"I know." Kaspar smiles. "And you are from where, Sam?"

I like how he says my name, so deep and heavy, *Sohm*. It's altogether different coming from his lips, like I'm suddenly someone new.

"New York," I tell him.

Kaspar half sings: *I vant to be a part of this . . . New York, New York.*

"That's the one," I say. I want to tell him that he has a terrible singing voice, but in the goofiest, most pleasurable way. But I don't, and as we talk, I realize we've never stopped shaking hands. He's holding mine in his own. I feel his thumb stroke, just once, the inside of my palm. Maybe it's nothing, probably it's an accident, but still, it feels electric. I pull my hand away. "Excuse me. I need to use the restroom."

"What is it, the 'rest room'?"

"Oh, nothing. I mean, I'll be right back." I walk away, staring ahead, certain he is watching me.

I wait for the bathroom, standing by the rack of newspapers, tapping my foot. A man exits, preppy but with dreads, a cigarette stuck in his mouth. Once inside, I lock the door and sit on the toilet.

I should leave the café, head back to the hotel. But what will I tell Kaspar? I don't need to tell him anything. I just met him. And are we even flirting? I think we are, but I don't know. Some guys tilt their head a certain way and wind up with a stranger in their bed. But me, somehow I've become clueless. And flirting sober, and in daylight? Forget about it. Besides, I have a dog and a boyfriend back in New York. "Fuck," I whisper. My mouth is dry and my heart is pounding, yet I could take a nap right here on the toilet seat. I stare at the graffiti on the bathroom wall, then at the poster on the door for Nena, who apparently has a new album out in two weeks. Ms. Luftballoon looks the same as she did on MTV a hundred years ago, just a bit shabbier in a Germanic Chrissie Hynde kind of way. I watch as the doorknob twists back and forth, slowly at first. Then a bang on the door: "*Mach auf!*" a woman yells.

"Okay!" I yell back. I flush the toilet, splash some water on my face, and stare at myself in the mirror. Tired eyes, unshaven face. What could Kaspar see in me? Then I notice a note taped onto the corner of glass, handwritten German in black marker: *Angestellte! Hände waschen nicht vergessen!* I wonder if it's some weird sign meant for me. It seems crazy, but I'm feeling superstitious. I rip it loose, fold it twice, and slip it in my pocket. I'll translate my secret message later. I wash my hands, but there are no more paper towels. Kaspar must have used them all to clean his spill. I shake my hands dry and wipe them on my jeans as someone pounds at the door again. I walk out and there is a short woman holding a cigarette and a baby. "*Jahzoose!*" she says, her voice slicing through me. She pushes past me and slams the door.

I return to my table. There's a glass of beer on it. Kaspar cradles his own beer, a foam moustache drawn over his lip. He says, "I think maybe you are thirsty."

"Oh." I look outside; gray clouds turning darker, each day a little shorter. On the stereo, Edith Piaf sings about the rain. I take a sip of beer, and then another. I feel a warmth, butterflies. Something new is happening. And so I begin to gather my stuff. "Thank you, but I have to go. I have a meeting." It's not a lie, exactly. It's just that the meeting isn't until tomorrow.

"Sam." He leans back in his chair. "You are here how long?"

"Not long," I say. "About a week."

"And you are here for the work?"

"Very much I am here for the work." In other countries I often find myself speaking English like a foreign person, assembling words in a peculiar order.

"And what is the work for you?"

"I'm an art advisor."

"An art advisor?" Kaspar mulls it over, seemingly confused.

I think about explaining what I do, but I can barely complete a sentence. "I'm here to see an exhibit, actually." I hand him the leaflet from the gallery.

"Ah, yes, I know it. The *Ostalgie* show at Zukunftsgalerie."

"That's the one."

"I would like to see it. It is funny that already there is nostalgia for the nostalgia. I was thinking we are done with this in Germany. But this is Berlin. We are always looking back."

"And what do you do for work?"

"Many things. But mostly, I am an artist." He holds up his sketch-book, a rough drawing of a young woman.

"Oh, it's lovely." And it is: a depth of feeling from very few lines, the woman's hair tumbling in just three strokes of charcoal, her eyes half moons of unalike sizes.

"I am starting it just yesterday. My mother, when she was young."
He closes the sketchbook, suddenly embarrassed. "It is nothing, it is
just a drawing."

"No, it's good," I tell him. "And it's cool that you're an artist." What a
dumb thing to say. I sound like some wannabe hipster uncle.

Kaspar raises his eyebrows. "In Berlin, everyone is an artist."

I think of Jeremy. "Or a DJ."

"Yes." He laughs. "So already you know what it is like in Berlin. It is
not so exciting, I do not think, next to New York."

"To be an artist in Berlin sounds great to me," I say. "Very romantic."

"Romantic?"

"Berlin is an intense city."

"New York I am sure is intense also."

"Definitely. Just not in a way that I like."

"I do not know if I understand."

"Well in New York you don't walk into cafés in the middle of the
day all lit up by candlelight." I look at the couple nuzzling like cats in
the opposite corner, at the woman reading a worn paperback of *Anna
Karenina*, hunched over her espresso. "You just don't."

"Berlin is a nice city," Kaspar says. "But it is not all cafés and candles."
He stares at me, not saying anything for a moment. I look into his eyes
and see the reflection of candle flickering on my table. "Tell me, are
you staying here, in Prenzl'berg?"

"No. In a hotel by the Hackescher Markt."

"Ah. You and the tourists."

"I guess so. I didn't know."

"There are some nice streets." His tone changes; perhaps afraid he's
offended me. "And where you are, it is central. By your hotel you are near
many of the galleries. So maybe this is good for your first time in Berlin."

"Right. And then yesterday a friend took me around this area and
I fell in love with it."

"Yes. To me, this is the best *Kiez* in Berlin."

"What's a *Kiez*?"

"It is how we call a neighborhood. But not an area that goes on
for kilometers; a *Kiez* is what is around you, just a few streets. Most

Berliners do not leave their *Kiez* unless they must." He points out the window. "I live just five streets away, on Kastanienallee. I love it. But now the yuppies are coming—the *Schickimickis*—and it gets more crowded. But I am thinking this is okay. A neighborhood cannot live as a secret, not in Berlin." He takes a sip of beer. "So who is it, the friend who takes you around Prenzlauer Berg?"

"Oh, just the nephew of one of my clients. It was sort of a work kind of thing."

"Ah," Kaspar says. "Sort-of-a-work-kind-of-thing," he repeats this slowly, trying it out, like it's one long German word. He writes something down on a paper napkin, taking his time. I listen to the song now drifting from the stereo. At some point, Edith Piaf somehow dissolved into Nik Kershaw's "Wouldn't it be Good."

"So, Sam, on some days I work at this gallery on Sophienstrasse."

"You work at a gallery?"

"It is not far from your hotel. Perhaps not as famous as the Zukunftsgalerie, but it is a good space. Maybe you visit." It occurs to me that Kaspar must know exactly what I do for a living. He hands the napkin to me. "It would be nice to see you."

"Thank you." I stare at the mess of Kaspar's writing, all these words, all over the napkin. "This is in German."

"Yes. I know."

"Is this the name of your gallery?" I ask, pointing to some words.

"No."

"What is it, then?"

"Just a note," he says. "You read it later."

Just a note on a napkin. I fold it carefully, slip it in my pocket. Now I have two secret messages in need of translation. I wrap my scarf around my neck and put on Daniel's hat. Kaspar looks right in my eyes. I begin to stand up. "I should go," I tell him.

"Ah yes, the meeting."

"Right." I look at my watch and tap it, another dumb New York move I instantly regret.

Kaspar leans back in his chair. "Sam, I like your head."

"What?"

He points to my face. "Your head, it is nice."

I touch my face. "My head?"

"*Ja*. It is cute."

I feel myself turn red. My head is cute? I didn't know Germans were so forward. And precise. But what about the rest of me? I touch the back of my neck and the top of my head. And then I realize what he's meant. "Oh," I say. "My hat." I pull it off and look at it: Daniel's green hat with the snowflakes on its rim. "You think my hat is cute."

"Yes, this is what I have said, no?"

"I thought you said—"

My scarf slips off my neck and falls to the floor. We both bend down to pick it up and our heads crash into each other. We both yelp. I say "Ouch!" and Kaspar says "*Autsch!*" and I think how funny it is that there is a German word for "Ouch." We laugh, holding our heads, eyes meeting under the table. "You are okay?" Kaspar asks. I nod. He picks up the scarf and hangs it gently around my neck. He's so close that I feel his breath, smell the beer. He reaches out and almost brushes my cheek. But he stops. "Hmmm," he says, looking at me, still holding the ends of my scarf.

"What?"

"It is, I do not know. It is funny."

"What's funny?"

"You, here, and the water. Everything. I do not know." He releases me and leans back in his chair. I don't say anything. I just look at him, past him, through the window, at the water tower outside. I wonder who lives in that giant brick thermos and what the apartments are like, if they're all curvy and sliced up like pieces of cake.

Kaspar looks out the window, too. "Tonight they say it snows."

"Really?" I say. "In October?"

"*Ja*, in October. It is of course early for Berlin. But sometimes things just happen."

We stare out the window. The sun sets beyond the Wasserturm, the weather already changing, the sky rippled gray and tangerine. Trees rustle in the wind. A swarm of leaves dance in the street.

It's going to snow. I've lost touch with everything, even the weather. In New York, I live a life of no surprises, all carefully orchestrated. I check the weather forecast five times a day. A storm practically needs written permission from me before it can pass through. But in Berlin things just happen. It's been so long since things just happened. I've sort of lost my way, and it feels okay.

I put on my jacket, wrap my scarf around my neck, and walk back to the hotel.

It's Going to Snow

By the time I reach the hotel, it's cold and windy. Though it's dark and my feet are tired, I feel more awake than I have in days. I walk into the lobby and find Magda, still at reception. I give her the obligatory nod, stroll past her and push the elevator button. As I wait, I hear the clack of her fingernails typing into the computer. "*Hallo*, Samuel," she calls. I look into the mirrored elevator door and see her reflection. At some point in the afternoon, she reassembled herself; she's now wearing a black turtleneck and hoop earrings so wide you could punch a fist through them. Her hair is folded several times on top of her head, stacked this way and that in an asymmetrical bun, an elaborate piece of origami.

I stare back at her in the mirror, sliced into diamonds. "How are you, Magda?"

"How am I?" She raises her eyes from the computer. Tiny black glasses rest at the tip of her nose. "I am well."

"That's good."

"Samuel is having a good day, *ja*?"

"I guess so," I say. But it has been a good day. Though my body is thumping from coffee and Kaspar, my headache is gone, my brain chemistry rebalanced. Somehow, I've slipped back into myself. "Yes," I say. "It was a good day. It is."

"Samuel, this is wonderful." I look at her, caught off guard by the lightness in her voice. Magda must be having a good day, too. "And the sun," she says, "it comes out for you today."

"Yes, but now it's cold again." The elevator door opens but I walk over to Magda's desk instead. "Windy and wet. More of the *Schmuddelwetter*."

"*Sehr gut!*" she says, pleased.

"But this time I'm prepared." I show her the blue umbrella I picked up at the pharmacy. "Though now they say it's going to snow."

"*Schnee*? In October? I do not think so."

We look out the window. One of the space-age ladies strolls past the hotel in a Russian fur-cap, red earflaps tied at her chin. Magda shakes her head disapprovingly. "Well, that's what I heard," I say.

"This would be wonderful," Magda tells me. "But totally impossible."

"You know, Magda, your English is excellent."

"Really? You are thinking this?"

"Absolutely."

This obviously pleases her. She leans back in her chair, the bun of her hair perfectly immobile. "Someday, Samuel, you must tell me about the good life in New York."

"Okay," I say. "I'll do that."

"Have you been yet to Austria?"

"Not yet. I'm still getting used to Germany."

"Not the country, Samuel. You are so silly. Austria is a restaurant, in Kreuzberg. The best schnitzel in town. I make a reservation for you before you leave."

"That would be lovely." What's this new mood, this helpful tone? Who knows, maybe it was the breadstick. I remove the paper from my pocket, my first secret note. I unfold it and hand it to her. "Can you translate this for me?"

Magda stares at it, then lowers her glasses. "It says: *All workers must clean hands*."

"Oh." I could probably have figured that out. "Well, there you go."

"You are strange, Samuel."

"Am I?"

"Yes." And then, if I'm not mistaken, she actually giggles.

"Magda," I say, encouraged by her mood, "there's actually another note I'd like you to translate."

"Another?" She furrows her brow. "Is it a game?"

"Nope." I shake my head. "Sorry to burst your bubble."

She twists her lip. "Burst your bubble? But what does it mean?"

"A bubble is a thing that floats in the air, or is in water."

"Like a boat?"

"Nope. It's just a thing. With air. It's nothing."

"Sorry to burst your . . ." She starts to write it down.

I glance at her pad. "It's b-u-b-b-l-e," I tell her, "not b-u-b-e-l."

"Ah, okay. Do I get the 'burst' right?"

"Yes. But Magda, forget it. It's just a way of saying it's nothing that exciting."

I unfold Kaspar's napkin. The truth is I was so nervous at Anita Wronkski that I barely looked at it. Now I see that he's drawn a cloud in the center of the napkin. Inside the cloud, it says *"Kaffeeklatsch."* Lots of writing surrounds the cloud. Magda presents her palm to me and I place the napkin in it. She studies it for a moment, removes her glasses and looks at me. "Ah. I understand."

"What? What is it?"

"Kaffeeklatsch."

"Yes, what's that?"

"Who is K.?" She points to the initial, signed at the bottom of the napkin.

"Just someone I met."

"He? She?"

"Yes," I say. "One of those."

"Ah. Well, K. is wanting to meet you *übermorgen*, the day after tomorrow."

"Really?"

"Four in the afternoon at the corner of Sophienstrasse." She raises her eyebrows. "Nice street for *Kaffeeklatsch.*"

"Yes, but what's *Kaffeeklatsch*?"

"It is how we call a coffee date. You will get coffee. You will talk. But really, who knows?"

"What do you mean?"

"In Berlin, *Kaffeeklatsch* can mean many things."

"It says all of that? On the napkin?"

Magda nods. "*Ja*. And here at the bottom it says: *Next time, no spill*."

"It's a long story."

"I see. Well, Samuel, K. will meet you there."

She hands the napkin back to me. I look at it. "There's no telephone number, in case I can't do it."

"No, there is not. Oh, Samuel, it feels almost like a movie." She smiles blankly and tilts her head. "The American in Berlin. Will he go to coffee with K? And what will happen?"

When I enter my room, I notice the blinking light on the telephone. I sit down on the bed and listen to the message, which zaps me back into my other life: "Hey, it's me. Me is Daniel, in case you've forgotten. So I'm sitting here with Harry and I think he misses you. He's moody today, needy. He's doing that thing where he follows you around the apartment and all you hear is the clicking of his nails against the floor. He's doing it now, can you hear it? Anyway, I have a confession: I slept with him last night. And it was good. He's warm, and I needed a cuddle. I guess we're both feeling a bit lonely. But that doesn't mean *you* can go for a cuddle in Berlin. Because you can't. So don't. I wonder what the German word for cuddle is. Well, this is costing a fortune, and we know how cheap you are. Just kidding. Sort of. Call when you can. What time is it there, anyway? Okay. *Auf Wiedersehen*, as they say."

I hang up the phone, take off my shoes, and lie back in bed. I'm not that cheap. And I'd have paid him a hundred dollars if he'd just said, "I love you."

My nickname for Daniel is Daddy Longlegs. He's streamlined like a rocket, all wiry and tall. He's always wrapping his arms around me. "You're so little," he says, looking down at me. I'm not short, but I only come to the bottom of Daniel's chin. Sometimes when we're waiting in line for a movie, he rests his chin on the top of my head. I don't think Daniel expected to wind up with someone so much smaller than him. He probably thought he'd find the dashing rescuing type, which is just not me. His head almost hits the ceiling of our elevator and scrapes the top of the subway car. It's sad to sit next to him on an airplane, his knees smashed into the seat in front of him, rubbing against the in-flight magazines. He says that I'm greedy in bed, at least when it comes to cuddling, that I'm always the one being held. But that's just how we fit.

Daniel is an architect. Every so often he designs a house, but his favorite projects involve buildings in which people gather and do things rather than just live—schools, libraries, office buildings. He likes communities. He loves history and being around people, and it shows in his designs: gleaming structures with open floor plans, sky-lit staircases, floors lifted from an abandoned building, carpet woven with fibers from plastic bottles, stone yanked from the bottom of the Yangtze River. Everything is recycled and repurposed, even me, our romantic partnership borne from nine months of friendship. I think Berlin might drive him crazy with excitement, all the sharp angles giving way to bursts of color, the spheres and glass sitting alongside slabs of concrete. The past and the present smashing together. I have this weird impulse to call Daniel back and tell him about Kaspar. "I met the cutest German guy," I'd say. "I felt that thing, you know, when we first came together."

I go to the window. The TV Tower sparkles in the sky. You can even see a few stars. It's hard to imagine snow is on its way.

I crawl into bed and fall asleep quickly, effortlessly, which never happens. A dream begins to coalesce, but when a man coughs in the hallway, I wake up. I look at my watch. I've slept only ten minutes. I'm disoriented, sweating, heavy. It's that deepest, darkest, hushed pocket of quiet that can only happen after a nap in a hotel room at the end of a long day, when you feel like half your life has slipped outside of you and fallen onto the floor.

I notice, for the first time, the slight odor of stale cigarettes. The carpet, the paint, everything has absorbed the nicotine. It makes me want to smoke, but everything in Berlin makes me want a cigarette. It's a giant tease.

I remember leaning out the window of Daniel's old apartment and having a cigarette after we'd have sex. I wasn't allowed to smoke in his apartment. There was one night in particular, when Daniel first told me that he loved me. It was freezing outside, but I had my shirt off. "Sometimes I just look at you," he told me. "In your cargo pants." That's all he said. I remember the feeling, hanging out the window, the cars honking, the arctic air slapping my face as fountains gushed in front of the fancy building across the street. I stubbed out the cigarette on the windowsill. Daniel was shirtless, too, in his pajama bottoms, lying face down on his bed with a pillow over his head. I went over and lay on top of him. "I love you," he mumbled, his head against the mattress. I rested my cheek on the pillow, my body lying against his, and we fell asleep, just like that. I still remember the smell of his hair that night, like nectarines and summer, from that shampoo he once used, and the feeling of his skin, so warm. I will give up cigarettes for you, I thought. I will give up so much for you.

I should call Daniel back, but I'm not ready. Something has happened during my sleep. I open the curtains—the moon obscured by clouds, the TV Tower disappearing. I lift the window and freezing air flies past me into the room. Maybe Kaspar was right. Maybe it can snow in October.

The phone rings, but I don't pick up. The light blinks, and I listen to my message. "*Hallo*, Samuel Singer. This is Ingrid from Zukunftsgalerie. I confirm for tomorrow your meeting with Klaus Beckmann—half past eleven at Café im Literaturhaus in Charlottenburg. Also your name it is on the list for the opening this weekend. Will you be on your own, or will you attend with guest? You tell us tomorrow."

Young and Stupid

I look at my watch. It's nearly midnight. I was so tired that I must have passed out again. I roll out of bed and a spectacular glare hits my eyes. It's almost radioactive, the thin, perfect layer of snow that covers the street and blankets the tops of the sleeping trams. The cable wires are coated, too, slick and frozen.

I unlock the window and run my finger along the railing. I look for the woman stringing her laundry on the clothesline, but she's nowhere to be seen. A shirt flaps in the wind, heavy and damp from the snow. It's the only sound I hear above the deep, collective hum rumbling through the streets; an altogether different noise from the high-pitched blare of New York. A man leans out his window across the street. He looks stunned by the snow and the icy wires that float in front of him like bolts of lightning. He brings his hand to his mouth in what appears to be disbelief.

Snow is a miraculous thing. It can halt an entire city, cause it to lie back and exhale. It can, at least for a moment, make anything beautiful.

I step onto the balcony. The space-age ladies are there in ski boots and Russian fur-caps. They pace in front of the trams, hands in their pockets. A tram pulls into the station and they disperse like a pack of startled birds.

I call Daniel back. I don't tell him about the café, the water tower, the snow. I don't tell him, of course, about Kaspar. He talks about a cantilevered office building in San Francisco with high-speed elevators. "You're not listening to me," Daniel whispers. He talks quietly when he's pissed off. "What's going on?"

"Nothing." I draw a face on the damp of the window with my finger. I make two dots for eyes, then wipe the whole thing away. "I'm just tired."

"You're always tired," Daniel says. "Do you have any idea how often you say that?"

I could remind him that it's midnight here, six hours later, but what's the point? He's right. I am always tired.

He asks, "So what did you do today?"

I turn on the television and put it on mute, some game show with Germans shrieking about mattresses that appear from behind closed doors. "Why are you being like this?" I ask Daniel.

"Like what?"

"This constant inquisition."

"Damn it, Sam. You called me. I asked about your day. It's an innocent question."

Harry has begun to bark in the background. I wonder if he senses a familiar whiff of unpleasantness from Daniel's end of the conversation. A discussion officially becomes an argument when Harry joins in, barking orders to shut up. When we fight, Harry retreats to the kitchen and stands next to our oven, facing the wall. Sometimes he even shakes. Daniel says he's a drama queen, but it's the saddest thing you've ever seen. Lately our dog has spent a lot of time next to the oven, staring at that wall.

Daniel says, "Sam, seriously, what's going on?"

"I don't know. We're just so far away from each other. I'm across the ocean."

"Thanks for the geography lesson."

"Oh, Daniel. Whatever."

"Whatever right back at you. At least I'm trying to talk."

I stare at the TV and half watch an advertisement for shrimp-flavored potato chips. On a countertop, a potato man dances with a sexy shrimp lady in a pink boa until they fall into a deep fryer and start kissing. "Our children will be delicious!" the shrimp lady inexplicably exclaims in English through a cartoon bubble. "You know I hate talking on the phone," I say.

"Oh, please. You're a salesman."

"I am *not* a salesman. You always say that. It's like you don't even know what I do."

"Well, it is a little vague at times."

I resist telling him to fuck off. "Can't we just have a normal conversation?"

"What is normal?"

"Fine, not 'normal.' Nice. Let's have a nice conversation." Or, I think, let's get off the phone. It's midnight. There's snow outside. There's Klaus, *Kaffeklatsch*, and five more days in Berlin.

I walk over to the drawer and find the remaining sliver of pill. Maybe I should go out and finish what I started at Polar TV. I wonder what Daniel would think of me balancing half an ecstasy tablet on my finger while we're talking on the phone. But I also wonder what he's hiding at home. "Sam, it was nothing," Daniel says. "I had dinner with him."

"I thought it was lunch."

Daniel sighs. "I wish you hadn't gone to Berlin. I feel like we're both walking around, alone, different versions of ourselves."

That's the entire point. I look out the window, fogged over from the snow. I notice drops of water releasing from the cable wires snaking below me. The snow is already melting. "Remember when we would call each other and talk for hours about nothing?"

"We weren't living together then. And we talked about everything."

"We talked about nothing."

"Maybe you're right," he says. "We were so young and stupid. But it was heaven."

"That was only eight years ago, Daniel."

"Eight years. If we'd had a baby, he'd be talking."

"He'd be more than talking," I say. "Or she . . ."

"You know I want a boy. Our baby would be brilliant. And gorgeous. Could you imagine? He'd have your eyes."

I don't say anything. Daniel often talks about our fictitious baby, but I can't go there, because I actually want one. I don't want to contemplate the impossible merging of our genes. I don't care if it has my eyes, or if it's a boy or a girl. But we're nearly forty and I've pretty much given up. We've got files bursting with information and the right books on our shelves, but there are always a few hundred reasons Why Not. Besides, who can compete with Daniel's buildings? He gives birth several times a year. To him, maybe, we have enough. Then I realize I'm carrying around half an ecstasy tablet in my hand. Some father I'd be.

"Eight years," Daniel says. "You were so cute back then."

"Thanks a lot."

"Oh, stop. You know what I mean. And you're even more handsome now."

"I'd really like to believe that."

"Good. Because it's true."

I lie back on the bed, cradling the phone. In the old days, before Daniel and I lived together, when my bed functioned as a couch, a desk, a place to have sex and a dining room table, I'd lie back and light one cigarette after the other, using a half-empty can of Coke as my ashtray. My room would be engulfed in haze, a layer of smoke dangling like clouds between my bed and the ceiling. My eyes burned and my comforter reeked of nicotine, but I was happy. Young and stupid.

I think of the cigarette with Jeremy and put it out of my head. I'm always putting things out of my head. If I've come to know anything, it's what I can't have. And now, our bed at home is just a place to sleep. The sheets are nicer, with a thread count fit for a pharaoh. But there are no crumbs anymore. No mysterious smells, weird stains. After the cleaning lady comes, Daniel strips the sheets and remakes the bed. He says she doesn't do it right.

"I miss you," Daniel says.

"Oh really?"

"What are you doing right now?" Daniel loves to ask this, as if I might be fixing an oven or writing a screenplay while we talk on the phone.

"I'm talking to you." But really I'm drifting away, watching the snow melt. Snow I haven't told him about. Snow that shouldn't exist. I look at the television, at the German weatherlady and her six-day forecast:

a smorgasbord of sun and clouds and rain and temperatures in Celsius that mean nothing to me. "I hate this," I say.

"You'll be back soon."

"Not that. *This*. Whatever's going on between us."

I hear sirens on Daniel's end of the line, a fire truck rushing by. "When are you meeting with Beckmann?"

"Tomorrow." I sigh.

"Just go and be your charming self. Maybe you'll discover some amazing artiste and we'll get super rich."

"We're doing fine, Daniel."

"But I want a house! In the country!" He says this playfully, but it makes me sad, longing for the days when we talked constantly about the future, our future, together.

"You just want me to be your sugar daddy."

"You know it. And remember, you never know the future." Daniel has always loved this expression, but it confuses me. Because he's right, you don't know the future, so I just assume something bad will happen. Daniel says if you expect bad things to happen, they probably will. "Well, I'll let you go," he says. "*Ich liebe dich.*"

"You love dick?"

"God, you're hopeless. How are you even surviving there?"

"Barely," I say. "I'm scraping by."

"*Ich liebe dich* means 'I love you' in German."

"Of course it does. I wonder how you say 'I love dick.'"

"That would be *Ich liebe Schwänze.*"

"Where did you learn that?"

"Well, Sam, I did some traveling before I met you. Gotta know the basics . . ."

I think of Daniel when we were younger. He was such a beautiful creature—tall, muscled, and golden haired, like something Michelangelo would throw onto a fresco or carve out of stone—and when we walked down the street, heads would turn. He seemed to take this for granted. His beauty, so effortless, was just part of his existence. I've always wondered what that would feel like.

When I hang up the phone, I look out the window, at the snow, and think of Kaspar. Maybe tomorrow, when the meeting is behind me, I'll head over to Sophienstrasse and find the gallery where he works. Or perhaps I'll just wait for *Kaffeeklatsch*. I wonder what it means that I can hang up the phone with Daniel and think of Kaspar.

The next morning, I order eggs, toast, and coffee to the room and spend an hour getting ready for my meeting with Klaus. I select the blue shirt from Barneys that Daniel gave me for my birthday and set it on the dresser. I can't figure out what to wear. Berlin seems so determinedly casual yet effortlessly chic. It's a tricky combination. I'm not as fashion savvy, or nearly as daring, as when I was young, when I'd go dancing in a vest, army boots, and a kilt. One morning after I left a club, a car pulled up beside me and a man leaned out the window. "Two hundred," he said. "For what?" I asked. "For you." He rolled his eyes and sped away. It's sort of nice, that someone wanted to buy me once.

I put on my jeans and the blue shirt. I can't get my tie right; the tail is too long, the knot clumsy. It's ridiculous, but Daniel usually does this for me, and I've forgotten how to do it myself. So I throw the tie on the bed and unbutton my collar. I wear the John Lobb shoes that Jeremy admired. Daniel is always telling me to make more of an effort. I slip into my blazer, throw on my jacket, and head downstairs. As I pass reception, Frankie looks me over. "Very nice," he says. "Armani?"

"What?"

"Your coat."

"Ah, well, I don't know."

"Hmmm. Okay, ciao." He returns to his glossy magazine.

On the way to the Friedrichstrasse train station, I pass the Neue Synagogue, an ornate structure of brick and terra cotta, its golden cupola reflecting against the silver sky. The building survived Kristallnacht, looting, fires, bombings; and despite its name is apparently the oldest synagogue in Berlin. Guards with guns stand in front of the barricades that line its entrance. Ten years ago, this display would have freaked me out, but now I'm used to the Storm Troopers walking around Kennedy

Airport with boots and rifles, a gaggle of cops marching through the N Train, men and women in fatigues patrolling Grand Central. When they began to make announcements on the subway to be aware of suspicious packages, I'd watch eyes fall to the carrying case on the floor by my feet. I'd bend down and cup Harry's warm body with my hands. He's just my dog, I'd think to myself. But for that moment, he was a dirty bomb, a nuclear explosion, a disaster waiting to happen.

I keep walking and stare at the pavement. Looking at the ground is perhaps my most indigenous behavior as a native New Yorker. You don't look up, you don't smile, you just go on your way. It amazes me when people smile at me on the street, or say hello. I think they're nuts. As I enter the station, I crash into a woman running down the stairs from the platform. "I'm sorry," I say to her.

"*Passen Sie doch auf!*" she yells, tossing her hand back. She flies past me and then is gone.

On the train platform I think of Daniel, when we were in our twenties. Daniel designed his first building, I had my first clients. We moved in together and adopted a dog. For a while, New York was still my city, and the world felt open. I would fly through weeks just to get to the weekend, to spend every minute with him. But something happened. Time slowed down. I began to feel alienated by my city, my body, my boyfriend, my work. I became an empty vessel, popping pills to help me sleep, keep my hair, calm me down. Then the towers fell, and for a while there was this strange elixir of total dread and togetherness. There were signs for the missing and that terrible smell was in the air, yet sometimes it felt like we were all sitting around a campfire feeling warm and fuzzy. And soon enough, everyone carried on: having babies, moving into houses, leaving the city, far away. I don't know what I expected, but watching everyone drift away took me by surprise.

As I wait for the train, I look out at the city. Berlin stretches out, boundless and flat, more like a desert than a bustling metropolis. A forest of cranes looms over the east, and in the distance, the newly rebuilt Potsdamer Platz pulses like a video game. I'm struck by how many opportunities I've had to gaze at the expanse of Berlin, its tentacles reaching for miles in every direction. There are few chances to see

Manhattan like this, at least not from within. You're trapped inside blocks, the vastness of the world only perceived by looking up at a sky interrupted on every side by buildings. But isn't that the whole point of living in New York—the shared certainty that nothing of consequence exists beyond it?

The snow is gone and the sun has returned, the sky burnt and orange. The epic, endless city looks radioactive, its metal beams and glass absorbing and reflecting the glow. The TV Tower looks molten too, beautiful and scary, like it could explode: the end of the world, and the beginning, all at once.

The World in a Wagon

Café im Literaturhaus is housed in an enormous nineteenth-century villa set on a tranquil side street in Charlottenburg. I walk through the lush gardens, past a bookstore, and up the stairs to get to the front door. When I arrive at eleven thirty on the dot, the café is buzzing. I ask the hostess for Klaus Beckmann and she immediately leads me to a corner banquette in the salon room.

Klaus is tall, with a bushy blond beard and pale blue eyes. He's wearing jeans and a button-down shirt that is tucked only in the back, a tie thrown over his shoulder. He stands to shake my hand, and as he moves toward me, I notice he walks with a slight limp. We sit and he tells me that his wife is joining us; she's gone to the ladies' room, "or the loo, as she calls it."

It's obvious Klaus is a regular at the café and that this is his banquette. Newspapers and art catalogues are strewn across the table, an open notebook sits in front of him, and an ashtray filled with cigarette butts all give the illusion that we're sitting at his desk. "You've just missed Mayor Wowereit," Klaus tells me, "famous for being the first politician to declare his love for Madonna. What an arse-fucker."

"Oh Klaus, stop." A stunning woman approaches our table. "Mayor Wowi is charming and smart. Klaus just dislikes him because he's popular."

"Well, it does not help," Klaus says.

His wife introduces herself as she slides into the banquette. "Sabine Beckmann," she says. "And I am pleased to meet you." Her voice is refined and full of texture. Her blond hair is pulled back in a ponytail, and though she's apparently wearing no makeup she is luminescent. She points to a table across the room and tells me that the mayor sat there with a mysterious younger man, that they ate eggs and toast and drank double espressos, oblivious to the roomful of stares.

Klaus turns to her. "But Sabine, how do you know the espressos were doubles?"

"Because I asked the server on my way to the loo," she responds.

"My wife, the starfucker."

"I was only curious." Sabine turns to me. "And across from us is Max Raabe. He's quite famous, too. A singer in the Weimar tradition. A dandy, you might call him. He is always immaculately dressed and never out of character."

Klaus rolls his eyes.

Right now, Max Raabe, a middle-aged blond with slicked-back hair, sits cross-legged in a pitch-black velvet blazer, a silk scarf wrapped around his neck. He's encircled by three younger men who laugh and smoke, but Max Raabe sits stone-faced, as if he must be surrounded by clouds of smoke and laughter at all times but not indulge in any of these activities himself.

When our waiter comes, I ask for the same meal as Mayor Wowereit, essentially what I ate a few hours ago at the hotel. I order this mostly out of laziness. Looking at a German menu can be exhausting, and yet the act of asking for an English menu, especially when you're with Germans, feels mildly humiliating.

Klaus asks what I've done in Berlin. I stretch the truth and tell him I've made a slew of gallery visits but worry I'm being coy about specifics. Luckily for me, he doesn't seem that interested. I tell them about the Philharmonic and my walks through Prenzlauer Berg. "Everyone lives there now," Klaus says, "but I cannot keep up. The new Ossies are so young and hip. At some point, you grow tired. I am fifty-two, Sabine is forty-three . . ."

"Klaus!"

"Stop being vain, Sabine." Klaus grabs her arm. "Look at her, she is beautiful, it is madness such a person thinking her age is a problem."

"Klaus, you just told our new friend that you feel old and tired . . . because of our age."

"What I mean is, sometimes you go to the market and get your bread and cheese, and then you go home and that is the day. In that way I suppose I am bourgeois."

"You may have the poster of Rosa Luxembourg above your desk," Sabine says, "but you are bourgeois in other respects, too."

"Well, it is true, I never thought I would live again in the West." Klaus looks at the well-dressed people in this handsome restaurant, classical music humming in the background, Max Raabe floating in his river of smoke. "Yet here we are."

"But the gallery takes you out of the neighborhood nearly every day," Sabine says. "Klaus rides his bicycle each way to Rudi-Dutschke-Strasse, four kilometers back and forth."

"Yes, despite the limp I have the legs of a lion. Besides, the rail system in Berlin is corrupt. I will not support it."

Sabine turns to me. "My husband, the communist living in Charlottenburg, eating croissants with Mayor Wowi."

"I offer no apologies. The croissants here are like Proust's madeleines. I could dedicate my life to them. Besides, it is not where you live, or what you eat, that makes the man."

"It can be amusing, Klaus, how you curve the words to your own sense of worth."

"Sabine, that is a strange sentence and we can discuss it later. Let us not argue in front of our new friend."

She places her hand on top of his. I look at her long fingers, her perfect nails. "You are right, Klaus. And despite the appearances, we are very much in love," she tells me. "This is just our thing."

"Yes." He strokes the back of Sabine's neck. "It is just one of those things."

Sabine coos at him, then turns to me. "So, do you like Berlin?"

"Absolutely, I do."

"Today is nice, but the weather has been shit," Klaus says. "Sorry."

"The *Schmuddelwetter*? It fits my mood."

Sabine smiles when I say this. "And it snows for you."

"I was awake when it was still on the ground. It was fantastic."

"Come back in February, when every street is covered in ice and you fall on your arse every day." Klaus sips his tea. "And the people? What do you think?"

"To be honest, I can't say I've felt entirely welcome."

"Ah, yes." Klaus nods. "The Germans and the Americans, always there is a tension. Right now, it's your Bush."

"It's that simple?" I ask him.

"You blame a country for its leader." Klaus lights a cigarette. "This is nothing new. You elected him. There is war. That was that."

"Well I didn't vote for him, just so you know."

He exhales a stream of smoke. "It makes no difference. Your people have spoken. Remember where you are right now. Every German is given the responsibility of our past."

"Must you smoke?" Sabine asks.

"Yes, Sabine. I must." He waves away the smoke and turns to me. "I forget, you Americans live in a smoke-free world now. It is about the control. All of this attention to health is very unhealthy."

"But we are getting this way, too," Sabine says. "Everything bio-organic at all the shops. It is a good thing."

"Blech," Klaus says.

"I used to smoke," I say, "but not anymore." I neglect to mention the cigarette I shared with Jeremy. "Now in New York, people huddle up and smoke in front of buildings and bars. They look desperate. But here, it feels folded into the culture."

Klaus smiles. "The way it should be?"

"Maybe it should bother me," I say, "but here it feels sort of right. Like how it was."

"So many people," he says, "prefer how it was to how it is, no matter what the was was." We all sit there and decipher this, even Klaus, who only continues when he realizes he has, in fact, made sense. "One of my artists, she lost her cheek. Cancer. She talks like this now." He sucks in his lips and makes a horrible slurping sound. "I have no illusions.

I am an addict." He puffs his cigarette and blows smoke slowly in the air. "And I will kill myself."

Sabine turns to me. "They say Mayor Wowereit will seek to abolish smoking in restaurants and bars."

Klaus shakes his head. "This will never happen. Nicotine is the petrol of Germany. There would be civil war."

Sabine smiles and pours some juice into my glass. She seems used to navigating her husband's tricky personality. Still, it seems like an excellent time to change the subject. "So, have you been to New York?"

"Yes," Sabine says, holding up three fingers. "Thrice." Her English is nearly perfect, if a little formal.

"I do not like the trains in Berlin," Klaus says, "but in New York I will ride the subway ten times a day."

"You're kidding."

"In Berlin, everyone is the same. Okay, so we have our Turks, our most recent slave import, but that is about it. But New York is color! New York is drama! You take the subway and you see the world in a wagon."

"It is a melting pot," I say. "The cliché is true."

"When I am in New York," Sabine tells me, "Klaus has his meetings, but I just sit in cafés. I'm an actress, so I like to study people. And it is nice to travel because no one knows my show. If someone stares at me, maybe it is because he is thinking that I appear interesting, and not because I'm on a television program. But I find New York intimidating. Everyone wants something so urgently. But what do they need? And then I shop and buy things because I think this is what I should be doing."

"She is a capitalist at heart."

"This is not true, Klaus. But I just snap into it. It makes me jealous and a bit sad."

"Berlin reminds me of New York," I say. "But an older version, back when I was growing up."

"You are sentimental," Klaus says. "This is nostalgia."

"It's more than nostalgia. It's something about the way the city looks and feels."

"The graffiti," Klaus says. "The art on the street."

"That's definitely part of it," I say.

"Berlin is a painted city," Klaus says. "This is one of the great pleasures of living here. Because where there is art on the street, there is freedom and tension. There is possibility."

"It is too much," Sabine says. "Some of the graffiti is quite artistic, but then you go to the park and someone has written something terrible on a Käthe Kollwitz sculpture, in front of the children. It should be stopped."

Klaus squashes his cigarette in the ashtray. "No, Sabine. That is how they express themselves. This is telling a dog not to piss on a wall. And you cannot decide what is beautiful and what is not." He turns to me. "Tell me, have you been yet to the Jewish museum in Kreuzberg?" I shake my head no. "Do not go," he says. "All of Berlin is in love with it, but to me it is disgusting. Everywhere in this museum, there is a plaque with writing: 'Daniel Libeskind wants you to feel this, Daniel Libeskind wants you to think about that. Daniel Libeskind wants you to consider the devastation of the Jews by looking at this shoe and that sock.' Fuck you up the ass, Daniel Libeskind. You are an architect from America. Do not tell me what to think."

"Oh, Klaus," Sabine says, as if she's been through this a hundred times.

"We are getting better about examining our past. But a museum should not be a mirror for the man who built it. It is for the people. Hopefully with the new memorial by the Tiergarten, they will finally get it right."

Klaus looks off to the distance. It occurs to me that I haven't asked about his emergency in Bonn. But no one has brought it up, so I decide to leave it alone. My eggs and toast arrive, and although they are perfectly adequate, they can only disappoint after Klaus' celestial description of his croissant. As I eat, Sabine tells me about her television show, *Ost und West*, a prime-time soap opera about three generations of Berliners living on both sides of a now-invisible wall.

"I play an architect," she says. "My character, Anna, grew up in the West, but now she lives in the East, which is the opposite of my own experience."

"My partner is an architect," I tell her.

"Oh, really? I've done my research. Anna is an interesting character. Very precise."

"She plays the bitch," Klaus says flatly.

Sabine looks at her husband. "Well, yes, I suppose she can be a bit hard."

"Last year, Anna is the editor of a magazine," Klaus says. "And now she is an architect."

"It is not real life," Sabine says.

Klaus leans into me. "If Sabine was in America, she would be a star, she would be rich. But here, Sabine is just a worker. The network treats her poorly. In Germany, we distrust celebrity."

Sabine takes his hand. "Klaus, you don't have to speak as if I am not here."

I'm beginning to wonder if this is, in fact, just their "thing," or if something deeper is going on. I turn to Klaus, switching topics. "So, did you grow up in the West?"

Klaus shakes his head. He tells a story about growing up in the East: his parents spying for the Stasi, betraying friends. When his father exposed a neighbor's plan for escape, the neighbor's wife came over and stabbed him in the stomach while the family ate dinner. "Some things you do not forget," Klaus says, full of a strange detachment. "I have strong memories of both East and West. So like Sabine, I do not really know where is home." He stubs out his cigarette. "When the Wall fell, the city was again reborn. But Berlin is always becoming. The city can never just be. She is wild and rebellious and of course this is appealing. But . . . the city is broke."

"A good place to make art," I say.

"Indeed. Everyone has space and time, exactly what you do not have in New York. The rents are low, so our artists have large studios, and there is always space to start a gallery. Here, if you want to sit by the lake with your friends underneath an umbrella all day and talk about art and philosophy and then fuck by the water, you can do that. This is the nice side of our shit economy . . ."

Sabine interrupts. "But Berlin is always disappointing people. We are the city that never quite delivers on its promise."

"I think this is powerful," Klaus says. "We are in a constant state of beginning."

"Or reinvention," I say.

"Yes. It is our condition."

"And we have our past," Sabine says.

Klaus grabs his wife's hand and kisses it. "Yes. We are a city of ghosts, but also a city of the future. That is why I named my space *Zukunftsgalerie*. It seemed only perfect to put the 'gallery of the future' inside a bread-making factory built one hundred years ago, taken over by the Nazis, and then blown to bits in the war. In Berlin, everything was once something else."

I think of Jeremy and the Wasserturm. "Someone said that same thing to me just a few days ago."

"Because it is inescapable. The past is everywhere, and this never changes. It is the blood of the city."

"A bit like your *Ostalgie* show."

"Please, Sam, call the show by its name, *Immediate/Present*. We have not had our opening and already all of Berlin is calling it 'the *Ostalgie* show,' even you, the newly arrived American. *Ostalgie* for me is complicated. It is ironic that at this moment *Ostalgie* is the ultimate in capitalism. I thought our show was making comment on it, but when people come to the early viewing—"

"They were crying," Sabine says.

"Really?" I say. "That's incredible."

"People used to visit museums and churches and weep," says Klaus. "They would look at a Madonna or stare at a Raphael for an hour and fall apart. But it is different now. Have you been to Rome?"

"Many times," I answer.

"The McDonalds next to the Pantheon, now that's God having a laugh."

"Or punishing us," I say.

"This is why I love the art on the streets," Klaus continues. "You turn a corner and there it is on the wall of a building, something from the people of the city, something you did not expect. Because art must surprise. I will take the terrible scrawl on the Kollwitz sculpture if it means I also get the painting on the back of the building that makes me stop and look at it and remember it still three days later. But now people do not want to connect. They do not want to experience the art."

"They want to have *had* the experience," I say.

"Exactly! It is an important difference. People have now these digital cameras, and they come into the gallery taking pictures. And I think, are you going to look at this photo again? No. You are not experiencing the art, you are photographing it with your shit camera."

"Now I do half of my work on a computer," I tell them, "sitting inside, emailing JPEGs to clients."

Klaus shakes his head. "JPEGs. Clients. Computers. Email. I hate them all."

I tell him that my BlackBerry broke when I arrived here. "This is lucky for you," he says. "Now you can really be in Berlin. Do not replace it, for everything breaks for a reason. I refuse to write emails, or to look at them. My assistant reads them to me if they must be read."

"The gallery of the future does not have email," I say. Sabine laughs.

"Quite right," Klaus says. "In the future, we are already past it. Could you imagine it, opening your email and there is a photo of Michelangelo's David, or that Rothko sends you a JPEG of his newest creation? You miss everything about it. It is degrading for the art, and for the artist."

"Warhol would love it," Sabine says.

"That is cliché, Sabine. Anything with a touch of future or reproduction, people say 'Andy would love this. He predicted it. He invented it.' He did not. The capitalists thought he was speaking to them. And the East Germans were thinking the same thing. That is the power of Andy. But if everyone had a camera, do you think Andy would have been standing with them, taking pictures? No. Andy would be doing something else. He would be living on the moon."

I nod. It makes a certain sense that, at least in his imagination, Klaus is on a first-name basis with Warhol.

"And these JPEGs that you send to your clients, Sam, I worry where this is going."

"Me too," I say, although I fear I'm only feigning a similar urgency.

"But our artists do not appear to mind it, as long as they get their cash." Klaus pauses to eat the last bite of his croissant. "Now, Sam, I am sorry to disappoint you, but at this show I have nothing to sell."

"Nothing?"

"Nothing. And there is no plaque telling you what to feel," Klaus continues. "You see a tube of lipstick or three bottles of Vita-cola, an old television playing the *Sandmann* show, a record player with an Ostrock record on it. You see, you hear, you touch. Nothing is behind glass. You have your experience and you walk away. This is how to present art."

"I get it," I say. "Although the promotional materials talk a lot about *Ostalgie*. And they were sent to me by email. And presumably . . . approved by you?"

Sabine laughs. Klaus says, "My manager insisted we write something, so we could get in the papers."

"What a socialist," Sabine says.

"I know. Fucking Otto, what a shit."

We leave the café and wander the side streets of Charlottenburg. Beautiful men in suits talk on their mobile phones. Pencil-thin ladies stroll by in sunglasses, even though the sky is thick with clouds. Klaus says to me, "Funny that you did not come to Berlin for the art fairs."

"I know," I say. "I missed them by just a few weeks."

"I am against them completely," Klaus says. "Stalls are for horses, not art."

"Well, then I don't feel so ridiculous." I stare into the window of a salon, Berliners lathered up and getting their hair done at lunch.

"And are you here with your partner?" Sabine asks. "The architect?"

"We tried to make it work," I lie. "But he couldn't get away."

"The buildings must be built!" Klaus says. "Well, I am sorry that your partner has left you alone in our city. But there are worse things than to be alone in Berlin." He winks at me, then claps his hands. "So, we had our chat. And in four days you come to the show."

"Absolutely."

"And bring a friend. This is Berlin, surely you will pick something up in the next few days, some stray boy looking for a hot meal."

Sabine elbows him. "Klaus!"

"What? He is a nice looking American, and he is from New York. You will have men falling all over you," Klaus says, "Are you Jewish?"

"Yes," I nod.

"Even better!"

"Klaus, this is enough," says Sabine.

Our conversation is interrupted when we notice a group of people standing on the corner, staring at us. I look at Sabine. "Is your television show very popular?"

"*Ost und West* is on each evening at seven thirty. And we are repeated again the next afternoon. The show is the most popular soap opera in Germany. About eleven million people watch it."

"So are you famous?" The question slips out of my mouth, and the answer is obvious.

"Just a bit," she says.

"I have a TV in my room," I say. "I'll have to watch it."

"If you like," Sabine says. Klaus has turned silent. I'm not sure if he's merely disinterested in her profession or if he actually looks down on it. "Maybe it's not art," Sabine continues. "But people like it, and that means something. Right now my character is pregnant. Her husband betrayed her, and so she left. Now she has a new lover—Sebastian, a man from her past in East Berlin."

"And whose baby is it?" I ask her.

"Even I do not know this yet. But I hope it is Sebastian's, because he is so good. He is poor, and humble, a hatmaker, and kind. He loves me very much."

"I love you," Klaus says. "And Sebastian does not exist. Nor does Anna the architect."

"True. But it is my job to make her real."

"I do not know why they give you a baby," Klaus says. "You are not even pregnant."

"The writers make me pregnant because I am forty-three and this is quite old. So if they want to give me a baby, it must be now, before I dry up." Sabine puts her hands in her pockets and walks ahead of us.

"Aye, fuck," Klaus says. "Now she is going into one of her brown moods."

Sabine turns around, walks over to me and grabs my arm. "I am sorry, Sam. I did not sleep so well last night."

"I understand. And now I know what I'm doing tomorrow evening at seven thirty."

"It would make me happy to think that you are watching. Happy, and a little nervous."

I ask her what station it's on, and she says channel four. I open my bag and write this down in my pad. I remove my bottle of water and take a few sips. "Americans and their plastic water," Klaus says. "You are like babies with bottles." He puts his thumb in his mouth and sucks on it, flashes his eyes at me.

"Klaus, that is not kind."

"Oh, Sabine, get off it. Our friend knows, I am not serious." Then he gets close to me and tickles my ribs. I'm so startled, I spill water onto my coat. "Let us go this way," Klaus says, pointing to a busy street. "We walk you to your train."

If there are few signs of Western culture in East Berlin, the Kurfürstendamm more than makes up for it. Down the street from the KaDeWe, Germany's largest department store, there's McDonalds, Starbucks, the Gap, and then the luxe stores—Gucci, Chanel, Prada—straight off Fifth Avenue. And though its side streets are beautiful and cobblestoned, Charlottenburg feels like many other charming European cities I've visited. It doesn't have the ragged, unfinished exoticism you find on the other side of town. West Berlin was split up by the English, French, and Americans. East Berlin was controlled entirely by Russia. The Wall may be down, but the distinct vibes of East and West still announce themselves loudly.

We cross the street and pass the Hollywood Media Hotel. I glance at the ridiculous murals painted onto its entrance: Hitchcock, James Dean, the Statue of Liberty, Marilyn Monroe. I turn to Klaus. "You know, I've read about you."

"And what have you discovered?"

"Well, that you and your artists used to show up to the openings naked."

"This is old news, and a bit of mythology. Back then I was more about theater, about provoking. Now we do other things."

Sabine laughs. "As you see, there is no more provocation with Klaus Beckmann."

Klaus continues. "Before the Wall fell, I directed plays all over Germany. For my first show, we did *Die Meistersinger*. Do you know it?"

"I don't, but my father loves Wagner."

"It is also Hitler's favorite opera, so tell that to Daddy. *Die Meistersinger* is five hours long, but when I do it, it was forty minutes. We throw out the scenes we do not like, and then we mix in text from other sources. Of course, this is making everyone angry. I was known as '*der Textwrecker*.' But when I look back, I realize I was in the future. We were sampling."

"Mix Master Klaus," I say. "Mashing things up."

We laugh. "Your father, maybe he would want to kill me, messing with his Wagner. But maybe it would shake him up, which is what I like to do. This is how I met *meinen Liebling*, my darling Sabine. I cast her as 'Beautiful Girl Number One.' Wagner did not write that part, but this is one of the advantages of being the Text Wrecker." He grabs Sabine and kisses her. "You are still my Beautiful Girl Number One. Always."

"Oh, Klaus," she says. "Now I fear *you* are being nostalgic."

"Well, it was a different time. But I grew bored with theater. After reunification, I started the gallery. And one day I looked at my teapot and realized I use it each morning for twenty years, on both sides of the Wall. It is not a special teapot, but if it broke, I would be destroyed. We have an intense relationship to these objects. This is what led me to the objects of the DDR, and the products we used every day, the hundreds of things that disappeared after the Wall comes down."

"I have to tell you, the show sounds fascinating," I say.

"It *is* fascinating," Sabine says.

Klaus continues. "When I open the Zukunftsgalerie ten years ago, the state gave me money to do it. You see, Sam, in Berlin there are demonstrations on every corner and always people are whining. And sometimes I am one of the complaining people, too. Because people like to cry about something. It reminds them of being a baby. Needing something is powerful. Why do I smoke? Because I like the taste? No. I smoke because the empty space between cigarettes is filled with a crazy need, and bringing satisfaction to that need feels good." Klaus, of course, takes this opportunity to light a cigarette. His first inhale is deep and dramatic, his exhale almost ecstatic. "But sometimes in Germany, if you need something from the state, all you do is ask. So I have Deutschland to thank for everything."

"We don't have anything like that in the states," I say.

"Berlin, she is poor as piss, but if you want to do your art, this is your place. *Immediate/Present* would not exist without it."

"Well, I'm excited." I say, "And it sounds like the show is moving."

"Moving? Where is it going?"

"And maybe even accessible," I tell him.

"What is it, accessible?"

I think about how to explain this. "Something that many people . . . most people . . . can enjoy."

"Oh," Klaus says with a groan. "This is terrible."

"But it's true," Sabine says. "It will be an emotional experience for many Germans."

"It takes six years to put together the show," Klaus says. "And now we open at the peak of this *Ostalgie* nonsense."

"It is not nonsense," Sabine says. "It is wrong to think the people are false for feeling what they feel. Think about your teapot."

"Hmmm. Beautiful Girl Number One, she knows everything. But I want to dig deeper. With nostalgia, the past becomes what one thinks it should have been, but never was. Historians always rewrite history from the moment of now. This is why I call the show *Immediate/ Present*. To many eyes, this exhibit is about the past. But really, it is about this moment, today. And Sam, please see it twice." Klaus wiggles two fingers in the air. "You know the openings—people leave speaking about who they saw and the wine they spilled on their dress. How can a sculpture compete with free beer and cheese? Even art has its limits."

Klaus puffs his cigarette. "Sam, *Immediate/Present* is a happening. It is never the same. So promise you will come back."

"Okay," I say. My plane ticket back to New York is for the morning after the opening, so it's unlikely that this can happen; and it's just been confirmed that I've flown four thousand miles for an art show at which there's nothing to buy. Nonetheless, I tell him that I'll try to figure it out. My visits with clients, curators and gallery owners are often filled with proposed trips to their summer homes and dinners that never materialize. I just say yes and move on.

"I really do wonder how it will be for you. It will have a different effect."

"Of course I'll let you know."

"Let us eat dinner after the opening. We take you with our group to the Paris Bar and then to our home for a glass of sherry and Sabine's baked pears. Bring your date if you like. We discuss the show in private."

"So," Sabine says, leaning into me, "I think he likes you."

Klaus stubs out his cigarette. "Well he must eat, *ja*? We must feed the American."

The Best Schnitzel in Town

I'm so pleased to have the meeting behind me that when I return to the hotel, I decide to call Jeremy. He sounds surprised and happy to hear from me. I ask if he'd like to have dinner tonight, and he quickly accepts. Our conversation is short, I think, because we're both shocked that our slightly awkward day wandering through Prenzlauer Berg has resulted in two friends going to dinner, or something like that. I just hope we'll have more to say to each other tonight. I'm certain that beers will be ordered to ensure that we do.

Magda had recommended Austria ("the best schnitzel in town"), so I go downstairs and ask her to make a reservation. "They have nothing after eight," she says, cupping the phone. "I make a reservation for half past seven, if this is okay." Magda sometimes mixes up her Vs and Ws, and so she pronounces it *reser-way-shin*, which I sort of love. A chink in her armor.

"Seven thirty is perfect." Then I remember Sabine's television show. I'll have to watch *Ost und West* another night, or perhaps catch the repeat tomorrow afternoon.

Magda hangs up the phone. "So . . ." She clasps her hands under her chin. "What is it? *Ein Geschäftsessen?*"

I roll my eyes. "Magda, like I know what that means."

"Is this a business dinner?"

"No. Just a friend."

"Samuel has a friend," she says. "This is nice."

"Yes. It is nice."

Magda raises her eyebrows. "Is it K.?"

"No. This is somebody else. He lives in Friedrichshain."

"Ah, a Berliner." She tilts her head. "And a man."

"Well, yes, but he's from Albany."

"Albany, it is in California?"

"Albany is in New York. It's the capital of the state."

"But the capital of the state of New York, it is not New York City?"

"Nope," I say. "It's not."

"This is silly." She waves her hand in the air and mumbles something in German, as if she can no longer be bothered with me or anything to do with my country. "Albany? Absurd."

"Well, I guess, but I mean, what's the capital of Germany?"

"Berlin, of course. Where else? You live in New York, Samuel. You should change it. We did it, you know. It was Bonn, the capital of Germany, *die Hauptstadt*. Then the Wall falls, and we change it to Berlin." She claps her hands twice, as if she'd done it herself.

"I'll see what I can do." I walk toward the elevator. "Thanks for making the *reservation*," I say, enunciating it slowly and correctly.

"*Kein Probleme*," she snaps. "And what is it that he does in Berlin, your dinner companion from the great capital Albany?"

I can tell that Magda has the relationship all wrong. She's solved some puzzle in her head, but she's placed the pieces together incorrectly. It's Kaspar, I want to tell her, that you should be thinking of (if you're thinking that way at all). And don't forget about the boyfriend and the dog back in New York. Don't forget, but she never knew.

I walk back to her. She stares, blinking, waiting for me to say something. I look at the thin silver chain around her neck, which drops into the V-neck of her sweater and disappears. I stare down at her hands, which I've never thought to do, and notice the gold band on one of her fingers, twisted backward so that whatever jewel there might be is hidden in the darkness of her palm. She has her history, too. She is her own puzzle.

"How long will it take me to get to the restaurant?"

"It is maybe fifteen minutes to Kreuzberg. You take the U-Bahn to Gneisenaustrasse, but it is not so easy from here."

"Can you call a taxi?"

"Yes. Or—" She looks at the row of clocks behind her: New York, Moscow, London, Tokyo, Sydney, Berlin. "I am finish with the work in thirty-four minutes. I will drive you."

Her offer lingers, so unexpected that it just floats in the air.

"Really?"

"My flat is just five streets from the restaurant. It is not a problem, Samuel. You will come." She stares into the computer and starts typing. "See you. *Bis gleich.*"

Magda's offer becomes an order, and thirty-four minutes later, after I shower and change clothes, I meet her downstairs. It feels strange to leave the hotel with her, to walk through the Hackescher Markt together—receptionist and guest—as unexpected as going home after school with your kindergarten teacher.

Magda's tiny green car is hidden in an alley by the tram station. Her secret spot, she tells me. Copies of newspapers and magazines—*Der Spiegel, Die Zeit, Zitty*—are piled onto my seat. I place them on the floor, as there is no backseat. Magda, not surprisingly, is an aggressive driver. As we zip through the curvy side streets of Mitte, a half-full bottle of Coke Light sloshes around and rolls over my feet. It's rush hour. Berliners on bikes swish past us, ringing their bells as they fly by. Things get more peaceful as we cross the river. Magda turns on the radio, and we listen to a man speak German in hushed tones, causing her to sigh and, every once in a while, to laugh.

"What's he talking about?"

"Oh, it is not important, Samuel. You would not understand."

As we drive through Kreuzberg, the terrain changes. Enormous slabs of apartment buildings hover over squares, satellite dishes dangling from every terrace. With scores of black windows and balconies dotting their facades, the buildings look like concrete beehives. We pass kebab shops, Turkish women wearing hijabs and pushing carts filled with groceries. Even from Kreuzberg, you can see the TV Tower glistening in the distance. We drive past a restaurant called Henne, a red rooster lit up in neon above its entrance. Magda tells me that the restaurant serves only one entrée—half a chicken—and utensils are not allowed. "Why?" I ask her.

"I do not own the restaurant, Samuel. But the chicken, it is good."

Soon we drive onto a quiet residential street, and everything changes with the turn of a corner. We pass cobblestone boulevards lined with majestic apartment houses, their facades painted in warm shades of yellow, blue, and orange, and lit by the soft glow of streetlamps.

I look at the clock in the car; it's not even half past six. As I feared, once we park on Bergmannstrasse, Magda invites me to her apartment for a glass of wine. I accept, as I'm not meeting Jeremy for over an hour, which she knows, and I don't even have the address of the restaurant or any sense of where I am. For the moment, I'm in Magda's hands. Daniel says you don't know a city until you've been inside the homes of at least three locals. Apparently I'll be eating baked pears in Klaus and Sabine's living room at the end of my trip. I don't know about local number three, but I suppose a visit to Magda's apartment, however unlikely, is a good enough place to start.

The courtyard of her building is beautiful: tall, flat columns, heavy stone stairs, ornamental trees glowing golden in autumn dress, two red benches, a stone table adorned with lit candles dripping wax down its base. All of these things are just here, keeping each other company in the dark. Some cities die as night approaches, but Berlin just seems to slide into a second day. A gray cat sleeps in front of the stairs. "*Hallo,* Blitz," Magda whispers as we step over it. "Is it a boy or a girl?" I ask. "Boy," she says. "He lives with Frau Schneider upstairs, but really he belongs to us all."

We climb the narrow stairwell, which twists and turns and passes the doors of four other flats. The only light comes from a single candle sconce on each landing, and I wonder, who lights them each night? Outside one apartment is a basket containing fresh eggs, a bottle of milk, and the *Berliner Morgenpost.* On the door of another apartment is a sign that reads FRANK & NAUHEIM. Magda turns to me and smiles. "My flat, it is on the top." I nod up to her. She looks beautiful in the candlelight, almost delicate.

What a place to live, I think to myself. For the first time, I realize that people actually live in this city, wake up here every day. And then it hits me: I feel that twinge of envy and awe that makes you imagine that you will pack your bags and leave your life and move onto a street just like this one, into a building just like this, guided to your apartment—your flat—each and every night by candlelight and quiet.

Watching Magda as she climbs the stairs, I realize that, until now, I've really only seen her from the neck up. I hadn't realized she's so tall and lithe and elegant. As we arrive on the fifth and final level of the building, she turns to me. "My trip to the gymnasium, every day, up and down these stairs. Good for the legs."

When she opens the door to her apartment and switches on the light, the first thing I notice is a puppy sitting in its bed, waking up. Through the hallway I see an open living room and a bank of tall windows facing the street. Then I notice the stench and the turds scattered about her wooden floors. The dog is so thrilled to see Magda that he runs over, barks, and pees on her foot.

"Aye! Schnapps, *nein, nein, nein*! Always, with the shit." She removes her shoes and grabs a roll of paper towels that she has left by the front door. Magda shakes her head as she bends down to clean the mess.

The dog runs over and jumps up on my legs. I bend down to him, and he licks my cheeks. "He's adorable," I say.

"He is, how do you say, a mix: part Snoopy dog, part Schnauzer. He is a baby, just"—she thinks for a second—"four months two weeks ago he is born."

Despite his age, Schnapps looks very serious, already possessed of a gray-white moustache and big brown eyes that stop you in your tracks. He looks like an analyst who has misplaced his glasses, like he knows something about you that is secret. "Frau Schneider walks him two times while I am working at the hotel," Magda tells me. "But Schnapps, he prefers to make bathrooms on my floors."

While Magda cleans up the mess, I walk around her living room. It's full of little touches Daniel would appreciate: a ceramic gnome table—kitschy, nerdy, chic all at once—holds up a stack of art books (Arbus, Klimt, Richter, Dada); a solid oak table sits in her dining room, a jar with a red sunflower floating in the water posed on its surface. A tiny Buddha lamp on her credenza, bejeweled and obviously hand-painted, emits a golden light.

"I must be giving Schnapps his dinner," she says, disappearing into the kitchen, the puppy following behind.

I steal a glance at the cluster of photographs on one of the shelves: a pretty girl in a school uniform, obviously Magda; and then Magda with what must be her parents, both smaller than her; and finally three different pictures of Magda with a handsome blond man. Three different ages, three different looks. In all of them, Magda has a smile that is big and open and full of teeth, a smile I have not yet seen on her face.

I walk over to the windows overlooking the street. The terrace is filled with plants, all unfamiliar to me: two flowering and two flat-topped mini-trees, like dwarf versions of the cypress trees you see in Italy. A clay pot filled only with dirt has a dozen cigarette stubs of different brands stumped out into it, evidence, perhaps, of a recent get-together. I stare out the window and watch as Berliners enter buildings with bags of groceries, bottles of wine. Two men walk arm in arm, briefcases by their side. With a sense of awe, I watch Magda move around her apartment, my picture of her developing, the colors filling in.

Magda lights a candle, and a faint smell, not unlike chai tea, fills the air. I usually hate scented candles—they remind me of my twenties, my slutty, sullen bachelorhood, when in between boyfriends I'd light candles, take baths, and write cheesy Post-it notes to myself to rouse my spirit and quell my depression—but here the scent is lovely and performing its duties nicely as the puppy-turd smell evaporates. "Now, I will get the wine," Magda says.

"And I need to pee," I tell her, instantly embarrassed that I've said something so crass and American.

Magda points me to a hallway toward the opposite end of the apartment. "I am sorry for the mess," she calls out, disappearing into the kitchen. "I was not expecting *wisitors*." She grunts and corrects herself. "Visitors," she says, and then, "reservation."

I walk into the bathroom and look at the massive claw-foot bathtub, at the cluttered shelf under the mirror, filled with miniature bottles of shampoo and bath gel that must be lifted from the hotel. I look at the shower curtain with its cheerful sea theme, the trash can overflowing with cotton balls, lipstick-stained tissues, and assorted feminine mysteries, the cactus sitting on a windowsill. It's clearly a room that was not expecting company, but still it is charming. It's a nice surprise to discover that Magda, who'd existed in my mind as some automaton, lives in a world as cluttered and human as the rest of us. "I was married," she calls from the kitchen.

"Married?" I crack open the door. "Really?"

"Yes. I still am. We are just, how do you say, taking a break? The man stuff, in the bathroom, it is not mine."

I wonder what constitutes "man stuff," and if everyone is taking a break, or thinking about it. It certainly is in the air. Then I look at the shelf and notice the bottle of *Rasiercreme* and the black razor, the mug with two toothbrushes jutting out of it, the pair of bathrobes hanging from a hook behind the door. I wonder if the blond husband visits; if he takes a break from the break.

"That is why Schnappsie has come to live with me," Magda says as we both return to the living room. I sit down on the couch, slip off my shoes. Magda scoops the dog out of his bed and holds him in the crook of her arm. Schnapps drapes his paws over her arm and drops his head down so that he is floating, almost flying, through the air like a dancer, as Magda moves around the room. They glide toward the stereo, and Magda puts on a CD—Dinah Washington.

"Soooo . . . sadly," Magda says, "it appears that I need a man by my side or I will melt or disappear. We all need a good warm man in bed, *ja*?" Magda waits for a response, some sort of affirmation or clue, but I just sit there. "Well," she says, "Schnapps, he is good, for now." The dog stares at me, fighting to keep his eyes open as he drifts across the room. He is, like his owner, totally relaxed, and I feel lost and homesick, pining for Harry, and Daniel, and a past version of things back home. Magda returns the puppy to his bed. "Sometime, maybe, you tell me a little of your story," she says to me.

"Sometime," I say. And she smiles at me.

Magda excuses herself and disappears to the kitchen. "When it is time, I walk you to Austria."

"You don't have to do that."

"I know it," she calls out.

I walk over to the wall of bookshelves. I scan her collection of books, their spines of different sizes, colors and titles forming an abstract mosaic of German gibberish, and her alphabetized compact discs—Massive Attack, Moby, Portishead, Radiohead, Röyksopp, Nina Simone—not so different from the music collection of a New Yorker, the sounds of a thousand dinner parties around the world.

This is how Berliners live, I think to myself. But that's not true. This is how Magda lives, one Berliner, and this is what she is really like, or what she is like today, when, as she hands me a glass of wine (a new type of red, she says, from Cologne), we suddenly take our masks off.

We pick at the tray of food that Magda has quickly assembled: red olives, cheese, sliced brown bread. She seems so relaxed in her own environment, drinking wine, feet tucked behind her on the couch, Schnapps sprawled across her lap. It's so easy, in fact, that we almost lose track of time.

She asks about my job. "Are you liking your work? Is it interesting?"

"I'd say it's interesting-ish."

"Interesting-ish?"

"Meaning kind of interesting. It's a strange business. I spend a lot of time with insanely wealthy people. Some of my clients accumulate their collections piece by piece, with great care. It can actually be a beautiful process, very intimate, and in its own way, creative. Other people buy a house on the beach and call me to say, 'Fill it with art.'"

Magda nods. She gets it. Working at a boutique hotel in Mitte, I can only imagine the assortment of transitory creatures she interacts with each day.

We discuss the gallery scene in Berlin, how it's shifting from Mitte to Kreuzberg and beyond. When I tell Magda about the galleries I plan to visit, she surprises me by quickly editing my list using her own knowledge of the local art scene. Many of her friends are artists, she explains, and because of the hotel's proximity to the galleries, it attracts plenty of guests from the art world.

Magda tells me that she's studied English since she was a teenager and asks me to correct her if she says something imperfectly. "I do not like to be wrong," she explains.

"It's a deal," I say.

"Visitors," she says again. "Reservation."

I nod my head. "Correct."

We chat about her childhood in Heidelberg, and how she always wanted to wind up in Berlin. After she graduated from university, she couldn't decide if she wanted to be a journalist or a pastry chef. When she moved to the city and went to drop off her résumé at what was supposed to be an East Berlin newspaper, she found the offices closed and the building converted into a hotel. Magda met the owner and started work that day.

"Is it our hotel?"

"Yes. The owner is thinking I was pretty, and he liked that I wanted to work as a journalist." Five years later, she was the manager of the Hotel Hackescher Hof. "I do not think we can know it," she says, "where we will be tomorrow. I think I know this now."

I nod and take a sip of wine. "I was an artist when I was younger."

"Really?" Magda looks surprised.

"Yup. A painter."

"This is incredible, Samuel."

"And now I'm just a salesman."

"This is not true. Your work, it is more interesting than that."

I shrug my shoulders. "Interesting-ish. The painter who sells other people's paintings."

"The journalist who gives you the key to your room." Magda smiles softly and sighs. "Excuse me, Samuel," she says, depositing Schnapps in my lap. "It is almost time to go. I must get ready. I will be just six minutes." And she disappears into her bedroom.

I sit on her sofa, listening to Dinah Washington as she tells us to grab our coats and hats and leave our worries on the doorstep. I stroke

Schnapps under his chin, clearly his secret spot, and watch as he drifts to sleep in the crook of my arm. I think of Harry, how while I hold him he stares up at me with an intensity I find profound and moving, and how he sometimes tries to stay awake just so we can keep gazing into each other.

Schnapps and I both manage to nod off during our daydreams before I open my eyes, startled, to the sound of boots clomping and the song fading out: *It's real crazy on the sunny side of the street.* Magda emerges from the bedroom smelling like flowers and licorice. I look up at her, embarrassed, half-awake, feigning alertness. "I saw you," she says.

"It was just a minute." I nonchalantly check the sides of my mouth for signs of drool.

"You and Schnappsie are sleeping like little babies. It was cute."

"I was relaxed," I say, stroking under the dog's chin as he stretches his paws.

"*Gut,*" she says. "Now you can wake up."

I stare at her. Magda has changed into black jeans and boots and a gray sweater that, somewhat surprisingly, has a small hole revealing a glimpse of her cleavage. In New York, I'd think this was decidedly tacky, maybe even trampy, but here in Berlin, fashion has its own vocabulary. Somehow you can wear a sweater with a peephole between your boobs and make it seem chic. Still, it's hard not to notice Magda's new outfit, her new smell, and wonder what exactly she's doing after she walks me to the restaurant to meet Jeremy.

"Wow," I say. Schnapps jumps off my lap and runs to her.

"Wow?"

"You changed."

"No, Samuel. I am the same." She takes a final sip of wine before removing our glasses from the table and carrying them to the sink. Schnapps follows her, his tail wagging.

"I mean, you changed outfits."

"Outfits? What does it mean?" She looks concerned.

"You're wearing different clothes," I explain.

"*Ja.* I am going to someplace, after I walk with you to Austria."

"Oh. I didn't know."

"Do you think I have nothing to do but to drive you in my *Auto*, take you to my flat, feed you wine and escort you to meet your mystery friend?"

Schnapps tap dances out of the kitchen, then watches Magda as she retrieves her keys. He starts walking in circles, whining. "I was just wondering where you were going, Magda. I'm not saying that at all."

"I am tee-zing with you," she says, looking at her watch. "Samuel, it is time to go, or your friend, he will be waiting in the restaurant. It is a ten-minute walk to Austria."

I put on my shoes. Schnapps watches Magda as she turns off the stereo, wraps a scarf around her neck, and checks herself in the mirror. She removes the clips from her hair, which drops down past her shoulders, cascading to her lower back. She runs her fingers through her long and shiny locks, the color of milk chocolate, and sculpts them into a studied mess. I stare at her, my new friend emerging somewhat shockingly from her former context, the tight-bunned German manageress.

Schnapps breaks my trance. The puppy is familiar with this routine. He knows what comes next is Magda's exit, so he starts barking. She ignores him and hands me my jacket, then sits on the couch and adjusts her boots. "So," she says, standing up again, "how do I look?"

"Magda, you look beautiful."

"*Gut.*" She removes her glasses and flashes her blue eyes at me, then puts them back on. "*Auf oder absetzen?*"

I look at her blankly and shrug. "On or off," she explains. "The glasses."

"I like them," I tell her, though I don't know where she's going.

"Hmmm. Okay," she says, straightening her glasses in the mirror. I watch as she crosses the room, leaving behind a trail of perfume and a devastated puppy. "*Der Hund*, he does not like when I am leaving." Schnapps is now growling at her, planting his legs at her feet. "Ignore him," Magda says. "I am thinking that Schappsie, he is a lee-tle in love with me."

"I think you're right."

"It is nice, *ja*? Sometimes, it is nice."

I watch Schnapps stare at Magda with such desperation that it breaks my heart. I think of Harry back home, how he so effectively blocks our front door with his little body that Daniel or I must pick him up and move him before we can leave the apartment, how he sits on our carpet every night, pointed toward the front door, waiting for Daniel to return home. He always knows when Daniel is on his way. "You know what?" I say. "I love dogs."

"Samuel, what a silly thing to say." Magda clomps over to the table and blows out the candles. She puts on a black raincoat, ties the belt around her waist and claps her hands. "Okay, let us go, now. I love dogs. Samuel, so silly."

I suppose I'm relieved that the Magda I knew from behind the reception desk has not disappeared entirely. I get up from the couch and walk over to her. "Well, I *do* love dogs."

"I know it," she says. "I am again teee-zing with you. You are just so—how you say it in En-gleesch?—sometimes you are *leicht auf den Arm zu nehmen*." She giggles. I assume she's just called me cheesy or stupid or corny or probably a combination of all three, which of course in German takes nine syllables.

"We have a dog at home," I say. "In New York."

Magda turns toward me, her eyes flashing. "We?"

"Yes, we." I take out a picture of Harry from my wallet and hand it to her.

"Ah," she says, looking at Harry sitting on the grass with a smile on his face, the tip of his tongue dangling from his mouth. "It is nice dog, the *Dackel*."

"What is a *Dackel*?"

"The vee-nir dog, of course."

"Don't you call it a dachschund?"

"No, we call it *der Dackel*."

"But isn't dachshund a German name?"

Magda rolls her eyes, impatient. "I think so, Samuel. I do not know."

Schnapps has resorted to tugging at Magda's jeans as she begins to turn off the lamps. "Aye, *mein* Schnapps, *nein, nein, nein!*" She bends down to scold him, but he starts furiously licking her face. "Okay! It is enough," she says, standing up. "The dog, he likes always to eat my face after I am painted in the lipstick." She goes to a jar on a table by the door, removes a biscuit, and dangles it in front of Schnapps. At the sight of it, the puppy jumps wildly in the air. Magda clicks her tongue and starts talking in a playful voice: "Aye, Schnappsie! *Für dich*!" She throws the biscuit across the room and Schnapps runs maniacally to retrieve it. "Magic," she says, opening the front door to let us out. "Every time I do it, and he just runs. They are cute but so stupid, *ja*? I wish it, that a cookie could make me forget all my troubles."

On the way to the restaurant, we pass an enormous cemetery, so lush it's like a tropical rain forest behind black gates. It's dark now, and a veil of evening fog, illuminated by the streetlamps, clings to the ground. Children bike through the streets, calling out to each other. One of them has turned on his headlight and pedals for half a block with his hands in the air. His laugh echoes in bumpy staccato as he flies down the cobblestone road. "It's cold," I say, closing my jacket.

"Good for the schnitzel," Magda says, marching ahead in her boots. "Samuel, you will get the dumpling or I will be killing you, okay?"

"Fine," I say.

"Do not get the beer of the *Haus*, it is . . . what is the word? *Ab-ge-stan-de-ne Pis-se*."

"What does that mean?"

"How are you saying in English? It is the piss that stands in the glass too long."

"You have a word for that?"

"Yes, of course. We have a word for everything."

"I'm not sure there's a word for that in English, but I promise, I won't order that beer."

"Good. I like things to be a certain way."

"Yes, I've noticed." Magda looks back at me, folds her arms across her chest.

"So do I," I say, and we keep walking. I take out my green hat, the one with the snowflakes, and put it on.

"This is a silly hat," Magda tells me.

"Thanks." I look at the cemetery, at the stone crosses atop monuments and a beautiful brick mausoleum with blue metallic doors. Enormous trees tower into the air, saturated with the deep reds and yellow of fall.

"Tell me, who is it, the stranger you eat with?"

"It's a long story. He's sort of a friend of a friend."

"With you, everything is sort of this, kind of that."

"I guess."

"Everything is always so *ish*. Does that work?"

"It kind of works."

"And how is he named, the friend of a friend?"

"Jeremy."

"Aye, this is sounding very French. A terrible name."

"Nothing French about him. And he's just a kid."

"Like the boys on the bikes?" she asks as one whizzes by and rings his bell.

"No. He's twenty-four or something."

"Ah, Samuel! Twenty-four—remember it?"

"Just a little bit," I say. "A blur."

"A blur?"

"A haze," I explain. "Foggy."

"Ah yes. A blur for me, too, then. But sometimes there are the things I am remembering too well."

"What do you mean?"

Magda looks pensive. "I do not know how to explain it. I am now thirty-seven, can you believe it?"

"Me too!"

"*Nein*! Really?"

"Yup."

"*Mein Doppelgänger*."

"Exactly."

We both laugh.

"So!" She claps her hands, taps my shoulder. "Samuel. Guess what?" Magda starts running ahead, strumming her fingers along the cemetery gates.

"What?" I catch up with her. "What is it?"

"Samuel, you and me," she yells. "*Wir sind sehr alt!*"

"What's that mean?"

"Ah!" She laughs loudly, then groans. "We are so old!"

"Tell me about it."

"Aye! How did this happen?"

"I don't know."

She stops and looks into my eyes. "My man, where is he? Now he is a photo on my shelf and I am the sad old Frau alone with her Schnauzer." She shakes her head and grunts as if she can't believe what she's just said.

"Oh, Magda, don't go there."

"What is it, Don't go there?"

"Just . . . let's talk about happy things."

"Are there happy things, Samuel? What happy things? Tell me now."

I think for a second. "I love my dog," I say.

"Aye, enough with *Hunde*!" Magda looks up at the sky. "Oh, Samuel look at the moon! And listen to the leaves falling!" She steadies herself against the gates, puts her hand to her head. For a moment it looks like she might pass out. She crouches down on the ground in a pool of leaves.

I go to her. "Are you okay?"

"Oh, I am feeling so red. With the wine in my cheeks." She sighs and looks at me. Her cheeks are indeed flushed, her big blue eyes staring into my own. I offer my hand but she shakes her head and stands up again, brushes off her knees. "Samuel, tell me something else you are loving. What is it that is making you happy?"

I usually dislike these sorts of questions, spontaneous inquiries that seem general and frivolous but are actually sneaky and deep; and coming from Magda at this moment, it feels almost urgent. And then, I remember: Daniel kissing me against the cemetery gates after a cousin's funeral. In our black suits, his hands in my pockets, leaning against a stone marker. We'd been together for only a few months, and even after a long, glum service, we couldn't keep our hands off each other. We couldn't help but feel totally alive.

"*Hallo*? Samuel?" Magda snaps her fingers. "Where did you go?"

I look around, take in the hush. The ivy hugging gravestones, the alien insects churning in unfamiliar voices as night approaches. The three boys zoom past us on their bicycles again, ringing their bells, nodding to us, the big yellow moon rising behind them. "You know what? I love Berlin."

"Really?"

"Definitely."

"So, this is surprise for me. Berlin, it is a little boring, no?"

"Boring? No way. God, no."

Magda walks into the middle of the street, boots dragging against the cobblestones. "Samuel, the big man from New York."

I catch up to her. "Remember, New York isn't even a capital."

"Albany, so stupid! So maybe it is true. Berlin is okay. But remember it, sometime you tell me about the good life in New York. I want to hear every lee-tle thing."

"I'll tell you. It'll probably bore you, but I'll tell you."

"*Gut*. Another bottle of wine, another night, *ja*? And we talk of Berlin and the city of New York and how we love the dogs, just for you, okay? And we can talk of men? Or women? Or Männer *und* Frauen? Is it both?"

"Magda, You're so nosy!"

"Nosy? What is it?"

"Wanting to know everything. But the 'know' and 'nose' aren't actually related." I tuck my hands in the pocket. "Men," I say finally. "We can talk of men."

"Ah!" she exclaims. "I said it! We are trying to guess it at the hotel. Herr Singer, he is *schwul*!"

I'm slightly mortified by the revelation that the hotel staff has been debating my sexual orientation. I think of the list of information Frankie told me about, tucked away on the computer screen: *switched rooms, coffee with milk at breakfast, probably gay?* "You were all talking about me? Being a swoo-le?"

"*Schwul*," she corrects me, pronouncing it sch-vool. "Yes, everyone at the hotel. You Americans, sometimes it is hard to know."

"Really? I don't think that's true."

"Astrid, she is believing that you have a Frau. And Gert says that a woman is calling for you, a Mrs. Singer, but we think this is your mother."

"My mother called? No one gave me that message."

"You must always ask for your messages."

"Um, I do."

"But Frankie, he was not so sure. He says a man is calling you every day. I think Frankie, he is liking you just a lee-tle in that way."

"Oh, come on," I say.

"Do not be getting too excited, Samuel. If you are man and you are moving, Frankie, he will be in love with you. And he is liking everything American: *Friends*, Marlboro, Britney, you. He is not so bad, really. He just needs love, like *mein* Schnappsie, or he barks and is very annoying."

"That's just weird," I say.

"I was certain that you are *schwul*, but tonight you make me confused for a minute and I did not know."

"And how did I make you confused?"

"You know, when I, how did you say it?" Magda thinks for a second. "When I *changed* my clothes?"

"Yep. Very good."

"When I changed into my *outfit*," she says proudly, "and you are looking at *meine Brüste*."

"Magda, I was looking at your breasts because they were on display. Like a painting in a museum!"

"No!" Magda gasps. "Really?"

"Yes! With a little frame around them and everything. How could anyone not look at your boobs?"

"A painting at a museum?" She giggles, opening her jacket, looking down. "I like it." She zips up. "This is *gut*. Samuel, this night, it is a nice night."

"I think so, too"

"*Gut*." Magda smiles at me. She grabs my arm and we walk like this for a while, saying nothing, just two friends strolling down the street.

How did this happen? When did this happen? I'm surprised by how comfortable and close I feel with her next to me, arm in arm, friends. "So how is he named?" she asks.

"Who?"

"Your man."

"Oh. Daniel."

"Dahn-you-elle" She stretches it out in the same way she says my name, Sahm-you-elle. "Dahn-you-elle," she says it again, as if she's mulling it over before throwing it away. "What a silly name."

"Well, Magda, that's his name. You're a tough cookie."

"I am a cookie?"

"Forget it." Beyond the iron gates of the cemetery, a sculpture of an angel, robed and bored, leans against a broken column. Someone has placed a rose on its hand.

"So tell me, are you calling him Dan?"

"Definitely not," I say. "He is in no way a Dan."

"I see. And are you in love with him very much?"

"I think so. To love, to be in love—after all these years, I can't tell the difference."

"Hmmm." Magda tilts her head. "There is a difference, I think."

I unlock my arm from hers, remove another picture from my wallet, and hand it to her. She walks over to a streetlamp and examines it. It's winter in the snapshot. Daniel and I sit on a bench in Central Park bundled in puffy jackets. He's wearing the hat I've got on right now. Behind the bench is one of those giant gray rocks, arching like the back of a whale, its tip covered in snow. Daniel's legs are draped across my lap, and he's squeezing my hand. We have huge smiles on our faces, frosty air coming out of our mouths. Magda studies the picture. "Look at you, Samuel. When is this from, is it ten years or so?"

"Oh gosh, no. Not even five."

"Ah. You are looking like little babies."

"I feel like we were babies back then."

"Your man, he is nice to look at."

"That he is," I say, peering over her shoulder.

"His legs, they are so long."

"Yes, they are."

"I am thinking you are correct. He is no way a Dan. And you, Samuel, you look happy in the photo." Magda looks into my eyes, trying to find, I think, the man on the bench with the smile. We stare at each other, until finally I take the picture and return it to my wallet.

"So tell me, who is it, the boy from Albany, at the restaurant?"

"Magda, it's not like that. I told you, he's just a friend."

"Okay," she says. "Just a friend."

"Really, Magda, he's straight."

"Straight?"

"Yes, and remember, he's American."

"Well, of course," Magda says. "How else can you speak at your dinner."

"That's not fair," I say. "We're doing okay."

Magda stops and looks at me. "This is because I like you, Samuel. Another Berliner, he may not tolerate your ignorance."

"Wow, Magda. That's a little harsh." I stare at her. "What do you mean?"

"Ah, well okay. You do not even know how to say good morning when you arrive at the hotel. I remember it, you walk up to the desk, and you say, Hello, I am Sam Singer, and I have a room here . . ."

I don't like the way she sounds imitating my accent, as if I'm some dad on a sitcom. "Magda, it was the crack of dawn. And I'd been traveling for a hundred hours. What do you expect? I'm not some ambassador checking into the U.N."

"Come, Samuel." She tilts her head. "We turn here."

We make a left and leave the graveyard behind. I follow her, but I'm upset. "Gosh," I say, stopping in front of a barbershop.

"*Gosh?* What is it?"

"Just, does that really bother you? The not-speaking-German thing?"

"Sometimes, yes. It is un-nice, to be knowing so little. I watch your silly movies, I buy your bad music, I plug into *meinen* iPod; can not you greet me in my language?"

"I'm sorry, Magda, I didn't realize."

"It is okay. In Germany we are used to this, *ja*? Probably in all of the world. It is what you do, sometimes, you people make a hobby not to realize."

"Well, I'm sorry you feel that way, but please don't lump me in with 'you people,' whoever they are. I'm not doing that with you." Magda looks at me. I stop in the street. "And you know, Magda, you do work at a hotel."

She pauses, blinking, contemplating what I've just said.

"I'm just saying, isn't it your job to deal with people who don't speak your language?"

She does not answer. "Let us keep walking," Magda says, grabbing my arm again. "We are having a nice night, *ja*? And Austria, it is right here on the corner."

Get Ur Freak On

Austria sits at the end of a quiet street, and even from the outside, it glows in a warm yellow light. As we pass through the front door, I look at my watch and realize we're late; our epic walk made four blocks feel like ten miles.

It's nearly eight and every table is full. Mounted deer heads, moody landscape paintings, and candle sconces are strewn across wood-paneled walls. People smoke at the bar, at the tables, as enormous trays of meat, potatoes, and beer swirl through the air. Everyone—the customers, the servers, the bartender—seems deeply involved in conversation. Diners lean toward neighbors at nearby tables and pat each other on the back.

I lay my jacket on the saddle of a wooden horse by the entrance as Magda chats with the host. And then I notice Jeremy sitting at the end of the bar, smoking a cigarette. Though he's still wearing combat boots, his red hair has been slicked back and darkened by some gelatinous product. He's wearing khaki pants and a striped button-down shirt. He's shaved and cleaned himself up for our dinner, which I find strangely moving. I walk over and pat him on the back. "Well, hello," he says, a trail of smoke seeping out of his nose. "Sorry, can't help it." He stubs out his cigarette. "I'm a goddamned chimney."

"When in Rome . . ." I shrug my shoulders and we shake hands. "Don't you look nice," I tell him.

"Why, thank you, sir. I've heard about this place. Figured I should make myself semipresentable. But look around. It's like we're at a lodge at the tip of some mountain. This is seriously old school."

"Indeed. And hey, sorry we're late."

"*Null* problemo. Wait, *we're* late? Who's we?" He turns around and notices Magda standing behind me. She comes forward, and I introduce them. I watch her small hand disappear into Jeremy's much larger one. He greets her in German, and they talk back and forth a bit. I'm surprised to watch Jeremy transform as he chitchats with far greater prowess than I expected, twisting his mouth around the rough edges of the words.

"Ah," Magda says, turning to me. "Your friend, he speaks *Deutsch.* This is *gut.*"

"I don't speak it so well," Jeremy says.

"*Nein,*" she says. "*Du sprichst wunderschön.*"

Jeremy instantly turns pink and laughs under his breath.

"What did she say?" I ask, feeling separate.

"I am saying he speaks German beautifully," Magda explains. She leans against the empty stool next to Jeremy. "Yeh-rah-mee," she says, "can I *buhme* a ciggie?" Jeremy doesn't even answer, just watches as she reaches over and slides one slowly out of the pack in front of him. She uses only her index finger. "Marlboro Man," she laughs, placing the cigarette between her lips. "I do it only on special nights."

Jeremy fumbles with the matches and nervously lights her up.

"*Danke,*" Magda says softly. She takes off her jacket and folds it in her lap. Magda's naughty sweater has just made its debut in Austria, and Jeremy is unable to conceal his interest. Magda whispers into my ear, "Your friend, he is not *schwul.*"

"No, he's not. I told you he's straight."

"Ah, okay. Straight, this I understand now." She laughs, exhaling a stream of smoke that envelops us all. I feel the bar vibrate suddenly and notice Magda's purse tottering on the edge. The computer-chirp chorus of "Get Ur Freak On" seeps out of the bag. "Oh, *mein Handy,*" she says.

Jeremy nods his head. "I *love* that song," he exclaims, as if it's the most meaningful coincidence, a sign of profound connection.

Magda opens her bag and removes her tiny red phone. She looks at the caller ID and sighs. "Please, you will excuse me . . . but you boys, you get beers, okay?"

"Should we get one for you?" Jeremy asks.

"No, I go soon. Get one and I take maybe a few seeps, *ja*?"

"You can share with me," Jeremy tells her.

"*Sehr gut.*" Magda turns to me. "Remember what I have said to you?"

"Yes, Magda. Not the house beer that tastes like stale pee."

"*Genau*, Samuel. Ask for the Kapsreiter, it is delicious." Magda grabs her jacket, wraps her scarf around her neck, and takes her cigarette and phone from the bar. Jeremy and I watch as she walks outside and stands in front of the restaurant window, talking on her phone. The bartender comes over and we order the beer.

Jeremy turns to me, starts humming the chorus from "Get Ur Freak On." "*Mein Handy*," he says, imitating her. "Oh. My. God."

"What?"

"What an incredible creature."

"Magda?"

"Dude, are you kidding? She is HOT. How do you know her?"

"She works at my hotel."

"No fucking way."

"Yes, way. I guess we've sort of become friends."

"Sort of?"

"Definitely sort of," I say. "Baby steps. She's prickly."

"She's like an angel. And what the fuck is that outfit?"

"Yes, Jeremy, I know."

"She's working that librarian look, which is so fucking hot, with those smart-girl glasses. And then she takes off her jacket and it's like peek-a-boo time at the Schnitzelhaus. What is *that*? I love it! These German ladies seem so prim and proper and then they come to dinner dressed like *that*?"

"That's a lot of décolletage," I say.

"If that's pretentious for smokin' hot, then hell yeah. She is gorgeous. That skin, those indigo eyes . . ."

"Indigo?" I roll my eyes.

"Yeah. Indigo." He looks outside and throws her a little wave. "And she's so smart and funny, too."

"So, you fall in love easily?"

"In Berlin, like five times a day. But how can you not? It's as if every beauty gene has been distilled here to create the most exquisite goddesses on Earth."

"Be careful where you say that, Jeremy."

"You know what I mean. And they're all hip and sexy, but without any attitude."

"Trust me—Magda has plenty of 'tude. And her romantic situation is . . . complicated."

"Everything is complicated." He sighs. "Oh, *l'amour*."

"You're insane." I laugh, sipping my beer

"Seriously, have you ever seen so many gorgeous women? Like when I'm walking down Karl Marx Allee and the sky is spitting hail and I'm fucking freezing and missing my favorite sweater thank-youverymuch Sam . . . and then some perfect girl appears like a goddamned apparition, and I'll stop and think, I could marry you, be a devoted husband to you, cook for you, make babies with you. But Magda, she's in another league. She should be worshipped in a temple."

We stare out the window. Magda is still talking on the phone. She catches my eye and puts a finger in the air as if to say *one minute*. "We were having such a nice night," I tell Jeremy. "And then on the way over here she reamed me out for not speaking German."

"Oh, she was probably just playing with you."

"Exactly."

"And she does have a point."

"Jeremy, I barely had time to pack for this trip. I've been to Prague, and it's not like everyone expected me to speak Czech."

"That's because everyone speaks English there."

"Everyone speaks English here too! Or they're supposed to. So I said to her, you know, Magda, you do work in a hotel."

"You said that? With that snarky tone in your voice?"

"Yes, I guess."

Jeremy winces. "Ouch, man."

"I know," I sigh. "I feel a little bad about that."

Jeremy glances back outside, then sits up straight. "Oh, here she comes. Damn, she put her jacket back on. Damn, damn, damn. Get her to unzip it."

"You get her to unzip it."

"Believe me, I shall try."

Magda twists through the crowd and makes her way to us. She reaches over Jeremy's shoulder and crushes her cigarette in the ashtray. "Okay, boys. I must go." A final stream of smoke leaks through her nostrils. Jeremy looks at her and smiles, dazed, as if he's sitting in a theater watching the most spellbinding movie. He hands his beer to Magda and she takes a sip. "Samuel, I am seeing you tomorrow at the hotel?"

I think of my plans and get a twinge of anxiety as I wonder how I will accomplish everything. I've put off so much already, it's starting to pile up, and the trip suddenly feels like it's collapsing. I stare at my towering mug of beer and remember the wine I consumed earlier at Magda's. I haven't let myself drink this much in years. "I have a meeting," I sigh. "First thing in the morning, actually."

"Then I see you later," Magda says. "I am working until eighteen hours."

"Well actually . . ." I do the math in my head. "After the meeting, I may go to Sachsenhausen."

"Really?" She cocks her head. "Why Sachsenhausen?"

"Because I feel like I should go."

"Samuel, it is far out on the S1. It takes almost one hour. And also, once you arrive in the boring town of Oranienburg it is a long walk from the station."

"Yes, I know," I say. "The end of the line."

"I do not know it," she says, "why people they come to Berlin and want to go see bad history part of Germany."

"I don't know if I *want* to go see it."

"It does not exist anymore," she says.

"But it's still there, Magda. So it does exist."

She turns to Jeremy and places her hand next to his. "Yeh-rah-mee, did you go?"

"Actually, I did," he tells her. Magda looks disappointed. "I mean, what can you say? It was, it is, pretty bleak."

Magda stares into her lap, silent. Jeremy looks at me as if to say, *What now?* Magda looks up. "Well, Samuel, you are doing as you wish."

"Thanks, Magda."

"And do not forget, you have also *Kaffeeklatsch*."

"You're right. Good memory."

"So maybe I see you after your big day?"

"I hope so."

"*Und mein Freund*," she says, patting Jeremy on the back, "it is good to meet you. It is nice to meet a friend of Samuel."

"*Gleichfalls*, Magda," Jeremy says.

"Tell me," she says to him, "where is it, your flat?"

"I live in Friedrichshain," Jeremy answers.

"Yes, Samuel tells me this. By the river?"

"Closer to Frankfurter Allee."

"Ah," she says, as if she's just sized him up by the revelation of his geography. "You and zee punks."

"I like it," he says, shrugging his shoulders.

The host places our beers on a tray; it's time to move to our table. We all get up from our bar stools. Jeremy leans into Magda and speaks softly to her in German. She shakes her head and laughs, then kisses him on both cheeks. He clumsily moves around, almost catching her lips. "*Tschüss*," she says, and waves goodbye. I watch her dissolve in the crowd as I'm led with Jeremy to a corner table in the back room. We're seated next to a man who is dining alone, eating Schnitzel under a moose head.

I fold the napkin across my lap. "What did you just say to Magda?"

"I asked her to stay for dinner."

"She's on her way someplace."

"Where?"

"I don't know, Jeremy. She wouldn't tell me." I peruse the constellation of antlers on the wall behind Jeremy. I suddenly have the random curiosity of what it would feel like to rub my head against the pointy horns. Maybe it would feel really good. "And besides, I invited you to dinner, not her."

"Dude, relax. First off, *you* brought her here. And anyway . . . she's not here, is she? Please, do as the Germans do, drink your beer and chill. It's really the best strategy." He takes a sip. "But I wonder where she went."

Me too, but I only admit this to myself.

A diminutive waitress with a shock of white hair lays menus on the table, then points to the blackboard, which is filled with the day's specials. Jeremy leans his head against the wall, just missing a small pair of antlers. "So my lady is a mystery. What should we order? I can speak the language pretty okay, but the food stuff eludes me. There's like a gazillion different regions and they each have like seventeen different words for lettuce."

"Magda told me to order the dumplings and the schnitzel. Actually, it was a command."

"Let's do it then. You can't play the point-at-something-on-the-menu game in Germany. You'll wind up with a bowl of lamb arteries or some sausage made of pancreas."

Jeremy orders for us. He seems delighted to serve this purpose, as if my utter incompetence with the language has made him realize how much he's actually learned. "*Wunderbar!*" the waitress sings, wobbling away.

"I also ordered more beer," he says. "That Kapsreiter was awesome. Magda knows her pilsner, which is like such a turn-on for me."

"I'm beginning to think dust would turn you on."

"Probably, if it was wearing a skirt."

"That was intense," I say. "The Sachsenhausen thing."

"Well, yeah."

"When she asked me why, I couldn't explain it."

"In New York you go to a Broadway show or take, like, the Circle Line. But Berlin is different. You're surrounded by history, and a lot of it is pretty bleak, even though, at this point, most people weren't even alive when the super dark shit happened. So it's the older people that genuinely freak me out. Like this woman who sits outside the *Imbiss* selling flowers, right by Frankfurter Tor. She's like ninety-seven and has bug eyes the size of golf balls. You walk by and she smiles at you. And you think, okay, so where were you, Frau Blumen? Back during 'bad history part of Germany'? But you'll see tomorrow at Sachsenhausen when you're surrounded by kids on class trips. It ain't the Statue of Liberty."

"Can you even visit the Statue of Liberty anymore?"

"Who knows. Someone's gonna blow it up, right?"

"And besides," I say, "now everyone goes downtown and stares into the big gaping hole." I roll my eyes.

"Yeah. Ground fucking Zero. Nine fucking Eleven. I hate that crap. It's like, must we nickname everything? Anyway, my experience in Berlin is that people's eyes kind of glaze over if you talk about the Nazi stuff. The Wall is a better story with a happy-ish ending. But you can't think about all that's happened too much or you'll just get freaked out. Anyway, enough doom and gloom. Here comes the Schnitzel."

Magda was right. Our meal is delicious—two gargantuan plates of perfectly golden veal cutlets with cucumber salad, potatoes and cranberries; cream-colored dumplings the size of my fist. Jeremy asks about my meeting, and I tell him about Klaus and Sabine and our walk through Charlottenburg. I'm relieved that I actually accomplished something today; for the first time on this trip, I feel like I deserve a night out. Jeremy slices a dumpling with his fork. "So . . . tell me about Magda."

"She's just the manager of my hotel."

"Come on. You can write books, poems, encyclopedias on women like Magda."

"Well, I told you she's a little snappish."

"Turns me on. Can't help it."

"Then you're in the right city."

And with that, I bring a final forkful of schnitzel to my mouth. I stare at it, the crispy brown corner of veal drizzled with lemon juice, mourning its passing before I devour it.

After dinner, before I can get the check, Jeremy asks the waitress for something. "Just one more beer," he says. "And espresso for both of us."

I look at my watch. "It's a little late for coffee, Jeremy."

"Nonsense."

"What do you mean, nonsense?" I throw two fingers in the air to flag the waitress.

"Dude, what are you doing, hailing a fucking taxi?" He lights a cigarette and pushes the pack toward me. "So, where we going?"

"It's almost eleven, Jeremy."

"Sam, the night is young! We're in Berlin. Let's go out."

I watch as the smoke from his cigarette dances upward, twisting through the maze of antlers before splitting across the wooden ceiling. "I need to get some sleep."

Jeremy points to our waitress. "Look, here comes our espresso already. You'll be up all night."

"Yeah, I know. And I have a big day tomorrow."

"Oh, yes," he says, cigarette dangling between his lips. "The camps."

"And, hello, my meeting?" And maybe even Kaspar, if I can bring myself to meet him.

"Sam, there are like fifteen places we could go to right now that would blow your motherfucking mind away. You want a silent disco? Tango in a warehouse? A techno party in the basement of an old department store?"

"Jeremy . . . I'm pooped."

"Fuck that. What happened to the guy who got off the plane, popped an E and danced the frickin' night away?"

"It didn't quite happen that way."

Our waitress places our espressos on the table. Jeremy picks up his tiny cup, stares into it for a moment, and then drinks its contents, defiantly, in one shot. "Whatever, dude. I want that guy. Bring that man back."

"That man is thirty-seven and still recovering from that night."

"So you're thirty-fucking-seven, Sam, big fucking deal. Madonna could be your fucking mother."

"Jeremy, you're talking a little loudly." I do the arithmetic in my head. "And Madonna could *not* be my mother."

He looks around the restaurant, probably wondering if he could lure anyone to go out with him tonight: the young woman in the corner, the table of handsome blond men across the room, even the old guy next to us, finishing his pudding underneath a moose head. Jeremy shakes his head. "Sam, you're in Berlin for Christ's sake!" He throws his arms in the air, the cigarette drooping from his teeth. A few people turn and look at us, amused. "The boyfriend, the job, that shit New York energy, they're all back home, waiting for you. Sleep when you're home. You're here now—why don't you live a little, instead of trying so hard not to?"

"I hate people like you."

"You *need* people like me. We're like fish in a mutually beneficial relationship. What's that word?"

"Symbiotic."

"Exactly. Symbiosis. I eat your scraps and you get your teeth cleaned."

"What the hell are you talking about?"

"Come on, Sam." Jeremy pounds his fist on the table, which startles the man sitting next to us, who drops his spoon. "Let's stay out all night and watch the sun come up."

I think about Debra and her stupid theory about Yes people and No people. I assume my role. "No," I tell him.

Jeremy just goes on. "Let's go out somewhere, then chill at the Lustgarten with some beers, watch the sun hit the Palast der Republik. It'll blow your mind, it glows like fucking lava."

I stare into my beer, my face reddening. Sometimes I wish I liked to drink more, that it didn't make me feel like I'm floating underwater when I'm just out to dinner with a friend. "Jeremy, seriously, please don't do this to me."

"I don't know," Jeremy says. "You're a cool guy, but it's like Aunt Deb said . . . you're a little uptight."

"What? She said that?"

"Just have a coffee, Sam. Let's go out, pretty please?"

"Debra said I was uptight?" I take an experimental sip of espresso. "Me?"

"She said you could be a little negative."

"Negative? What a terrible thing to say."

Jeremy asks the waitress for the check. "Sam, just pay the bill. You're coming with me."

Zugunglück

It's past midnight when we walk through the doors of SO36. Some DJ from Stuttgart is playing minimal techno—vocals hacked to bits, pouring out of speakers as processed bleeps. Jeremy tells me it's the thing right now in the underground clubs of southern Germany, as if it's some new Beaujolais or a rare truffle from Düsseldorf. As we pass the dance floor, he yells in my ear: "I fucking love this song!"

"What song?" I ask. "There is no song." I can't believe I let him drag me to this club. "*One* hour," I tell him. "And that's it."

"Hey Sam, can I—" Before he finishes, I hand him twenty euros. "I'm totally paying you back," he says.

While Jeremy heads to the bar, I cross the crowded, sticky dance floor to the men's room, the rattle of broken glass beneath my feet. Men stare at me with their piercings and faux-hawks. I'm dressed inappropriately for this club in every way possible. It's hot, and the room seems to be perspiring. I remove my sweater and unbutton my shirt. There's a line for the bathroom and a drunk girl starts talking to me in German, but I ignore her and head back to find Jeremy. My foot scrapes against the floor. I look down at my shoe and see a shard of glass sticking out of the sole. I sit on a bench and remove it, hoping that sooner or later Jeremy will find me.

A boy walks up to me. He's wearing white jeans and a tank top that says BULLSHit.

He can't be more than twenty-two, with a pink Flock of Seagulls haircut, complete with a single braid falling past his shoulder. He sits down next to me and scatters the broken glass with his feet like shells on the beach. "It's wack, isn't it?" He's American. "They'll have to switch to plastic soon, like the Brits."

"Plastic beer bottles?" I ask. He nods. I think about that plastic island drifting through the Pacific, the garbage patch that's four times the size of Texas. "That's depressing."

"Yeah, but in the UK they're killing each other at soccer matches. It's mental."

"Well, okay, then. I don't want anyone to die."

"But those Brits are crazy motherfuckers. They'll still find some way to shove each other into gates and call each other arseholes." He cracks himself up, then introduces himself. "Lawrence," he says, holding out his hand. A surprising name for a boy with a pink mohawk.

I tell him my name. Well, actually, I scream it over the music. "So, how did you know I spoke English?"

"I had a feeling. You just look American."

"That's more depressing than plastic beer bottles."

"Yeah, well . . ." He pulls out a joint and lights up, takes a hit, coughs. The aroma is strong and sweet and smells like rain, like wet grass. "Want some?"

"Nah. I'm a little drunk. And I can't find my friend."

Lawrence folds his lip and makes a sad face. "Poor Sam."

"I never know what to do when you lose somebody at a club. It's not like they can make an announcement."

"Just stay on the bench with me. Trust me, the whole point of this place is to get lost. I've been trying all night." He takes another hit of pot. "So, where you from?"

"New York. You?"

"Ohio." Lawrence starts singing. "Why oh why oh why oh, why did I ever leave Ohio?" He laughs, looks at me. "Know that song?"

"I do not," I say.

"Yeah, why would you." Lawrence leans back and starts rubbing my knee. "Don't worry, Sam. Your friend will show up. They always do." He stares ahead, but his fingertips begin to travel up my leg. "Eventually."

I look down at his hand. "What are you doing?"

"What do you think I'm doing?"

He glides his fingers up and down my thigh. Here, no one notices. Three men walk by holding hands. Couples of every combination kiss on the dance floor. One shaved-headed woman is topless, endless tattoos of snakes and ivy swirling down her back.

I can't figure out what I'm doing here. I'm supposed to be in bed, resting for tomorrow, which according to my watch, is now very much today. I try to think of something to say, but instead Lawrence passes me the joint, and this time I take a hit. As the smoke fills my lungs, I barrel over, coughing. "Jeez. That stuff is strong," I say, clearing my throat.

"Yeah." He stares at his joint. "It's, like, grown in water."

"Is it?" Wet grass, I think. Rain.

"My guy calls it *'Zugunglück.'* It's German for 'Trainwreck.'" He giggles. "Just you wait."

I rub my eyes. Great. I just smoked something called "Trainwreck." Already, I feel a wave running over me. "Don't worry, honey," Lawrence says. "You'll be okay."

I feel my body turning warmer, the music sounding fuller, his hand running down my leg. I watch his joint burning, drifting above me like a firefly. He turns his head against the wall. I examine him while his eyes are shut: his long pencil arms, the blue vein snaking down his narrow bicep as his finger slides down my leg, then strokes my knee, his skinny legs spilling out of his hips like an afterthought. He's a strange character, but his face is undeniably beautiful, his young skin smooth and iridescent. I lean my head against the wall, too. Suddenly, I can't even hold it up. "It's loud," I say.

"Yeah." We look at each other. His head moves closer, creeping against the wall. "So, like, what do you think?"

"Think about what?"

Lawrence laughs, his lips next to mine. "I don't know." His hand is now a few inches from my crotch, rubbing my jeans, his face next to my face. I feel nauseous and hot and vaguely disgusted, and despite everything, I feel myself get hard. We both look down at my crotch, at the tent forming in my pants. A shirtless and shaved-headed muscleman twice Lawrence's size and age comes over and grabs his hand. "Well, here he is," Lawrence says as he's lifted from the bench. "See, I told you. They always show up. Good luck finding your friend, sweetie."

The muscleman leads Lawrence to the center of the dance floor. Lawrence sways beneath a beam of light, his eyes closed, his arms dancing upward, a beatific, sleepy smile on his superstoned face.

Jeremy finally appears with two beers, a cigarette dangling from his mouth and a story about some gorgeous girl in boots made of bubble-wrap who came *this close* to dancing with him. I'm so happy to see him that I almost hug him. He sits down next to me. I don't tell him about Lawrence, his wandering fingers, or the hit I took from his joint. In Berlin, I can edit my life as I go, choosing what facts to report and which to omit. "You can go home now," Jeremy says. "If you want."

I take the bottle from him. "Why now?"

"Because you've earned it. What time is it?"

"Don't you have a watch?"

"No way." He rolls up his shirt and shows me his red hairy wrist. "I don't do time."

I look at my watch. "Well, it's after two."

"No shit. Sam Singer, out 'til the wee on a school night."

"Jeremy, you don't know me." I sip my beer, slosh it around my mouth. "Mothafucka."

Jeremy gasps. "*Excusez-moi*? That is *Herr* Mothafucka to you. Sam, I like you better drunk. Much better."

"Well thanks, I guess." I laugh. "Right back at ya." I look toward the dance floor and laugh again.

"Why are you giggling?"

"I am *not* giggling." I try to hold it together, but I can't.

Jeremy turns my head toward his, looks into my eyes. "Oh my God."

"What?" I pull away from him. "Why are you staring at me?"

"You're totally stoned."

"No, I'm not." I shake my head like he's insane for even thinking that. I laugh nervously, then snort. "Gosh, why did I just snort?"

" 'Cause you're high as a kite. Look at you! Your eyes are bugging."

"It was one hit," I explain, putting my thumb and index finger tightly together. "Just the littlest bit."

"Hey, whatever floats your boat. But man, you play the prude, and then I leave you alone for ten fucking minutes and you get all drugged up."

"You're right." I move closer to Jeremy and lay my head on his shoulder. "I'm terrible."

"Aw, is my wittle Courtney Love all sweepy?"

"Yes, actually. Is that okay?"

"Sure. Just don't pass out on me. So like, what did you smoke?"

"Sho-gun-something. It's *stroooong*. It was grown in a river or something."

Jeremy shakes his head. "What a pussy."

"I know." I cover my face with my hands. "I'm such a big pussy."

"Jeez, Sam, it's like, who knows what was in that pot? You should be careful at a place like this."

"Well, thanks for bringing me here, Jeremy. It's not like I have to be up in four hours and pretend to be an adult in front of other adults. Adults who are German. And probably mean." I laugh a little. "Are we really in Berlin?"

Jeremy smiles, but I can tell he's shocked that I'm behaving like such a moron. The music is blaring, the lights pulsing, and there are four men making out on the bench next to us, but I feel like I'm alone in my bedroom about to slip under the covers. Jeremy rests his head against mine. "Well, Sam, all I know is we just flirted our asses off. Without landing, but whatever. The point is we flirted."

"What are you talking about?"

"Who was that boy you were chatting up?"

"You saw that?"

"Dude, of course. While I was trying to dance with Bubble Boots, I saw a certain pink-haired gentleman getting a little cozy with you."

"Trust me, it was nothing. We were talking about beer bottles. And he has some Conan-the-Barbarian boyfriend. They're like dancing on the dance floor."

"Whatev, Sam. Apparently he managed to get you high." Jeremy throws a cigarette in his mouth.

"He's not even my type."

"Yeah, he was a little wisp of a dude. You can do better, methinks. So tell me, what *is* your type?"

"Uh, hello?"

"Hello, what?"

"I'm in a relationship?" I show him my hand and wiggle my fingers as if there's a ring on one of them. But there is no ring.

Jeremy rolls his eyes. "Yeah, okay, so what's your type?"

I think of Kaspar. And then of Daniel. And then I think of nothing at all. "Daniel," I say. "Daniel is my type."

I stare at my fingers. I can't feel them. I look around. A few people dance under the disco ball but there are also people who stand on the side, faces like ghouls, broken glass at their feet. The night has turned that corner again, when it's too loud, too dark, and you just want to start over or fast forward. And I drift toward home, before I left: the burst of Indian summer. The subway. The message on Daniel's phone. It all starts to come back to me with a pot-induced clarity, like everything that's happened is just floating in front of me. A tsunami of anxiety rises from nowhere. Damn that Trainwreck. Now is not the time.

Jeremy grabs my shoulders. "Sam, what's wrong?"

"Nothing." And just like that, I feel my eyes well up. "Everything is fine."

"Come on, Sam. I'm taking you home."

The Drugs Don't Work

I need to sleep but my heart is beating fast, like it's jumped outside of me, pulling me out of the room. That's the thing with drugs. Sometimes you wish there was an off switch to make it stop. But it doesn't work like that, and I find myself beneath the covers, an after-hours cliché, lying in the fetal position, my life flashing behind my eyelids with a clarity not suitable for any time of day. I've left the curtains open, and the TV Tower blinks in the distance, but I may as well be in New York, three weeks ago, because that's where my mind takes me. Indian summer. That queasy feeling.

I was on the train, trying to read my book, Harry tucked under my seat. In front of me, some mother tried to read to her daughter. "Sometimes Poppleton did not want spaghetti," she said. "He just wanted to practice his harmonica." The girl squealed. The mother grabbed her wrist. "Hillary Hunter Feldman!" she said with that shaky New York voice. "Please! S-T-O-P."

"No," the girl screamed. "I want off train!"

So did I, and I wondered why only children and crazy people have the right to let it all out. Lately I felt two beats away from standing on a corner with a handmade sign explaining my own life story in three sentences.

I was used to the crazy people, but it seemed like New York was suddenly disproportionately filled with children. I watched as friends got married and had babies. They disappeared—sometimes literally to another city, but most often they disappeared into parenthood and family life. It was an adjustment. When I grew up in New York, my mother practically threw me over her shoulder like a gorilla baby and marched through the urban jungle unfazed. But times had changed. Dinner parties became playdates; Daniel feigned interest while new versions of our former friends talked endlessly about nursery schools and nannies. But I'd get lost in the eyes of every toddler I met. We'd return home exhausted and invariably with some mysterious stain on our clothing. But still, I found myself wanting a family. It's what I'd always imagined, what I'd hoped for. The future looked empty without it.

I researched constantly and mostly in secret. As for Daniel, I just didn't know. He was less restless, more ambitious, busy conquering New York one building at a time. So I put it on hold. This enormous thing went on the ever-growing list of someday-maybes: beach vacation, more sex, country house, possible child. You can talk about it for days and stuff a filing cabinet with information, but there's no baby without a baby.

Hillary finally escaped with her mother at Columbus Circle. I opened my book, but I knew these things came in waves. The subway doors opened and closed and chomped into each other, my least favorite sound in the world. Then another bad sound: "In front of the train, stop blocking the doors. No one leaves!" The conductor yelled at us like we were delinquents.

The guy next to me rocked in his seat, listening to music with his eyes closed. His butt rubbed against the side of my pants, his elbow pressed my ribs, the tinny sounds of hip-hop leaking from his headphones. Even as a native New Yorker, I've never adjusted to this forced intimacy, this violation. "It's my shit," he chanted, snapping his fingers.

A thin woman in glasses entered the car. "First," she bellowed, "let me apologize for the disruption." I sighed, closed my novel, and put it in my bag as she began her pitch.

Daniel wondered why I didn't just take cabs everywhere. Over dinner, I'd say, "On the subway today . . ." and he'd roll his eyes as he anticipated the next horror story. "Sam, why do you pretend you're poor? It's so boring."

Daniel had made his peace with New York. Like so many friends who grew up in college towns, on farms or mountaintops, Daniel had always dreamt of Manhattan, the end-all-be-all. But I grew up in New York. For me, it was just a continuation, or maybe the end-of-the-line, and I often felt like a crack baby, unknowingly addicted to the thing that was destroying me. Maybe I was meant to live on top of a hill, a hermit in a hut baking pies. But I'd never know. New York was inside of me, and despite every impulse to flee, I'd never leave.

Daniel was practical. He made simple, logical adjustments to life in the city. It wasn't just that he took taxis everywhere. Instead of Broadway he walked down West End Avenue, where the architecture was more beautiful, the trees lusher, the street less crowded. He'd buy enormous books on art and design, giant biographies of obscure architects and disgraced aristocrats, and slice them into chunks with our kitchen knives. He'd use packing tape to bind them into mini-books so he could carry the section he was reading wherever he needed to go.

When we reached my stop, I strapped Harry's bag across my shoulder and climbed the stairs to Seventy-Ninth Street. Every time I took those stairs, I'd wonder how I wound up on the Upper West Side. I was a downtown boy. Living near Riverside Drive was as likely as Brooke Astor squatting on Avenue D. As I climbed the stairs, I was jostled by a group of school kids. I bent down on the street, let Harry out of his bag, and put him on his leash. A man pushed past me with his briefcase. He looked into my eyes. "Fuck you," he said.

What? I thought. What did I do?

There's this place in my chest, some invisible organ between my heart and my stomach. It secretes a specific chemical into my system, my odium juice. It amazes me that people don't flip out, lose it every day on the subway, because there I was dangling from a thread.

It was five o'clock, the sky was blue, and it was warm. The entire city slid back effortlessly into the heat, but I was queasy in my stomach. My brain had switched to falling leaves, crisp air, darkening skies. Soon it would be winter, my favorite time of year.

I passed the Apthorp, the colossal apartment house on Broadway. There was a table by the curb lined with plates of cookies and Entenmann's boxes, a mother/daughter bake sale for the Democratic Party. It was voting season, there was a war going on. A sign beside the Rice Krispies treats read: *Weapons of Mass Deliciousness.* The mothers were fired up. Their daughters did their best impersonations of being fired up, too: *Stop the madness! Buy a brownie!* I wondered if the girls understood what causes their cakes would benefit or if they were just in love with their liberal mommies and their huge pre-war apartments. Children seem so in love with their parents these days, entwined in intense relationships, epic romances, walking hand in hand down streets, hugging in restaurants, arguing like old lovers.

They were selling iced tea and bottled water for two dollars each. My heart was still pounding from the train, from the weather, and I was sweating. I bought an Evian, and a redheaded girl handed me my change and thanked me. "I believe in gay marriage," she said.

I cocked my head, startled. "Well, that's good."

She bent down to Harry. "Can I pet your dog?"

"You can, but he'll probably bark." I took a napkin from the table and dabbed my forehead.

"So he's mean?"

"Not at all. Just misunderstood."

"Good 'cause my mom says 'Mean dog, mean owner.'"

"He just puts on a tough-guy act. He's a dachshund." I picked him up. Harry licked my face. "It's what they do."

I bent down to her. The girl, unafraid, stroked Harry's chin. "What's his name?"

"Harry," I told her.

"Harry. I like it. Who's he named after?"

"No one. We just liked it."

"Good," she said. "That's the best reason." She began stroking Harry's neck. Harry tilted his head toward the late day sun and closed his eyes. I smiled, suddenly relaxed. "You found his spot."

She kept petting Harry and looked at me. "Do you have a husband?"

"A husband?" I laughed, disarmed by the girl. I wanted to question why her gaydar was so acute, but I just went on. "I sort of have a husband. But as you know, we can't get married."

"You don't have a ring."

"No." I looked at my right hand, then the left. "I don't."

"You should be able to get married and adopt a baby."

"I agree. But I can adopt, you know." Just last week I had emailed an agency in Evanston, Illinois, and requested a brochure. Just to see. I almost told her this. I hadn't even told Daniel. "And there are other ways."

"Do you want to?"

"That's kind of a personal question."

"Whoops. Sorry."

"But you know what? I think I do." I stared at this girl stroking my dog's head. I wanted to slip her in my pocket and take her home. If only it was that easy. Look what I picked up at the bake sale, I'd tell Daniel.

"You seem like you'd be a great dad," she said.

"I do?"

"Yeah, of course, look at you and your baby Harry." She held my gaze for a moment. Sometimes I think kids know when they're piercing right through you. "You should do it," she said. "Like, tomorrow."

"Well, I'll see what I can do." I handed her my three dollars back. "Here. Keep the change. But keep it for yourself."

"No way! Do you want some babka?" she asked, slipping the money into her jeans. "It's from Zabar's."

"No, thanks." I walked away, carrying Harry in one hand and the water in the other. This eight-year-old turned my day around.

I walked into my building and got the mail: bills, the *New Yorker*, and, with uncanny timing, a manila envelope from the adoption agency. I ripped it open. There were reams of information, pictures of smiling families, and so many forms. I was excited, but overwhelmed.

Jonathan and Ellen were in the lobby with their beagle, Brutus. Since they adopted their puppy, they were always around—in the lobby, on the street—teaching Brutus how to sit and be extra friendly, like them. I often wondered what they thought when I opened the mailbox, marched to the elevator, and didn't crack a smile, not even at their puppy. Daniel is afraid that our neighbors think I'm antisocial. But I just want my privacy, or as much anonymity as I can steal in a building of two hundred strangers. Daniel was raised with knee-jerk Midwestern politesse. I sometimes watch in awe as he smiles and engages in elevator conversation. But then he winds up in strangers' apartments while they pour him tea and show him pictures of their cat's back surgery. On this day, though, I surprised myself and actually said "Hi, Brutus." Harry even wagged his tail. Jonathan and Ellen stared at us, dumbfounded.

I opened the door to our apartment and Harry rushed in barking. The vacuum was chugging, fans were whooshing, a timer bleeped on and on. We were having two of Daniel's work friends over for dinner. The fragrant smell of Daniel's apricot chicken drifted through the living room, but already the contentment I'd felt from the encounter with the girl was disappearing. Daniel always opens the windows before guests come over, takes out floor fans and starts blowing them at full blast. Harry hides under the bed, his ears flopping from the squall.

"Why do you have to do this?" I asked Daniel. It was a stupid question. He'd been doing this for years. For someone who seems so defiantly relaxed about everything, Daniel has a weird, deep thing about germs and cleanliness. Why were we having people over for dinner, anyway? I wanted to sit down with Daniel and tell him about the girl, and maybe, even, the envelope; discuss where we were going, what was missing, and what was wrong. But Daniel wasn't there these days. He was next to me, but he wasn't there. *Oh, Sam,* he'd say, *can we not have one of your lifey conversations? I love you but I can't deal.*

"What?" Daniel yelled. "I can't hear you."

I walked over to one of the fans and turned it off. "You can't hear me because of the damn fans." We didn't laugh, or kiss each other. We never even said hello.

"We're having guests." He turned off the vacuum cleaner. "What if we smell?"

"I don't think we smell, Daniel."

"You don't know that. We can't smell ourselves anymore. We've been together for too long."

I shook my head and went into the bedroom. I bent down to find Harry. And there it was: Daniel's phone. It was on the floor, face down, right next to the legs of his nightstand, as if it too, was hiding under the bed. I picked it up, and, as if on cue, the phone buzzed and lit up. I looked toward the living room, but the vacuum was back on again. And then, seized by a strange feeling of fate, I flipped open the phone and saw the message: *Hi D that was fun when do I see u again? xoBrad.* My heart fell on the floor. Not this, not again. I grabbed Harry so hard he actually whimpered. I held him and kissed his forehead. I placed the manila envelope under some shirts in my dresser drawer.

We continued to get ready for dinner. Eventually, I turned to Daniel. "You know that opening I was invited to? The one in Berlin?"

"Yes." He nodded. "Klaus Beckmann. What about it?"

"I think I'm going to go."

A Knock on the Door

I can only vaguely recall how I got back to the hotel. The last thing I remember is Jeremy dropping me off. "Just go to bed," he said, then hugged me and walked away. But Jeremy has no money. I wonder how he got home. It was the middle of the night, the trains probably weren't running, even the space-age ladies would have disappeared. I'm an idiot. The last time someone brought me home due to inebriation, I was eighteen and home was a dorm room.

I call the Haus 4 Gallery and leave a message for Leopold Koch. I'm sick, I explain, and cancel our meeting. I apologize for the late notice and promise to stop by the gallery before I leave Berlin. Life is a series of white lies. The trick, I suppose, is keeping them simple and not getting caught.

My mouth is dry, my head splitting. I skip the breakfast room and drink an entire liter of Coke from the minibar, which, as always, feels like fuel from the gods after a night of debauchery. The sugar and caffeine pour through me, coloring me in. Thankfully, this hangover seems short lived; perhaps I'm getting used to late nights, little sleep, and variable substances drifting through me. I open the dresser for a change of attire and see the half tablet of ecstasy hidden under a shirt. I cup it in my palm, this tiny yellow thing, like it could fly away.

They say that ecstasy makes you nostalgic for a moment as you're experiencing it. That's sad, and even a little cruel—you're feeling contented and connected but also aware that the feeling will soon disappear. All that's left is the memory, the residue.

Once upon a time, ecstasy was my pill of choice. It even delivered Daniel to me, as we kissed so suddenly underneath a disco ball. When you share your first kiss under the influence of a pill, you think, was it just the pill? Was it even real? Or maybe it was more real than anything before it, or anything since; perhaps the pill simply opened the door. But in Berlin, the pill can't do its job. *Ostalgie* surrounding me, New York haunting me from across the ocean.

I wonder where the rest of the pill could take me. There's only one way to find out, but nothing good will come of it. The drugs don't work anymore. So I go to the toilet, lift the lid, throw the pill in the water and flush it down.

I walk to the Tiergarten and head into the park. Endless rows of hulking trees stand like soldiers, amber leaves falling in the breeze. The sky is blue, and the sun warms my cheeks. It's hard to believe it snowed just a few days ago.

I used to go into Central Park looking for love. When I was single, looking for love was the only reason to leave the apartment. There had to be some possibility that I would find it, and if there wasn't, then what was the point of going outside? On weekends, I'd walk through the park, trying to lock eyes with a stranger who might hold the key to the rest of my life. Sometimes he jogged past me, or he slept on the grass, his shirt off, his spine twisted toward the sun. Perhaps he zipped past me in a flash, a blur of promise on rollerblades. Or maybe that was him, reading the *Times* on a bench, looking thoughtful in his glasses, his baseball cap twisted backward. I'd think, he's happy to be here, in the park, alone. He doesn't notice me. But maybe, like me, he's waiting. And then my eyes would return to the pavement, safe in the gray.

I'd return home loveless and defeated. I once called a friend and said, "Every time I look in the mirror I think I look older." And she said, "You look older because you are. Every day a little more. So stop staring at yourself in the mirror." She practically rolled her eyes through the phone. "If you look for problems, you'll find them, Sam. It's as simple as that."

But when you look for love, it eludes you. In a big city, you can get lost. And you give up, bracing for a life of one-night-stands and takeout and old friends growing older. Uncle-dom. Everyone drifting away.

Then, of course, it happens, at the end of a harsh winter, one that dumped forty inches of snow on the city and sent winds whipping over the Hudson, right down Horatio Street. For months, the wind rattled your windows so much that you spent days and nights with your windows locked and the shades pulled down. The radiator hisses, the pipes clank. You've endured that unique brand of Manhattan dry heat that leaves you headachy and shriveled-up like dried fruit. But suddenly the days are longer, the snow has melted, and out of nowhere, you sense a whiff of possibility in the air.

The sun is out, warm on your face, and it makes you crazy. You always feel this energy shift, when winter turns to spring and it seems like the entire universe is orbiting around the city. Just thinking about it makes your heart beat faster. The sludge in your blood turns to espresso, and you come out of hibernation.

There's a party, a friend of a friend. You're lazy, and you hate parties. But this one is three blocks away, and you feel that stirring, so you go. You smoke, you drink. People you barely know hug you like you're best friends. You're in Manhattan, so half a dozen strangers ask what you do. At this particular moment, your work is something people find interesting and a little bit hip. You're lucky, because this is a city that explodes with envy. People want to hear about success, touch it; or talk about failure, the definition of which, in New York, is anything other than great success. But it's been an hour and you've had enough chitchat. It wasn't worth the three blocks, the shower, the shave, the deciding-what-to-wear. What are you doing at another party? You don't like drinking, or talking to people, or talking about yourself. You were more at peace in your winter tomb.

You go into the bathroom and lock the door. You look in the mirror and realize you're slightly drunk. And you wonder if you'll wind up going home with someone. After all, you're still in your twenties, reasonably good-looking, with a beer in your hand; it just seems to happen. You run the faucet, splash some water on your face, then lower your mouth to the spout and drink. You always do this when you're out, because you hate hangovers almost as much as you hate parties. And you stand there, wondering how long you can just stay inside. You wonder how many hours you've spent in strangers' bathrooms, head against the door, feeling alone and separate.

The radiator hisses. A knock on the door.

You look around the bathroom and feel your cheeks flush, staring at some stranger's scented candle, their carefully curated reading material displayed like art at a museum, their mismatched hand towels (charming or self-conscious depending on your mood), and the view from their tiny bathroom window of a Spanish restaurant on Jane Street. You hear the chatter and laughter of New Yorkers seeping through the door, all of them strangely wanting to be among each other after a depleting week of doing who-the-fuck-knows-what. What are they even talking about? Silverware and plates clanking at a dinner party, that's what they all sound like, Portishead and Tricky playing in the background. Then you open the door, and there he is.

When I first saw Daniel, I actually gasped.

Now I walk through parks and all I see are young people; bodies twisted into each other like pipe cleaners, couples engaged in conversation or lying next to each other with eyes closed, connected by the spaghetti strands of headphones. It doesn't matter what they're listening to, it's the white wires linking them that get me. The way they're connected. And though I'm coupled now too, it still feels the same when I'm in the park. I'm alone, disconnected, feeling uncertain. Because I will always be looking for that stranger. I will always be looking for love.

And now, I stand at the edge of the Tiergarten. Where the Wall once stood. Right here in front of the gate.

I think about Jeremy and our walk in the park. I've become scared that I'm not seeing the real Berlin. "You and the tourists," that's what Kaspar said. I wonder if such a thing as the "real" Berlin even exists. Because how do you experience a city, or a person, or anything, fully and definitively? You're always the variable, the wild card, just a piece of the set and setting. And my mind right now, I don't know if it's the drugs, this city, the people I've met, or my own reaching into the past.

I'm enveloped by *Ostalgie* which is invisible but everywhere and totally contagious. I'm stuck inside my head, which feels like it might implode.

In New York, tourists pour through Times Square, invading my city, blocking traffic so much that there are now barriers herding them like sheep. They take pictures of places New Yorkers never go, things we don't want to see. That's not New York, I want to say. But maybe I'm wrong. It *is* the city on postcards, in pictures, in movies. Who am I to say it's not real?

But if there is no definitive version of anything, I wonder which version of Berlin I'm experiencing, and how my heavy brain is impacting my stay. Before last night it was filtering the city like a cup of coffee, too dark, too strong. And now, on a crisp Berlin morning, so clear and blue that I can only assume it is random and as special as a holiday, the faint white wisp of a moon lingers in the sky, hovering next to the TV Tower. I wonder if this same moon is visible in New York, and where it lives back home, if it hangs above Broadway or over the Hudson. But then I realize it's not even dawn in Manhattan. Daniel and Harry are, I hope, tucked away, oblivious to me and the sky a few time zones away. The moon, perhaps, floats above the river, while my boyfriend and my dog sleep.

I remember riding down in the elevator after I picked up Daniel's cell phone, thinking: I need to find something new. Find another place with a new history and throw myself into it so I can disappear. But it wasn't a real thought, it was a fantasy. And I didn't really know this until I was in Berlin, where I would find the doppelgänger's building with the trees and the candles and the wayward staircase, the lonely American boy, the cat named Blitz, a man named Kaspar, the painted streets, the exploding city.

The phone rings as I'm showering. I grab a towel and run, dripping wet, to answer it, wondering if it's Magda. The television is muted, and the opening credits for the afternoon rerun of *Ost und West* have just come on: the TV Tower, a slab of the Wall, cafés and coffee cups and a succession of graffiti-stained buildings, a sun-dappled street.

"*Hallo,*" I say.

"Who's this?" a woman's voice asks.

"It's Sam Singer. Who's this?"

"This is your mother, Samuel. What is this, *Ha-llo*?"

"Sorry. I guess I'm talking like a Berliner."

"Don't do that. And by the way, that receptionist is rude."

"Man or woman?"

"A snippy man."

"Oh, that's Frankie. He's harmless."

"Well I don't appreciate his tone."

I stare at the TV. I watch Sabine in the credits, tossing her hair back, beaming. The show's title *Ost und West* is spray-painted on the side of a building. "Is everything okay?" I ask. "Where's Dad?"

"He's out with Herman. Your father is such a lady now that he's retired, going to the opera and museums and these silly lectures and lunches. I can't imagine what on earth they talk about."

"They probably talk about museums and opera and being retired."

"I'd rather die. So how was the opening?"

"It's not until the weekend."

"Then what about the galleries?"

"They've been good. I've only been to four or five so far."

"That's nothing, Samuel. Isn't that the whole reason you're there?"

"I'm here to meet with Klaus Beckmann. Which I've done, by the way. I've been here for less than a week."

"Well, it feels like forever." My mother tells a story about a cat on a leash that scratched her on the elevator as I watch Sabine on TV. Her character visits a doctor, who examines her pregnant belly. Together, they look at the baby's beating heart on the sonogram. The doctor smiles, but she turns away and begins to cry. "So tell me about Berlin," my mother says. "Is there a Starbucks?"

"Down the street from the hotel. And I passed another one by the Brandenburg Gate."

"Oh good."

"Good?"

"It's cold in New York but I still need my iced latte. Your father switches to hot drinks in October, but not me. Too obvious."

"Mom, why are we talking about Starbucks?"

"I don't know, Samuel. You clearly don't want to talk about work. And so what if Starbucks makes me happy?"

"That makes me sad."

"What makes me happy makes you sad? What a cruel thing to say."

"Well, Mom, sorry, but there's other stuff going on in Berlin."

"I bet."

"And in the world. Besides lattes."

"I read the newspaper, Samuel. I stay informed."

"Mom, I have a meeting." And a TV show to watch. In a flashback of the Wall falling, Sabine's character walks through the rubble. She is greeted by friends and relatives but looks beyond them for something else. Someone is missing.

"You never talk to me anymore," my mother says. "If your brother was there he'd call me every day. Probably twice a day. But then, he wouldn't be in Germany."

"I'm going to get off the phone now."

"How's Daniel?"

"He's . . . fine. We haven't spoken in a few days."

"What? Why? What's wrong?"

"Nothing's wrong. I'm busy, he's busy."

"We're all *busy*. You must miss him. When your father traveled, I'd stare into my Grape-Nuts and sink into the most horrible depression. I couldn't wait to have him back home. I love your Daniel. You know that, don't you?"

"Yes, I do."

"You should marry that man."

"As if that's even possible."

"I remember that first dinner when he walked into my kitchen and did all the dishes. All of them."

"Even the egg slicer," I add, because she tells this story so often.

"And I thought, who is this beautiful blond man in my *Sweeney Todd* apron, so charming, so adept at housekeeping? I loved him instantly. Don't let him go."

"Mom, you're so dramatic."

"I hear something in your voice. I've been sensing something."

I push my head into the pillow. Maternal premonitions, however accurate, are exhausting. "I don't like you retired, Mom. You have too much time to think."

"Daniel takes care of you, you know."

"Look, this is not a productive conversation. And it's probably costing a fortune."

"I'm calling you through the computer, Samuel. The guys downstairs showed me how when they took out the air conditioners. I can call Egypt if I want. For free."

I can't get online to check my email, but my sixty-five-year-old mother has figured out how to make illegal phone calls on her seventy-pound Dell.

I watch the TV. Sabine's character, Anna, walks into her office in a wrath, pregnant and sexy in a black business suit. She sucks in her stomach, and the baby bump disappears. She throws papers off drafting tables as she stomps toward her office. She swings open the door, and there they are—her husband kissing another coworker. A man. She twists her lips into a knot before the scene fades to a commercial.

"So what about Berlin?" my mother asks. "I bet it's grim."

"Actually, it's beautiful."

"Berlin is *not* beautiful."

I could tell her about the cobblestone streets of Prenzlauer Berg, the lovers feeding each other cake, the ephemeral blanket of snow. But she wouldn't understand. "Well, Mom, I'm the one who's here. And it's kind of amazing."

"It's *Germany*."

"So what?"

"Samuel, you romanticize everything. It's always been your Achilles' heel."

"Whatever that means."

"It means you have the artist's temperament. So, how are those Germans?"

"They can be a little cool at first."

"I bet."

"It takes a while. But then they crack. I think a lot of it is the Bush thing."

"Samuel, you know I hate our president so much I could slit his throat with my own fingernails. But that doesn't give any German the right to judge us. Bush is not our fault."

"That's not what's happening, Mom."

"Look, I understand you're there for work, but that doesn't mean you can have a good time. We're Jewish, Samuel."

"This is ridiculous. You raised us with a menorah one year and a Christmas tree the next."

"Sometimes we had both."

"Exactly. You served pork chops at Passover and now you're pulling this?"

"I'm not pulling anything. You're in Germany. *Germany*! And you were bar mitzvah'd."

"I was bar mitzvah'd to alleviate your guilt. We had a party. They played Duran Duran. I got money and bought a VCR. It didn't mean anything to anyone."

"Well, maybe I feel badly about that."

"Maybe you should. And I think you and Dad should come here sometime. My experience of Berlin is that it's very thoughtful about its past. There are reminders everywhere."

"I'm sure."

"They're building a Holocaust memorial by the Brandenburg Gate."

"What took them so long?"

"Whatever, Mom. Berlin has this energy—it reminds me of New York, back when I was a kid."

"No, it doesn't."

"Remember what it was like, when everything was gritty but sort of glamorous? It was dangerous, but there were sparks in the air."

"There you go again. You were always stuck in your head, painting your pictures. Your brother, he was pragmatic. He was playing with trucks."

"Remember what you always say about New York. You say, 'I miss the dirt.'"

"Well, I do miss the dirt sometimes. Giuliani, that creep, turned us into a shopping mall."

"Exactly. The dirt is here, Mom. And it's incredible."

"Samuel, it was different in New York, it's true. But remember, you couldn't walk through the park *during the day.* Every night on TV they'd say: *It's ten o'clock, do you know where your children are?* There was Bernie Goetz, and Hedda Nusbaum and that creep husband of hers, and the city was broke, literally broke. You couldn't even take your kids to *Annie* without some prostitute propositioning your husband, or your nine-year-old son for that matter. Okay, so the city's cleaner, and we've gotten older. That's what happens. You're romanticizing New York, Samuel. And you're definitely romanticizing Berlin."

"Well you know what, Mom? I love Berlin. Sorry."

"You don't *love* it."

"Yeah, I do. Talking to you has made me realize how much I like this city. So once again, your nagging has resulted in the opposite of your desired outcome."

"Fine. Go have fun in your city of death."

"You're being crazy."

"Don't call me crazy. Listen, Samuel, don't forget what's happened there, that's all I'm saying. It's okay to move forward, but you can't just erase the past. And look, I'm not pretending to be some super Jew, and I'm not saying that your father and I did everything right. We clearly didn't. But it's still our blood, Samuel, it's our history. You're of a different generation, but I feel the ghosts. I was closer to them than you."

"Okay."

"When I told Sylvia you were going to Berlin, the first thing she said was that her grandfather was shot to death by a lake just outside of the city."

"You didn't tell me that."

"I'm telling you now. So when you cross the street, it's important you remember where you are. Remember the past."

"Okay. I get it."

"Good. And go to Sachsenhausen, Samuel."

"How do you know I didn't go?"

"Because if you'd gone, we'd be having a different conversation. I'm going to check in with your Daniel. He probably misses you terribly."

"You do what you need to." I look at my watch. "Look, it's almost four, and I need to meet someone for coffee."

"Sammy. Be good."

"I'm meeting an artist," I tell her. Which is true of Kaspar, but still.

"And stop being so nostalgic. It's not healthy."

"Who just told me to always remember the past?"

"The past is fact, Samuel. Nostalgia is just a fuzzy dream in your head. Nostalgia is memory with a really good director."

Painted City

I think about shaving but don't. If I shave, it'll seem more like a date. So I'll leave some stubble. It'll look more casual. Maybe even a little more desirable? I don't know what the fuck I'm doing. I slip on my jeans and, after some deliberation, the black cashmere sweater Daniel bought me last year. I put on my coat and the hat with the snowflakes, the one he likes, and head downstairs.

Frankie is at the front desk. He half smiles at me. I'd expected to see Magda, assumed she'd be working since she told me as much last night. There's a bowl of apples on the counter, some new flourish. Today, Frankie's hair is slicked back. With his smooth skin and crazy cheekbones, he looks positively statuesque, albeit in a black shirt made of rubber. "No," he says. "No one has called for you, okay?"

"That's not what I was going to ask," I tell him. Frankie folds his arms, waiting. "When do you expect Magda?"

"I am working through evening." Frankie yawns, flipping through a copy of *Zitty*. "Magda is on holiday."

"Holiday?" This doesn't make sense. I want to explain that I saw her just last night, that I was drinking wine in her apartment. Then again, after we parted ways at Austria, my own evening took a few hundred unexpected turns, so who knows what happened to Magda. "But Magda told me she'd be here today. When will she be back?"

Frankie shoots me a look. I peer over the counter and see a pile of tabloids from Germany, America, and England: *Bunte*, *Bild*, *Us*,

OK, Hello! I've interrupted his quiet time, forcing him to do something besides staring at pictures of Posh Spice. "I do not know when Magda returns."

"Is she in Berlin, or did she go away?"

Frankie gathers the magazines on their sides and taps them up and down as if he's straightening important business files. "Excuse me, Herr Singer, do I look like Mommy? I am not *der Babysitter*. I do not know where she is."

"Fine." I'm getting tired of this energy. And after the call with my mother, I'm over it. I grab an apple from the bowl and walk away.

Frankie calls after me. "But I will tell her that you are curious to know where she is."

"Great." I button my coat and head for the door. "Thanks."

As I begin to leave, Frankie says, "Herr Singer, let me ask one question." I turn around, unsure what will come next. "I want to go to New York. More than anywhere in zee world. Tell me where you are living? In the city center, or in Queens?"

"I live in Manhattan."

"Ah, in the heart of it all! The Big Apple!"

"Yep." I glance at the clock on the wall. I have fifteen minutes before *Kaffeeklatsch*, and I'm only five blocks away. I'll just be a wandering wreck if I don't occupy myself somehow. I walk back toward the reception desk. "You know, Frankie, it's quite expensive in New York."

"I read about it," Frankie says. "The clubs, the celebrities. Do you know many celebrities in New York?"

"Not intimately, but I've met a few."

"Who? Tell me! Leo? Whitney? Meryl? J-Lo?"

"What a list," I say. "No, none of them. But I did meet someone here in Berlin, an actress."

"In Berlin?" Frankie is skeptical and throws his nose into the air.

"I think she's maybe a little famous here. She's on television, but of course I'd never heard of her."

"Who?" He taps his fingers impatiently on the desk. "Tell me."

"Sabine Beckmann," I say. "She's on—"

"*Nein, nein, nein!*" He pounds his fist on the desk, startling me. A copy of *Hello!* goes flying in the air, an apple falls out of the bowl. "You meet Anna Vogel from *Ost und West*?"

"The architect?"

"Yes! *Genau*! Zee architect!"

"Yup. We had lunch."

"Lunch? No! Herr Singer, this is incredible! Anna and Sebastian, they are so beautiful. But now Sebastian, he is living in the mountains with the monks and she will have the baby alone."

"Does Sebastian have a shaved head?"

"*Ja*! And a beard. So sexy. But you know, I do not think this is his baby. Thomas is the father. I know it." He puts his hand over his mouth and starts to whisper. "But Thomas, he is her cousin. Of course, Anna did not know this when they are making sex together because, you know, Thomas, he has a new face."

"A new face?"

"Yes of course. Since the ski accident of last year." Frankie sighs, catches his breath. "But Anna, she has still that disgusting husband. *Ein Schwein*!"

"She has three men? That's a lot."

"*Ja*, I know it." He raises an eyebrow. "So tell me everything."

"There's not much to tell. Sabine is very nice. Beautiful, of course. I met her husband as well . . ."

"Husband? No!" His eyes flash. "How is he named?"

"Klaus," I say.

"Ah, Klaus!" He swoons. "They must be the most beautiful, *ja*? What skin!" Frankie twirls in his seat. He motions toward the sofa so that I will sit down and tell him more. He clasps his hands and lowers his chin into his palms, his eyes wide as the ocean. I sit on the couch and he throws me another apple. For the moment, at least, he is mine.

"Actually," I say, "I'll be right back." I run upstairs to my room and grab the white bag by the door. When I return to reception, I place the bag, overflowing with dirty clothes, on the counter. "I'll tell you everything," I tell Frankie, "when I pick up my laundry in the morning."

Berlin is a painted city. There is graffiti on virtually every street, blanketing vestibules, crawling up poles and streetlamps, covering archways, alleys and traffic signs. The art on the street folds itself into the architecture of the city until it becomes ubiquitous and invisible at the same time. The facade of the apartment house next to the hotel is painted with vines and flowers as real ivy twists up the building, plants dangle from its windows, and trees shoot up from the street.

And here are those English phrases again, which render the graffiti more pointed and mysterious; as if their meaning is italicized, infused with hidden layers. Outside the window of my hotel room, across the way, someone has painted, in big black letters on the face of a satellite dish, *Don't Watch Stupid TV*. On the side of Kunsthaus Tacheles, stenciled in ten-foot type: *How Long Is Now*. And on a dirty wall near an U-Bahn station, untamed strokes of silver have christened it *The Wall of Piss*. And now, walking to meet Kaspar, I pass the window of a gallery with a photograph of a sleeping rhinoceros hanging on a white wall. Stenciled onto the window of the gallery, in white letters: *Stay Now. You Are So Beautiful!*

Art is everywhere, and it speaks to me in a way that has eluded me for years. Klaus was right: it's here, all around you, stopping you in your tracks. I've learned to approach art expecting to dislike it—to enumerate its flaws, illuminate its derivativeness, and quantify its merits through dollar signs and of-the-moment gimmickry. Daniel may call me a salesman, but it's more than that: I'm a professional snob, a curator, a stylist, and a magician. I forecast trends in the art world the way the farmer's almanac predicts a season of snow. But in Berlin art feels necessary and urgent. I don't know if it's just the fact that I'm experiencing everything purely and on my own, but I feel cynicism falling away and a sense of purpose returning. I feel myself waking up.

Kaspar waits on the corner, leaning against his bike. He wears sneakers, yellow and purple, with black laces. He is sockless, his jeans rolled up just above his ankles. Even Kaspar is a canvas—jeans splattered with paint, blue jacket frayed at the bottom, yellow threads trailing behind him like sparks. His fingernails are painted, too, chipped and black. A bike chain dangles from his neck. It's sunny, and the air just hangs there, prickling my skin like electricity.

I look at his long neck, his green eyes visible even from across the street, the dark eyebrows and eyelashes that seem painted on. His cheekbones cast moon-sliver shadows over his jaw as if in charcoal; his elaborate nose so unwieldy that it only adds to his beauty. Like so many things in Berlin, he leaves me breathless. Looking at him now—holding his bike upright with one hand as I walk toward him—I feel like I need to sit down or take a nap right there on the sidewalk. He is even more than I remember him, so fragile, like glass, and everything comes into focus as I approach him. He waits for me, his foot hooked under the spoke of the wheel. I watch as he removes the chain from his neck and drops it into his bag. And then he opens his mouth, his red lips smiling, revealing that small gap between his teeth. "*Hallo*," he says.

"Hi," I say.

Kaspar leans in, perhaps to kiss my cheek, but instead, nervously, stupidly, I extend my hand to him. "Oh," he says, taking my hand, "it is good to see you." He stares at me, appraising my mood. "So, I think we get a coffee at the Kunst-Werke. Then maybe we take a walk."

"What about the bike?"

"It will come with us," he says. "I take *mein Fahrrad* everywhere."

We walk with Kaspar's bicycle alongside him. It's simple and red, the kind you don't see anymore. He leads it down the street like a dog, stroking the back of the seat.

I've walked so much that my feet hurt. After I spoke to my mother, I soaked them in the tub while watching Sabine on TV. At the end of the show, her character collapsed onto the floor of a colleague's office while rummaging through his files. The colleague, a beautiful man in a suit, hid in a closet. When she fell to the floor, Sabine clutched her stomach in pain and cried out: "*Mein Baby!*" The man watched as she writhed in pain. Alone in the room, they both had their secrets. I can relate. There are many things I should be doing today. Going for coffee with Kaspar is not one of them. I know this, and my heart begins to pound. "You walk fast," Kaspar says. "I must jump on my bike to keep up with you."

We head toward the Kunst-Werke, a cluster of galleries and artist studios in an abandoned margarine factory. The KW is one of the hubs of the art scene in Mitte, at the top of my barely dented to-do list. How lame that it took *Kaffeeklatsch* to get me here. At least I can use it to justify my afternoon with Kaspar.

Two red KW flags hang above the entrance, a dozen bikes parked under its arches. Kaspar glides his bike into the rack and loops the chain around its neck. A cobblestone path leads to the courtyard, which is filled with sound installations. Gurgles of audio pour out of metal boxes placed throughout the yard, attached to benches, perched on walls, hanging from trees. Voices echo from nowhere and everywhere as if at an invisible cocktail party.

Café Bravo is a glass-and-steel cube built into the corner of the courtyard. It's filled with Berliners sitting at yellow tables and blue banquettes, artists and student-types drinking beer and coffee. It's light outside, but each table is adorned with candles.

Kaspar leads us to a table and we sit next to each other along the banquette, a wall of glass behind us. Couples of every combination sit like this in the café: next to each other, not across. So they can be close, so they can touch (which they all seem to do), so they can watch everything and everyone around them while they eat cake. Someone's sheep dog sits patiently at the door. On the stereo, a woman sings: *Love comes in and fills up everywhere.*

Our waiter comes over. Kaspar kisses him on both cheeks. They speak quickly in German. At first I think Kaspar is ordering food, but then he looks at me and smiles. He's a different person, talking to his friend—gesturing with his hands, laughing. I'm jealous of their ease, the way they communicate at normal speed; the slow-motion sentences that make up my conversations with Berliners render me an adult and a first grader at the same time. If Kaspar and I could say what we wanted rather than what we merely can, I wonder what would actually come out of our mouths.

Kaspar orders for us: beer, cake, and coffee. "The perfect meal," he tells me.

At the bar, a beautiful curly-haired man kisses his lover, then takes a drag from his cigarette. I turn to Kaspar, distracted by the way his stubble has grown darker since I saw him last. I imagine what it might be like to kiss him like the two men at the bar. A long, lazy afternoon kiss. Then our waiter returns with our meal. "I like how they give you a cookie with your coffee," I say.

"They are giving you a cookie with your coffee in most any place in Europe."

"It feels different here."

"I think you are falling in love a little bit."

Kaspar and I share a slice of almond cake with layers of cherries and white frosting. We eat in contented silence, looking at each other every so often. He stretches his arm behind me, along the banquette. People must assume that we, too, are lovers. I look up, through the glass ceiling, to a sky that is blue except for one gray cloud. And suddenly the cloud bursts open with rain. Streams of water pour down the glass walls.

The woman next to me reaches over and says hello to Kaspar. One side of her head is shaved; on the other, pink braids sprout like the wiry hair of a plastic doll. Bracelets jangle on her wrists like Christmas bells, a blue flower tattooed on her neck. She's so pale that you can see the veins under her cheeks. She is translucent, like a seashell, a ghost in a leather jacket. I almost slip into a daydream watching her fingers slide a cigarette out of the pack in front of her, the rain pouring outside. "*Hallo*," she says to me, a cigarette dangling from her mouth. She turns to Kaspar. "*Hast du Feuer?*"

"*Nee*," he tells her. "Sorry."

"*Kein Problem.*" The pink-haired woman leans into the candle on our table and lights up. She sits back, and an eruption of smoke seeps out of her nostrils. I breathe it in, the salty gray tobacco smell.

"I sort of want a cigarette." I sigh.

Kaspar shakes his head. "No. It is not good."

"So I'm with the one person in Berlin who doesn't smoke?"

"This is correct."

"I don't smoke, by the way."

"*Gut.*"

"I used to, though. It's hard not to smoke in this city."

"Really, it is not so difficult."

I look at his arm stretched out behind me, the vein running down his bicep, the tattoo on his forearm, the black band around his wrist.

He catches me staring, and smiles. And so I blurt out a question, just to fill the space. "How old are you?"

"What a question! If you must know, I am twenty-seven."

"Really? I thought you were older."

"Aye!"

"No, it's just, you're very tall."

"Yes," he laughs. "The tall people, we are all very old."

"And you're, I don't know, self-possessed."

"What does it mean, self-possessed? Is it like a scary movie?"

"Not at all." I consider this for a moment. "It means, you seem comfortable in your own skin." The rain has stopped, and I look at him through the light streaming from the window; his long legs crossed to the side of our table, his arms stretched across the banquette, his golden-green eyes. He looks like a leopard in the Serengeti, licking its paws in the sun. "It's just . . . I don't know." We stare at each other, both waiting for me to wiggle out of this. "You're a man."

He looks away and laughs softly.

"Which is nice."

"I agree. And you, how many years is Sam?" His Adam's apple drops down when he says my name, like an anchor.

"How old do you think I am?"

"No." Kaspar leans back. "I skip it. A gentleman never plays this game."

I take the last bite of cake. "I'm thirty-seven."

"*Nein!*" He gasps, covers his mouth. "It cannot be."

"Oh, it can be. You're just pretending to be surprised, right?"

"I was thinking you are thirty at most."

"Me? Are you serious?"

"Yes, I am serious. This is what I have told my friends. He is thirty, at most."

I take a sip of beer. Kaspar's glass is empty. "Maybe that's why I came all the way to Berlin," I tell him. "To hear that."

"I think there is more for you in Berlin." He looks away. Before I fumble for a follow-up, he goes to the bar to get more beer. I stare at him, his long twisty legs. His perfect little butt. Oh, what I could do with that. I don't know what I expected from our coffee date, but now it feels dangerous. And I wouldn't presume a man such as Kaspar would be interested in me. Then I remember Magda's explanation of *Kaffeeklatsch*: *You will get coffee. You will talk. But really, who knows?*

Kaspar returns with beer and another piece of cake, a slice of pure white, the color of snow. We clink glasses. He's next to me now, against me, closer. With his fork he cuts the cake into four perfect sections. One more beer, I think to myself, and then I'll go back to the hotel. A man, wet from the rain, enters the café with an umbrella. A blue bird flies in behind him. No one stirs. The bird flies around before settling down on the edge of a nearby table, eating crumbs from an abandoned plate.

I lift a forkful of cake to my lips. "How are you so thin, eating all this cake?"

Kaspar shrugs his shoulders and pats his flat belly. "I am young," he says, the sort of thing only a young person would say.

"So does thirty-seven seem old to you?"

"*Ja*, of course," he laughs. "Old man."

"Great," I say, though it's true that an irritatingly dramatic measurement of time, a decade, separates us.

"I like it." He turns to me. "You are older brother."

I look at him, slightly disturbed, a little turned on. "And do you have an older brother?"

"I do now." He stares at me. I take a large sip of beer. "So," asks Kaspar, "when is it, your birthday?"

"July," I say.

"Ah. *Ein Kreb* . . ."

"If that's a crab, yes. Cancer."

"I am often with the crabs. Very nice, many hugs at home, but emotional and often depressed. The last man, he baked bread in the morning and was always crying. It was sad."

The last man. What does that make me? I'm a terrible person. I've already heard about a bread-making ex, but I haven't even mentioned Daniel. For several minutes we barely speak. This usually makes me nervous, causes my leg to shake, to get up and escape. But here— with Kaspar and a solid beer buzz, the hum of German conversation enveloping us, good music percolating on the stereo—the silence feels comfortable. I'm still a bit hung over from my night with Jeremy, and I've forgotten how the exhaustion of an epic night out can make you feel strangely relaxed the next day. The waiter returns with yet another round of beer. "Are you trying to get me drunk?"

"*Ja*. Drunk and fat."

"I'm on my way."

"No." He reaches his arm in back of me. "You are good."

"So, you've talked about me to your friends?"

"I have told you this?"

"Yes. You did."

"Well, then, perhaps." My heart is fluttery; the beer is making my skin tingle. Kaspar locks eyes with me, trying, I think, to get a read on me, his leg snug against me, his hand on his knee, right next to mine.

Two women sit down next to us. They throw their purses onto the table and thrust their bags against me; I have no choice but to scoot even closer to Kaspar. The women sigh at the exact same time. "You know Sarah," one says. "She's such an emotional person."

"Oh, I know. She's so the template of the person I don't want to become."

It feels jarring to hear Americans speak here, like I've been pushed off the bed in the middle of a dream. Kaspar turns to me, places his hand on my shoulder. "Come, I will show you my flat. You can meet my bird."

Six o'clock and I hear church bells in the distance. Kaspar brings his bike on the tram. The car is stuffy and crowded. A few students with backpacks drink beer. A group of Italians fan themselves dramatically with their *Berlino!* travel guides. A tiny man is dressed head-to-toe in leather. He carries a briefcase, also leather, apparently on his way home from the office. An old lady lays her cane across her lap. I sit down beside her. A hound pants next to its owner, its tail wagging lazily in our faces. Two lanky girls in T-shirts and skinny jeans sit opposite me, staring at their mobiles.

Kaspar and his bike are parked in front of me. He reaches down and scratches the hound's wrinkled neck, the fatty folds stretching across it like an accordion. I like seeing this bond between Kaspar and the dog. Then I notice a spider dangling from the ceiling. It lowers itself over the old woman's hat. She is oblivious, but several of us marvel at the insect hanging just an inch above her.

We exit the tram. It's turning dark and we walk in silence. I hear the wheels of Kaspar's bike clicking and turning, children playing in a nearby park, and the hum of drilling so deep and low it sounds like whales at sea. The streetlamps have switched on, and bicycles fly past us with illuminated beams.

I don't know what I'm doing, following this beautiful man home, apparently to meet his bird. At least this will help my mission of seeing the apartments of three locals. *I did some traveling before I met you*, Daniel said to me. I think of how he said this, and what he meant. But I feel strangely at peace. Maybe it's the beer and the arrival of another Berlin evening, which at the end of each day seems to fall down from the sky. Perhaps it's this city, its expansiveness and quiet, which I've begun to notice, actually soothes me.

Kaspar leads us down Schönhauser Allee, and once again I find myself walking alongside cemetery gates. This cemetery is enormous, stretching for blocks and shielded from the street by giant gray walls. Kaspar tells me that it's an old Jewish cemetery, the largest in Berlin, and that many artists and writers are buried there.

I ask if we can go inside. Kaspar leans his bike against the gate. I follow him through an entrance. The graveyard is overgrown with ivy and gnarled trees. It's far more foreboding than the cemetery Magda and I passed on the way to Austria. Gravestones are doubled over and cracked, markers covered with dead leaves, stone memorials cave in on each other. Along the exterior walls are larger plots. Some are enormous and ornate, others far smaller, but what unites them is that they're all in some form of disarray.

I walk over to a plaque, which Kaspar translates. The sign honors the men who attempted to evade Hitler by hiding among these tombstones. "They were found by the Nazis," Kaspar tells me, "and hung on trees." Standing in the middle of it all, submerged in dark and silence, you feel the layers of death. You feel the ghosts. For the first time, I feel the undeniable darkness of the city, its history choking me. As if my mother conjured this from across the ocean.

It's a relief to step onto the street again. We walk down Kollwitz-strasse, where cemetery walls are surrounded by modern apartment houses. I look up at an illuminated balcony; a dog lies on its side and stretches its paw, watching us go by. On the street, a boy runs into his father's arms. Death, decay, history, and construction; everyday life and childhood. Everything rubbing up against each other in this tight space.

Our unexpected detour has put me in an uncertain mood. I look at Kaspar, who stares at the sky. Perhaps he's feeling something similar, wondering why we spent twenty minutes in a graveyard on our way home to meet his bird; why I slowed down the momentum of what-ever this is. I think of my own Jewishness, and the fact that it didn't come up as we walked through the cemetery. That I didn't bring it up. Did I obscure my identity?

We turn onto a street filled with thrift stores, cybercafes, and record shops. Students eat curry from the Imbiss. Boys in hoodies smoke cigarettes and hug their skateboards; two baby-faced men in black suits each carry a bottle of champagne. We pass a beer garden and a *Fotoautomat* on an empty lot. At Kaspar's suggestion, we take a round of pictures. I sit with him in the booth, our butts squeezed next to each other on a stool no bigger than a dinner plate. He's relaxed, making faces, but I'm self-conscious, just sitting there. For the third photo, he puts his hand under my arm and tickles me. I jump up, startled. And then, before the final photo, Kaspar puts his arm around me and pulls me close. And I think to myself, *oh*. Daniel flashes into my mind. A ring on my finger would come in handy at moments like these.

When the strip of photos falls into the slot, I see that the tickling worked: Kaspar got a toothy smile out of me, the kind I usually avoid. And though my eyes are closed in the final shot, Kaspar's arm is around me, and we look connected. He wants me to have the photos, he says, so I take the strip and put it in my bag. We walk just half a block. "Here it is, *mein Zuhause*," he announces. I stare up, frozen. The address of his apartment building on Kastanienallee is lit up and spelled out across the facade, strewn this way and that like magnetic letters across a refrigerator door. This has been our destination since leaving Café Bravo, so I don't know why my arrival at Kaspar's building feels like a surprise.

Walking through the red doors of its entrance, I feel nervous and slightly drunk. We pass through an archway covered with graffiti and lit from the ground by strips of neon. Ivy crawls up the wall behind rows of scooters and bikes. In the courtyard, an alfresco living room has been assembled from tossed-away furniture: wooden stools, a plastic table, an old leather club chair. To the side, under an awning wrapped in Christmas lights, sits a tattered sofa as big as a boat, a string of lanterns hung above it. Two young men sit on opposite corners of the sofa, smoking cigarettes, blowing rings into the air. Both wear puffy jackets with a furry trim. A portable heater sits in front of them, burning orange like a fireplace. "Hey, Kaspar," says one of the men.

"*Hallo*, Jan." Kaspar smiles.

"*Das ist der neue Mann?*" asks the other, examining his nails.

Kaspar leans his bike against the sofa. "See you later," he tells them. One of the boys whistles as Kaspar puts his hand on my back and leads me away.

"What did he just say?" I ask.

"Jan and Karl, they sit in the yard all day," Kaspar tells me. "Like two old *Frauen* watching everyone come and go."

"They don't have jobs?"

"This is Berlin. Their job is to open their mail and look for checks from the state." He leads me toward the staircase, then steers me gently with the back of his palm. Though I'm buried beneath a sweater and coat, electricity shoots through me.

We make our way up the stairs. Music pours through doorways, rusty radiators hiss like snakes. "Almost," he says, as we climb one final flight. Like Magda's apartment, Kaspar's flat is on the top floor, the fifth. And as he fumbles for his keys and pushes in the door with his shoulder, my heart feels like it's going to explode.

Don't Sweep Your Wife Away

Kaspar switches on a light. An old chandelier illuminates a tiny apartment. It would be a stretch to call it a studio; it's just a square room, albeit with super high ceilings and ornate but cracked moldings. Two walls are covered in different wallpaper, each with its own distinct pattern. A row of shelves lines another wall, crammed with books, photos, and art supplies. A single bed is tucked in the opposite corner. Suspended on the wall above the bed is a giant red plastic K. I remember when Magda, translating the napkin, tilted her head and asked: "Who is K?"

Kaspar hangs our jackets by the front door and removes his sneakers. I take off my shoes and place them next to his. "My flat, it is not large," he says. "But it does not cost much. And I like the view." He walks to the other side of the room and opens the curtains, revealing a wall of windows. Two slender glass doors open to a balcony overlooking the street. Kaspar turns on a string of red lights that twist carelessly along the perimeter of the terrace. He opens the doors and we lean outside. You can see Mitte and the TV Tower blinking in the distance. It's such an incredible feature that the apartment's smallness is totally irrelevant.

Kaspar closes the door. Next to the window stands a metal birdcage, which holds a small bird. He places his finger inside. The bird hops onto it, and he glides it carefully out of the cage. It's unlike any bird I've ever seen: pure black and white with golden eyes. Kaspar whispers,

"*Hallo, mein Baby*," and rubs the bird against his cheek. "This is Varhole," he says, bringing him close to my face. "Var-hole, meet Sam."

"Hi, Varhole," I say. "Is that a German name?"

"It is American. Well, no, I am thinking it is first in Polish, *Varhole-a*, but he make it shorter. You know, the artist, the can of soup, Marilyn Monroe."

"Oh, Warhol," I say.

"*Ja*." Kaspar laughs. "*War-hall*," he repeats, exaggerating my American accent. "I name him this because he is looking like a photocopy of something else, black and white. But the copy, I think it is more beautiful than the original." The bird strolls up Kaspar's arm and perches behind his neck. "He maybe is feeling shy. Yesterday it is his birthday. Three years he is living with me." Kaspar walks over to a stove in the corner of the room. A pipe sprouts out of it, leading up to the ceiling. It's like something out of "Hansel and Gretel." He opens a bag of coal and throws a few pieces into the oven. "The building is very old. But I like old things," he says, looking at me.

"Hey. I'm only thirty-seven."

"Yes, older brother." He smiles, revealing that gap between his teeth. I study the row of sneakers and boots lined up neatly by the front door, the slabs of wood piled on the floor, perhaps waiting to be painted, and the stacks of canvases ready to be primed. The familiar smells of turpentine and linseed oil are trapped in the air.

I follow Kaspar to a corner of the room that functions as the kitchen—a plate warmer with a kettle on it, a single cabinet, a French press, a sink, and a blue refrigerator that barely comes up to his knees. He bends down and opens the refrigerator door. I see the edge of his underwear, the ridges of spine tight against his skin like a chain. He must know I'm staring at him, but he seems so unselfconscious, his shirt riding up his back, exposing a few more inches of perfect skin. "If you like it, I make a cup of tea." He stands up and hands a bottle of Warsteiner to me. "But I am thinking this is better."

"More beer?"

"*Ja*, of course." He sets a few items of food on the counter. "Or also I have wine, if you prefer it."

"I shouldn't."

"Why not?"

"I'm tipsy," I explain. But I take a sip anyway.

"What is it, tip-see?"

"A little bit drunk."

"No. It cannot be. We have only, what, one or two Pilsners at Café Bravo."

"Three, actually, and I'm a lightweight." I look around. There's nowhere to sit. The chair at his desk has books stacked on it. I consider perching on the edge of his bed, but that might be too much for right now. So I sit down on the shaggy yellow rug and lean against his dresser. Kaspar lights a few candles in glass jars. He pulls a cassette from the bookshelf and puts it in his stereo. It starts up halfway through the Cure's "Close to Me." "I like this song," I tell him.

"I am making this tape just a few nights ago. It was during the snow, after I meet you at Wronski." He tilts his beer toward me to say cheers. I bring the bottle to my lips and take another sip. I stare at the row of cassettes on his shelf, Kaspar's messy handwriting decorating their spines. It's nice to know that someone still uses cassettes besides Osama bin Laden. And that someone still makes mixtapes. I once spent entire days creating mixes, making sure every song was right—curating a mood, capturing a moment. They were my love letters, my time capsules, the novels I never wrote.

I ask Kaspar, "How do you say 'mixtape' in German?"

"Ah! It is so clever, because in *Deutsch* we say . . . '*Mixtape*.'"

"Of course."

Kaspar taps his fingers along his legs and bobs his head up and down. He looks silly and adorable, dancing around the room with his beer. Warhol flies to the top of his cage and walks along it. "I work at a lee-tle club on some nights. On Dunckerstrasse, in an old church."

"What do you do there?"

"*Barmann*," he says. "I make drinks. They are long nights, but with my two days working at the gallery, I pay for the flat. Maybe you will come? Sometimes we play the Cure."

I make a mental note to myself: *Some nights. A church on Dunckerstrasse.* "So you were right about the snow," I say. "My friend didn't believe me. She said it was impossible."

"Ah, well." He turns to me. "I am right about many things."

I take my beer and walk over to Kaspar's bookshelves. There's a faded picture of a teenage boy on a rocky beach with his unsmiling family. Another picture: a boy in a scout uniform, his black hair parted to the side. "This is you," I say, and he nods. I pick up the photo. "You have freckles."

"I do still," he says, sliding his T-shirt over his shoulder, exposing a few inches of dappled skin. I laugh nervously. Kaspar clearly enjoys being a flirt. It's not that I was ever a prude. But I mostly skipped this part and went straight into the bedroom.

I study Kaspar's eyes in the picture. They are as green as they are right now, gleaming against the candlelight, the sort of eyes that make it impossible to look at anything else. When do I tell him about Daniel? I'll do it when the cassette shuts off. But then the next song comes on: the Verve, "Bitter Sweet Symphony."

I return the picture to the shelf, next to a few trophies for who knows what, and peruse a row of books: *Harry Potter und der Stein der Weisen; Das Wörterbuch der Synonyme; Bauhaus 1919–1923*. I notice a few figurines on the shelf below. I pick one up: a plastic strawberry lady with legs. "This is Korbine," Kaspar says, coming up from behind. He hands me a plate of sliced sausage and cheese and continues. "It was my father's. A cartoon from when he was a boy. She tells us to pick up fruit in the forest, to eat a healthy diet. Well, she told us. After the Wall, she is retired. Maybe now she is living by the sea eating fried fish. I hope this for her."

"So you grew up in the East?"

"Just a few kilometers from where we are now, In Pankow."

I pick up another figurine, a black creature in the shape of an electric plug, with isolators on its head and a crazy grin. "And this is Korbine's friend, Wattfrass. He teaches us to conserve energy. In the DDR they teach about recycling and working hard. Nothing could be wasted. But you see this still in Berlin."

I think of the lights outside of my hotel room, how at night I must press a button to illuminate the hallway for half a minute, and the gumdrop-shaped recycling containers lined up on street corners. I pretend not to notice that Kaspar has walked over to his bed and now lies across it, watching me.

He points to the red K above his bed. "My uncle took this from an old food market after the Wall came down. It was a gift to celebrate. I was just a boy." He looks at the figurines on his shelf. "Now they make copies of everything from when I was a child and sell them in shops."

"*Ostalgie*," I say.

"Yes. I think this is strange. Some of my friends ask me questions: 'Kaspar, what was it like before the Wall?' Like I am grandfather. But I am not a museum, I am just a person, and I am young. But this is very Berlin. The city is changing always, and it has no money. Trendy is all we have, and next year there will be something else." He sits cross-legged on his bed. "You cannot live in the past forever. But I should make money on the internet. People would pay a lot for the strawberry-head."

"Keep her," I tell him. "I sold my *Star Wars* figures and I still regret it." I thought perhaps I'd share them with my children one day, but when Daniel went through our closets last year, he felt like purging, and we sold everything on eBay.

"*Star Wars*. I saw it for the first time when I was at university. It was so big and American. I loved it."

I go to the window and stare at the TV Tower, its candy-cane antenna blinking in the distance. "The only thing that stays the same is the giant disco ball in the sky."

"*Was?*" He walks over to me. "Oh, the Fernsehturm. I hope they tear it down."

"Really? I kind of love it."

"It means something to me that it cannot mean to you. My father hated that tower. He was there when the country was destroyed and rescued and then split up again. When I was a boy he would say, 'Kaspar, they built the Fernsehturm to intimidate us. But it will not work forever, I promise you this.' And he was correct. He thought he knew everything, but my father, he did not know this new Berlin. He is dead just five months before the Wall is coming down."

"I'm sorry."

"Every day I miss him. I think this is strange. You have your life and you see the war, the Wall, your city divided in two. Then you die, and you leave a Berlin that in five months does not exist anymore. But this is what happens. People die, and cities change. I am sure in New York, also."

"New York is always changing. But that's different. The history in Berlin, it's hard to believe."

Kaspar lies on his bed. I'm cross-legged on the floor. "When I was a boy, Prenzlauer Berg was broken streets and dirty buildings bombed in the war. Now they make it beautiful, everything renovated with plaster and paint. I think I am happy about this. But sometimes I do not know."

"But you've stayed."

"Yes. This is my *Kiez*, and this is my home." Kaspar turns to me with sleepy eyes, looking almost bored. The beer, perhaps, or maybe he expected something different from this night, something different from me, not some existential riff on our two cities. Warhol chirps on the windowsill, staring ahead. "Soon it will rain," Kaspar says. "Warhol, he knows always when it will rain. He sits at the window and he waits."

I notice the plastic clock on his desk, in the shape of a cow. It's nearly midnight. Many hours have passed since we met on that corner, and the day feels appropriately epic. I should go home, but right now home is a hotel room, and probably all that's waiting for me is a blinking light on a phone next to a bed, signaling a call from Daniel that will just make me feel more alone. I should feel guilty, perhaps, a hand-some Berliner feeding me sausage and beer in his apartment. But I don't. What I do feel remains undefined: my life floating above me, an entire night happening to someone else. I turn to Kaspar, who has been examining me as my thoughts drift. He looks up at the ceiling, as if he knows what's next. So I say it: "It's getting late." I get up and walk toward the window.

"Not for Berlin." He shrugs. "For Berlin it is early."

I look at my shoes standing by the door. Put your feet inside of those shoes, I say to myself, and leave. Instead, I point to the clock. "So what does the cow do when the alarm goes off? Does it moo?"

"*Ja*, it does moo. And the cow, she is funny. When the alarm comes, she talks. The cow is speaking English, but with a Japanese accent."

"And what does the cow say?"

"So . . ." He stands up and walks toward me, wraps one hand around my waist. "Maybe you hear it in the morning?"

"Oh. Wow."

"Yes. Wow."

"I can't."

"Ah, yes, the man in New York." He pulls his hand back. "*Die Frau.*"

"How did you know?"

"I did not see a ring on your finger, but you have the air of someone who is taken."

"I do?"

"Yes. You do."

I suppose I shouldn't be surprised, given how long Daniel and I have been together. But I thought perhaps I was hiding it better. "That's interesting," I tell him. "And sort of wrong."

"I am wrong?"

"Well . . . it's complicated."

"Of course. Everything is always complicated. Because here you are in my flat."

"That's true."

"At midnight." Kaspar walks over to his desk and picks up the clock. He presses a button on its back, and the alarm goes off. The cow's eyes light up and its tail, just a piece of string and plastic, swings back and forth. The cow moos twice, then speaks: *Wake up. Don't sweep your wife away.*

"That is fantastic," I say.

"A gift," he says, "from the last man."

"The baker?"

"Yes."

"What happened to him?"

"My favorite thing about him was maybe the cow, and I have it now. So perhaps it was a great success." Kaspar returns to the bed, lies on his side, his body twisted toward me. But he seems distant now, slightly annoyed, and who can blame him? He wrote me a note on a napkin. He talked about me to his friends, brought me home to meet his bird. There's nothing like the revelation of a partner back home to cut through possibility like a jackhammer. "Tell me about the Frau in New York," Kaspar says. "How is he named?"

"His name is Daniel."

"I hope he is exciting. And very pretty."

I sit down and lean against the bed. I stare at a corner of Kaspar's apartment: yoga mat, box of laundry, crate of records. "I'm sorry. I don't know what I was thinking."

Kaspar crawls down the length of the bed and props himself on his elbows. He looks down at me. "It is not great," he says, his breath against me, warm, filled with beer. "But it is okay."

The candlelight casts distorted shadows on the wall, Warhol's head a giant flickering blur. I can't think of what to say, so I fill the blank space with yet another question. "Have you ever been to New York?"

"My friends, they return from New York with this energy and shopping bags and the dark eyes. They are shaking from the excitement."

"That sounds about right."

"I am not wanting to shake with excitement. I am wanting to just be. And why go to New York when it comes to you?" Kaspar slides down next to me onto the floor. He pushes my leg down. My foot, I now realize, has been tapping anxiously for who knows how long. "You are nervous puppy," Kaspar says, still holding my leg with his hand. "You are discombobulated."

"You're right. I am."

"Remember, Sam, don't sweep your wife away." His hand rests on my knee, an invitation. "The cow is wise."

I take a sip of beer. "You know, back in New York—"

"No," he interrupts, putting a finger to my lips. "We will not talk of home. And I should not have asked about the man."

"Okay," I say. "No more New York."

"What is it, New York? Just a place in the movies." Kaspar gets up, dims the chandelier, then switches it off entirely. The room glows only with candlelight and the lights on the balcony. He returns to me now, an apparition. He grabs my hand and lifts me up. "You are here now. Let me have my dream of you."

"Are you sure you're talking to me?"

"Yes, I am sure. And Sam, I like our conversation, but maybe it is possible for just two minutes not to talk?" With his thumb, Kaspar strokes my lips, just once. In the candlelight, I see his eyes are surrounded by a golden ring; his chin, covered in stubble; the swirls of hair poking out of his T-shirt, and then the end, or the beginning, of yet another mysterious tattoo, this one crawling up his chest. I hear him breathing. I feel it, too. He touches his lips to the side of my face, his nose snug against my ear. His skin smells spicy and sweet, like something cooking in the oven.

I look at Kaspar. He presses his lips to my ear. "Please do not smile like this or I think you are making a flirting thing."

"I thought we weren't supposed to talk."

Warhol flies across the room and lands on his cage. He must have given up on the rain. Kaspar's fingers rub against my stubble. "This here," he whispers, "is maybe my most favorite part of a man."

"Kaspar," I say.

He strokes the back of my head. "Just a little, how do you say—*ein Schläfchen*?" He closes his eyes and rests his head against my shoulder.

"A nap?"

"Yes. *Ein bisschen Schmusen*, a cuddle. Come onto the bed. We sleep." He lies down and pats the mattress next to him. "Two friends, two brothers."

"I can't." But I lay my head next to his anyway.

"So . . ." he whispers. "Let us discuss *den Kuss*."

"The what?"

"The kiss," he translates.

I move closer. "Where did this come from?"

"You see, Sam, *der Kuss*, it was not always about sex. It was once a sign of friendship, or a display of respect. One Roman emperor, he was allowing his most important noblemen to kiss his lips."

"Interesting."

"Yes. And the not so important ones are allowed to kiss only his hands."

"I didn't know that."

"The ones who are below even these less important people, the dirty peasants, the emperor is allowing them to kiss only his feet."

"How do you know this?"

"There are books," he says. "It is fact."

"Really?"

"Yes, Sam. So it is your choice. What do you want? Hands? Lips? Feet? Because at the least, you can kiss *die Füsse*," he says, wiggling his toes, which are covered by a black sock with skulls on it. "Tell me, how important are you to me?"

"I'd like to think I'm very important."

"Yes. So then, as the emperor of Kastanienalle, I must command you to kiss my lips."

"I'm not sure I can do that."

"Sam, you are not at home. There are rules in this kingdom. I am sorry, but you have no choice. If there is no kiss then I must punish you."

"This is a weird game."

"A game? No. You come to my city without showing to me a simple sign of respect? The entitlement! Typical American, he must be punished. You must not refuse the king a sign of respect. Not in Berlin." Kaspar reaches over and touches his lips to the side of my face. "That's all it is," he says quietly, kissing my cheek, stroking my chin with his fingers, working his way toward my lips. I feel his tongue run against my skin and I get instantly hard. "Just a show of respect. Two friends, or brothers, spending a night together while the husband is away. You choose."

"You know, you speak very good English."

"Sam," he whispers. "No speaking."

"How come you get to talk?"

"Because I am king."

"You're tipsy."

"Maybe a lee-tle." He wraps his arm around me, and I watch shadows dance across the wall. It's perfect the way his body feels against mine, how we fit. He moves closer and I feel him behind me. "Two brothers," he says, "just spending the night together. There is nothing more." The Smiths come on the stereo—"Cemetry Gates."

"I love this song," I tell him.

"I do, too."

A nostalgic rush runs over me. I remember walking along Seventy-Ninth Street, the sidewalk sparkling with bits of glitter and glass. For months I'd listen to *The Queen Is Dead* on my Walkman on the way to school, nothing else. I'd stop and think, *I will remember this moment, this music, the way the sun is shining, the way the park looks as it looms or lurks—depending on the weather, depending on my mood; the way the leaves rustle and fall to the ground, yellow and orange.* It was fall. It was always fall, or spring, when I'd have these moments, when I was alone, of trying to remember. The two seasons of transition feel so palpable in New York, so full of possibility. Winter and summer just seem like bookends. Looking back, it's strange, how I tried to preserve a moment and, like a dream, the moment broke into fragments and disappeared.

"It's strangely appropriate," I tell Kaspar, "considering our walk a few hours ago. I'll meet you at the Cemetery Gates . . ."

"I was maybe seeing the future when I make this mixtape." Kaspar smiles and offers a charmingly bad, Manchester-by-way-of-Berlin Morrissey impersonation: *All those people, all those lives, where are they now-ow?*

I close my eyes, butterflies in my stomach, wondering what the next song will be. And then the rain arrives, pouring in sheets against the window. Kaspar moves closer, his arm still around my chest, one leg fastened over me. "Do you want to know more about this kiss? Because there is more to tell you."

I turn toward him. "Why do you know so much about kissing?"

"It is something I am liking very much."

"A hobby?"

"Yes. A hobby."

"So do you kiss many men?"

"No. I am, how do you say, selective. An expert."

"A connoisseur."

"Yes, a connoisseur. This is perfect to tell you what comes next. About the kiss."

"Which is?"

Kaspar shifts on the bed. He hovers above me, props himself up on his elbows. He looks different from this angle; his nose large and a bit crooked, and I notice his ears, how small they are, and the vein that quivers on the side of his neck. It's been so long since I've seen a man from this perspective, staring at me while I lie below him—a man other than Daniel, whose appearance from every angle seems as regular and expected as just waking up each morning.

Instead of dropping down toward me, Kaspar climbs off the bed. He sways to the music, the dreamy tones of German trip-hop this time, lost in some music I don't know. He pulls me up and places his hand against my back, softly at first, but then he draws me close. I look up at him. I feel small; Kaspar, though slender, towers above me by at least half a foot.

"Sam, do you know it was in France that the kiss first becomes an accepted practice in courtship, and in love?"

"The connoisseurs."

"*Genau*. And around this same time, dancing also becomes popular." He bends down and rests his head on my shoulder, runs his fingertips down my back. "And every dance ended," he says, "with a kiss."

"That's a nice story."

Kaspar laughs quietly, but there is something different in his laugh. "Well, it is not so much a story. It is fact. Every dance ends with a kiss."

"Or so it was," I say. "You know, your English . . ."

"My Engl-eesch, it is okay because at university I study the English literature."

"Sneaky. I remember when we met, you said '*I speak not zoh good Engleesch*.'"

"I am shy."

"I don't know about that." I look at the birdcage. Warhol stares at me from his perch on top of his house. "Warhol was right about the rain."

"Yes. The bird is funny. He waits all night for the rain. But when it comes, he flies back into his house." Kaspar gazes into my eyes when he says this, his hands still grasped around me. He leads us to the birdcage. Warhol hops onto his finger. Kaspar returns him to the cage and places a blanket over it. He's holding onto me the entire time.

I look out the window. The rain has stopped. "I should leave," I say. "I should go home."

"Sam, the day we meet at Café Anita Wronski, before the snow—I felt something."

"You did?"

"Yes. And I did not know that you will meet me again."

"I didn't know, either. But here I am."

"And you will leave. I know this. I know there is the man back home. But can I tell you one thing more?"

"What?"

"If you were mine. I would never let you go."

And everything just stops. He holds me, for how long I can't really tell. Long enough that another rain passes. Long enough for me to notice that even the thunder sounds different in this city, the rumbles deeper and longer. And the raindrops, so quiet this time against the window, inexplicably remind me of home.

It's three in the morning when he walks me downstairs. The moon is yellow and muted. Two girls stand on the corner smoking cigarettes. One of them wraps a scarf around her neck and twirls down the street. They laugh. But Kaspar and I are shy and awkward. "So," he says.

"So," I repeat.

Kaspar places his hands on my shoulders and looks down at me. "The photo strip," he says. "May I have from it one photo?"

I remove it from my bag and rip it carefully in half. I hand one section to him. "You can have two."

It's hard to describe the eerie, beautiful hush of Prenzlauer Berg at night. The city breathes. Some of the familiar sounds of Berlin are still there—a tram slicing down the street, a lone drunk laughing in the distance, a bike whizzing by. But the night is the only time that the sounds of construction evaporate. I've grown so accustomed to the echoes of drilling and cranes twisting and construction workers calling out to each other that the silence of nighttime becomes a noise unto itself. In the distance, I hear the clomping of boots as people walk down cobblestone streets. But mostly, the streets are deserted. Everyone must be tucked away, asleep inside their apartments, or out in a club or a bar ingesting beer and smoke.

I walk along another park, shadowy and dark. The streetlamps give off a faint glow, as if they're on the muted strain of back-up generators. The city doesn't blaze anything like New York. Instead it's an urban forest—streetlamps rise like trees; plumes of mist levitate above pavement—and as I turn to cross the park, something appears in the haze. At first I think it must be a dog, but this animal moves differently—slowly, stalking, almost like a fox. I must be imagining things. I'd never walk through Central Park in the no-man's land of 3:00 a.m., a strange creature slinking past me. But I feel safe as I walk back to the hotel.

If you were mine, I would never let you go.

When Kaspar said this it felt like a threat, my life reduced to a *What if?* But what does it matter? All of this will soon disappear. I'll wake up from this dream. I'll go home to Daniel. I'll look back and remember this night—the way Kaspar held me when he said those words, the rain pounding at his window. Or perhaps I won't think of it at all.

A bike flies past me. During the day, they're everywhere, as common as people walking on sidewalks. But in the dark of Berlin, they seem like creatures of their own, speeding by and creating a momentary vibration in the air. They look like UFOs as they soar past me, a single white beam flying out of their hulls, which seems appropriate, as there is something about Berlin that feels like another planet, some other universe.

I cross Torstrasse and look up. The TV Tower hangs in the black sky, blinking slow and lonely as a valley of stars gleams over the city; a silver satellite, my talisman, leading me home.

When I finally turn onto Grosse Präsidentenstrasse, two of the space-age ladies stand in the street in vinyl raincoats. A layer of mist clings to the pavement. One of the women talks to a tiny old man with a moustache, trying, I think, to close a sale. She tilts her head to the side and bends down, rests her head on his chest. They start slow-dancing in front of the sleeping trams as if they've danced like this for their entire lives, an old married couple, an Ella Fitzgerald record playing on an invisible turntable.

I watch as the man reaches up to the woman, caresses her neck, and pulls her down to him. Every dance ends with a kiss.

A Ghost of Me, While
I Was Gone

The lobby is empty when I arrive at the hotel. There's no one at the desk. All I hear is Elvis Presley's "Blue Moon" pouring desolate from the stereo. Even the fish in the tank appear to be sleeping, drifting in the water.

I pass the courtyard on my way to the elevator, and that's where I see him: Frankie slouched in a chair beside the koi pond, a burnt-out cigarette dangling from one hand, his mobile in the other. His legs are twisted in some awkward position of sleep, a blanket wrapped carelessly across his chest. I stand by the door and consider waking him, but it's four in the morning. The front door is locked, the streets empty. It's best to just leave him alone.

As I head toward the elevator, I see something move. Another lump of person, this one curled up in the leather club chair in the lobby, snoring. I walk toward the person, who, though obscured by a coat, is so instantly familiar that I kick its foot. The coat falls. Jeremy opens his eyes and looks up at me. "Sam," he says, groggily.

I shake my head, confused. "What on earth are you doing here?"

"I was in the 'hood. I came by to say hello. You weren't here so Frankie and I hung out for a while."

"How do you know Frankie?"

"I didn't. Now I do. Then I guess we both fell asleep." He examines the row of clocks above reception until he finds Deutschland. "Holy crap."

"Yeah, I know."

"Where've you been?" He rubs his eyes. "We know you love your early nights, so frankly, I was worried."

"Well, don't be."

"It's just that last night . . ."

Last night. Which night does he even mean?

He continues. "In the club?"

"Right." SO36 feels like weeks ago. "Look, it was a long night, and I had all that wine."

"And beer."

"Yes, wine and beer."

"And pot—"

"Yes, the Trainwreck." I sit on the couch beside him, but I don't take off my coat. "Thanks for bringing me home, by the way."

"You were a fucking mess."

"Really?"

"Well, nothing I haven't seen before. But I wanted to check in on you."

"You could have called."

"Yeah, I called twice, and you weren't here."

"Oh. I've been out for a while."

"I gather that. And you totally don't owe me anything from last night—I'm not that kind of guy—but maybe you could have rung in the a.m. and said 'Thanks, bro, I'm all right now.'"

"You're right. I apologize."

"You were *gone* last night, Sam. Like, on another planet. Talking to yourself . . ."

"Oh, God." I shake my head, embarrassed.

"I was fucking worried."

"Look, I'm touched. But I'm fine."

"You're the only friend I have in Berlin."

"Jeremy, you've been here for nine months."

"Thanks for rubbing it in. It doesn't change the fact of it. No one else has taken me to dinner or talked to me about anything. I've had a good time with you. It's a compliment. You should take it." I nod my head to say okay, fine. Jeremy looks toward the reception desk. "Aw, shit. Where's Herr Pissy Pants?"

"Frankie? He's asleep in the courtyard."

"Oh. He asked me to watch over things while he shut his eyes for a few minutes."

"Well, good job."

"He's working a double shift. He was beat."

I think about Magda and her non-appearance at the hotel yesterday. Frankie said she was on holiday, but I know she'd planned on working. Tomorrow, I'll figure out what's going on and make sure she's okay. "Jeremy." I sigh. "I appreciate your concern, seriously. But it's been a long night, and I need to go to sleep. Like, now."

"Fine. But before I go, explain to me this: Where in the hell have you been?"

"It's a long story." Jeremy surveys me up and down. "Stop looking at me," I tell him.

"I'm sensing something. Your smell, your eyes . . . everything."

I sniff my hands, the sleeve of my coat. "What do you mean, my smell?"

"Uh-oh. Has someone been a naughty boy? What, did you get some man-on-man action?" He stares at me. I look away. "No!" Jeremy exclaims. "This is so exciting! Tell me everything."

"There's nothing to tell, Jeremy."

He looks at the clock. "At four-sixteen a.m., there is always something to tell." He yawns. "Oh, man."

I can't decide what to do. Part of me wants to make him disappear. But it's late. He's here. And he cared enough to bring me to the hotel after the Trainwreck and returned to see if I was still alive. So I offer an invitation. "Do you want to come upstairs?"

"I'm not into you that way, dude."

"Oh, please. And didn't people stop saying 'dude' in 1989?"

"Dude is classic."

"Jesus. So here's the deal: go home, or come to my room. But staying in the lobby is not an option. I'm tired. I have work to do in the morning, and this time, I mean it. Stay with me if you want—sleep in, have breakfast, whatever. But . . . I don't want to talk."

"Do we share a bed?"

"Absolutely not. You're on the couch."

"Is it a nice couch?"

"It's a couch, Jeremy."

"Do you have a bathtub?"

"Sleep in the tub if you like."

"This place is sweet," he says, looking around. "Swank."

"Less so than you think. I can barely get my laundry done."

"If you saw my slum closet in Friedrichshain, you'd understand."

Jeremy's coat, which he's used as a makeshift blanket, falls to the floor. I pick it up, toss it over my shoulder, and offer my hand. I pull him up from the chair. He's even heavier than he looks—it's like lifting a bear. Jeremy stumbles across the lobby in his combat boots and looks into the courtyard. "We better wake up, snooty-toots," he says, stretching his arms.

I examine Frankie through the window, his mouth hung open, his cheek twitching. "The front door is locked," I say. "Let's let him be."

"Nah. The kid asked for a wake-up call." Jeremy marches into the courtyard. He taps Frankie on the shoulder like a cop waking a bum on the street. "Wake up, man." Frankie's eyes flutter; he takes the back of his palm to his forehead. He looks at us, confused, mutters something in German, then begins to stretch. "Sam, let's go," Jeremy says, and we head to the elevator. "So, where's Magda?"

"She doesn't work at night," I say. "She'll probably be here in the morning."

"Well, I hope so."

I hope so, too. Then I realize. "Jeremy, is *that* why you came?"

"No way, man. I came to see you." A pause. "Okay, maybe I was multitasking."

"Oh, come on." I press the elevator button, again.

"She casts a spell, Sam. You can't deny it."

"Actually, I'm going to deny the spell."

"I usually go for girls around my own age, but something about her . . ." He thinks for a moment. "She's a woman."

"Somehow, Jeremy, I don't think you and Magda are meant to be."

"You think she's out of my league."

"It's not that. First of all, she's sort of involved with someone."

"Sort of? I can totally deal with sort of. Sort of is key!"

"How can you deal with sort of?"

"This coming from the gentleman who wanders home at four in the morning."

I shoot him a look. "Jeremy, this is not my home, and you are not my babysitter. Come on, let's not loiter in the lobby."

"Who uses words like 'loiter'?"

"I do. Don't make me reconsider your spending the night."

"You're so frickin' uptight. Even Frankie says so."

"What do you mean?"

"He was telling me that you changed rooms a hundred times."

"Twice!"

"And that you're obsessed with doing your laundry."

"Hello? It's a hotel! My clothes are dirty! I smell like a German ashtray and disco balls. And why are you guys sitting around talking about me doing laundry? That's a really good use of your time." I cross my arms. "I have no privacy."

"Dude, *relax*. You're too easy."

"How am I supposed to relax when apparently everyone thinks I'm uptight? You, your aunt—who, by the way, has a giant stick up her butt when she's not saying 'yes' to everything—and the snotty receptionist in his stupid rubber shirt who judges my clothes."

"Oh my God, calm down, Sam. Is this what D. has to deal with?"

"But what does it take for me to prove I'm not uptight? I take ecstasy at Polar TV, I smoke God-knows-what at some skanky after-hours club, I'm drowning in liquor, I never sleep, and where do you think I've been all night?"

"That's what I keep asking you!"

"Well, I am not uptight, okay? So everyone needs to stop saying it."

"Actually, Frankie got it wrong. He said 'Herr Singer is 'asstight.' Which still works, in its way . . .'"

"Asstight? What a bitch."

"Yeah. And he thinks you're old, which is funny."

"Hilarious." This is not funny. This is mortifying. "Why were you talking about my age?"

"He was asking about you," Jeremy says. "All these questions. So I told him you're a pretentious art dealer, you're thirty-seven, whatever, no big deal. And he was like, 'Herr Singer *ist* seven-*und*-thirty? *Er ist alt!*'"

"What does that mean?"

"He's old! Which of course you totally aren't." I stand there while Jeremy tries to dig himself out of this. "But me and Frank, we're in our twenties. You know how it is."

"How is it, Jeremy?"

"Oh, I don't know," he says. "Younger."

I'm regretting the invitation to let Jeremy spend the night, but now it's too late. He's the puppy you bring home and then put in the closet because it won't shut up and needs too much. And if there's one thing my night doesn't need, it's another chapter tacked on at four in the morning. "Just relax," Jeremy says. "Let it roll."

"You let it roll. I'm sick of everyone insulting me here."

"Fine, let's go to your pad." He puts his ear to the elevator door. "By the way, where is this thing?"

"The elevator? It's probably taking a cigarette break on the third floor. Nothing works in this place." And with that, the elevator lands and the doors creep open. We step inside.

He looks at me in the mirror. "Do you have beer?"

"It's four in the morning, Jeremy."

"Beer was invented for four in the morning. And will you stop saying my name like you're my mother?"

"I have a meeting in five hours."

"Okay, whatev. We'll be lame and crash. But just so you know, Michelangelo and Thomas Edison slept only four hours a night. Martha Stewart and Napoleon, too."

We arrive on my floor and walk to my room. When I push the door open, Jeremy runs inside like it's Christmas morning. He kicks off his boots, runs his hands across the freshly made bed, then lies down on the couch.

I usually love to return to my hotel room at the end of the day, everything clean and in its place. But there's something eerie about returning after a night spent somewhere else. The curtains are open, exposing my room to the eyes across the courtyard. My desk lamp has glowed through the night, illuminating my unused bed, with its two pointy pillows sitting strangely at the top and two white blankets folded into rectangles beneath them, like a couple with their arms crossed. A tray of chocolates sits on my nightstand, and next to it, the flashing light of the telephone alerting me to a message. It's just an empty room, I think to myself. Then I see that the maid has folded my pants neatly on the back of a chair and placed my shoes beneath it—a ghost of me, while I was gone.

Jeremy starts snooping. "Okay, I see why you moved. This room is incredible!" I follow him into the bathroom. Everything stares at me, unused and accusing: the triangle tips of the toilet paper, the perfectly straight towels, the unopened soaps and bottles of bath gel on the countertop. "I'm taking a bath. Is that okay?"

I hang my jacket and lie down on the bed. I'm still in my jeans and Daniel's sweater, which smells of beer and smoke and coffee. Of Kaspar and Berlin.

Jeremy runs the bathtub. "Just a short bath, Sam. It's been months."

"Fine," I say, "I'm going to sleep." But who am I kidding? I can't sleep when I'm so out of my routine. Just a few days ago, I didn't know anyone in Berlin. And now, in one night, I've left one man's apartment while another man is in my room running a bath for himself. Restless, I take off my sweater and throw it in the closet. I pick up my book; the first sentence is about a river flooding in Istanbul. But all I can think about is Kaspar. And Daniel.

Jeremy wanders back into the room. He clocks me in my T-shirt and does a double take, as if it's weird to see me so exposed, casual. He removes his socks and places them neatly in the corner, by his boots, to demonstrate his good behavior. "I poured some lavender stuff into the tub—hope you don't mind. I love me some bubbles." He spots the chocolates on the bedside table. "May I?" he asks, and I wave my hand as if to say, whatever, go ahead. I pretend to read.

As Jeremy eats his chocolate, he eyes the phone. "Sam, I think you have a message."

"It's probably from you."

"Nope, didn't leave one."

I look at the flashing light. "I'll listen tomorrow." It's almost definitely Daniel and I can't deal right now. To prepare for his bath, Jeremy begins to take off his shirt. I see the edge of his white skin, and the mass of red hairs swirling across his belly. "You can hang your clothes behind the door."

"Oh, okay," he says, clearly embarrassed. He lifts his shirt, disappears into the bathroom.

He leaves the door open a crack. I lie back and rub my temples. I feel a headache coming on. A river is flooding in my book, a town will soon be under water, people will probably die. I hear the faucet stop and the whoosh of Jeremy lowering himself into the tub. "Oh. My. God. This feels fucking a-mazing. Hey, can you bring me a beer?"

"No," I say. "The minibar is a rip-off."

"Please. You're loaded."

"Totally not loaded, Jeremy. I just do business for people who are."

"Do you have any pot?"

"Of course not."

"It's a pity to waste a bath without some weed."

"Poor you."

I hear splashing from the tub and then he calls out again. "So, like, with you and D., it's nonstop sex-making, right?"

"Excuse me?"

"It's no big deal. If I was gay, trust me, I'd be schtupping all the time."

"It's not necessarily like that, Jeremy. At least not for me."

"What, are you guys in some sort of . . . arrangement?"

"That's personal, Jeremy."

"Sorry."

And a really good question. "Yes. No. I don't know."

"Huh. But it's good when you guys are shaking the sheets, right?"

I put down my book. "It is what it is, Jeremy. Daniel and I have been together for a long time. We're just like any other couple."

"Well, that's no good. So, like, what's the point of being gay if you don't have sex all the time?"

I think about whether I should dignify this with a response. But it's an unexpectedly complicated question that, if I'm honest, I've asked myself before. And I'm stumped. After all, I was just in Kaspar's apartment. After all, there's Daniel doing who-knows-what. "Jeremy. I'm trying to sleep."

"So what, then, are you guys gonna have a baby or something?"

"Why would you say *that*?"

"You said you're like every other couple."

Jeremy's on a roll with yet another topic not suitable for the crack of dawn, or any time of day. "I might like to, actually, but not anytime soon."

"Why? You have the dough to make it happen. Isn't that the new frontier?"

"It's not just about money. And I don't want to talk about this. We had a deal."

"Okay, fine." I pick up my book again. In just three sentences, a baby drowns in the river; the first of many, I'm sure. I rest my head on the pillow and close my eyes. Then Jeremy starts speaking again. "Sam, don't you love German? I mean, the language itself."

He's lucky that I'm tired, and that the book sucks; it's either dead babies floating through Istanbul or talking to Jeremy while he takes his lavender bath. "I don't know," I call out. "It's not the prettiest language."

"Fuck pretty. Go to Paris for pretty. Everything in German is one word: *Sportspark*, *Flughafen*. *Brustwarze*." He pronounces this slowly and with a German accent: *brooste-vartz-ah*. "Know what that means?"

"What?"

"Think about it. *Brust* is 'breast.' *Warze* is 'wart.' Breast Wart. *Brustwarze* is Nipple! Lightbulb is *Glühbirne*, which is literally Glow Pear. Isn't that genius?" I don't answer but Jeremy goes on. "*Zahnfleisch* is Tooth Meat, and means . . . chewing gum. Even the simple things are awesome, like *Einbahnstrasse* . . . which means One-way street."

"But that's exactly how we say it in English."

"It's different. German is the language of the future. No spaces in between words, like Web addresses. And you can just make shit up as you go along, combine whatever you want. It's like playing with Legos except the plastic things are words."

"Oh my God, Jeremy. Get out of the tub and go to sleep."

"You still haven't told me where you were tonight."

"I was walking around."

"I believe that—a five-hour walk in the rain? Whatever, dude. You'll tell me eventually."

The funny thing is, I probably will.

I hear the bath drain, Jeremy lifting himself out of the tub. I hear him take an endless, droning frat-boy piss. He emerges in his jeans and hoodie and flops onto my bed, his wet hair red and dark and flat against his face. He burps as he lands. I get up from the bed. "You're disgusting."

"Yeah, but I smell like a field of poppies." He sniffs his skin in self-approval. "Thank you, Sam. I haven't stank this good in months."

"Oh man, how much of that stuff did you use?"

"Whatever. You love me."

"Just remember, you're sleeping on the couch."

I head into the bathroom to wash my face. The room, humid from the bath, smells like flowers and strangers.

I deliberate telling Jeremy about Kaspar. Maybe it would be good to talk about it. But the problem is that once it's out, it's real, and you can't take it back. Something did happen, and I'm not sure what it was. What it is. And I need to ask someone. I can trust Jeremy. We're up, he's here, maybe I'll just get it off my chest. But when I come out of the bathroom, brushing my teeth, the decision has been made: Jeremy is miraculously asleep.

I should be relieved; I won't have to deal with his further interrogation. But now I can't sleep—especially with my new companion sprawled sideways across my bed.

Anxiety ripples through me as I think about Kaspar and wonder about the phone message—if it's from Daniel, or yet another work thing I've invariably blown off. I picture Daniel and Harry. They feel so distant that I feel sick, knowing that we'll have to reintroduce ourselves, that my hotel room sat empty for most of the night and there was a not-great reason for this. Now that the opportunity to tell Jeremy has passed, I wonder if it will remain my secret.

I go to my toiletry bag, pop half an Ambien. I've never been so hopeful for the side effect of temporary memory loss.

As the pill settles in, I open the window and stick my head outside, the dawn sky hazy blue. One of the trams comes to life: the motor hums, lights switch on. A taxi stops on the corner and a young couple gets out. They walk up to the hotel, their trendy suitcases rolling behind them, jittery against the cobblestone. My day ending as someone else's begins.

A Needlepoint in Time

I wake to the sounds of a steady rain and Jeremy snoring next to me. Somehow, I managed to fall asleep not on the couch, but right beside him. He's still in his jeans, but sometime during the night he took off his sweatshirt and socks. One of his feet dangles off the side of the bed. I stare at his calves covered in bright orange fur. I throw a blanket over him. I look at him lying there, my strange new friend.

I leave the curtains drawn as I shower and get ready.

I'm lucky—really lucky—that I woke up in time for my meeting with Greta Hoss. I'm grateful for Ambien's whiplash effect, the way it can knock you out, only to startle you awake just a few hours later, a light slap across the face. I call downstairs, hoping Magda picks up, but it's not her. This woman's voice is way too friendly. "Sorry," I say, and hang up.

I write a note on the hotel stationery and leave it on the bedside table:

J—Have breakfast, charge it to the room. Try the nougat croissant. If you see Magda, please tell her I'm looking for her. Meet me at HENNE in Kreuzberg at 7 p.m. for an early dinner (i.e. a dinner that ends). The chicken place with no cutlery. On me, of course. Ciao, Sam.

It's nice to have friends with nothing to do. You can tell them to meet you someplace, and they'll probably just show up.

As I settle into my corner table in the breakfast room, Frank Sinatra's "Fly Me to the Moon" is playing. The two British ladies plan their final day in Berlin: the Charlottenburg Palace, one more strudel at Café Einstein, and a trip to the KaDeWe to buy chocolate and scarves. They begin discussing Harvey again.

"You'll just confront him tomorrow, won't you?"

"Not sure I'm up to it. I've got that feeling again, those bloody butterflies."

"Darling. Five days in Berlin and we're back where we started? You need to move on. Maybe we should stay on a few more days."

"Don't be ridiculous. Six days is quite enough. This city makes Wales seem cheery."

"Right you are, Ruthie. And this tea is crap, isn't it?"

"It is! I wasn't going to say it, but it is! There's really no place like home."

"Even with Harvey the Wanker?"

"Yes, even with him, the bastard. And we have each other, right then?"

As the ladies clink their cups in a show of solidarity, they examine me, the lonely foreigner in the breakfast room. One raises her teacup as if to say, I know you, lonely man who speaks no English, I see you drinking your coffee and now that I'll never see you again, maybe it's time to say hello. I nod back, then stare out the window. It's easy to cultivate an air of mystery when you travel by yourself. No one knows what you sound like, or even what language you speak. All they know is your face and clothes and the egg on your plate. But I've listened to these ladies for days, following their lives like installments of an early morning radio play.

The ladies leave and once again I'm alone in the breakfast room. Granted, the hotel is small, but where is everyone? Are the guests still out techno dancing in the vaults of an abandoned department store, or sleeping in, recovering from a night of debauchery? I barely see anyone in the hallways or the lobby. The hotel, like Berlin, must be perpetually half-empty.

Astrid walks over. "*Guten Morgen*," she says, pouring me coffee. From her tray, she places a carafe of steamed milk onto the table, followed by a soft-boiled egg in its porcelain cup and a piece of thick brown toast. And from her apron pocket she deposits a tiny spoon onto the plate. She knows me by now, all my needs contained on a breakfast tray.

I finish my meal and contemplate my day: first my meeting with Greta Hoss at Café Orange, and then a few galleries. There's also Sachsenhausen, though I don't think I can squeeze that in before dinner with Jeremy. Maybe tomorrow. I'll need a nap at some point, and I suppose I'll call Daniel and check in with work back home.

I open my guidebook and organize my day with the transit map. It's always satisfying to master another city's transport system, to finally figure it out. Astrid comes over with more coffee and a nougat croissant wrapped in a napkin, so that I may take it for later. "So," she sighs, "more rain." I look into the courtyard; the day looked promising at dawn, but now it's gray and I hear thunder in the distance.

"Astrid, can I ask you something?" She turns around, waiting, open to my question. "Do you know where Magda is?"

"No. I do not." She walks away.

It's unexpected how much it bothers me: Just when Magda and I had turned a corner—*doppelgängers*, she called us—she disappears. If she fails to materialize this morning, perhaps I'll search for her.

I stare out the window. The sky has turned dark and green, nauseous, and it starts to hail. The icy drops assault the courtyard, bouncing off chairs like Pop Rocks. One chair sits off to the side. The blanket Frankie used to cover himself last night, wadded on its seat, gets instantly drenched. Astrid appears in the courtyard—an enormous umbrella hoisted above her—fetches the blanket and throws a plastic cover over the table. She runs back inside. The koi pond sways like a stormy sea. I have no choice but to sit with my coffee and wait it out.

I'm well past the halfway point of my trip. When you travel, the first part of your visit is full of possibility. You're jet-lagged, disoriented, a bit cranky, but everything is new. And then you cross a line, and when you wake up one morning, the rest of your stay feels like the end, a reminder of all you haven't done. You're already wistful for what happened yesterday. You see yourself eating schnitzel and currywurst, drinking wine in people's apartments, wandering the city with strangers who have suddenly become friends. Streets you got lost on finally make sense. You no longer forgive a shitty weather day. And everything you do is just a drumroll to the inevitable: the airplane seat, half a dozen time zones, an entire ocean, home. And I must return home. After all, there's a ticket with my name on it.

Astrid dries herself with napkins and slumps in a chair, her black jeans drenched, her blond hair plastered against her neck. Lightning flashes in the distance.

I look out the window at the pounding rain and think of the morning before I left for Berlin, when similar weather woke me up—a tremendous thunderclap followed by a churning roll. At first I thought it was a bomb. Daniel and I sprang upright in bed. Harry whimpered. And then the rain came—one of those angry, drenching Manhattan downpours that reminds you that you're on an island, as tropical sometimes as Jakarta. I watched as empty streets swelled like streams, and lone taxis sludged down West End Avenue like rowboats. It was one of those storms that ended just as suddenly as it began, and then the sun came out, brilliantly. Daniel went back to sleep. I fed Harry and then stood with him in the elevator. I discussed the storm with our neighbor. She, too, had been startled awake. I told her that I had thought it was an explosion, a bomb. "That's funny," she said. *Not really*, I thought.

As I walked Harry, I passed the man who sleeps in boxes on the church steps next to our building. "Hey, my man," he called out to me. "It's just a needlepoint in time." Harry barked at him, but I knew exactly what he meant.

I had to get to a meeting with a new client in Tribeca, a young French banker named Damon Dufort. Half my clients seemed to be insanely wealthy Europeans, newly arrived to the city with the dumb wide eyes of toddlers running into a playground. They'd discover (or re-discover) the city by following me around, eating at restaurants, looking at art. I'd interpret their taste and subvert it just a bit, challenge them. People like a little danger, to feel they've discovered something new. There was always a honeymoon period. They'd buy a bunch of work, and then eventually the affair would taper off, though occasionally it would resume after a new infusion of cash or a change in life circumstance. But even if I never saw them again, they'd often remember me and recommend me to friends. I thought I was ill-suited to this line of work, but somehow it kept perpetuating. It wasn't what I had imagined for myself, but it paid the bills.

The subways were flooded, but I didn't know it. Daniel and I had stopped watching television or listening to the radio in the mornings. All the news was ridiculous, repetitive, and scary. I'd even stopped reading the *New York Times*. I'd ask Daniel if I missed anything in the paper, and he'd just say, "Oh, you know, there's just stuff about stuff."

As I walked to the subway station, the air was even thicker than before the storm. The sun in New York can do that, spin moisture into another dimension. Down on the subway platform, everything felt swollen and close. There was no train, and no announcement about why, just the standard confusion as rows of sweaty New Yorkers lined the volcanic strip of concrete. When the train finally wormed its way into the station, I fought my way into a car. The proximity to so many strangers, as always, felt humiliating.

The subway inched out of the station and headed downtown. The train wheezed and sighed, and then it just stopped, an exhausted animal whose legs caved beneath it. A garbled voice informed us that due to flooding, there would be "no movement." The lights flickered on and off. It never fails to amaze me how New York can be so broken down, just held together with spit and glue.

I stood with my satchel locked between my feet, trying to remain composed. If Damon bought just one painting this morning, I wouldn't have to work for a month. His taste was refined; he always ordered the best wine, wore the most expensive clothing. His taste in art followed suit. It's one aspect of this job that I've always liked; I can work hard and then be lazy for a while, if I want.

I thought about the fact that I had to pack for my newly planned trip. But no matter how much I tried, I couldn't stop thinking about the text on Daniel's phone. Who was Brad, and why was he asking for another date? And did his name really have to be Brad? I didn't know how to bring it up with Daniel, or if I even should. There had been other men, with crumbs left for me to discover in a variety of ways. When had the rules of our relationship changed? And had we really ever established them? We had lived in limbo for so long, with assumptions and avoidance and mazes and walls. It was incredible how many walls you could erect in eight years, how much you could share and yet how much else you could still hide: texts from strangers, open laptops illuminating what you really did that day, manila envelopes hidden in drawers. But perhaps we'd both been careful not to look.

I felt my shirt, soaked from sweat, my heart beating faster. The woman seated below me swatted her way through the *New York Post* while the man next to her flicked the pages away with his hand. "You're on the subway," he snapped. "Not your couch."

I stood on that unmoving train for twenty minutes. There was no explanation given, no announcement at a time when explanations were key. The towers had fallen a few years prior, and anything abnormal hinted at disaster; I'd imagined my own death in an exploding city at least five times a week. Then the train would move, or the sirens would pass, or a smell would disappear, and I'd live another day after all.

My particular car was halfway in the station and halfway out, which felt fitting. I hadn't slept well. I'd stopped going to the deep place of sleep at night; it was dark, my eyes were closed, but there was no rest or release. Just blank space, and the next thing I knew it was morning and I had to take the dog out.

And then it just happened: I collapsed onto the floor, suddenly, yet surprisingly slowly. Like a falling tree, someone told me later. When my eyes opened, all I saw was: *Get a Lawyer. 1-800-ENGLISH. Don't Let Impotence Ruin your SEX life! Learn English with the best. Zero Trans Fat. Lead paint can kill you.* And then I saw the eyes looking down. And immediately, I thought: *They're staring at me. I'm that guy. I'm on the floor.* A woman bent down. "Are you okay?" Someone asked, "Was it a seizure?" A child said, "Maybe he's paralyzed."

Things happen. People faint on trains. But I couldn't believe it was me, that I had just stopped—a tape reaching its end, clicking off.

I looked up and focused on an advertisement: *Are You Happy?* A relatively simple question, although what New Yorker would say Yes while lying on the floor of the subway in a Ted Baker suit? I kept reading. *Do you have Vague Feelings that something bad is going to happen to you? Is everything, always, falling apart? Maybe you have Generalized Anxiety Disorder.*

I lifted myself up, dusted myself off, and apologized to my fellow riders. I thanked the few helpful faces and said to the child, "Don't worry. I can move."

I was late to my meeting, but I spun a good story. And I unexpectedly brokered the sale of six works by a rising young painter who worked with hand-applied pulp pigment and stencils. Damon Dufort liked the fact that I rode the subway. He thought it was charming, a little eccentric, and displayed thrift. Damon took me to lunch with his wife at Odeon. She was newly pregnant, and I was only the third person they told. She grabbed my hand when she told me, squeezed it. I looked at her hand holding my own, examined her smile, so open. I feigned excitement but inside I felt a surge of sadness and jealousy. This beautiful couple was discovering a new city, buying art, making friends, and creating life while just an hour before I had collapsed on a train. My phone vibrated endlessly in my pocket, probably Daniel. I turned it off and finished my meal.

When Daniel and I ate dinner that night, he made some vague assertion that if he could get away from work, he'd join me in Berlin. We both knew it wouldn't happen, and for me, it was essential that it not. Didn't he realize why I was leaving? He must have, although maybe that too was hidden under the bed like everything else.

We walked Harry around the block. I didn't tell him about the train. I didn't bring up the text message. I didn't tell him I'd sold enough art that morning to float myself for a year. Daniel watched a two-hour documentary about china—not the country, but the plates. Then he folded my shirts and helped me pack.

Ich Bin Ein Berliner!

Greta Hoss is formal in appearance and manner; her blond hair is tied back, and she wears a beige business suit. She looks like the sort of person who sells you a mortgage or opens a savings account for you, but in this case happens to be an expert on the Berlin art market.

We sit at a tiny table at Café Orange, an enormous restaurant that is thankfully just a few blocks from the hotel. The café is, of course, painted orange, with epic ceilings and colossal windows facing the street. Greta takes out a binder and shows me the work of two artists—one is a printmaker whose work consists of bold, monochromatic, brightly colored flowers and fruits (lemons and tulips, pomegranates and poppies); the other artist, using wax and tar, creates three-dimensional simulacra of German seascapes. "The wax must be heated to 54 degrees Celsius to melt and is hand-created by the artist from *Bienenwachs* and honeycombs along the Rhine in Düsseldorf," Greta tells me. "His use of tar is influenced by his father's tire business, but I think the results are rather pleasing." She studies my face, and her well-practiced intuition deduces my lack of enthusiasm for either artist. She closes the portfolio and folds her hands across her lap.

We talk about *Ostalgie*, because I bring it up. "The people got what they wanted," she says. "The unification process was incredible. I was there. But euphoria does not last. The dream of 'one people' collapses like the Wall, and now we have *Ostalgie*. Like art, it is just an idea, an abstraction. Or perhaps it is like beeswax from the Rhine. Just something to talk about."

We discuss Klaus and his upcoming show. "Do you know him?" I ask.

"Everyone knows Beckmann," she replies, with a hard-to-read expression.

"I'm going to the opening in a few days."

"Yes, *Immediate/Present*, a rather pretentious title. Or, the '*Ostalgie* show,' as everyone is calling it. It is troubling to me. Many Germans forget, this was a dictatorship, the DDR. A brutal regime. And I find it very curious, because in Berlin, there will always be a Wall, whether we see it or not."

Over two macchiatos and a few bites of a cheesecakey thing called *Quarkkuchen*, Greta fires off questions about my taste in art and my experience so far in Berlin. "I understand," she says after a final sip of coffee. She writes down an address on a slip of paper. "Go here, to this exhibit in Wedding. The artist is Manfred Butzmann. You will know why when you are there. Do it tomorrow. They are closed today. And I assume you go already to the galleries on Auguststrasse."

"Of course," I say. Though I've only been to one.

She suggests I walk to a nearby gallery on Gipsstrasse featuring new work by one of the artists in her book. "I know you do not like pretty, but it is three streets away and worth a look."

"Who says I don't like pretty?"

"It is a good thing." She stands up and shakes my hand. "In German we call this *Urteilsvermögen*. A discerning eye is how you might say it. A pleasure to meet you, Herr Singer. Ring me after Butzmann if you like."

I go to the gallery on Gipsstrasse and walk into a white room. A man and a woman sit on a bench, facing opposite directions, mesmerized by the giant waterfalls and rivers on the walls. But the work leaves me cold. Perhaps Greta was right. If this is pretty, it's not my thing.

After a few more gallery visits, I take the U-Bahn to Kreuzberg. I don't remember the address of Magda's apartment, so I try to retrace my steps in reverse; I use my guidebook to find Austria and walk past the cemetery on Bergmannstrasse. In the daylight, you can see the towering evergreens, the streams passing through the grounds, the immaculate bouquets left on gravestones. I turn left at the next corner and follow another street until I see a familiar square and, at the far end, Magda's ivy-covered apartment building. I survey the cars parked along the street, but there's no sign of Magda's tiny green automobile. I walk through the gate and pass the courtyard, toward the front door of her apartment house. On the top floor, the curtains are drawn across her living room windows.

I glance at my watch. I have some time before I meet Jeremy for dinner at Henne. I guess I'll just wait.

If Magda emerges, she'll think I'm nuts. I can only imagine her finding me at her front door: *Samuel, why are you here? This is absurd.* She'd have no interest in my explanation. She'd push past me and go up to her apartment. Because really, what excuse could I offer? *Oh, hi, happened to be in the neighborhood, thought I'd check on the manager of my hotel?* It's useless. I'm here because I care about her. But there's no denying that I'm being slightly stalkerish. Still, I have a hunch that something is wrong. If Daniel were here, he'd say I always have these hunches, and nothing is ever wrong. But I can't shake it, and really, who is he to talk? Perhaps nothing is wrong if you don't look too closely.

I sit on the steps, my head against a column. Opera wafts from someone's window, a big-throated woman singing in Italian over cellos and horns. A young man in a pinstriped suit and a fedora passes through the courtyard with his bicycle by his side. He parks the bike in the rack and then approaches the doorway, a black scarf wrapped around his neck. He checks his phone, tucks his newspaper under his arm. He's dapper and clean-cut, like something out of Savile Row, except for metal spike passing through his earlobe. He looks at me, probably wondering what I'm doing here, loitering, so I smile and nod. While he fumbles for his keys, I press the buzzer for M. Schubring. The man unlocks the door and enters the building. I let the door close behind him and wait for Magda to answer because I don't want to appear to be an intruder. But of course she's not home and the door shuts in my face.

I wait on the steps for an hour. Long enough for the day to fall into dusk, for me to regret not wearing my wool sweater and wonder a few dozen times what the hell I'm doing here. The streetlamps switch on. Then Blitz appears. The cat slinks around and eyes me suspiciously before leaping onto my lap and collapsing. I'm a dog person. I've never loved cats. I always thought they were unemotional and not to be trusted. But feeling Blitz's warm body vibrate against my leg, his paw stretching languorously past my knee, it's an undeniably nice feeling. Daniel always says that we'll have a cat when we have a house in the country. He says it with such certainty.

I stroke the cat's head and he pushes into my palm, humming his approval. After a few more minutes of Blitz's seduction, a window flies open above me, in the apartment below Magda's. An old lady leans out, a shock of long white hair falling past the windowsill like an ancient Rapunzel's. She surveys the courtyard as the opera, now louder, leaks from her window. She waves, but I can tell she wonders who I am, this stranger with the cat on his lap. "*Hallo*," I say. I could attempt some invented sign language to tell her I'm waiting for a friend, but she doesn't seem the type that would play along.

"*Was machen Sie hier?*" I can't tell if this is a question or a command.

"I am waiting for Magda," I tell her.

"*Magdalene?*" She points to the window above hers.

"Yes!" I say, nodding. "Magdalene." What a beautiful name.

She shakes her head. "Frau Schubring *ist nicht da.*"

"Ah." I know enough from her brutal inflection that Magda is clearly not home. "Okay."

"I have dog," she says, holding Schnapps up to the window.

I smile. This must be the neighbor who takes care of the dog. "Ah, Schnappsie!" I say this warmly and with enthusiasm so the woman will realize I know Magda well enough to know her puppy. Schnapps seems to remember me. Though he's being hoisted out a window, Michael Jackson-style, he stares at me, his tail twirling so maniacally he could fly to the moon. Schnapps begins to whine and bark, his paws swimming in the air, so she puts him down in her apartment.

"*Schönen Abend,*" the old woman says in a curt voice that lets me know our conversation is over. She makes a clucking noise with her tongue and calls out: "Blitz! *Komm jetzt!*" The aristocratic feline morphs instantly into an anxious servant, leaping out of my lap and zigzagging up a row of window boxes to her windowsill before disappearing into her apartment. The window slams shut.

It's freezing and dark, and I'm feeling stupid. I didn't even get back to the hotel for a shower or a nap. At least I'm slightly less worried about Magda. Her puppy is safe with her neighbor, her disappearance likely planned. And though I didn't understand what the woman said, she didn't seem distraught about anything besides the American dumbass sitting on her stoop. I think about leaving a note for Magda, but what would it say? Besides, I've no paper or pen, and she knows where to find me. I brush a few leaves off my jeans and move on.

I stare at the apartments on this street, shadows passing in windows, all these lives being lived. A boy zooms past me on his bicycle, ringing his bell. The end of my trip looms, and I see it hanging there in front of me. I'm tired just thinking about what it will take to get me home: Packing. All this work piled up at the end. A few meetings still to come. The opening. The goodbyes. A trip to the airport, the long flight home. I start walking to the train. Time to meet Jeremy for chicken and beer.

Henne appeals to my indecisiveness: you get half a chicken, potato salad, cabbage, and a piece of bread. A fork is permissible, but don't even think about asking for a knife.

The restaurant is famous for more than its chicken. A signed picture of JFK hangs above the bar. Apparently, Kennedy was supposed to dine here in 1963 after his legendary eight-hour motorcade through Berlin. He wound up missing dinner, so he sent this photograph as some sort of consolation. During this same visit he delivered one of his most famous speeches, the one in which he announced, "*Ich bin ein Berliner!*" All of West Berlin turned out to throw flowers in the path of his motorcade, trying to shake his hand, screaming "Ken-ah-dee! Ken-ah-dee!" with an intensity that startled the president. Berliners waved signs proclaiming things like, "Next time, bring Jackie." But there was no next time. He was assassinated a few months later. The Wall curved directly in front of the restaurant, where it separated Kreuzberg from Mitte. Henne serves the same half-chicken dish now as then, although of course today it's organic, milk roasted, and raised on a farm.

"You're giving me a headache," I tell Jeremy, who's reading this information out loud from some tattered guidebook. "We're here because Magda says they have the best chicken in Germany." I'm also intrigued by this no-knife thing; you gotta have a gimmick, but this strikes me as a particularly odd quirk.

"I love me some poultry," Jeremy says. "And this place, it's definitely got a vibe."

You can feel the history in Henne—the dark interior aged from decades of smoke and chicken grease, its nicotine-stained walls jammed with cuckoo clocks, moody landscapes, and black-and-white pictures of the Wall. The restaurant has two levels, and we sit on the upper floor, tucked in a corner lit only by a flickering sconce a few feet away.

Jeremy studies the beer selection with a seriousness usually reserved for weightier matters. When our server comes over, I fold my hands while Jeremy orders for us. It never fails to impress me to hear him speak the language so effortlessly. "You sound butch when you speak German," I say. "Very commanding."

"*Danke*, Herr Singer."

"I'm glad I have you. You order and I just play along. It's kind of relaxing."

"You're my lady." Jeremy winks at me. The waitress returns with two giant glasses of *Schwarzbier*—the darkest beer I've ever seen, the color of licorice. "It's black beer," Jeremy explains. "Specialty of *das Haus*." He pops a cigarette between his lips and lights up. He offers me one, but I wave it away. I don't want to get so addicted that I have to slap a patch onto my shoulder when I return to New York. "I heard they're going to ban smoking in restaurants."

"Yeah, like that'll ever happen," he says, exhaling. "So I'd like to make a toast." Jeremy raises his glass, the cigarette hanging from his lips. "To you, Sam Singer, for taking pity on a poor kid like me, for feeding me so well, for providing shelter and friendship and even a bathtub. Your kindness has not gone unnoticed." We clink glasses. I take a sip.

The beer is as thick as it is dark, and slightly spicy; a decadent drink to be sipped slowly on a chilly Berlin night.

I take another sip, but it's too special to be savored without its obvious soulmate. I lean into him and imitate Magda. *"Yer-a-mee,* can I *boom* a ciggie?"

Jeremy slides one out of the pack, puts it between my lips and lights me up. "Anything for m'lady."

I lean back to relax, but the smoke chokes my lungs. I can't believe I smoked so much when I was younger, that somehow it felt normal. Because when I smoke now, it makes my skin feel different. It makes my heart beat so fast that I feel like I swallowed a typewriter.

"So where's Magda?" Jeremy asks. "I didn't see her this morning."

I contemplate telling him about my afternoon spent on her stoop, but I don't. "She went away."

"Really? Where?"

"Not sure."

"Well, I hope she comes back."

"She will," I say, convincing myself.

I take a deep breath, relishing the beer and the cigarette buzz. It must be true what they say about nicotine—when it's swimming through your blood, it really does give you a sense of well-being. As Klaus remarked, it's the time in between cigarettes that's the problem. I hate the feeling of needing something so badly.

I fold my arms across my chest and survey the room. Next to us, an elderly couple eats chicken in contented silence. In the center of the landing, two women I'd thought were just friends caress each other's faces. Jeremy sees the women, too, and gives me a look to say, "Yep, here we go again." And in the opposite corner, two parents sit next to each other, looking amused by their young daughter who is relishing the excuse to eat a meal without utensils. "Why are you smiling?" Jeremy asks.

"I'm smiling?"

"Yes, you are."

"Right now, I feel happy. I like this city."

"Yep. Totally get it."

"I just feel different here." I take a drag from the cigarette and look at him. "The day before I came here, I fainted on the subway."

"What? Are you serious?"

"Yup. Passed out. Fell over like a tree."

"That's crazy, Sam. People don't just pass out like falling trees. Did you go to the hospital?"

"Of course not. It's New York. I went to Tribeca and sold a few hundred-thousand-dollar paintings to a French dandy."

"And D. let you come to Berlin after you blacked out on the subway?"

"I didn't tell him."

Jeremy looks puzzled. "Dude, you have to take care of yourself. And I mean that on multiple levels."

"I know." So much for drinking slowly; I finish the *Schwarzbier*. "There's some stuff I need to sort out back home."

"I'll say."

"But I don't have time to think in New York. I don't have ten minutes that aren't interrupted by something. I can't even walk Harry without having six random social interactions on the elevator." I think about telling him about the last few months: my nights spent awake in bed or arguing with Daniel, Harry trembling next to the stove; or taking the subway to the end of the line because I didn't want to go home. How lonely I've felt. How lost. But it's just ennui—privileged, urban, childless ennui—so boring and indulgent that it's sickening even to me. I could have a tumor growing nefariously within me, a dead baby floating through the river, a wall dividing my city. That would explain everything turning to black. But I don't have any of those things. "And now, I'm in Berlin and the energy has shifted. There's this stillness. There is something else." I feel my eyes well up, but I stop it. "And I know that I'm traveling, which makes everything feel different. But this time it *is* different. In New York, my entire life is on vibrate."

"Hey, you're preaching to the converted." He puffs his cigarette. "So, get off the wheel."

I feel emotional, a knot in my throat. "But I'm supposed to love New York. It's where I'm from. It's where everyone wants to go. And it's given me so much. Don't bite the hand that feeds."

"Fuck that," Jeremy says. "Bite that fucking hand right off. Everyone is in an abusive relationship with New York. I had to shake that sick bastard off me. Nothing there is real."

I'm quiet for a moment, startled by the bitterness in Jeremy's voice. The waitress places two fresh mugs of *Schwarzbier* in front of us. "Fine. So then tell me, what *is* real? Sitting here with you in Berlin, or my life in New York?" I flick my hand toward my life back home like I'm shooing away a fly. "Is it Daniel and the job back home? Or is it you, and this, and Kaspar?"

"Back up."

"What?"

"Who is Kaspar?"

I throw my hand down on the table. My beer splatters. "Shit."

"Man, I knew there was some secret diddle guy!" Jeremy imitates me from the other night: "Who, me? Yeah, I was just walking around Berlin at *four a.m.* In the fucking rain." He rolls his eyes. "You whore! Tell me everything."

I sigh, defeated once again by my big mouth. I blame the beer. "There was no sex," I whisper. "No diddling."

He clasps his hands and leans excitedly toward me. "But?"

"Okay, maybe there was a connection."

"*Maybe*? Is he hot?"

"That's inappropriate, Jeremy. I have a boyfriend."

"Oh, please." Jeremy tucks his hands under his arms. "Come on. Is he hot?"

"Yes." I picture Kaspar. His long twisty body, his green eyes. "A little bit."

"You're blushing."

"No, sir." I look away. "Where's our chicken?"

"Do not be embarrassed, Sam. Even I think German guys are hot. This whole city is a mindfuck. The guys look like girls, the girls look like guys, and everyone is fuckable."

"God, Jeremy, how do you talk like that? You're just so open."

"Because it's all talk. I sleep alone, you know that." He drops his head and gets this gloomy look on his face. His eyelids crinkle as if controlled by some secret muscle no one else has. "I'm lonely as shit." He slumps, this giant sliding down a tiny wooden chair. "Do you know what the OJ girl told me?" Jeremy looks toward the candlelight. "She said that when it rains at night, she thinks Berlin is crying."

"That's weird."

"I know."

"And beautiful."

"Yeah. She said that a city can't contain so much and not collapse in exhaustion, grieve for itself. 'Berlin must release something into the air,' she told me. And so it cries when the streets are empty, while Berlin sleeps. She thought that if the city didn't weep for itself, it might explode. That was, like, her theory."

"My God. That's intense."

"Right?"

"So what happened with this OJ girl?"

"She called it off. I probably came on too strong, plus I was too boring for her, I'm sure."

"I doubt that, Jeremy. You're not boring at all."

"I liked her. I have to admit, I cried."

"You actually wept?"

"I'm in touch with my feelings. No apologies, man, it's who I be."

"Do you cry a lot?"

"Well, I was a sensitive kid, and my folks were not the best parents. Ask Debra. There's this story about when I was a baby and my father would put me naked on the windowsill so I'd get used to the cold."

"That's insane."

"And remember, we lived in Albany. It was freezing. He just let me cry, thought it would make me tough."

"That makes no sense."

"Exactly. And it didn't work. I still need my sweaters, right? The world is just so full. Sometimes, I don't know what to do with it all. So when was the last time *you* cried? I mean, besides your ganja-induced breakdown the other night?"

I think about it. "You know, I can't remember." And I can't. I'm more used to the empty feeling, the exhaustion and effort of just pushing everything away.

"All this time I thought, jeez, look at Sam, he just needs to get laid."

"Fuck off. I have a boyfriend."

"Exactly. Old Chinese proverb says: He with the full glass gets nothing more to drink."

"Oh, stop." The waitress returns with more beer. The foam spills unapologetically onto the wooden table. "And by the way, how long has it been since *you* hooked up with someone?"

"Don't go there with me, comrade."

"Before the Wall fell?"

"Look, the ex-girlfriend in New York did a number on me. I was in love with her, before she went all loco. But whatever. I like to dream. I'm an excellent coveter. There's all this possibility, and sometimes that's the best part." He pauses, then smiles sadly. "If you want to know the truth, the last time I slept with a girl, I wound up crying."

"After?"

"During."

I actually wince. "Oh, Jeremy."

"I was just so happy to be with someone, to be smelling her hair and touching this beautiful creature. Of course, she got all freaked out."

"Was this in Berlin?"

"Maybe."

I want to reach out to him, but I just look at him blankly. "I'm sorry. That's sad."

Jeremy sighs. "Everything is sad. So the dream ended. Next subject, please." He stares into his glass. "Thank God for beer."

"Was it the OJ girl?"

"Of course. Her name was Ulrike."

"Pretty name."

"Man, she was lovely. She smelled like apples." He lights another cigarette. "I suppose she still does."

"What happened to her?"

"I just told you, Sam. She got freaked out." He removes a picture from his wallet and hands it to me. A beautiful brown-haired girl in a sweater, big brown eyes. "She didn't exactly give me this picture. And we only lasted ten days. But it's over, so why talk about it. Sometimes you gotta just move on."

"We should find her."

"No way, José." He exhales, smoke streaming from his nose. "Ulrike works at this ice cream place not so far from me. So now I walk on the other side of Simon-Dach-Strasse just so I won't see her." He looks away. "But that 'hood is getting totally yuppified anyway, so whatever, I can deal with not walking down that street."

"Jeremy, this is not good."

"You know what? It is what it is."

"I hate that expression. What happened to the Yes person who walks into buildings to see what's inside, the guy who just told me to get off the wheel?" Jeremy shrugs his shoulders. I lean forward. "Maybe tomorrow we should go get ice cream."

"Dude! It *snowed* two days ago. And just . . . no."

This is perhaps the first 'No' that's come out of Jeremy's mouth since I've known him. It feels heavy, like an anchor, so I know to move away. "So, I have to go to this art opening."

"You're shitting me. You're actually going to work?"

"I worked plenty today, I'll have you know. And yes. The opening is the day after tomorrow."

"*Übermorgen.* Man, I love saying that. I forget—what's the show?"

"It's about *Ostalgie*, which is—"

"About cute girls crying over rusty cans of OJ."

"Exactly. So will you come?"

"You mean be your date?"

"Well, yeah I guess you could say that."

"What about this Kaspar dude?"

I knew he would go there. "I won't see him again."

"Why not?"

"I can't do that. I've done enough."

"What about Magda?"

"Like I can even find her. Anyway, I'm asking you. Just come."

"You just need me to be your translator."

"Actually, Jeremy, I'm asking because I'd like you to come with me."

"Okay, I'll check my book and get back to you. What would you do without me?"

"You know what? I don't really know."

We're interrupted by the arrival of our meal, two perfectly golden chicken halves served with a hunk of brown bread and glass bowls filled with potato salad and shredded cabbage. A waiter brings two more glasses of beer. Jeremy takes a sip and leans into me. "I told them to just keep 'em coming."

"We're turning into alcoholics." I take a sip.

"*Nein*, we're turning into Germans!" He stubs out his cigarette and fastens his napkin under his collar. I unfold mine and set it on my lap. We try to figure out how to approach the chicken. I start picking at it. I feel rebellious just digging in with my fork and fingers, a caveman poking at his food. Maybe Jeremy got it right, turning his napkin into a bib. I put a piece of chicken in my mouth; it's moist, salty, perfectly fried. The crunchy skin alone would send you reeling. Jeremy throws his head back and swoons. For a few minutes, we devour our meal in ecstatic silence. I demolish the bread to soak up the beer inside of me. Jeremy spoons himself some potato salad, then plops some on my plate. "So where does this Kaspar live?"

"Prenzlauer Berg. I met him at Café Anita Wronski the day after I first met you. I went back to check it out. So if it wasn't for you, I'd never have met him."

"Don't you go blaming your sluttitude on me," he says. "You're extremely secretive, Sam Singer."

"Like you should talk, with this mysterious OJ girl."

"That was months ago, and I literally just told you everything." Jeremy leans back and rubs his chin. "So . . . then answer your own damn question. Is it real?"

"With Kaspar? I was definitely attracted to him. Everything about him. But I can't believe he was actually into me."

"You're totally cute," Jeremy says. "Look at you in your nice little sweater."

"Well, thanks."

"And you're so compact." He squeezes his hands together like he's making a ball. "Just a little dude."

"Am I?" But I know this about myself. I'm not short, per se, but Daniel calls me celebrity-size, like the Tom Cruises of the world. I suppose those are my general dimensions, without the movie star face. "Well, anyway, somehow we wound up in his apartment."

"Funny how that happens."

"There was this electricity between us. I hadn't experienced that in a long time, and frankly, I didn't know it was still possible. Anyway, whatever. I'm with Daniel."

"You're sort of with Daniel." Jeremy leans into me, a drumstick in his hand. "That's my sense of things."

"Jeremy, I have a life back home with Daniel. We have friends and neighbors and jobs and parents and a dog. Okay, so maybe I'm a little mad at myself for not acting on it. But I couldn't go through with it." Although that didn't stop Daniel. At least I don't think it did. I consider the *Schwarzbier* in my veins, and my big mouth, and stop myself from saying anything further. "Anyway, the Kaspar thing was not real. Daniel is real."

"You don't know that."

"But I do. I love him."

"How do you know?"

I consider this. I remember a night a few years ago, when Daniel and I had a few martinis at a friend's wedding. A song by Simple Minds came on, and Daniel grabbed my hand and led me to the dance floor. It was funny how the soundtrack to the bar mitzvahs and sweet sixteens of our youth had become the playlist for all these weddings just a decade or two later, and I told him this. Everyone around us treated "Alive and Kicking" like a fast song, but Daniel wrapped his arms around me, and I laid my head on his chest. It was someone else's wedding, but all eyes were on us.

I take a sip of beer. "Because we like the same songs," I tell Jeremy.

"What do you mean?"

"I mean, literally, we like the same songs. We enjoy the same movies, and often we read the same books. We differ once in a while, which keeps it interesting. But mostly, we just like the same things. Maybe you don't get this yet, but that counts for a lot. If you like sitting next to someone and watching TV or reading the paper, that's what keeps you together."

"Come on. *That's* the secret?"

"I mean, it's not everything. But it's something."

"Shit."

"Well, Daniel is also smart. And charming. And handsome, too." I pick at the chicken with my fingers. "Though lately, it's complicated. Lately, when I think about Daniel, I get upset."

"Always?"

"Not always. Well, pretty much. Unless I think about the past. But that makes me sad."

"That's lousy, Sam. Do you want to talk about it?"

"Not particularly." That icky feeling creeps into my stomach. I stare out the window as if this will push it all away. "I don't know why I'm feeling so many things. But I am."

"Travel does that, and you're confused. It's like, you came here for work. You should probably be out with some art person making deals but instead you're sitting here with me, eating chicken with your hands."

"So?"

"So, let's face it, apparently you came to Berlin for other reasons. Cosmic, perhaps."

"You've had too much beer. And so what if I came here for other reasons? I feel like I've left my life. I mean, look at you, for example. Who the fuck are you? I've known you less than a week. And now you're, like, my best friend and I'm spilling my guts to you." I dab my cheeks with a napkin. "I don't do that."

"Wait. Back up. I'm your friend?"

"Of course."

"Your Best Friend. Really?"

"Jeremy, shut up."

"I'm extremely needy."

"Yeah, I hadn't noticed."

I stare down at the carcass on my plate, bones so clean they could be displayed at the Museum of Natural History. The manager of the restaurant, pleased that we've ordered so much, insists we finish our meal with an after-dinner drink on the house (*"geht aufs Haus"*). Jeremy downs a shot of *Getreide-Kümmel*, a brandy, but I only manage a few sips of the cinnamon liqueur in front of me. It's too sweet, and I'm already feeling a little drunk. I pay the check and give the waitress a twenty percent tip, which Jeremy tells me is at least four times too much. The Germans may not love me, but at least I've been tipping like a king; that has its own kind of power. Jeremy dabs his mouth with his napkin and turns to me. "So," he says, inevitably, "what's next?"

We take a cab along Unter den Linden, its trees glittering with white lights, the Brandenburg Gate lit up majestically on all sides, standing in front of the Tiergarten like a dare. Jeremy points to the gate's iconic statue, the copper goddess driving a chariot drawn by four galloping horses. "You know, Napoleon marched through that gate. The little fucker liked the goddess so much that he removed the statue and had her shipped to Paris. So fucking French."

I look at the gate, one of those things so endlessly photographed that now that I'm seeing it in real life, it looks fake. "Another factoid from your walking tours?"

"*Natürlich.* But the Prussians kicked his tiny French ass and got the statue back. And when they put her back up there, they added the eagle on the wreath and the Iron Cross."

"Those were designed by Schinkel."

"Yeah, I know, Mister Pretentious. Then the statue was damaged in the war, and when the Wall went up, it ran right in front of the gate. So the gate was technically in East Berlin, but only the West had the molds necessary to restore the statue. The *Wessies* made nice and left a new statue right on the demarcation line. The East finally sucked it up and accepted it, but they sawed off the eagle and the Iron Cross as a little fuck-you. Then the Wall fell, and like everything else in this city, it's been restored all over again."

"I didn't know you were such a history buff."

"The walking tours usually wind up right here, so I know this area particularly well. Sometimes I try to pee in the Hotel Adlon, but they are total snots in there, so now I just go to Starbucks." He shows me the enormous field to the left of the gate, where the city is building its first major Holocaust memorial, the one Klaus told me about.

"What are they going to put there?"

"Rumor is a bunch of concrete slabs."

I stare out the window. Even in the dark, Unter den Linden is impossibly formidable, almost a joke of an avenue, an alpha-street. We pass the American Embassy, the British Embassy, then the opera house, museums that reach back centuries, and others just a matter of years. I see the memorials to Jews, to victims of war, to books burned, to Frederick the Great. We stop at a traffic light. Jeremy rolls down the window. "Wow, look at the moon."

I look out at the moon hovering over the Palast der Republik. "It's huge," I say. "Is it full?"

"Almost." Jeremy turns to me. "Hey, can we get out of the cab and walk a little?"

"Seriously?"

"Yeah. I've never been here at night, it's like we own the place. We can hitch another ride in a few minutes."

Jeremy asks the driver to pull over. I pay the fare and we walk toward Museum Island. Even though it's cold and dark, it feels special, this impossible mash-up of history surrounding just the two of us. I think about all the buildings I've seen enduring public surgeries to correct their wounds and the onset of age. How much history can one city contain? Bombed out, burned, bullet-scarred and crumbling, and it has all risen again. The linden trees rustle in the wind, and a sea of leaves falls onto the street. Jeremy walks through them, hands tucked in his pockets, and points to the sky. "You know, the moon is highly underrated."

"How so?"

"It just does a lot . . . controls the ocean, moves the planet, keeps everything in check. Plus, as celestial decoration, it's fucking beautiful."

You can see everything tonight: the stars, the blue and the black of the horizon, the craters on the moon's face. As we cross the Spree, boats slumber below us, moonlight reflecting on the water. Jeremy practically dances across the bridge, possessed by the moon and the quiet. I don't think he realizes how happy he is right now. I lean against the wall of the bridge and call out to him. "Jeremy, you're the coolest guy."

"Yeah, right." He turns around. "Really?"

"Look at your life. You dropped everything."

He walks over to me. "What do you mean?"

"You left New York."

"'Tis true."

"And you came here."

"Jeez, I know."

"Well, look at this place. We might as well be on Mars." I stare at the empty streets, the rows of giant trees, streetlamps rising like claws, every building distinct and incredible and of a different time. The Berliner Dom sits at the tip of Museum Island, its gigantic dome lit from below and flanked by four corner towers. Across the street, the Palast der Republik's massive block of dull copper reflects auburn against the sky. And then, above it all, the giant moon floats over the city, casting light on the colossal cranes that sleep above countless buildings, ensuring that Berlin will always be changing. This is what makes Berlin so remarkable—the past is everywhere, and history swirls through the air, but still, there's forward momentum, rebirth on every corner. It feels like the future. No spaces between words.

"You barely had any money. You didn't know the language. You didn't know anyone. Do you know how brave you are?"

"No," he says. "I don't."

"Well, you are. I grew up on East Seventy-Ninth Street and now I live on West Seventy-Sixth Street. I know it's New York, but it's still totally lame. Is it any different than growing up in Bumblefuck and just staying there?"

"Well, yeah, it is different. And besides, I had nothing to leave."

"Whatever." I start walking ahead, then turn back to him. "Jeremy, you're my hero."

The S-Bahn rumbles a few streets away, making that now-familiar slicing sound, knives being sharpened, as it curves past Friedrichstrasse. Jeremy catches up to me. "Now you've had too much beer."

"And whose fault is that? You *are* my hero. It's a compliment. Take it."

"That's like the nicest thing anyone's ever said to me."

"Well, it's true. I'm jealous of you. You came here and did this." I open my arms to all of Berlin, the stars, the sky.

"Yeah, well, I'm not sure what *this* is. And I've got to tell you, Sam, I'd like to fly around the world and stay in nice hotels just to look at art and stuff."

"I guess."

"And I know your relationship is complicated, but something is keeping you guys together. You have someone to go home to."

"I suppose the grass is always greener."

"It totally is. And as for you, Sam, I think you know what you want."

"Oh yeah, and what would that be?"

"I didn't say *I* know what you want. You need to go home and figure it out. And then do something. Come here, stay there, go somewhere else, whatever. I think you're just lost."

"Great. The lost and lonely American abroad. I guess that's me."

"Join the club."

And then an idea pops into my head. "Hey, how about one more beer?" I look at him, and beyond him, to the big white moon hovering over Berlin.

A Fool in Berlin

I pay the woman five euros. She's wearing black lipstick and cat ears on her head. Jeremy and I walk into the main room of the Duncker. The club is so tiny it could fit into the Limelight ten times over. Jeremy lights a cigarette. "What is this hippie music?"

"It's not hippie music. It's the Cocteau Twins!"

"Never heard of 'em."

"I thought you were a DJ."

"What's that supposed to mean?"

"You know—a music aficionado."

"We all have our preferred genres. Just because you specialize in art with recycled bra pads doesn't mean you have to know all about the Parthenon."

"Actually, it does. You need to know the history of things to understand what led to a point in time. And that goes for music, too."

Jeremy tosses his head back, pretending to be asleep. "You're a snob. Look, there are the classics like Afrika Bambaataa and Kraftwerk and Giorgio Moroder, and then there's this." He waves his hand in some mock-psychedelic dance move. "Which, let's face it, has not stood the test of time."

"What, because *you* don't know it?"

"Just saying."

"Who's the snob?"

Jeremy shrugs his shoulders, *whatever*. "I'm going to take a leak and get a beer."

"Fine," I shout over the music. "Just don't leave me here for long."

Famous last words. I stand in the corner as Siouxsie and the Banshees come on: "Cities in Dust." I watch the Prenzlauer hipsters, dressed in black, how they dance with their eyes closed. The air smells moist, thick with smoke and sweat. A man leans against the wall next to me, his shirt unbuttoned to the waist. He's got a beer in one hand and a cigarette in the other, the disco ball spinning behind him. A beer, a cigarette, and a disco ball—such symbols of this city, they should throw them on a flag or sculpt them atop the Brandenburg Gate. The lights flash like lightning and a wave of dry ice rolls across the floor.

I scan the club, searching for Jeremy. And then I look across the room and there he is, wiping the counter of the bar, oblivious to my presence: Kaspar. He's wearing a tight black T-shirt, his sinewy arms falling out of his sleeves like snakes. He's clean-shaven tonight, and so he looks like an angel, with those cheekbones visible all the way across the room. It's a shock to see him here, though not a surprise. *I'm a bartender*, he told me, *an old church on Dunckerstrasse*. It's why I'm here, of course.

Jeremy finally appears at the other side of the bar. Kaspar walks over to him. They talk for a moment. Kaspar hands him two beers, Jeremy leans in and gives him money, my money. What sort of dumb game am I playing? I picture myself just hours ago, sitting on Magda's stoop with Blitz on my lap and an old lady yelling at me. Is Jeremy the only person I've met in Berlin who I'm not currently stalking? Well, I couldn't get rid of him if I tried.

Jeremy returns, passes me the beer, and lights a cigarette. "Let me have one," I say. I'm almost done with this city; I may as well use it while I'm here. He sticks a Marlboro between my teeth and lights me up. The smoke fills my lungs, disgusting and great. "What took you so long?"

"It's a *story*," he says, a strange smile on his face. "I'll tell you later."

"Fine. Let's sit," I say, indicating the row of steps behind the dance floor. The beer buzz and the nicotine collide, and I nearly lose my balance, but I lead us to the fourth step, the top, so we have a view of the dance floor and the bar beyond it. The undulating bodies shield me from Kaspar's view, but I feel myself drift away, to some other place where we are next to each other; where I can gaze into his eyes and put my mouth close to his ear and then, maybe, begin to lick his neck. Why didn't I just do it when I had the chance? Why do I always have to be good? That's a complicated question, because here I am in another club, hypnotized by yet another disco ball. There's no halo over my head.

"Hey!" Jeremy taps my knee. "What are you looking at?" I say nothing. "Sam, what's going on." It's a statement, not a question.

"Nothing. Just watching everyone dance."

"It's sexy."

"Very," I say.

Depeche Mode's "Black Celebration" segues into some intense industrial music I don't recognize but Jeremy is clearly loving. A man speaks over a beat: *Your love is mine, tonight, it's fine, tonight, it's mine.* I continue to stare at Kaspar. The disco ball starts spinning in slow motion. I feel like I'm hallucinating, but I'm not on drugs. Jeremy sways back and forth, eyes closed. "Want to dance?" I ask him.

"Nah. I never dance," he says. "This is as far as I go."

"You're one of those disco voyeurs. The owl perched in a tree, watching everything."

Jeremy shrugs. I've got him pegged. Through the river of smoke, I see Kaspar lean over the counter, talking to a blond man. They smile and Kaspar touches his shoulder. Jealousy creeps over me. The man is beautiful and young, exactly the sort of person I imagine would be with Kaspar. But what right do I have to even a modicum of jealousy? I have an entire life in another city. I'm just drunk, a fool in Berlin. I turn to Jeremy. "Let's go. I'm tired."

"No way, sir. You lose dibs on tired at two a.m."

I look at my watch and groan. "Jesus." I start to get up, but Jeremy pulls me down again. "Come on, Sam. This is amazing." I watch him scan the dance floor, mesmerized by the sea of women lifting their arms like Greek goddesses on the side of an urn. Jeremy throws his arm around me. "Dude, I am so glad Aunt Debra introduced us!"

"Yeah." I peruse the bacchanal before us. "I bet she'd be thrilled."

"I shall distract you from your tiredness."

"Good luck with that." But it's Kaspar I need distraction from. Watching him with the blond man through the maze of heads, I feel lost. The doorwoman with the cat ears walks up to the bar. She kisses Kaspar and the blond man on both cheeks, takes the band off her head and places the cat ears on Kaspar.

Then the lights go black. Darkness. And the music stops. All I hear is the clanking of bottles and a few stray feet stomping on the floor. People begin to whisper, then whistle in anticipation. A synth squiggles and a few beats blast out of the speakers. This must be a signature moment when the night officially turns into after hours. Through the darkness, a white beam streams across the dance floor and hits the disco ball. Another blast of dry ice rises through the air. The ball turns, the crowd begins to chant. Something ominous, something German. The beat speeds up, gets slower again, before it rewinds itself, and then . . . silence. The lights fade into darkness, and all you hear is the hum of chanting and bottles rolling across the floor. It feels like anything could happen, the moment before a heart attack, the tide receding before a tsunami crashes to shore. Then the beat starts again. New Order. "Blue Monday." The crowd goes nuts. Jeremy leans into me. "This is old school!" he screams. "I'm in fucking heaven!"

"Wait. This you know?"

"It's the definition of four-on-the-floor."

We're the only people sitting on the stairs now; everyone is on the dance floor. Jeremy throws his fist in the air. "Bet you're not tired anymore!" he yells into my ear. "If I wrote this song, I could die happy. It's a masterpiece. Transcends pop, disco, wave, electronic, everything."

"Yeah, but it's not exactly goth."

"You crank. Since when are you such a purist? Berlin mashes it up!"

Jeremy leans into me and sings along, starts drumming the beat onto my shoulders. The club is wild, but it has the whiff of a deranged frat party, with some sloshed bro screaming lyrics into my ear. "How is everyone out so late on a weeknight?" I ask him. "Doesn't anyone have a job?"

"*Nein*," Jeremy yells. "Welcome to Berlin!"

I wonder how I can be so happy sitting next to Jeremy and yet also want him to disappear, or at least calm the fuck down. He's too much, even though part of me is envious of his unedited enthusiasm, his undeniable youth. Jeremy says he has nothing, that he's lonely and broke. But he's not trapped like me, suspended in the muck of soon-to-be middle age. I'm thirteen years older than him, but they may as well be dog years. He has possibility, and sometimes that's enough.

I stare at Kaspar through the smoke, wearing his cat ears, looking adorable. And I wonder why I can't say hello, why I'm keeping his presence a secret, why I'm unable to sustain a decent beer buzz without the floor falling out from under me. But Jeremy just smiles because he's in his element, drunk on beer at three in the morning, the pulse of a city orbiting around him, the night owl of Dunckerstrasse. And then he says, "Hey. What're you looking at?"

"Nothing."

"Are you having fun?"

"Of course I'm having fun."

But Jeremy follows my eyes across the dance floor. He's just put two and two together. "Sam, you are totally cruising the bartender!" He looks at me, jaw agape.

"I am not!" I yell, a bit defensively. "And how do you know a word like 'cruising'?"

"Hey, buddy, I spent four years in New York." He looks at Kaspar. "I get it. The dude is hot. Now *he's* your type."

"Don't be ridiculous."

"I'd like a prop-ah sandwich," he says. "And that fine piece of Deutsch-ass."

"Shut up, Jeremy. Don't pretend you know me."

"Oh, I know you." He points his bottle toward Kaspar. "And that," he says, "is your type."

"Well, just so you know, cruising requires the other party to return your gaze." I guzzle my beer. "And that is not happening."

"Perhaps that's because you're being all *lame* and *hiding*."

You don't even know, I think to myself.

"So," he says, "why don't you go buy us beers? Strike up a conversation like normal people do."

"No, thanks."

Jeremy looks toward the bar. Kaspar's arms are spread across the counter. He's deep in conversation with the blond man. "Sam, you better nab the bartender before blondie closes the sale. I'll guard the steps. Go on." He shoos me away. "Skedaddle."

"I have a boyfriend, Jeremy."

"Oh, dude, please."

"What is it with this city. Does the phrase 'I'm in a relationship' mean nothing here?"

"It's got nothing to do with Berlin. My parents spent twenty years screwing other people. They don't know that I know, but I know."

"Your family sounds fucked up."

"They did not set a good example. But still, I'm a romantic. Jaded perhaps, but undeterred." He stands up on the steps, looks out at the dance floor and opens his arms. "*Fräuleins* of Berlin, sweep me off my feet. I'm ready!" He looks like a Gorilla about to beat its chest and run through the jungle to find a mate.

I grab his leg, afraid of his spectacle. "Sit down, Jeremy! You're drunk."

Jeremy slides down to me. "Like anyone can hear me. Anyway, I'm not necessarily suggesting you *do* anything with the dude. But you can still flirt, right?" We look toward the bar, at Kaspar and his cat ears. Jeremy leans into me and meows. "Go on, Sam. Go get your kitty."

Kaspar glances in our direction and just maybe catches my eye. He looks confused. Then, a moment later, he smiles at me. My heart explodes. I turn to Jeremy, who, thank God, is looking in the other direction. I grab his sleeve. "Come on, let's get out of here."

"Really?"

"Yes, really." I pull Jeremy up by the wrist, and as we leave the club, I invite him to spend the night at the hotel. "But this time you're really sleeping on the couch."

We walk down Dunckerstrasse, looking for a cab. "The most amazing thing happened at the club," Jeremy says.

"Oh, right—when you deserted me." I'm relieved to be on the street, away from Kaspar, talking about something else. "So what's the story?"

"This kid from Frankfurt came over to me on my way to the bathroom. His English was lousy. He was like "You from New York, yes?" So, of course I told him yes. Then we go out into the yard for a smoke, and he tells me that he was at NYU for a semester a few years ago, when I threw my parties. And he came to the club—my club. Like, all the time!"

"Did you recognize him?"

"Nah. Back then I had to work the room, say hi to everyone. That was half my job. But talking to him now, it was like I was famous. Because Sam, when I threw those parties, I was the shit. We only had two hundred peeps a night, and it was a tight space, but it was something." He stares at the sky, dotted with stars, and sighs. "I didn't know what was next, but I did not care. Do you ever look back, and you're like . . . *that was a moment*?"

"Yes. And trust me, the older you get, the more your life becomes a series of moments." The streets are empty, and there are no taxis in sight. "Moments that have passed."

"That's morbid, dude."

"Well, it's the truth."

"But look at us. Aren't we having a moment right now, walking down Dunkerstrasse after an epic night, having shit luck trying to find a cab?"

"Time will tell." Although I have a hunch he's right.

"Anyway, this dude wanted to introduce me to his friends, but they were inside dancing. So we smoked our cigs in the yard and I told him I lived here now, and he was like, of course you do, Berlin is where it's happening. He said, 'Hey, Jerry'—because he could not get my name right—he was like 'Hey, Jerry, you make party here in Berlin?' And I was like, no, I don't do that anymore. And he said, 'Man, you should make party here, you must do it.' So I said, well, we'll see. Of course, I neglected to tell him that right after he went back to Germany we got kicked out of the fucking space. He was basically dancing at my funeral. But then he says, 'For me, this was New York—dancing at your party.'"

"That's incredible."

"Right? It was profound. But look at me now. Was that my peak?"

"Oh, Jeremy. You're still a puppy. Just be glad you gave that to someone."

As we stand on the corner, still looking for a taxi, a boy with spiky black hair walks up to us with a few friends. "Oh my God," Jeremy whispers. "This is him."

"*Ya-ree!*" the boy yells. He's a little drunk, or high, or both, and throws his arm around Jeremy. "This is New York!" he yells to his friends. The boy looks at Jeremy intensely in the eyes. "I miss it, these nights. I keep looking but I never find a night that is so good." He shakes his head, then makes a strange little bow to us, almost a curtsy. "Jerry," he says, again pronouncing Jeremy's name *Yar-ee*. "Thank you for making it for me."

"You're very welcome."

"The best music. The people. The feeling of a new city." The boy places his hand on Jeremy's shoulder. "I make envy on your disco." He kisses Jeremy on the cheek, then runs to catch up with his friends.

"Wow," Jeremy says, looking at me. "What was that?"

"You know what? I don't really know."

Hello, New York

The next day Jeremy and I walk down the stairs of the Hackescher Markt S-Bahn station. Two Heidi lookalikes with pigtails stand on either side of the entrance with baskets full of pretzels. I buy a pretzel and rip off a piece for Jeremy. He looks ridiculous, sporting a pair of giant red plastic sunglasses I bought for him at the flea market along the Spree for three euros. The glasses engulf half his face. On the train today he decided to teach me to count from one to ten—*eins, zwei, drei,* all the way to *zehn.* He's been drilling me all day. I keep stumbling on *sieben,* which is seven, and pronounced *zee-bin.*

Jeremy accompanied me to four galleries. My favorite, by far, was the exhibit in Wedding that Greta Hoss recommended. It featured the work of Manfred Butzmann, an East German artist who used rubbing techniques to capture the texture of floors and entryways after the Wall fell. He knew that many of these structures would disappear, or be destroyed, and so he preserved their histories by laying sheets of paper on the floor and rubbing over the uneven surface with pencil or coal, transforming a rectangular slab of floor into both a historical document and a work of art—the past etched on paper. He captured the hallways of apartment houses, hospitals, restaurants, discos, hotels.

I found the rubbings, framed and hung along the gallery's five walls, to be incredibly beautiful, oftentimes exposing the grain of wood accentuated by years of scrubbing, or the vein of a leaf, or the legacies of countless shoe soles walking across tile. The rubbings yielded unlikely patterns—a gash in the floor, a coin in a corner and a discarded paperclip would come together to suggest another object entirely. In one case, an oddly cracked tile suggested the image of a bird, which reminded me of Warhol, and the profile of a face, in which I saw Kaspar. An incessantly swinging door, which for decades rasped the floor of a busy café and left scratches along its path, immortalized its track with something resembling a comet's tail. Jeremy's favorite was a rubbing taken from a library; its wooden floors, scratches and shoe prints conjured a cityscape with buildings, clouds and sun. Butzmann's work is pure and effortless and, to me, profound—the past recorded and transformed, a moment preserved but inverted. And it captures Berlin, or my experience of it—everything becomes something else.

I'll have to ask Klaus about Butzmann when I see him at the opening; it seems like work he would appreciate, but who knows. As it turns out, Butzmann is alive and still making art. I left my number with the gallery in hopes that I can arrange a meeting before I head back to New York, and I'll let Greta know that her recommendation was spot-on, and thank her for it.

As we continue down the street I spot a few student-types in orange jackets carrying clipboards. I thought I was safe from this phenomenon in this city, but here they are, young people trying to get me to save the world. I try to walk past them, but one of the girls runs over to us. She speaks to me in English. "Hey, mister, it would be awesome if you could help us save the planet."

"I bet it would." I hate when people call me mister. Still, I take the clipboard and sign the petition.

"So what are we doing tonight?" Jeremy asks, impenetrable in his sunglasses. "There's a secret rave in Gorlitzer Park."

"Didn't raves die in 1996?"

"Not in Berlin."

"And how is it a secret if you know about it?"

"I'm on a list," he says. "Come on, it'll be an amazing event."

"Tonight, I'd like to be in my room before midnight, put on my eye mask and ear plugs and have an amazing event for one. I call it sleep."

"Whatever," he says, giving up. Jeremy signs the girl's petition and we move on.

Maybe my mother is right—I have been romanticizing Berlin. On the S-Bahn today, we suffered through a woman playing "Edelweiss" on an out-of-tune accordion while a few hours later, a shaggy mutt sprayed urine on the door of the S6, just missing my coat. Back in art school, a professor told me that you don't see flaws until you're ready to engage with the world around you. Nothing is perfect, he said, and beauty can delay this realization. I spent fifteen years riding the subway before I noticed my first rat. Now I see them all the time.

Jeremy and I head down Rosenthaler Strasse. There's a bookshop on Auguststrasse, and I need to buy something for Daniel. You know a trip is winding down when your mind turns toward the procurement of gifts for people back home. My mother is easy. I buy her a jar of jam and she acts like I've handed her a block of gold. But Daniel is another story. There's this book on German ceramics I've been eyeing in the store window for days. It must weigh approximately nineteen tons, but whatever, it's substantial, and I need to bring something home for him. I don't care if the book is in German. If Daniel can say *I love dick*, he'll manage.

I look at Jeremy and start counting to ten, adding a finger with each number that escapes my mouth. "*Eins, zwei, drei, vier, fünf, sechs, zwiebel . . .*"

"Dude, why do you want to turn 'seven' into a vegetable? It's *Sieben. Zwiebel* is *onion*. Got it?"

"*Sieben,*" I repeat, then continue. "*Acht, neun, zehn.*" I nod my head, enormously proud of myself.

"That's damn good. I'm going to celebrate with a smoke." He stops on a corner, removes his sunglasses, and lights a cigarette in the graffiti-covered alcove of an apartment house. As I wait, a man in a pale blue suit crosses the street dragging a silver case on wheels. Everything about him looks un-Berlin. He's groomed and vaguely familiar, and as he gets closer, he looks at me and slaps his knee. "Well, I'll be," the man says with a Southern drawl. "It really is you!"

"David?" I shake my head. "No way."

"My gosh, Sam Singer. In Berlin!" David kisses me on both cheeks. "Gotta be European, right?" He smells like hotel soap and cigarettes. Jeremy stands next to me, instantly perplexed.

I perform introductions. "David Monroe, this is Jeremy Green." They shake hands.

David looks Jeremy up and down, then plants his eyes on me: "So, doing the art thing?"

"Trying," I say. "How funny to see you."

"Everyone from New York is here. I already saw Melinda from *Art Forum* and what's-his-name from the Guggenheim. Even the Met has three curators scouring the *strasses* for hip new things. Three!"

"Yep, I know."

He pokes me and puts his hand on his hip. "And I don't know about you, but I've gotten into all sorts of trouble. So, Sam, where'ya staying?"

"Around here, actually."

"Really? I'm in Kreuzberg at that new art hotel."

"Which one?" Jeremy says.

"Yeah, right. All the rooms have a theme. Mine is a girl-on-a-swing-Fragonard thing. Just my luck. I'd be better off with some Bauhaus vibe or a room full of rubber, but I suppose you get what you get."

I'm relieved he's staying on the other side of the Spree. It took this encounter to fully appreciate my anonymity in Berlin. It's been miraculous, like a form of currency, a gift.

"Apparently Kreuzberg is *the* place," David continues. "Have you been there yet?"

"Indeed I have."

"Good. They say Mitte is over."

"Who's they?" I ask.

"Oh, I don't know." He tosses his hand in the air. "Everyone."

I look around. Kids going home from school, Berliners smoking in cafés, trams twisting down the street. I find myself feeling defensive about my *Kiez.*

"So how do you guys know each other?" Jeremy asks.

"David is a collector," I say.

"That's Sam's code for *socialite*. But it's true, I do collect. And I've known this one forever," David says, pointing to me. "Sam has a nice career going, no doubt. But once upon a time he was a rising star, an artist to watch."

"Huh." Jeremy looks at me strangely. "I did not know that." A tram twists past us as the light switches green.

"Yup," David says. "I actually own one of his prints."

"Yes, well, that was a long time ago," I say.

David folds his arms. "You were good, Sam. Still painting?"

"Nope."

"That's a pity. Say, come have a drink at my hotel. Half of New York is there, you'd feel right at home."

"That could be fun," I lie. I've never understood the appeal of the Hamptons or Fire Island. I like to flee New York, not follow it to the beach. My idea of a vacation is a hut in the woods and shades that pull down.

"Oh, come on, it'll be fabulous," David says. "So, Daniel let you come to Berlin all by yourself?"

"You know . . . he has work."

"Right, all those macho buildings to design. Anyway, seems like you found a friend." David appraises Jeremy once again. "And where do you come from?"

"Albany."

"Well, does it get more glamorous?"

I'm appalled by David's rudeness, but Jeremy can take care of himself. "I'm *from* Albany," Jeremy clarifies. "But I moved to Brooklyn five years ago and I live here now, in Berlin."

"We are where we're from, that's what I always say." David waves his hand in my direction. "Now *this* is the rarest of species, born and raised on the isle of Manhattan. You'd think Sam would be wild, but he's positively tame. Me, I'm from Texas, but I've lost my accent. You probably can't tell."

"Oh, I can tell," Jeremy says.

"Now your Daniel, didn't he grow up on a farm?"

"Milwaukee is not a farm," I say.

"Same difference. That boy might as well have hay coming out of his pretty white ears, he's so corn-fed." David turns to Jeremy. "Have you met him?"

"Daniel? No."

"Sex on a stick."

"What a lovely compliment," I say. "And how's David?"

"Wait," Jeremy says, "I thought *you* were David."

"I am," he says. "My man back home is also David. I'm David Monroe. He's David Koplovitz. We met at the Gay David Party."

"Of course," says Jeremy.

"Trust me, there are *lots* of us. Anyhoo, my David is fine, doing his real estate thing. The market is so good right now, I want to just buy things, but David thinks it's all gonna pop. I tell him, Dave, just shut up and enjoy it. Anyway, I hope he's wrong, because if it does pop, you and me, Sam, we're fuuuucked. Besides, David and I may have a child, so we need some . . . funds."

"You?" I say, more incredulously than I intend. "You. And David? A child?"

"Well, don't act all surprised, Sam."

"I don't mean to be rude, I just didn't see that coming."

"We are indeed exploring. Just call me Daddy Monroe!"

I feel something, almost a pang of jealousy. He lights a cigarette, some Capri-type thing. "Hey Sam, don't tell Dave. You gotta cheat when you're in Berlin, right? Life is a cabaret . . ."

"Don't worry about it," I tell him.

Jeremy looks like he's about to walk away, or run, but David turns his sights on him. "My David is a nice Jewish boy from the Bronx," he explains. "Jewish boys are so calm and sturdy. Who knew? Sure ain't what Mama Monroe raised me to believe." He points at Jeremy. "You should get one!"

"Oh, trust me, I will!" Jeremy says.

David turns to me. "You're Jewish, aren't you, Sam?"

"Yep."

"Thought so. Is it spooky, being in Deutschland?"

"That's a complicated question," I reply. It really is complicated, because for the most part, my Jewishness has receded into the background of my consciousness, neither here nor there. I didn't expect that—not in Berlin.

"Well, with those blue eyes and that nose, you blend right in."

"Wow," Jeremy says, coughing. I feel the blood rush out of my face.

"Hmmmm?" David replies, giving Jeremy the once over again. "But you, young man, with all that red hair and scruff, you look positively *Fiddler on the Roof.*"

"I'm Irish," Jeremy says. "And Catholic."

"You lie like a rug!"

"Anyway," I interrupt, "I like Berlin a lot."

"Me too," David says. "Great city. They should do something about the rain, though, and all that graffiti."

"So, where are you headed?" I ask, trying to be polite, desperate to detach.

"To the galleries on Auguststrasse."

"We're headed that way, too," I tell him. "We'll walk you a few blocks." I glance over at Jeremy, who rolls his eyes. I shrug my shoulders to say, *What do you expect me to do?*

We head down Rosenthaler Strasse, David's tiny suitcase thumping behind us. "All my files are in my attaché," he explains. "I'm just an old-fashioned girl in an old-fashioned world." He puffs his cigarette and makes a pout. "Gentlemen, where is everyone? It's like a goddamned ghost town." We pass the two-story Starbucks, encased in glass and metal. A chalkboard outside advertises an open-mic night for poets, philosophers and singers.

"I like all the space," I say. "You can breathe."

"So go to Wyoming and buy some cows. In a city I need to be surrounded by people, and lots of 'em. Going places, doing things."

"Yes, well." I look at Jeremy, sensing his impatience. I've tolerated David Monroe at parties and openings, but that's when he's surrounded by other people. I wonder if he's going to Klaus's opening tomorrow night. I wonder, but I'm not going to ask.

"And what's with all the candles in the cafés?" David asks. "*Très atmospherique*, I'll give you that, but can't someone in Berlin buy a lamp?" He takes a drag from his cigarette and looks at it, sighs. Then his phone vibrates loudly in his pocket. "I should take this," David says, patting his pants. "It's New York in my pocket. Y'all okay with that?"

"Of course!" Jeremy and I say in unison.

"Well, Sam and—I'm sorry. I don't remember your name . . ."

"Joachim."

"Hmmm, right, Joachim. Good to see you both. Happy hunting." David kisses my cheek and wiggles his fingers in the air. "Toodles." He walks away, picks up the phone, and says, "Well, hello, New York!"

We watch him cross the street. I turn to Jeremy. "Joachim?" Jeremy points to the street sign on the corner: *Joachimstrasse*. "You're terrible," I say.

"Forget my name twice in three minutes and I reserve the right to invent one. That guy was a douche."

"Oh, he's harmless. But sorry."

The *Ampelmann* traffic light shifts from red to green, and we head to the bookstore. "Just please tell me that dude is not your friend."

"The art world is surprisingly small, so I try to be nice. Why, did I seem like a jerk?"

"No, you held it together pretty well while he was being all racist and drooling over your boyfriend."

"Good. By the way, David Monroe totally knows your aunt."

"Of course he does," Jeremy sighs. "And by the way, I dig Mitte."

"Are you kidding? It's amazing," I say. "It's such a New York thing to be judgmental about everything. And passing judgment on neighborhoods is the specialty of the house."

"Actually, Berliners are just as bad. 'Hood snobbery is a modern urban epidemic." I spot the bookstore across the street. Jeremy follows behind. "So your Daniel is a pretty little thing?"

"He's not so little," I say. "He's a good-looking guy."

"With a wandering eye?"

"Whose eye doesn't wander?"

"I don't know. If I was with some perfect little *Fraülein*, I'd be content."

"Here we go again . . ."

"Well, it's true. I really don't think I'd look at another girl."

We reach the shop. I look at the book I plan to buy for Daniel sitting in the window; seventy-six euros and big as a boat. I open the door, setting off a round of chimes. The shopkeeper nods hello. I hold the door open for Jeremy. "All I know is you have your own distractions here in Berlin," he says. "If only David Monroe knew about your German boy toy."

"Oh, stop."

"And by the way, is there something you want to tell me?"

"No," I answer, stumped. "Why?"

"The bartender last night?"

"Yeah. What are you talking about?"

"If you think I don't realize who he was, you're a moron." Jeremy flashes his eyes at me. I'm still holding the door open, my mouth agape. He walks past me into the store and says "Kaspar." So quick, it's like a sneeze.

I can't believe it. I follow him inside and sigh. "What gave me away?"

"Sam, you took us to a goth club in the wee hours of the morning. It was a little random." I bring my finger to my lips to shush him. I look at the shopkeeper assisting a man with books on Norwegian lamps, but Jeremy goes on. "And when I bought the beer from him, I thought he looked strangely familiar. Then I saw you looking at him, and it clicked."

"Strangely familiar?"

"He had that hoop in his 'brow."

"So, I don't get it."

"The photos on your dresser . . ."

I snap at him. "You were snooping in my hotel room?"

"Um, no, sir. That photo strip was on fucking display. Propped up below the mirror. Right next to a picture of you and Daniel."

"The maid did that," I say.

He raises his eyebrows and clucks his tongue as if to say, *gotcha!*

I groan. I can't believe my stupidity. The shopkeeper crosses his arms and looks us over. I pick up a book on the history of gnomes and stare at the back cover. Daniel loves gnomes, so maybe I'll get this, too. I whisper to Jeremy, "Why didn't you say anything at the club?"

"I didn't want to embarrass you. You should have seen the slobbery look on your face. Only love can do that."

"That's not love," I sigh. "But you're right. I'm a moron."

"So what was up with you ditching him last night?"

"Kaspar? I didn't ditch him. Okay, maybe I went there to see him, but not to, like, *see* him."

"But he saw you, right? And you bolted. What if he thought I was your new boyfriend?"

"Oh, come on, Jeremy." Although the thought never occurred to me.

"It was kind of a dick move, Sam. That's all I'm saying. You may have hurt the dude's feelings. Even hot people have a heart."

"Can we change the subject?" I look at my watch. "I should get back to the hotel."

"You got work to do in the room?"

"Of course not. I need to watch a soap opera." I watched the repeat of Sabine's show earlier today. In the cliffhanger, Anna was in a car wreck on the outskirts of Berlin. In the preview for today's episode, it looks like Sebastian, having left the monastery in the Black Forest, makes his way back to the city only to find Anna clutching her stomach by the side of the road. "Hopefully," I say, "the baby will be okay."

"So, I have no idea what you're talking about. But can I come watch with you?"

"As if I thought you were ever going home?" The shopkeeper stares at me from behind the counter. I put the gnome book down and turn to Jeremy. "I need you to ask for the book on the history of German ceramics. It's in the window."

"That sounds awful," says Jeremy.

"Yeah, well, I'm going to buy it."

We head back to the hotel. The goliath of a book is now wrapped in stiff brown paper. Jeremy and I take turns carrying it down the street. "Can I take another bath?" Jeremy asks me.

"I don't know. The room will have just been cleaned, and I want it to stay that way." The streetlights switch on. It's windy again, and a paper bag flies past us. "And what if I want to take a bath? I like a fresh tub."

"You're so asstight," Jeremy says. "You must get comfortable with a little mess, my friend."

"Thanks, Yoda." I take the book from Jeremy.

He lights a cigarette and rubs his lower back. "I think I just sprained my sphincter carrying that terrible book for you."

"Hey, stop."

"What? Too much ass talk?"

"No. I mean yes, actually, but listen—you can't smoke in front of me anymore."

"What? Why not? Want one?"

"Yes, Jeremy, of course I want one. As soon as I smoked that first cigarette that *you* gave me, my body remembered everything. All that nicotine from my youth. It was like my cells said, Wow, maybe it's not over after all, we're still starving, we'd almost forgotten, yay. And then they said, We will get this pushover to smoke and won't let him think about anything else. I went into withdrawal from one lousy cigarette."

"Jeez, really?" Jeremy looks at his cigarette. "Sorry."

"And you shouldn't smoke either."

"I know."

"Whatever. Give me that thing." I take a puff from the cigarette. "Oh, I'm so bad." I look around, feeling guilty, as if I'll be thrown in jail by the *Polizei*. I guess that's part of the thrill.

"It's okay to be a little bad," Jeremy says.

"Yeah?" I breathe deeply as I contemplate this trip, a veritable parade of badness. "Hope you're right."

Jeremy watches me and crosses his arms. "Did you smoke a lot of pot back in the day?"

"Why?"

"Because you smoke your cigarette like a joint."

"Really?" I release the smoke from my lungs. "Well, yes, I guess I did."

"You were such a bad boy, Sam Singer. I wish I knew you back then."

"No you don't. I was a mess."

"Exactly."

As we near the hotel, we each take one last drag before Jeremy crushes the cigarette with his foot. "That'll really be the last one," I tell Jeremy, grabbing him by the shoulders. "Promise you'll help." He nods in agreement. "I cannot go back to Daniel reeking of cigarettes." I look through the window into the lobby. A black-haired woman with a Louise Brooks haircut sits at the front desk, a new person I don't recognize. "Where the heck is Madga?"

"You still haven't seen her?"

"No. And it's starting to bother me."

"What's it been? Two days?"

"Yes. Frankie says she's fine, but still. . . ."

We stare through the window at Fräulein Brooks, who is filing her nails. "She's pretty," Jeremy says. "But she's no Magda."

"Nope."

"You care about her, you know."

"Magda?" I still haven't told Jeremy that I spent yesterday afternoon camped outside her building, Blitz curled up in my lap. "I've only known her for a week."

"So what? You've known me for even less than that."

"It's different."

"No, it's not."

"Well, whatever, hopefully I'll find her before I leave."

"What? We have to find her! By the way, when are you leaving?"

"I don't want to talk about it." I stare at the yellow tram sleeping outside of the hotel, a conductor leaning against it, having a smoke. "I'm leaving the day after the opening . . . *Übermorgen*." I smile, pleased that I've managed to pick up something in German. But Jeremy doesn't respond. Instead, he walks to the corner and leans against a lamppost. It switches on, like magic. "Hey!" I call out to him. "Where are you going?"

He yells back at me. "What am I going to do?"

"You're going to come upstairs with me."

"No! I mean, what am I going to do without you here?"

"Oh, Jeremy . . . you'll be fine."

"Says you." He tucks his hands in his pockets, his back to me. "Everyone leaves. It sucks."

"You're the one who moved to Berlin."

Jeremy glares at me. I put the book down on the street and leave it there; it would take a sumo wrestler to haul it away. I walk over to him. "You can send me emails."

"You don't check your emails."

I crouch over, rubbing my neck. I think I twisted my entire body carrying that damn book. Daniel better love it. "We can talk on the phone."

"You hate talking on the phone."

"That's because I'm in Berlin, Jeremy. In New York, I'm tethered to the world every minute of the day. Trust me, I'm in a deeply committed and highly dysfunctional relationship with my BlackBerry. It's even come up in couples therapy." It's so cold that I see my breath in the air. "Come on! Let's go inside." I get behind him and push against his back as a joke, but it's like trying to push a tank. Jeremy throws the hood of his sweatshirt over his head. I grab his arm but he won't budge. "Oh, don't be a baby."

"Shut the fuck up," he says. "I'm not a baby."

"Great, then let's go." I take his arm again, and we walk back toward the hotel. I nod at the tram driver, who's been watching our lovers' spat. The driver crushes his cigarette with his foot. He picks up the stub and places it in a tissue, which he then puts in his pocket.

Jeremy collects the book from the street and I open the door for him. He leans into me as he walks inside. "So, you and D. are in couples therapy?"

"You know, on and off. We're never in the same place at the same time. And I don't just mean that geographically."

We walk through the lobby. The bar once again sits empty but has now been decorated for the approaching weekend: dozens of candles are lit throughout, Europop is drifting from the speakers, arrangements of autumn flowers have been placed on tabletops. It's such a strange ritual, this happy hour for no one. I nod to Louise Brooks at reception and show her my keys. She smiles flatly. She couldn't care less.

In the elevator, I ask Jeremy what he's doing for Thanksgiving.

"Nothing." He rests his head against the mirrored wall. I look up at the ceiling and see his reflection multiplied in distorted slivers, trapped in a block of ice.

"So you're not going home?" I ask him. "Your family's not coming to Berlin?"

"*Nein* and *nein*. And I don't feel like talking about it."

The elevator door opens and we walk to my room. I sigh. "The next thing you know it will be Christmas."

"And then," he says, "it'll be next year."

Reunification

We sit cross-legged on the couch, drinking Beck's from the minibar, watching *Ost und West* on TV. After a beer, Jeremy's mood softens, thank God. Maybe he's just one of those people who gets cranky when they forget to eat lunch, except in his case, lunch is beer. Whatever the case, I'm happy to be sitting next to him, riveted by the TV show and Sabine's transformation. The episode is almost exclusively about her character. I barely know the show, but you can tell that this particular episode is an event, bringing plotlines to a head, and that it will climax with a cliffhanger. It's different watching *Ost und West* with Jeremy sitting next to me, explaining what's actually being said; the way he whispers his translation into my ear while the action unfolds, as if we're watching a play at the theater and he has to talk in hushed tones.

Anna and her baby have survived the crash. Jeremy tells me that the doctor has scheduled a C-section because of trauma sustained in the accident. Before the wreck, Sebastian had a premonition, and so he walks all the way to Berlin. He goes first to Anna's apartment, then straight to the hospital and finds her there. Once they're together, the doctor informs them that it's going to be a boy. Sebastian climbs into bed with Anna. *I did not know that I missed you*, she tells him. *I was too busy hating you for abandoning me. Everyone leaves.*

Jeremy turns to me, silent. We watch a commercial for wasabi-flavored Kit Kats.

Ost und West returns. Anna lies in her hospital bed, delirious from drugs. She clutches Sebastian's hand and closes her eyes. In a flashback, we see Anna as a girl in East Berlin, saying goodbye to her father, Wolfgang, before he leaves the family, jumps into the river, and escapes the GDR. He tells Anna, *You may not see me for a long time, and perhaps you will be angry. But I promise we will be together. You will one day have a life you dare not dream possible. That is why I am going, my dear Anna. Do not hate me for abandoning you. I must do what is right.*

Wolfgang says goodbye to his wife and Anna's brother, but little Anna refuses her father's kiss. As he leaves the apartment, we see a tear fall down his cheek. It will take three years, many secret phone calls, and one botched escape before the father manages to move Anna's family to West Berlin. But the Stasi has been eavesdropping on Wolfgang's calls, and one of Anna's neighbors has been acting as a spy. A few days after the family's reunion, her father disappears, never to be seen again.

Anna flourishes in the West. She puts herself through journalism school by modeling on the side. She eventually becomes the editor-in-chief of *Die Berliner Presse*. Under her leadership the newspaper wins prizes for its coverage of the fall of the Wall and reunification. But Anna is haunted by memories. She sits in her flat—a sea of cranes necking like dinosaurs in a transforming no-man's-land right outside her window—and dreams of her childhood, of the dark apartment in the East, of her cruelty to her father. She can barely summon his face, but she remembers turning her back on him and refusing his kiss.

Anna goes back to school, studies architecture, and becomes a star at her firm. She relocates to Mitte and settles in an enormous loft. It is there that she meets Sebastian, a hatmaker with a store down the street.

It's good to have Jeremy translate for me. He fills in so many blanks. I did not realize, for instance, that Anna planned to give her baby to her best friend, who is newly married but barren. But since the near loss of her baby and her reunion with Sebastian, she's had a change of heart. She looks at her tummy and tells the baby, *I will raise you. I will name you Wolf, after my father. And you will live a life you dare not dream possible. I will never refuse your kiss.* And that's the end of the episode. Jeremy and I look at each other, emotionally exhausted. "That was awesome," he says. "I'm hooked."

Something to keep you company when I'm gone, I think to myself.

I decide to let Jeremy have his bath. He disappears; a moment later I hear water rushing into the tub.

The suit I'll wear to the opening is hanging in the closet and I wonder if I'll need to iron it. God forbid I should have to go downstairs and ask Louise Brooks for help. I run my hands across the pants. Thankfully, all looks wrinkle free. I haven't worn this suit since last winter. I put my hands inside the pockets of my jacket and pull out a taxi receipt and a note from Daniel: *Fed Harry. Walked him at 7:30, pee no poop. I'm sorry. I tried. I'm really trying, Sam. Don't forget I love you.*

My heart drops. This note needs no translation.

I examine the three remaining shirts Daniel assembled for me back in New York, stacked on the closet shelf. I'd have better luck solving a Rubik's Cube than properly folding a dress shirt. I find Daniel's willingness to fold my clothes deeply moving, even when things feel wrong between us. He knows how to do so many things, and he does most of them perfectly, and always with a smile. No wonder people trust him with their offices and homes.

I select the gray-and-pink shirt he gave me for Christmas last year and set it on the dresser. Daniel told me to wear it to the opening, and so I will. I look in the mirror. I haven't shaved in a few days and my hair is a bit too long. I keep my hair short so people won't notice it's not as thick as it once was. I squirt Rogaine onto the crown of my head like it's whipped cream and I'm an ice cream sundae. I hate getting older with a fury that's surprised me. I find myself staring at young people on the subway, jealous of everything about them. It's hard to know what you can get away with, what haircut, which sneakers, what jeans you can wear without looking like a dumbass. I don't feel wiser. I just feel thicker, more tired, and hairier in places other than my head. No one prepares you for thirty-seven. It's a bum deal so far, the mucky in-betweenness of everything. Time and genetics, they catch up with you. I could swim a thousand laps a day and never have the body I once had, or that Daniel still has now. My neurotic loop is interrupted as Jeremy calls out from the tub, "Hey, what are you doing?"

"Nothing," I say. "Looking in the mirror."

"You are a class A narcissist."

"Hardly."

"Come talk to me. It's safe. I've built a fortress of bubbles."

I walk into the bathroom. Jeremy's body is surrounded by ten inches of suds. There are bottles of soaps and gels lining the side of the tub, and a near-empty glass of beer. "It smells like Crabtree & Evelyn threw up in here."

"I gotta make this last bath count."

I walk over to the mirror above the sink and look into my eyes. I take the skin below my left eye and push it down with my finger, I release it, then do the same thing with the right. I look at Jeremy. "Do you think this eye is droopy?"

"Not at all," he says. "Especially not when you push it down with your finger."

I let go of the skin, run the faucet, and prepare to shave. "George Clooney had his eyes done. He told Oprah it's the one thing he needed to change. And if George Clooney had his eyes done, maybe I should, too."

"Kaspar the goth boy didn't think you look so bad."

I put shaving cream on my cheeks, giving myself a foamy beard. "What if Kaspar saw me as a father figure?"

"Oh, shut up."

"Or a big brother type."

"Face it, Sam, he thought you were hot. Why spend hours staring in the mirror and picking yourself apart? I have limited sympathy for such indulgences." He says this playfully, but I sense impatience in his voice.

"Just wait until it happens to you." I start shaving, steam rolling upward.

"Maybe you haven't noticed, but I already have a bit of a belly." He cups his stomach beneath the bubbles. I say nothing, though the truth is, I have noticed his paunch. But it's Jeremy. He's just a big straight guy, and on him, it seems right. Besides, what does he expect? He's practically a one-man brewery. "So you do think I have a belly."

"I think you look great."

"Oh, fuck, thanks a lot." He splashes me with water.

"It's just . . . I feel like I'm either eighteen years old, or a hundred and two. I never feel like I'm thirty-seven."

"Maybe that's what thirty-seven feels like."

"No one ever says, I feel like I'm thirty-seven."

"No they don't," Jeremy sighs. "So, can you bring me another beer?"

"And Kaspar is not a goth boy," I say to him. "He's a bartender at a goth club. It's not the same thing."

"The dude wears black nail polish, Sam. Get over yourself."

I return to the mirror. "And I have hair in my ears."

Jeremy rolls his eyes. "So shave it off."

"You don't understand."

"What's to understand? You're being a girl."

"I'm the girl? You cried the last time you had sex!"

Jeremy drops his hand into the water. "So what? It was *emotional*. I can't believe you're throwing that back in my face, Sam. So high school. Not cool." He slips under the bubbles, dunks himself, and reemerges. "Now be off with you. I have to get out of the tub."

I shrug and walk back into the room. The phone rings. My heart races. It could be Daniel, the Zukunftsgalerie, my nagging mother; it could even be David Monroe. "Well," Jeremy says, "are you gonna get that?" Jeremy emerges from the bathroom in a white robe that's at least three sizes too small, his orange hair plastered dark and wet against his cheeks like paint. I sit on the edge of the bed, frozen. "Fine, I'll get it," Jeremy says, picking up the receiver before I can stop him. "*Hallo*? Sam Singer's *Zimmer*." I flash my eyes at him, scared and embarrassed. Jeremy's eyes widen as he listens to the other line. "*Ja, hallo! Es ist* Jeremy. *Alles gut. Ja*, Sam *ist hier*." He laughs, nearly giggles. "*Natürlich!*"

Who is it? I mouth to Jeremy.

Jeremy holds up a finger, keeps talking. "Okay, Magda, *hier ist* Sam." He mouths *Magda*, and I grab the phone from him.

"Magda!" I yell into the receiver. "Where are you?"

"Downstairs," she says.

"What do you mean, downstairs."

"I mean, downstairs. You have a package."

I begin pacing the room. My hands are shaking like I've downed three espressos and a line of coke. "Where have you been?"

"Samuel, would you like your package? Shall I send Astrid up to the room, or are you busy with your friend?"

"Can I come down and see you?"

"I am working, Samuel."

"I was worried about you." I stare at Jeremy sitting in his robe in the desk chair, looking ridiculous. "You disappeared."

"This is absurd."

"I'm coming downstairs."

"Do not. I send Astrid."

"I'll come down and get the package." Before Magda can respond, I hang up the phone, rather violently. I slip on my shoes, smooth my hair in the mirror, and turn to Jeremy. "Do I look okay?"

"I mean, as good as you can look without an eye lift."

"Shut up," I say. "You stay here."

"Yes, sir. Can I have another beer? Pretty please?"

"Yes," I say and leave the room.

Magda wears a white-collared shirt with a black sweater tied around her shoulders. A diamond-encrusted skull dangles from one ear and a silver chain is wrapped around her neck a few hundred times. It's *The Preppy Handbook* meets Berlin dominatrix; you half-expect her to have a pencil behind one ear and a whip hidden under the desk. As I walk up to her, I feel excited, desperate, relieved, and a little angry. "Where have you been?" I clasp my hands on the counter waiting for an explanation.

"Samuel, it was only two days. I had things to do. How do you say it? I make blue."

"You make blue?"

"Yes. *Ich mache blau.*"

"I don't get it."

She rolls her eyes, impatient. "I am skipping the work."

"Oh. I guess I've been making blue a lot lately."

Magda throws me a look as if to say, whatever. She's wearing more make-up than usual. Some powder—or is that foundation, I never know—is making her pale, borderline kabuki. Her lips are painted deep purple and strangely shiny, as if they've been sprayed with Pledge. "Something's going on," I say.

"*Was?*" She sneers. "Nothing is going on. Is this what it is like in New York? Talk, talk, talk, *Blablabla . . .*" She opens and closes her fingers, flapping them Pac-Man style.

I grab an apple from the bowl. "Have dinner with me tonight."

"Do not be absurd," she says, returning her attention to the computer monitor. She begins typing, but I'm undeterred.

"I want to take you out," I say, rubbing the apple. "To a nice meal."

"No. It is not appropriate. You are guest at the hotel."

"So what? A few nights ago I was drinking wine in your apartment."

"Yes, I know it. This was wrong."

"It was not wrong," I say emphatically.

She looks back at the row of clocks on the wall, behind her head. "And tonight I am working until twenty-two hours." I start to do the math in my head. "This is ten o'clock, Samuel," Magda says.

"So? That's early for Berlin. We'll have a late supper."

She opens a drawer in her desk and hands a package to me, a small box wrapped in brown paper. "It is from K.," she tells me flatly. She looks back at the computer screen. "Goodbye, Samuel."

I stand next to the desk, holding the box. "When did this come?"

Magda shrugs. "It was maybe thirty minutes." She begins typing.

"How did it get here?"

"What do you think? That a bird dropped it?" She raises one of her eyebrows and looks at me. "K. brought it himself."

"Oh."

"And I told him that you are not here."

"You met him?"

"Really, Samuel, he is so young."

"Magda, it's not what you think."

"I do not think anything but that you have a husband in New York."

"Daniel is not my husband."

"Yes, Samuel, he is. And this reminds me, you have a message also. The new girl did not give it to you."

Magda hands a slip of paper to me. I look down at the message: Daniel. He called last night. "Oh, man." I set the apple back in the bowl.

"You are so busy today," Magda says. "A package from a K., a call from your husband, a boy in your room."

I have to stop myself from saying something nasty to her. I walk away with the slip of paper in my hand and the package under my arm. Two can play at this game. "Fine," I tell her.

"What is fine?" she asks.

I press the button for the elevator. "You don't know everything, Magda." I watch her in the mirror. She is staring toward the window. Then she looks back at me.

"Samuel?"

"What?" I ask, angry, frustrated.

"I should tell you . . . how do you say it? *Dein Hosenstall ist offen.*"

I roll my eyes. "What?"

"*Dein Hosenstall ist offen,*" she repeats. She flicks her hand toward me.

"Like I know what you're saying."

Magda shakes her head. She thinks about it, then finds the word. "Your zipper-thing, it is open." She points to my pants and spreads her hands.

"Shit." I can close a deal on a million-dollar lithograph. I won't leave the apartment without making sure the door is double-locked, the oven is off and the faucets aren't running. But leave it to me to walk into rooms with my fly down five times a week. My mother claims this as hereditary. "Thanks," I say, fixing my jeans.

"Okay," she says.

I look at her in the mirror. "Okay, what?"

"Take me to dinner."

"Really?" A wave of relief washes over me. Magda is nothing if not consistent: I must first be sent away, banished and insulted, before I'm invited back. The elevator creaks open, but I walk back to her. "So, you'll have dinner with me?"

"Yes," Magda says. "Frankie arrives at ten for the night shift. You and me, let us go to Gugelhof."

"Is that the restaurant by Kollwitzplatz?"

Magda nods. "They have excellent Alsatian food, good stews and krauts. I will get a table. We will drive in *meinem Auto*."

"Fantastic," I say. "And remember, I'm paying."

"Yes, I know. This restaurant is expensive." She purses her lips, failing to obscure a smile. "Maybe we sit where your President Clinton sat when he was in town."

"Great." The truth is, we could eat Döner under the train tracks in a Schmuddelstorm for all I care. I feel triumphant. I walk back toward the elevator. I hold the door open and smile at her. "I'll meet you here at ten."

She puts on her glasses and begins typing into the computer. "Samuel, go to your room before I am changing my mind."

"That's some nice English," I tell her.

"*Bis bald*," she says, waving me away with the back of her hand.

As I step inside the elevator, the phone rings at the reception desk. Magda coos into the mouthpiece, using a totally unfamiliar sing-song voice, so chipper and benevolent it might as well have a dot bouncing under each word: "*Guten Abend*. Hotel Hackescher Hof. How may I help you?"

When I return to the room, Jeremy is sprawled on my bed watching German MTV, another beer clasped between his hands. "So?" he says. "What happened?"

"I have news." I walk over to the TV. The video for Eurythmics' "Here Comes the Rain Again" is playing.

"They're doing an eighties thing," Jeremy tells me.

"This should be the official anthem of Berlin," I say, setting Kaspar's package down on the dresser, next to Daniel's book. I walk over to the TV, turn it off, and tell him about my dinner plans with Magda.

"Can I come?" he asks.

"Sorry. I have to take this one alone."

"Fine," he says. "Is Magda looking all *lecker*?"

"She's got a lot of look going on, actually. She's really insane, Jeremy."

"I don't care if she's crazy as cat shit. I love her. And so do you."

I guess I do. "What will you do tonight?"

"Same thing I did every night before you were here." He talks in a robot voice: "Go home. Smoke weed. Watch TV. Drink beer. Sleeeeeep." He gets up and stretches. "Hey, we should smoke together, before you go."

"I don't do that anymore." I go to the closet to assemble my outfit for tonight. Pale yellow shirt, black sweater, corduroys.

"Um, you did it with the pink-haired twinkie at SO36."

"That was different," I tell him. "And I was drunk."

"Great, we'll get drunk first." He tips his beer bottle to me. "I only have a finite period of time with you, Sam Singer, and I plan to use it well. Come over to my pad. We'll take a bong hit and watch TV. Trust me, you have not lived until you've seen *The Golden Girls* dubbed in German. It's fucking genius."

"I don't know how you smoke pot every day."

"It's torture," Jeremy says. "Actually, if you want to know something, meeting you has made me reconsider my weed intake. I'm thinking perhaps I should go easy on the stuff."

"Why? Do you see me as a cautionary tale?"

"No, the opposite. You *do* things. I don't."

"Really?" I put on the shirt and walk over to the dresser. "I don't think I do anything."

"Yes, you do. You have a life."

"I do?"

"Yeah. You have a career, friends, cities to visit, meetings to take. You have someone to go home to. You even have a dog. What's his name? Poopsie?"

"His name is Harry."

"And you come to Berlin and wind up with me as your best bud, some foxy German dude is salivating all over you, and then we turn on the fucking TV and the star is, like, your friend."

"Sabine? I just met her."

"Exactly! And now you have a date with the manager of the fucking hotel. Fine, so you blew off some meetings, but at least you have meetings to blow off. I mean, Sam, you're a little out of control."

"I never thought about it like that." I put on my sweater and straighten my shirt collar in the mirror. "But as for the home stuff, remember, it's complicated."

"You'll figure it out. I'm not worried."

"Yeah, well, remember, the grass is always greener."

Night is coming, and without the glow of the TV, the room has grown darker. I turn on a lamp and sit on the couch. Outside, the urban sprawl of Berlin emerges like a million Lite Brites.

"Whatever," Jeremy says. "You're a good guy, Sam Singer. You're my inspiration."

"If I'm your inspiration, you're in lots of trouble."

"I'm fine with that."

"And don't forget, when you met me, I was still coming down from an ecstasy trip."

"That day was heavy." Jeremy looks at himself in the mirror. He flattens his hair by patting it down and then running his fingertips through it, perhaps his version of a comb. "Man, it was freezing. We ate currywurst. Remember?"

"Of course." I slip on my shoes. "It wasn't that long ago."

"Well, it feels like forever. And I have to say, I like you better a bit more lucid."

"I thought you liked me drunk."

"The events of the past few evenings changed my mind. I think I like my Sam a little clearheaded."

"Yeah." I laugh under my breath. "Me, too."

Jeremy goes to the window and looks at the city glowing in the clear twilight sky. "And I like Berlin more like this, too. No city does the gloom so well, but if there wasn't a blue sky every once in a while, I don't think I could survive." He leans against the window. "Just look at that."

I walk over and join him. The sky is a dark iridescent blue, the silver orb of the TV Tower sparkling against it. "It's amazing," I say, hypnotized by the tower as it pulses above Alexanderplatz, a few wisps of clouds floating around it. I go over to the other window and look down at the tram stop. The ladies of Oranienburger Strasse haven't arrived yet, and in two days I won't be here to see them. "I'll miss this view," I tell Jeremy.

"It's perfect," he says, returning to the edge of my bed. The light from outside hits him so that he has a white slash across his face. "Sam, I'm scared. The winter is going to be brutal."

"Remember, winter in New York isn't exactly fun."

"Yeah, maybe it's cold and stuff, but it's not like you don't see the sun for three months. In Berlin, it's four hours of daylight and then the sun disappears, if it was ever out at all." He stares out the window. "It's already starting. I can feel it."

I think of Jeremy's sweaters, sitting in some storage space in Red Hook. I still have the combination to his lock sitting on my desk at home. Perhaps I'll drag myself to Brooklyn, liberate his winter clothes, and send them to Berlin. "Can you give me your address before I go?"

"Sure." Jeremy slouches. The white slash has moved off his face and onto the wall beside him. "This city is going to seem a lot emptier when you leave."

"Oh, Jeremy." I sit down next to him. "You managed before I was here."

"Well, my goal in life is to do more than merely manage." He looks past me, then out the window at the perfect sky.

"It'll be okay."

"Yeah," he says. "It'll be . . . fine."

We are silent for a moment. I remember when I first laid eyes on Jeremy; how enormous he seemed, how lost he looked. But I was lost too. I dreaded our meeting with so much energy it could have lit up an entire city. Sitting here now, it's as if our friendship was predestined. He's the strange kid who sits next to you in class one day and changes your life. Berlin would not have been the same without him. He pulled me out of myself.

I begin to have that feeling, the one you get, quite suddenly, when you realize that a trip has been good, perhaps even great, and that it's about to end. You experience a mixture of homesickness and angst and the anticipatory anxiety of reentering the life you left behind. Nostalgia begins to envelop moments as they are happening. At the end of a trip, time really does feel like money; something you can run out of, something you can lose.

I look at Jeremy staring out the window and my heart grows heavy. I have to return home. I will leave this city and this view. This room, my cocoon. The people I've met, the friends I've made. I don't think I've made a new friend in years. I wonder if the sense of peace is real, or if it is specific to this city and will evaporate as soon as I'm back in New York.

I turn to Jeremy. "You can spend the night if you want. Sleep on the couch again, take another bath."

"Really?"

"Of course. Order room service. Raid the minibar, go crazy."

"Seriously?" He finishes his beer and places the empty bottle on my dresser.

I take the bottle and put it in the trash can. "Well, don't Johnny Depp me. But yes, have a few beers and order some food."

Jeremy sits down on the edge of the bed again. Another shadow passes over his face; something has shifted. "Nah, that's okay. I don't think I want to get used to this, if that makes sense. But thanks."

"Okay." I sit down next to him. I want to put my hand on his knee, give him a hug or something. But I don't. "You're still coming with me to the opening . . . right?"

"Tomorrow?"

I nod. Tomorrow is my last full day.

"Sam, no offense, but I think I'll skip it."

"What?"

"Is that okay? I'm pretty lousy at goodbyes."

"All right," I say. "Me too."

The idea that I might not see Jeremy again hadn't occurred to me, and I don't think it occurred to him until this moment. I wasn't prepared to say goodbye at all, let alone tonight. It just hadn't crossed my mind. We hear laughter coming from the hallway. A door closes shut. "So, you're an artist," Jeremy says. "I'm not surprised."

"I *was* an artist."

"You still are, Sam. That doesn't go away. What happened?"

"The world is filled with creative people. And . . . life happened. God, I can't believe that just came out of my mouth."

"Yeah, really."

"I was part of a few shows, sold some paintings, whatever. And one day some journalist asked me what I was trying to say. You know, with my art. And I froze. Because I had no idea how to put it into words. It wasn't always like that. But I felt like a fraud. So I stopped, slowly, the way you do. Looking back, maybe that shouldn't have stopped me. The irony is that now I've adopted a perfectly passable vocabulary to describe other people's art. But it wasn't any one thing. And it's not that simple. I don't have a very thick skin."

"I bet your stuff is great."

"It was okay. I had a moment. Now I help other people have their moment."

"Do you miss it?"

"I don't allow myself to miss it."

"I don't know, Sam." Jeremy stands up, takes his wallet off the desk, and sticks it in his pocket. He digs into his jeans to make sure he has his keys. "There's so much we didn't do. We should have been all gay and gone to Schöneberg and perused the rubber shops. I should have walked you down Karl Marx Allee and shown you the insane Stalinist architecture, and brought you to the flea market in Mauerpark. And man, there are these giant lakes around here, and the abandoned amusement park. I'm such a bad guide."

"You're the best guide, Jeremy. Berlin is huge. It's impossible to see everything. And it's good when a city leaves you wanting more."

"You never even saw my apartment, or like, where I live."

"Next time," I say.

"Right. Next time."

End of the Story

We sit at a corner table by the window overlooking Kollwitzplatz. The remaining diners at Gugelhof lean back in their chairs draining bottles of wine, nursing espressos. A gaggle of waiters float about dressed in white shirts and striped aprons. The atmosphere is loose, relaxed; we've arrived just as other meals are winding down, a cold starlit night waiting outside. Magda sits up straight. She looks tense, her long day of work all over her face, trapped in her shoulders. "Shall we get some wine?" I ask her.

She looks up, thinking about it, then says "of course" and orders a bottle of Edelzwicker when the waiter comes over. She excuses herself to the ladies' room. I watch her cross the restaurant and disappear downstairs, then notice the table of businessmen laughing and smoking cigars at the end of the bar. At a table nearby, a handsome man strokes his date's neck with one hand while lighting her cigarette with the other. I think of Jeremy and all the dreamy scenes we've experienced just like this one. I wonder if he'll reconsider my invitation for tomorrow, or if that was it, back at the hotel. We never really said goodbye.

Magda returns to the table. She has her glasses on now, but she's let her hair down, her brown mane spilling past her shoulders, down her back. She's removed some of her makeup. Even with her tired eyes, she looks beautiful. But I can't help feeling something isn't right. "I feel better," she says. "A day at the hotel can be so long." She tells me about the man who left this morning without paying his bill for six nights, his credit card suddenly declined, his mobile phone and email account deactivated. "We are calling these guests *die Geister*," she says. "Ghosts. Because it is as if they were never there. They disappear. This is happening more than you think." She takes a sip of water. "So, what was in the package?"

I think of Kaspar's box, next to Daniel's book, both wrapped in brown paper on top of my dresser. "You know what? I haven't looked at it yet."

"Really? But how could you not open it?"

"I don't know." I shrug my shoulders. "I'll do it when I'm back in the room, I guess."

"Then you do not love him."

"Magda, don't be ridiculous. Who ever said I loved him?" I feel like I'm on an episode of Sabine's TV show.

The waiter brings over our wine, which Magda samples. She tilts the glass, closes her eyes, and breathes in the bouquet as if she's lost in a field of flowers. *Stay there*, I want to tell her, because she looks so content. She nods her approval, and the waiter pours us two glasses. Magda orders our meal, the *Baeckeoffe* to share, one of the evening's specials: lamb, beef, and pork marinated overnight in riesling, then stewed and served in a pot with vegetables and topped with a bread-crust lid. We clink glasses. "I like this wine," Magda says. "It is not too light. A good white for a cold night."

A stream of people begins to leave the restaurant, the front door chiming behind them. Though it's barely November, everyone has slipped into winter; many of our fellow diners are donning their furry hats, gloves and scarves. They venture outside with the good cheer that often accompanies the completion of a hearty meal on a chilly night.

Magda takes another sip of wine, stares into her glass. "He is just a boy, Samuel. You should not be so foolish. Did you kiss him?"

I wish she'd asked if I'd slept with him, so I could just say no and move on. But I confess all the same. "Yes, I kissed him."

Magda clears her throat, crosses her legs and stares out the window. "Poor Daniel."

I shake my head. "Don't worry about him."

"It is difficult for anyone in a relationship, Samuel." She looks into me with those enormous blue eyes. "It is not easy to be with someone."

"I'll drink to that." I raise my glass and take a sip. I stare out the window, a little embarrassed.

"K.," Magda says. "He is sexy."

"Yes. I know."

"What happened, beyond the kissing?"

"We took a nap. Can you believe it? Then I went home."

"Home?"

"You know what I mean, Magda. Back to the hotel, and that was that."

"So, you are a good boy."

"Mostly." I sigh. On this trip, I blew off work, skipped meetings, smoked cigarettes and pot, took ecstasy, went dancing until morning, and wound up in bed with Kaspar. And still, at the end of the day, I'm a good boy. "I'm so boring."

"Me too," she shrugs. "Frankie says always to me, 'Magda, you old'."

"He says that to you?"

"I could kill him sometimes." She takes a sip of her wine. "You want to know something? I never had dinner with a guest from the hotel."

"Never?"

"No. Well, except for Holger."

"Wait . . . the blond guy from the pictures? The robe hanging in your bathroom? Is that Holger?"

"Yes." She pauses, takes a bite of bread, then decides to continue. "He lived in Hamburg. His firm was sending him to Berlin and he would stay at the hotel maybe one week every two months. This is how it was beginning between him and me. I hide it from the girls at the hotel because it is unprofessional. It is not allowed."

"Does Frankie know?"

"Yes, of course." She smiles. "We know a lot about each other."

"So what does Holger do, exactly?"

"Samuel, let us not talk about it, okay? I do not know even where he is." She brushes the edge of her wineglass with her finger. "I should not be drinking. I am tired."

"Holger just disappeared?"

"No." Magda looks uncomfortable. "Have I told you already I do not want to talk about him? You are so *nosy*, Samuel. Did I use it correctly?"

"Yes, you did. And you're nosy, too, asking me a zillion questions about Kaspar."

"This is different. How many is it, a zillion?"

"I don't know, Magda. A lot."

Magda's legs are crossed, and I see one of her feet shaking. She stares at the cluster of businessmen laughing at a nearby table. "They are too loud," she scoffs. "So, okay, I will be forty and alone. So what? I have nice apartment in Kreuzberg. I have an okay job at the hotel, maybe it is not my dream, but it is fine. And I have Schnappsie, a nice puppy. I can live without a man. If I need sex, I can get a fucking friend."

"A fucking friend?"

"This is what you call it, yes? Wait!" She sticks her finger up at me, thinking. "Do not tell me. What is it? A fuck bunny, right?"

"Close. Not fuck bunny. Fuck *buddy*."

"*Genau!*" She leans over the table and whispers to me. "I will find a fuck buddy." She snaps her fingers as if she's just solved some problem.

"Magda, you may not need a fuck buddy. And besides, we've still got a few years 'til forty. And forty is not the end of the world."

"You are telling me this, the guy who is coming to Berlin and has his midlife crisis."

"Whatever." Is that what this has been, I wonder, a midlife crisis? "If that's true, that's so depressing."

"Yes. Forty is almost here, and it feels shit-ish."

"You wouldn't use *ish* quite like that. You'd just say 'shitty'. Or 'like shit'."

"Shitty," she repeats, trying it out. "Like shit."

I stare out the window, at the dark blank space of Kollwitzplatz. "It feels like the last day of school."

"What do you mean?"

"Because I'm leaving Berlin. And I have that feeling—everything winding down and you don't know what's next." I look at her. "I have the butterflies."

"Butterflies?"

"That nervous feeling. You know, butterflies flying around your stomach."

"Oh, yes, we are saying this, too. *Ich habe Schmetterlinge im Bauch.* But for us, it is more of a romantic thing."

"Interesting." I take a sip of wine. "You know Jeremy?"

"The boy from the great capital of Albany?"

"Yes. Well, I shouldn't say anything, but he likes you. Actually 'likes' is too soft a word. He's completely obsessed with you."

"Really? How silly." She looks around distractedly. "Where is my stew? I am starving."

"He thinks you're the ideal German woman."

"*Ja.*" She looks annoyed and laughs. "He is a boy. He does not know anything." She sounds almost angry. "You and me, we know this."

"Just take it as a compliment." *And I may ask you to look after him a little bit,* I think to myself. But I'll get to that later, if there's a moment that feels right. "He's a nice kid, and good-looking, too."

"Samuel, I do not want to be someone's mommy."

"Listen, Magda, he's important to me, he's my friend." I look into her eyes, which seem to be welling up. "It's just a little crush."

"A what?"

"Forget it. I didn't tell you for any real reason. It's not worth getting upset about."

"Oh really?" Magda leans back in her chair. "Samuel, look at me."

"Okay." I stare across the table. "What? What is it?"

"Samuel." She crosses her arms. "I am pregnant."

"Oh my God."

"*Ja.* Talk about foolish."

"Holger?"

"Yes, of course it is Holger. And now he is gone."

We stare at each other, silent, her face lit from below by the candle on our table, flickers of shadow dancing across her chin. Then I remember: the walk to Austria, the cemetery gates. Magda's cheeks so red, her kneeling down to the ground.

"When did you find out?"

"It was three days. I was not feeling so good."

We stop talking when the waiter arrives and places our dinner on the table, a steaming bowl of meat stew with chunks of tomato, potato and onion. He presents us with two plates and a ladle. Magda, ever the control freak, prepares a portion for each of us. The fragrant herby scent wafts straight up my nose. "So where did you go after you left us at Austria?"

"This is not important, Samuel." She brings a forkful of stew to her mouth and blows on it. "Why did I just tell you?"

"Because I'm your friend."

"That is silly. You are a guest. And you are going back to New York. You and your butterflies."

Despite our heavy conversation, we devour the stew. I didn't realize how hungry I was until now. I can't stop bringing forkfuls to my lips. "So, what are you going to do?"

"I do not know. I cannot manage the hotel and also be sexy in my tight black outfits if I am pregnant."

I didn't realize this was a goal. "That's the last thing you should be worrying about."

"Did I get it right? *Outfits*?"

"Yes," I sigh, rolling my eyes.

Magda nods her head. "*Gut*. So what will I do?" She looks out the window and points to the square beyond Gugelhof. "Move to Kollwitzplatz to be with the other mommies? Sit in the park with my coffee and go to the bio-market and buy organic everything? Then what? I do not think so." She starts to cry. "Ah, *Scheisse*." I hand her my napkin. "To make the German woman cry," she says. "It takes a lot."

I don't doubt it. "Do you want to leave? Take a walk?"

"No." She dabs her eyes with my napkin and composes herself. She clasps her fists on the table. "We must finish the stew. And then I want cake. Lots of cake."

"Okay."

She leans across the table and whispers. "This baby is hungry. You know how they are saying when you are pregnant, you are not liking to eat certain foods?"

"Yes."

"Well, I want to eat *everything*," she grunts. "It is disgusting. I could eat your napkin and your spoon both."

I push my utensils toward her. "Be my guest."

"Ha, ha, Samuel. It is not so funny."

"And what about Holger?"

"Samuel, I told you, he is not in my picture, okay? End of the story."

"But . . ."

"But what? Holger, he is another ghost. He is gone."

"Okay." I grab a piece of bread from the basket to scoop up the last bit of sauce from my plate. "So what have you been doing for the past two days?"

"I am thinking a lot, talking to myself. I plan to visit my mother at her house, and I drive almost there. But then I turn around. I could not tell my mother. She will not understand."

"Oh, Magda, I totally get it," I say. "So, where did you wind up?"

"Nowhere. Sitting here with you with a baby in my stomach. Now you know." She taps her wineglass. "Can I have maybe one more sip?"

"I don't know, Magda."

"Fine. But I want *Kuchen*." She waves the waiter over and speaks to him quickly in German. He nods and walks away. "One warm chocolate nut cake," she translates for me. "And one crème brûlée. Two espressos."

"Great." I hold up two fingers. "*Zwei Kuchen, und zwei Kaffee*." I say this with a purposely exaggerated German accent.

Magda's eyes light up. "*Sehr gut*, Samuel!"

I practically blush, I'm so pleased with myself. "Baby steps," I say.

"*Ja*," Magda grunts, "baby steps." She takes a deep breath. I can see her torment beneath the candlelight, the dark plum dents under her eyes fighting to break through the makeup. She lifts the glass of wine, holds it to the light and studies it, as if the golden liquid contains some secret message. "Samuel, what should I do?"

"I don't know. But I don't think you should drink any more wine."

"Fine." She pushes her glass away and takes a sip of water. "And what about you, Samuel, do you think about it?"

"What?"

"Children. Babies. With Daniel."

"Oh. Yes. Actually, I think about it a lot."

"And?"

"And it's not so easy."

"What are you meaning?"

I lean across the table and take a sip of wine. "Well, look at you. I mean, I know it's hard and a baby was maybe not what you wanted at this particular moment. But that can change. And it probably will. And if you have the baby, you'll figure it out. That's what happens to my friends."

"Your *straight* friends."

"Yes, exactly. Some of my friends call me and they say, oops, we're pregnant, shit, what are we going to do? Or now, it's whoops, it's baby number two and we're just not ready. But then they figure it out. And I'm not saying there aren't tremendous challenges, or that parenthood doesn't crash into your life and change everything. But they do work it out, somehow. That's been my experience, at least."

"So it will happen for you," she says.

"No, Magda. If I want a baby, it's complicated, however it could happen. All the research, and the planning. So much time. So much money. The blood tests, the agencies, the surrogates, the paperwork, tax returns, the bureaucracy . . ."

"What are you saying? I am lost."

"Exactly. It's so exhausting, so clinical. Seriously, I get tired just talking about it. Tired, and . . . depressed." I take a sip of wine. "I wish Daniel could just knock me up."

"Knock you up?"

"Meaning, I wish Daniel, or someone, could just fuck me and get me pregnant. Then we'd figure it out. Or I'd fuck them. I don't care."

Magda gasps. Our waiter sets our cake and coffee onto the table and scurries away. "Samuel!" She flashes her eyes at me. "You are being so dirty!"

"Well that's how I feel. And that's how babies are made. But anyway, I don't know what Daniel wants. He says he wants a baby. But you know, he also says he wants an apartment in Barcelona and some rare book on Shinto architecture from 1922." I take a final sip of wine. "I don't really know what he wants anymore."

"But he is almost your husband."

"Exactly. Almost. And I just can't get a read on him. So, I guess I've stopped wanting it." I look under the table. It's my foot that's shaking now. "I've stopped wanting many things."

"But do you want a child?"

"I think so. I don't know." But talking about it now, I feel that ache in my heart, that heaviness. I'm so used to pushing it away, I don't know what to do when it gurgles back to the surface. "I always thought that if I didn't have a child, I'd regret it." I look away, as if admitting this will make it less real. I stare out the window and watch the wind shake the trees. A flurry of golden leaves parachute onto the street. In a week, the trees will probably be bare. "Yes, I want a child. Of course I do."

"Samuel, at the hotel we talk sometimes about the people, our guests. It is a small hotel, and we are getting to know our guests very well. And we are saying sometimes that with the Americans, they are difficult to know."

"That's ironic."

"Why?"

"Well, you Germans aren't exactly the most open people I've ever met."

She holds up a finger and leans into me. "Let me finish, Samuel. What I am saying is that with the Americans, everything is on the surface, and often you do not get beyond that. Astrid says, 'Americans do not have a soul.'"

My mouth falls open. "Astrid said that?" Magda nods her confirmation. I'm shocked. Astrid has always seemed so kind, and soft. She was the one person who was nice to me during my first days in Berlin. Has she actually spent the entire week sizing me up while she filled my coffee cup?

"She did not say this about you, Samuel."

"Well, good."

"Just about Americans."

"That's crazy, Magda. We're guests at a hotel. You're giving us directions and handing us our keys. And as you've pointed out, we also have the language barrier to deal with."

"A barrier?"

"A wall."

"Fine. But what I am saying, Samuel, is that you are different. I see sadness in you. In a way, it feels very German. We are calling this *Wehmütig*. It is a nice sadness."

"Well, thanks, I guess."

"I am thinking that you would be a good father. If you would want it, you should do it."

"What, with all my sadness to give to the world?"

"Kindness, Samuel. With sadness comes kindness." She leans forward and smiles. "You are kind."

I laugh under my breath, a little embarrassed. "Thank you, Magda." I take a bite of my cake. "It's been hard, watching my friends start families. They move away. Literally they move away, but psychologically too, and, you know, what's left for me? I don't want to go out dancing every weekend or spend my summers on Fire Island."

"There is an island of fire?"

"Oh, just ask Frankie."

"Can I finish your cake?"

"Please." I push the plate to her. After my weeklong festival of schnitzel, beer, sausage, and cake, it's a miracle I still fit in my jeans. Magda slides her glass of wine toward me and tells me to finish it in exchange. I oblige and take a sip. "Maybe this is a horrible thing to say, but you're miserable and scared tonight. And I'm jealous of your misery. I'm envious of your fear."

"Why?"

"Because if you do have this baby, and okay, maybe you won't, but if you do, you will love this baby. And you will wake up every day and be grateful for it. I know it won't be easy, and some days it'll be impossible and you'll want it all to stop. But every day, you will look into your baby's eyes, and he or she will stare up at you, and you will be Mommy. You will know who you are, and why you are here." I look at my foot under the table, still tapping. "And when you go to sleep at night, when you're forty, sixty, or a hundred-and-two, you will know your purpose. You won't float through your life, not knowing what to do. That's powerful stuff, Magda. That's amazing." I take a deep breath and another sip of wine. "I want that." I've never felt so clear. "Anyway, we're not supposed to be talking about me. This is about you."

Magda just looks at me. I have no idea if she wants me to shut up or continue. She takes a spoonful of crème brûlée and holds it to her lips. "Go on," she says.

"No, I'll shut up." I bury my spoon into her dessert. "It's just, sometimes I wish it could just happen. And just to clarify, I have no regrets about being gay."

"Good."

"Trust me, I love men. But having a child, and what it feels like to be this age, our age. It's caught me by surprise, all this . . . blank space. I wish it could just, you know, that's where I have total vagina-envy. I wish some things could just happen."

"Almost by accident," she says.

"Yes, exactly. And then you figure it out." I scoop sugar into my espresso. Magda leans forward but says nothing, her eyes glittering in the candlelight. Jeremy was right; they are a shade of indigo. "What?" I ask, leaning into her.

"Nothing."

"What is it?"

She looks around the restaurant, then at me. "Nothing. It is silly."

"No, tell me. You're thinking something."

"You could move to Berlin," she whispers.

"Oh really?" I take a sip of my espresso. "And why would I move to Berlin?"

She leans back in her chair and rubs her stomach. "Maybe you have found your vagina."

"You can't be serious."

"Why not? Maybe I am your accident."

I look at her in disbelief. "Magda . . ."

"Listen, Samuel, to me. You go to New York and you think about this, about what you want."

"I think about what I want every day."

"I am not sure that you do."

"Magda," I repeat. "Come on."

"You come back in April. No more *Schmuddelwetter*. Spring in Berlin, Samuel, it is magnificent. You skip the terrible winter. I will suffer for the three of us." She smiles blankly and stares down at her belly. Does she mean her, me, and the baby? Does she mean her, me and Daniel? I don't even know.

"You *are* serious."

"And then you return in April, for the baby. You get a flat close to me in Kreuzberg. Remember, Samuel, it is not so expensive to live here. Not for a New Yorker. Or maybe we move to Prenzlauer Berg, as you like it so much."

"Magda!" I gape at her. I can see the excitement in her eyes, and hear it in her voice, too, energized by the spark of a new idea.

"And your work, you can do it here. You know already people in Berlin, and so do I. And maybe you keep your clients in New York, you fly there a few times a year and see your family, you do some business, and then you come back to us. And think of it, Samuel! Spring in Berlin. Oh, it is so lovely. And it is asparagus season, the most delicious *Spargel* you have ever tasted."

"Magda, are you inviting me back to Berlin to eat asparagus or to be the father to your child?"

She thinks about it and shrugs. "Why not yes to the both?"

"You're being very casual about this."

"Do you want that I get down on the floor and offer you a ring?"

"What about Harry?"

"The dog? Bring him to Berlin!"

"I can't."

"Why not? The wiener dogs originate from Deutschland. You will bring him home!"

"He's not my dog."

"Of course he is."

"Harry is Daniel's dog, too. He's our dog. I couldn't do that. And besides, even if he did come, wouldn't he need to be quarantined?"

"Oh, I do not know, Samuel. Your mind is crazy, how do you get to the dog so fast? We are talking about a baby."

"My mind is fast? Who brought up asparagus?"

"Fine. We figure it out, as you say. That is, only if you are thinking that maybe this is a good idea."

"But I don't really know you, Magda."

"Yes, you do."

"No, I don't."

"Yes, you do. *Mein Doppelgänger.*" Magda takes a sip from my wineglass. "Sometimes maybe you just have to do things, Samuel."

Just like that, I think to myself. "But what about Daniel?"

"Yes, what about Daniel?"

"I don't know."

"Maybe he comes to Berlin, too," Magda says. "Or perhaps not. You must find out what he wants and think about also what you want."

My heart beats faster. "A baby."

"Yes, a baby."

"We must be drunk."

"Or it is maybe the sugar," she says.

The restaurant is practically empty. The businessmen have settled their bill and walked out the door. We look out the window and watch them—drunk and happy, smoking and singing on the street, perhaps having closed a deal of their own. They shuffle into a pair of taxis. I stare at Magda. I don't know what she's thinking, but I go over every reason Why Not in my head. I could explain that I'm the world's worst candidate for fatherhood just on the basis of the past several days. After my week of debauchery—endless nights of drugs, kisses and a river of wine and beer, six straight days of making blue—I'm the last person who should be raising a child. But maybe that's just it. Maybe this *has* been my midlife crisis. What I want, what's been missing, has seemed impossible—until now. And maybe, just maybe, this is what comes next. Magda interrupts my thoughts. "You are right, Samuel. Maybe it is crazy."

"We should get the check," I say. "Should we find *die Teller?*"

"*Teller* is a plate, Samuel."

"Oh."

"*Kellner* is waiter. And both are masculine, *der Teller, der Kellner.*"

"Oh well."

She reaches across the table and puts her hand over my hand. "But the words, they are close to each other. And it is nice that you try." I almost blush, looking at her hand on mine. "They are in the same family."

We walk down Knaackstrasse, toward Magda's car. She'll drop me off at the hotel on her way home. It's even colder outside than when we arrived. Magda wraps her scarf around her neck. I tuck my hands into my jacket and put on my hat, Daniel's hat. Magda turns to me. "So, what did you do with your two days?"

"A lot of running around. Obviously you know that I saw Kaspar. And I hung out with Jeremy. A lot. He dragged me out, we stayed out too late. I even visited a few galleries and discovered an artist I like, so at least there's that. I should have worked more, but there's still tomorrow."

"And what did you think of Sachsenhausen?"

"You know what? I didn't go."

"Hmmm," she says. "Next time."

We pass Café Anita Wronski, which must be closing. Through the window I see a waiter blow out a candle. I consider telling Magda that this is where I met Kaspar—by accident, a glass of water, Daniel's hat with the snowflakes. But I don't. We walk toward the water tower and stand at the corner. It's still a perfect blue night, just deeper and darker, and now you can see a few dozen glittery stars. The moon is there too, just a pale yellow shadow. Tonight, it seems far away.

"Magda, I was worried about you. You just disappeared."

"I know. I could not talk to anyone. When I returned home, Frau Schneider told me there was a nice-looking American man waiting for me all afternoon. I could not believe it."

"But how did you know it was me?"

"Frankie, he is saying you are looking for me. And then Frau Schneider told me that Schnappsie was excited to see the American man in his green hat. She watched you from her window, sitting on the stairs with Blitz on your lap. '*Er sieht gut aus*,' she said."

"What does that mean?"

"She is thinking you are handsome."

"I thought she wanted to get rid of me."

"*Nein*. Frau Schneider knows everything about everyone, and she knows about Holger. She was excited that maybe I find a new husband."

We both laugh quietly, but then we look at each other and smile shyly, because it's not that funny anymore. After all, fifteen minutes ago we were talking about me leaving New York. We were talking about a baby. Magda turns to me. "I thought it was strange, Samuel, you coming to find me."

"I thought it was strange, too."

"Strange, but nice."

Outside of Bar Gagarin, a few Berliners huddle on lounge chairs and smoke cigarettes, warmed by heaters and the wool blankets draped around them. I think of Jeremy and our first afternoon together, soaking up the warmth under the canopy of Anna Blume. That feels like so long ago. Magda looks at them longingly and groans. "I want a ciggie."

"Me too," I say, kicking a rock down the street.

"Maybe we could *buhme* one," she says, gesturing toward the people at Gagarin. "But I guess we should not do it?"

"Nope. We shouldn't."

"They have delicious Pelmeni," Magda tells me. "Chicken dumplings with cream."

"You're already hungry again."

"Probably."

We stand in front of the Wasserturm. I turn to her. "Did you know the basement of this tower was used as a torture chamber?"

"I did know this. And now, it is an apartment building."

"It's just crazy," I say. "How everything used to be something else. Do you realize this? Or do you not think about it, because you live here?"

"I do realize this. A city changes every day, but Berlin is something else. To live here, you must be okay with the ghosts." Magda looks up at the water tower. "My friend Martin lives there with his husband, Dirk."

"Really?"

"*Ja*, but not in the basement, of course." She points to a dark window. "They are sleeping or maybe not home, but it is this flat, on the third floor."

"What's it like?" I ask. "Are the apartments curved and cut up like a slice of cake?"

"Cake? You are so silly. They are small apartments, one on top of the other. Not very nice, really." Her eyes widen. "Sorry to burst your bubble, Samuel." She grabs my arm as if she's hit an ace. "Hey, I used it!"

"You totally did! Very good!"

Magda throws her fist in the air. She locks arms with me and we look at the building. "But the location, it is lovely. In the spring, the cherry trees are blooming, and in the summer, the hills of this park, they are filled with wild roses. And living also in the hills are bunnies."

I look at her, amused by this sudden onset of tour guide enthusiasm. "As in rabbits?"

"Yes." She purses her lips playfully like a bunny, then grows silent. "Maybe you will see."

"You're lucky," I say, looking at the stars, at the TV Tower blinking in the distance. It's a city haunted by ghosts, but there is no denying its beauty. "To live here, to have this."

"As we say: *die Kirschen in Nachbars Garten schmecken immer ein bisschen süßer.*"

"Wow. What does that all mean?"

"I do not know if it is the same expression for you. It means the cherries in the neighbor's garden always taste a bit sweeter."

"Oh, yes. We say, 'The grass is always greener.'"

"Hmm," she says. "I think I prefer the cherries to the grass."

"Yeah." I laugh. "Me, too."

A swarm of black creatures fly by, squeaking as they pass overhead. "Are those bats?"

"Yes, we have many bats in Berlin."

"I thought I saw a fox the other night. It was late. I don't know if I imagined it."

"It is quite possible," she says. "We have also wild pigs in Berlin. But soon, the animals are disappearing for winter. It will be too cold for them." She shivers. We unlock arms and she rubs her hands together. "And it will be too cold for me, too. Everything has a cost, and for us living here, besides the ghosts, it is the Berlin winter."

Magda looks up at the sky as if winter is right there in the stars, about to fall down on us. I picture Jeremy, alone without his sweaters. I'm going to ship them over when I get back to New York. Maybe I'll even ask Magda to check in on him. It's worth a shot. And then, a light switches on in the tower. "Ah look," Magda says. "Martin and Dirk, they are home! I will get my handy." She pulls out her mobile phone. "Should I send an SMS? Maybe you can see the flat."

"No," I say. I'm too happy looking at the stars, Magda's arm now locked in my own. If I've learned one thing on this trip, it's that sometimes you don't mess with a moment. "It's late. And besides, I'd rather have their apartment live in my imagination." Sliced like a piece of cake.

"I understand," Magda says. "If this is how you like it."

We stand in the middle of the cobblestone street. I think about how strange it is, that I've walked down this same block with Jeremy, then Kaspar, now Magda. I wonder what it means—one street in this enormous city, nine times the size of Paris. The light in the apartment switches off again, darkness. A bike whizzes by, ringing its bell, its beam pointing down the street. It's hard to describe the hush of Prenzlauer Berg at night. The city just breathes. I wonder what Berlin might look like in spring, this little park with its towers covered in graffiti, its hills filled with rose bushes and rabbits. New lives being born.

"Samuel?"

"What?"

"Are you dreaming?"

"I guess I am." I bend down and pick up an acorn off the street, hold it in my palm. "When I first came here, it seemed like the leaves were just beginning to fall. And now look . . ." I kick a sea of red and yellow leaves at my feet. "The trees are almost naked." Magda laughs and kicks some leaves, too. A few swirl in the air. We watch as a breeze carries them down the street. My teeth begin to chatter from the cold, but I feel entirely content.

Magda tucks her hands in her pockets, looks up at the stars, and sighs. "What a night."

"Indeed." I squeeze the acorn in my hand, then put it into my coat pocket. Maybe I'll bring it home to New York.

"Samuel?"

"What?"

"I must tell you something." She leans into me, rests her head on my shoulder. "I love you."

The words. They just linger in the air, but I feel my heart open, crack, ache. It seems too stupid, too predictable to say something. Because right now, for at least a moment, I have everything I need. So I take my arm and put it around her. I look up at the sky. "I think I get it now," I say.

"What? What are you getting?"

"I make envy on your disco."

"Samuel, really. You are so strange sometimes."

ACKNOWLEDGMENTS

I Make Envy on Your Disco has had many adventures on its way to publication. The road was long and sometimes twisty, but when it ultimately leads to Zero Street, all is right in the world. A fitting end, or beginning, to the story.

On that note, I'd like to thank my editors Timothy Schaffert and SJ Sindu for their dream of Zero Street, for their intelligence and kindness, and for believing in this book. To Courtney Ochsner and the entire team at the University of Nebraska Press, thank you for your thoughtfulness and care. And to Hilary Zaid, my Zero Street book sibling, your wit and generosity have been a blessing from day one.

Thank you to the brilliant Jennifer Belle, whose workshop and support nurtured the seeds that grew into this novel. To Carolyn Turgeon, who I met there and became a one-of-a-kind creative soulmate. To Joi and Tink and all the OG writers in Jenny's workshop.

A shout-out to Doma, that miracle of a coffee shop on Perry Street where I began this novel, and which is, like so many great things in any city, now gone.

To Steve Adams, for pretty much everything. For Steven Ball, ditto. Your wisdom and smarts provided more sustenance than you both already know. To Deborah Koplovitz, my beautiful snowflake and biggest cheerleader.

This novel benefitted from many great readers. In addition to those already mentioned, big thanks to: Rob Bannon, Sandra Bauleo, Chris Berger, Mark Berger, Zoë Chapin, Colin Dickerman, Jonah Disend, Alison Dominitz, Tracy Doyle, Kevin Emrick, Karen Fricker, John Havard, Scott Huff, Kait Kerrigan, Evelyn Leong, Julia Lewis, Sam Magid, Galadriel Masterson, Katharine Mehrling, Sophie Muller, Patrick Myles, Michael Paoletta, Marlo Poras, Jeffery Povero, Peter Rehberg, Kim Schmidt, Jeffrey Seller, Darius Suyama, Liz Timperman, Nathan Vernon, Barbara Whitman, and Soo Jin Yi.

Thank you to the insanely lovely Todd Doughty. Billy Goldstein. David Ebershoff. Joy Harris. Susan Petersen Kennedy. To PJ Mark for your support of this book, and a durable friendship.

My deepest gratitude to a handful of people I am astoundingly lucky to know: Franki De La Vega, Kellan Dore, Stephanie Downes, Terry Nauheim Goodman, and Sarah Marshall.

I'm indebted to Brian Savelson and to Wendy Taeuber for walking and talking in Berlin, in New York, and for always being there even when you're halfway around the world.

Thank you to Aaron Goodman for taking an idea and transforming it into something iconic and fun.

I'm forever grateful to Marc Schubring, for your embrace and singular spirit, and to my soulsister Uli Frank, I seriously don't know what I'd do without you, or what I did to deserve you. Uli and Marc, Berlin was always great but you made it into a Technicolor dream.

Thank you to Kerstin Höckel, who threw me a little party on Kollwitzstrasse the night I wrote my ending. To Frank Hüllmandel and Dirk Nickel for hosting me at 80a. To Randy Pence and Jen Ellerson, for Berlin inspiration. To Arielle Tepper, for letting me work on a Broadway play while being on another continent. And to David Binder, for so many happenings and decades of friendship.

All my love to my sister Marianne, to my rockstar nieces Lotus and Jazmin, and to Tom . . . Boom! To Char Rachita for her giant heart, to my entire Ohio family. And to Fritz and Patty, I'm the luckiest son-in-law (and I'll see you on Sunday!). No one shows up like my cousins

Samantha Levine and Penny Sanders, and for that I would like to express my gratitude.

This book benefited from two dachshund muses—first Shorty, and now Buddy. Legends. Bosses. Supreme cuddlers.

For my grandfather, for teaching me that everything was possible, and that most of it was supposed to be joyful and fun.

For Berlin, for teaching this jaded born-and-bred New Yorker he could fall in love with another complicated city. And for New York— you bitch, I still love you.

For Shax Riegler, for bringing me Berlin and so much more. There is no story I could ever read or history I could ever learn that would be richer than what I've experienced with you. *Du bist mein Zuhause.*

This novel is dedicated to the memory of my parents. I lost both of them this past year, only ten months apart. To my extraordinary, brave, and creative father, Norman Schnall—I don't know how to express all that you meant to me. And to my remarkable, curious, and huge-hearted mother, Carol Schnall—I feel you in me right now. Mom and Dad, thank you for everything.

IN THE ZERO STREET FICTION SERIES

Forget I Told You This: A Novel
by Hilary Zaid

I Make Envy on Your Disco: A Novel
by Eric Schnall